A *Dangerous* LEGACY

Books by Elizabeth Camden

A *Dangerous* LEGACY

ELIZABETH CAMDEN

BethanyHouse

a division of Baker Publishing Group
Minneapolis, Minnesota

© 2017 by Dorothy Mays

Published by Bethany House Publishers
11400 Hampshire Avenue South
Bloomington, Minnesota 55438
www.bethanyhouse.com

Bethany House Publishers is a division of
Baker Publishing Group, Grand Rapids, Michigan

Printed in the United States of America

ISBN 978-0-7642-1881-1 (trade paper)
ISBN 978-0-7642-3113-1 (cloth)

Library of Congress Control Number: 2017945296

This is a work of fiction. Names, characters, incidents, and dialogues are products of the author's imagination and are not to be construed as real. Any resemblance to actual events or persons, living or dead, is entirely coincidental.

Cover design by Jennifer Parker
Cover photography by Mark Owen/Trevillion Images

Author is represented by the Steve Laube Agency.

17 18 19 20 21 22 23   7 6 5 4 3 2 1

New York City
1903

The amount of female attention her brother garnered never failed to amaze Lucy. Even when he was wearing grubby coveralls and carrying a sack of plumber's tools, girls flocked around Nick as though he were Casanova. Lucy watched from a few yards away as they waited for the streetcar after a long day at work.

Nick was fiercely intelligent, handsome, and had an easy laugh, but what would those girls do if they knew that anyone who befriended him would be targeted for complete and total ruin? Few people lingered for long once they drew her uncle's attention. She and Nick had been raised since birth to be on guard against underhanded attacks from Uncle Thomas, but it would take someone with a backbone of steel to stand alongside them once her uncle got wind of it.

To the outside world, Lucy and her brother looked like normal, hardworking people. Nick was employed by the Municipal Water Authority, and she worked as a telegraph operator for the Associated Press. They didn't have much of a life outside of their jobs. The lawsuit consumed everything they had, for she and Nick were the only two people left standing to carry on the forty-year battle that had eroded their spirit, finances, and even their safety.

Lucy cut through the trio of girls flirting with her brother. "Nick, I need to speak with you."

His smile broadened when he saw her, and it didn't go unnoticed by his admirers.

One of the women sent Lucy a surly glare. "Who's she?"

"That's the girl I've adored from the moment I first clapped eyes on her," Nick said. "Of course, at the time she was a squalling infant and I was only three years old, but sisters can grow on you."

The girls pealed with laughter and swatted Nick on the shoulder. He didn't seem to mind, grinning down at them with a reckless smile that worked like a magnet on women. One of the girls even reached up to tug on a lock of the wild, dark hair he wore far too long.

"Nick?" Lucy pressed, a little less patient this time. "Can I speak with you? We've got a problem."

He must have noticed the tension in her voice, because he picked up his tools and followed her a few yards away. "What's going on?"

"I got word from Mr. Garzelli that a stranger was spotted poking around his building. I'm worried Uncle Thomas might have sent someone to sabotage the new valves. Mr. Garzelli has cut off water to the building until you can check it out."

Nick's mouth narrowed to a hard line. He'd spent the past two weekends installing pumps and an ingenious set of valves in a Lower East Side tenement building. It meant that two hundred people living on the upper floors could have water pumped up to their apartments for the first time. The valve had been invented by their grandfather. Such an ordinary-looking piece of hardware, but one that was worth millions and had sparked decades of litigation. Not that the people living in the tenement cared about her family's bitter lawsuit. All they wanted was to stop lugging buckets of water up five flights of stairs every day.

The stranger sniffing around the tenement building worried Lucy. Their installation of those valves wasn't technically illegal, but if Uncle Thomas found out about it, he would make them pay. She wouldn't put it past him to have someone sabotage their work. Mr. Garzelli was probably right to cut off the pumps until Nick could verify it was safe.

"You want us to go over tonight?" Nick asked. It had been a long day for both of them, and the trip across town would take an hour each way, but they didn't have much choice.

"It would be best."

He nodded, his expression grim. "I get it, but I'd rather go to Uncle Thomas's fancy mansion and cut the water to *his* house. See how he likes it. See how he likes—"

"Stop," she said, laying a gentle hand on his sleeve. "Don't let him rattle you. We'll handle this, just like we've handled everything else over the years. We just need to keep our heads on straight."

An hour later, they were in the basement of a tenement in one of the worst sections of the city. Nick lay flat on his back, pointing his fancy new flashlight beneath a complicated system of valves and pumps, looking for signs of sabotage. Lucy sat on an upended bucket, handing over tools as requested and trying not to breathe too deeply. It smelled bad in this part of town, with grimy streets, overcrowded apartments, and very little running water flowing to the hundreds of residential buildings. Each time she visited this section of town, the stench penetrated her hair and clothes, making her wonder how anyone could bear to live here. At least the people lucky enough to live in this building had running water thanks to Nick and her grandfather's valve. Everything about life for the people who lived here got better, cleaner, and healthier as soon as they had enough pressure to supply water to all eight floors.

Footsteps sounded on the stairs as Mr. Garzelli joined them. Nick slid out from beneath the valves and rolled into a sitting position.

"So someone has been sniffing around?" he asked.

Mr. Garzelli nodded. "He was a skinny guy. Old. Shifty-looking. One shoulder was twisted up almost like a hunchback. It was that weird shoulder that made me remember him. I've seen him around a couple of times before. My oldest boy caught him trying to get in through the basement window, and he ran off. And I saw him last weekend when you installed the valves."

Nick began putting his tools away. "It was a good idea to call me, but it doesn't look like there's been any harm done. You should probably get a better lock on that window, though."

"I know you've been in some kind of court business over those valves," Mr. Garzelli said. "You're not going to get in trouble for this, are you?"

She and Nick risked awakening a sleeping giant every time they installed her grandfather's invention in another of Manhattan's endless tenement buildings, but Nick shrugged and flashed an easygoing smile.

"I'm more afraid of my baby sister than I am of that lawsuit," he said.

"Miss Lucy?" Mr. Garzelli asked incredulously. "I don't believe it."

"You've never seen her when I burn dinner." Nick hefted his sack of tools over his shoulder. "Just don't blab to anyone about these valves. You can't exactly hide the fact that you've got hot and cold running water throughout the building, but no need to mention my name, right?"

"Okay, you got it, Nick," Mr. Garzelli said with a hearty handshake.

The sun had already set by the time Lucy and Nick returned to Greenwich Village. They lived on the fourth floor of a brownstone walk-up that had once been a prestigious building but had fallen on hard times in recent decades. Much like her own family.

She twisted the key in the lock to the apartment, stepped inside the darkened interior, and immediately knew something was wrong. Her nose twitched. Cigarette smoke?

That was odd. No one should have been in the apartment today. Their mother had moved to Boston after their father's death almost a year ago, and they no longer had money for servants.

When her eyes adjusted to the dim interior, she scanned the room, looking for anything out of place. Nick's half-assembled pumping valves lay scattered across the dining table, their mother's leggy orchids lined the windowsill, and books were crammed into every vacant table space and cubby. Their once-fine furnishings had witnessed several generations of use and no longer had any pretensions of grandeur, but everything had the comfort of a much-loved blanket. Their family had once been happy here.

"You weren't home today, were you?" she asked.

Nick strode inside and tossed his sack of tools onto the sofa with a thud. "Nope. Why?"

"Don't you smell cigarette smoke?"

He paused to sniff the air, then shrugged. "The lady who lives upstairs smokes like a freight train. It's probably coming through the ventilation pipes."

"Are you sure about that?" Nick was a plumber, not an expert on ventilation, but he seemed unconcerned.

"I'm not *that* paranoid," he said as he headed to the kitchen sink to scrub his hands.

He might not mind the faint acrid scent, but it was worrisome. Everything looked precisely as she'd left it, but her skin still prickled with the hunch that someone had been in their apartment while they were gone.

She took a deep breath and wished her father were here. He had been the rock on which their family depended, but toward the end of his life, she'd sensed he was losing hope. She'd often caught him standing before the window, staring down at the street below with bleak eyes, as if the demons were finally catching up with him. The week before he died, she'd arrived home from the office early one day and caught him staring at a paper clenched in his hand, his face carrying a sickly pallor. She flew to his side and asked what was wrong, and he startled. That was the first time she saw pure, undiluted fear on her father's face.

He had stuffed the paper into a maroon satchel and denied anything was wrong, but she knew he was lying. His hands had been trembling as he locked the satchel in his desk drawer.

After he died, she went in search of that satchel, but it was nowhere to be found. She and Nick turned the apartment inside out in search of it. They even pried up the floorboards in the kitchen, where they hid the only treasure left to their family. The treasure was still there, but no sign of the satchel. She never did find it, and Lucy couldn't help but think that it somehow contributed to her father's death the following week. He'd always had a weak heart, and whatever was in that maroon satchel had petrified him.

Lucy heated a can of baked beans for their supper. She and Nick alternated kitchen duties, and it was always a simple affair. After ten hours of staffing a telegraph station, she didn't need anything fancy. All she cared about was easy.

It didn't take long to wolf down the meal, and she volunteered to clean up afterward while Nick flopped on their worn sofa and paged through the day's mail. They both worked long hours, but she spent hers at a desk while Nick performed physically demanding labor deep beneath the city streets as he helped install the massive underground pumps that kept freshwater moving in and out of the city.

Water flowed from the tap as she rinsed the cooking pot. Even though they lived on the fourth floor, their grandfather's valves in the building's basement supplied the perfect amount of water pressure to their apartment. They lived in a clean, respectable building with an excellent supply of water, but only a few miles away, the city teemed with over a million people crammed into tenements without proper plumbing. At least there was one more building in the city that now had running water.

She flashed a smile of accomplishment Nick's way and noticed him staring at the floor, his shoulders slumped as he held a letter in his hands.

"What's wrong?" she asked, turning off the tap.

"This is from our lawyer. Uncle Thomas is after us again."

She stiffened. "What is he claiming this time?"

"He's accusing us of acting in bad faith. They want the judge to throw our case out."

"Bad faith" could mean almost anything, but there was only one truly underhanded thing she and Nick had been doing, and it was the sole reason they'd been able to stay ahead of Thomas Drake's swarm of lawyers all these years.

She set down the dish towel, holding her breath. "You don't think he knows, do you?"

"If he does, we're done for."

Lucy sighed and nodded, wandering to the worn dining table, exhaustion setting in as she plopped into a chair. It was getting hard to keep fighting Uncle Thomas and his family, who lived like European royalty at their mansion in upstate New York. The Saratoga Drakes had been using the fortune from her grandfather's invention to launch legal salvos at the

Manhattan Drakes for decades. Lucy had no proof yet, but she sensed the Saratoga Drakes might have somehow been behind her father's death. The doctor said it was a heart attack, but Lucy couldn't be certain.

Was the lawsuit worth it? Her gaze tracked to the faucet. How easily most people took clean water for granted, but she never did. Neither did Mr. Garzelli or the rest of his two hundred tenants.

Yes. The lawsuit was worth it, even if it meant she became a spinster and had to fear the scent of cigarette smoke leaking through her apartment's ventilation system. She had an obligation to her father and grandfather to keep fighting the Saratoga Drakes. Her uncle had a fortune, an army of lawyers, and three rounds of lower court decisions on his side. Most importantly, he had no soul, and that let him fight with the single-minded zeal of a jackal.

But she and Nick had a weapon the Saratoga Drakes knew nothing about. For two years it had served to keep them one step ahead of her uncle and all his scheming. It was a risky weapon that could land her and Nick in jail, but with luck, it would also finally turn the tide in the Manhattan Drakes' favor.

Chapter
TWO

*L*ucy sat at her booth in the cavernous office of the Associated Press on the sixth floor of the Western Union Telegraph building. Forty-five people worked in this office, receiving coded messages from all over the world. With the clicking of dots and dashes coming across dozens of telegraph machines, the noise in the office probably sounded like chaos to most people, but Lucy focused only on the stream of Morse code coming from an operator in Boston who was sending her a report about the opening of another segment of the Boston subway.

A buzzer sounded on the desk beside her, but she ignored it as she continued translating the message. The buzzer was a summons from her supervisor, but it was standard procedure to finish receiving a message in progress before responding to a summons. In the news business, speed was everything. Their office even had a series of pneumatic tubes into which they placed freshly delivered stories so they could be whisked away at an awesome speed to another floor in the building for further distribution.

Ten minutes later, she stepped into Mr. Tolland's office and managed to catch a fat copy of the *Times of London* before it smacked her in the chest.

"They've scooped us again!" Mr. Tolland said through gritted teeth. "Our reporter in the field swears he immediately submitted his story about the Chinese invasion of Manchuria, but the telegram did not arrive at our office until an hour ago. And yet the *Times* had the story yesterday."

Lucy knew better than to interrupt Mr. Tolland when he was on a rant. After all, he was angry with Reuters, not her. The newspaper industry was a fiercely competitive business, and a few hours could make the difference between having a bonanza day or being old news. Lately, whenever a story was wired in from the Far East, Reuters had consistently beaten them to the punch.

Both Reuters and the Associated Press were news agencies. Newspapers from all over the world contracted with one of them to provide stories of national and international interest, which were wired in and republished in local papers. The British news agency Reuters had dominated the industry since it was established in 1851. The Associated Press was the American equivalent, but they were new and still struggling to establish a foothold.

The Associated Press embodied American capitalism. They were efficient, competitive, and no one could transmit bulletins to their affiliated newspapers faster than the AP. Lucy ought to know. She was one of the agency's best telegraphers and could type and translate Morse code as fast as she could speak. She loved transcribing stories from AP journalists in sunbaked African plains or the fjords of Scandinavia. Thanks to the transatlantic cable that joined New York to all the major cities of Europe, news could be wired across the ocean in less than five minutes. The AP was known to print stories occurring in London before the *Times of London* even got their presses cranking.

American reporters were scrappy, fast, and famous for sending stories over the wire as they happened. It was a privilege to be part of this vast network of dedicated professionals committed to spreading the news of the world to anyone willing to open the pages of a newspaper.

There was only one huge, glaring flaw in the AP's business model. There was no undersea cable across the Pacific Ocean. Stories from Russia and the Far East had to travel through a network of overland cables through British colonies in order to reach the United States. And who did they pay to transmit those stories?

Reuters.

Any time a journalist working for the AP wanted to send a wire from China or Japan, it had to be sent over a Reuters cable and across British colonies. The AP paid plenty for the privilege, and it had been working well until recently. Lucy could pinpoint the day, even the very hour, their stories from the Far East started slowing down.

It was the day Sir Colin Beckwith took over the administration of Reuters' New York office. Everything changed the moment he entered the building, even though her boss refused to believe it.

"I suspect the problem may originate with Mr. Beckwith," she said. She refused to use his stuffy British title. They were in America, and she had no obligation to bow and scrape before Reuters' golden boy.

"Sir Beckwith is far too much of a gentleman to tamper with our stories," Mr. Tolland said.

Never in her life had Lucy seen a man so high in the instep as Colin Beckwith. He'd actually been humming "God Save the King" the one and only time they met in person. It was on New Year's Eve in Central Park, and Lucy had done her best to block the mortifying night from her memory. She doubted he

15

even remembered it, for every subsequent time she encountered him at a streetcar stop or in the elevator, his gaze slid past her with no sign of recognition. A mercy, really.

"The delayed messages started shortly after Mr. Beckwith arrived in the New York office. I'm certain—"

Mr. Tolland cut her off. He was the one who had negotiated the deal with Reuters, so he had a vested interest in believing the plan was proceeding like clockwork, despite all evidence to the contrary.

"Our contract with Reuters is explicit," he groused. "Stories arriving at the New York office are to be delivered to us within two hours of receipt. Reuters would be in breach of contract if they deliberately slowed our stories. I want you to check the pneumatic tubes to see if they're malfunctioning."

Lucy had inherited her family's technical know-how, and that skill had helped her rise quickly through the ranks at the AP. In addition to sending and receiving messages, she was responsible for ensuring the pneumatic tubes were in working order. The tubes used vacuum pressure to shoot small canisters carrying mail or other documents from floor to floor.

"I'll look into it immediately," she said.

Thousands of magnetic clicks filled the air as she stepped onto the main floor of the office and headed to the sending stations at the end of each aisle. She examined the pneumatic tubes' conduit pipes, air vents, and flex hoses, all of which were properly connected. She would need to inspect the central power station in the basement and the access station in the Reuters office to confirm all was in order. It was a fool's errand, but she needed to do it to pacify Mr. Tolland and safeguard her job.

But first she was going to head straight to the source of the trouble: the office of Sir Colin Beckwith. Next week was another court hearing against the Saratoga Drakes, which meant another lawyer bill needed to be paid. She was not going to let her job be endangered because of Colin Beckwith's loose definition of fair play.

❦

Reuters and the AP occupied different floors of the same office building at 195 Broadway. The Western Union Telegraph building was a spectacular ten-story edifice built specifically to send and receive telegraph and telephone messages from all over the world. The awesome network of wires and cables coming from the building made it the natural place for both Reuters and the AP to set up operations. Their presence made 195 Broadway the heart of the news industry for the entire North American continent.

Lucy climbed the two stories to the floor occupied by Reuters. The differences between the AP and Reuters offices were stark. Whereas the AP's lobby was full of office supplies laid out in military precision, the foyer of Reuters displayed flags from dozens of colonies and territories of the United Kingdom, a portrait of the king, and a life-sized statue of a rearing lion. A large silver urn provided hot tea alongside platters of shortbread and wedges of Cheshire cheese, all served on real china. The AP had a public drinking fountain.

The secretary at the front desk spoke in an elegant British accent. Reuters was entitled to hire whoever they wished, but couldn't they staff the clerical jobs with New York residents? The AP always hired local people from the area for clerical positions at their foreign offices.

"Is Mr. Beckwith available?" Lucy asked.

"Do you mean *Sir* Beckwith?" the secretary asked pointedly, managing to look down her nose at Lucy even though she was seated.

"That's the one." She'd choke before using his title. She didn't wait for the secretary's response, instead heading back through the corridor to the corner office belonging to the director.

Lucy had seen Colin Beckwith many times in the four months since he'd arrived from London. He wasn't terribly tall but still cut a dashing figure with high cheekbones, flawless attire, and the smooth, cultured accent that sounded as if it came straight from Buckingham Palace. With sky-blue eyes and perfectly groomed golden-blond hair, all he needed was a laurel wreath crowning his head to make him look like he'd just stepped down from Mount Olympus to mingle with the peons.

She needed to root out the cause for their delayed messages from Asia, and that meant she was going to have to swallow her pride and speak with him again. She just hoped he didn't remember their first meeting.

The door to his office was open, revealing a palatial desk and an open window overlooking downtown Manhattan, but no sign of Mr. Beckwith. A familiar rattle caught her attention, and she took a step inside the office. Once across the threshold, she could see him hunched over a corner table with his ear cocked to a miniature telegraph sounder, almost as though he was receiving an actual message.

"Mr. Beckwith?"

He shot her an annoyed glance. "Hush!"

He immediately turned his attention back to the rapid-fire transmission of clicks coming from the magnetic sounder. Colin Beckwith understood Morse code? That was impressive. No one in the AP's top management could send or receive messages, and only the very best operators could translate in their head without jotting down the letters as they went. He was decoding as he listened. Her respect for him inched up a notch. He couldn't be a completely inept blue blood if he could translate Morse code on the fly.

His face looked spellbound as he concentrated on the message coming off the sounder. Enraptured. He was actually holding his breath as he listened to the taps coming off the telegraph machine. Something about a man that passionate about life was intrinsically appealing.

Stop! The last thing she wanted was to let this unwieldy attraction get the better of her again. Besides, what sort of news provoked such rapt attention from Mr. Beckwith? Did Reuters know something the AP didn't? It wouldn't do to let them scoop her employer on another story, so she cocked her head to listen. Even from across the room, she was able to make sense of the clicks coming from the sounder.

```
Gentlemen of India, 118 dash 10. Oxford 146
dash 5.
```

Lucy blinked, not sure what to make of the strange message that enthralled Mr. Beckwith. His hand clenched so tightly his knuckles were white, and emotions flitted across his face as he digested the news. She turned her focus back to decoding the message as it came over the wire.

```
Williams took five wickets. Barnes caught
at cover point off Grigson from a no-ball.
Fielding all around very smart.
```

Cricket scores! He was listening to *cricket scores!* They hadn't yet received today's update from the Philippines, where three thousand American troops were stationed, but it was good to know Reuters was on top of the latest cricket news. She folded her arms and waited for the end of the transmission, forcing her breathing to remain calm. She had stood up to bigger opponents than Colin Beckwith, but it was dangerous to let a rival see any hint of agitation. Her father had taught her that long ago.

At last Mr. Beckwith closed the circuit, adjusted his collar, and rose to his feet. He dressed very formally for the office. Few men wore high-stand collars anymore, but it gave him a refined appearance that was hard not to admire.

"Miss Drake, correct?"

She startled. "How did you know my name?"

"You told me," he said with a teasing glint in his eye. "New Year's Eve, eleven o'clock, standing in front of the vendors near 86th Street. You wore a scarlet knit cap, and your brother was ready to strangle me."

Heat gathered in her face. So he did remember. She squared her shoulders, determined not to revisit the event. "Mr. Tolland is frustrated with the lack of timeliness of AP stories from the Far East," she said. "I've been sent to investigate the possibility of a problem with the pneumatic tubes, but I suspect the slowdown may originate elsewhere." She glanced pointedly at the telegraph station. "Perhaps on a cricket field in Oxford."

He scrutinized her with a curious light in his gaze. "Did I hear a hint of reproach in that comment? Why, yes, I think I did. Come inside and tell me what egregious sin I've committed. I have so many failings and am probably guilty as charged."

He held a chair for her, then rounded his desk and took a seat, fixing her with a pleasant smile that probably thrilled the peasants in Europe. She didn't care how thick he laid on the charm, she needed Reuters to live up to their contractual obligations, and until he arrived in New York, they had.

"The AP has been experiencing delays with our messages from India, Russia, and all of the Asian nations."

There was no waver in his composure. "And?"

"And I think you know something about it."

"About a delay? Nonsense. Our contract with the AP would not permit it." He smiled with the innocence of a freshly bloomed rose.

"The slowdown did not happen until you were appointed director of the New York office."

"Are you suggesting I have something to do with it? The cheek."

"I am not a big believer in coincidences."

He tutted. "Whatever happened to American get-up-and-go? Whatever happened to a sense of competition? I thought you took pride in being faster, better, and cheaper. That you worked around the clock to deliver and never whined about being second best."

Her chin lifted at that *second best* jab, but she kept her voice calm. "The AP doesn't mind paying for a service. If you'd care to peruse your contract, you will find that's what we bargained for until our cable is ready."

The Americans were on the verge of completing an undersea Pacific cable that would render this contract with Reuters irrelevant. As soon as the Pacific cable went into operation, the AP would no longer need this cumbersome workaround. In a few months, the final link of the undersea cable would connect Hawaii to the Philippines, and Reuters was still bitter over the deal. They'd tried to negotiate landing rights for a cable in Hawaii, but the Americans now controlled the island and refused to permit it.

"I suspect the time is near when you'll be asking to lease our Pacific cable," she said. "I can't imagine we'll extend the courtesy if you don't honor your existing contract with us."

"Sour grapes are so unattractive," he purred.

"Then you admit you've been slowing our cables?"

"Why would I admit to something that would put us in violation of a contract? You seem to have an irrational sense of urgency. The AP is still getting their bulletins, every word of them. Why the rush?"

Because the AP was hanging on by a thread, barely able to

operate on the razor-thin profits from their subscribing news-papers, while Reuters was so heavily subsidized by the Crown that they fitted out their office with lavish furniture and relaxed for a catered tea each afternoon. Reuters had been a thriving company since its founding in 1851 and was in no danger of folding if they lost a few subscribers. Reuters could afford to be fat and lazy; the AP could not.

"As you noted, it is important for us to be faster, better, and cheaper than the competition."

Her train of thought was interrupted as a bird flew through the open window and circled through the center of the office.

"Oh my heavens!" She darted to the far side of the room as the flapping bird careened toward the desk. Rather than appear startled at the invasion, Mr. Beckwith stood and extended his arm. The bird settled onto his hand and twitched a little as it straightened its ruffled feathers.

"Good girl," Mr. Beckwith murmured to the ugly bird, pass-ing it onto a perch beside his desk. He unfastened a tiny canister attached to the bird's leathery claw. "Have you any experience with homing pigeons?" he asked as he extracted a tiny strip of paper from the tube.

"I didn't realize anyone still used them."

"Not many people do, but it was how Reuters made a name for itself during its early years, and I believe in keeping tradi-tion alive."

The pigeon pecked at a lump of seed-covered suet, scattering kernels and bits of fat onto the floor. It was a plump, dull gray bird that looked dirty to Lucy's eyes, but she was intrigued as Mr. Beckwith passed her the strip of paper to inspect. Miniscule dots and dashes crammed a surprising amount of information onto the six-inch strip. She decoded quickly. Dinner tonight was a formal affair, and he must wear tails and a top hat.

"Wouldn't it have been easier to pick up a telephone?" she asked.

Mr. Beckwith tossed the piece of paper onto his desk. "Telephones are unreliable, and we all know that telegraph operators are notorious eavesdroppers. Not that *you* would ever commit such a gross error in etiquette, I'm sure."

She declined to comment. Telegraph operators *were* infamous for listening in on the wires. During overnight shifts when the wires were slow, they chatted with one another for hours. As many as twenty stations could be connected through a single line, and any telegraph operator along the line could listen in without anyone noticing. Sheer boredom often prompted operators to send messages on everything from office gossip to sporting scores to politics. Those who didn't chat sometimes simply lurked and listened.

She glanced at the strip of paper. "And tonight's dress code warrants top-secret delivery by homing pigeon?"

"My butler thought so."

"You have *a butler*?" She thought butlers had gone the way of homing pigeons.

"Just because I'm stationed in the hinterlands doesn't mean I ought to surrender all the comforts of civilization. Of course I have a butler. A footman, a valet, and a housekeeper, too."

He flashed that smile again, a man on top of the world, as though the angels themselves had set him there.

"With all that help, I'd expect you'd be a little quicker getting things done here at the office. I'd like to see if Reuters can step up to the plate and fulfill their obligations regarding the Pacific cables."

"And I'd like a raspberry torte with chocolate drizzle for afternoon tea. That doesn't mean I'm going to get it. If the Americans don't like the way we handle their business, they can go get their own colonies." He beamed that insufferable smile at her again. "Now, if you have no further accusations or insults, it's time for me to get back to the telegraph. News from the Cambridge cricket match is due shortly."

Lucy knew a dismissal when she heard it and left without saying good-bye.

Colin remained motionless for a full minute after the door slammed. Lucy Drake was as attractive as he remembered. He wished she wasn't.

It had been four months since he first caught sight of her on a snowy New Year's Eve in Central Park. Thousands of people crowded the park for the fireworks at midnight. The pond was open for ice skaters, strands of electric lightbulbs illuminated the area with a festive glow, and vendors did brisk business selling warm eggnog, hot chocolate, and toasted chestnuts. He had only been in America for three days, and it was his first time to witness the amazing cross section of people enjoying the park. Millionaires in chinchilla furs mingled alongside immigrants wrapped only in woolen blankets, but it seemed perfectly normal to everyone at the celebration.

It would have been fascinating had he not been frozen to his core. Why hadn't someone warned him how viciously cold New York could be? It was freezing! The cold penetrated straight through his thin topcoat, and he would have returned to his townhouse if he hadn't been so enchanted by the spectacle before him.

He stood in line at a vendor's cart for a mug of hot chocolate, blowing into his cupped hands and humming "God Save the King" while stomping his feet as he waited for the girl in front of him to finish haggling over the price of toasted chestnuts. Why couldn't she pay the extra nickel and move on? Although he had to admire the way her red cap perched at a jaunty angle over her glossy black hair. Any girl who had the courage to wear such a saucy cap was probably a lot of fun. He only wished she wasn't such a penny pincher.

"Oh, for pity's sake," he finally interrupted. "I'll pay for the blasted chestnuts. Just fetch me a mug of hot chocolate, please. Hopefully before I catch my death of frostbite." He covered his mouth and blew on his hands again, and the girl turned around to gape at him.

He was gobsmacked. She had a pretty face with a narrow chin, but it was her dark eyes that captured his attention. They were full of laughter and sparkled in the light from the streetlamp.

"I don't think you can actually *die* of frostbite, can you?" she asked.

A young man with wild hair and the same dark coloring stood beside her. "You could if it catches gangrene. I think it develops seepage in the worst cases."

The girl turned back to Colin. "Well? Do you have seepage?"

"What I have is an urgent need to buy something hot. I'm serious about paying for your meal, although a simple sign posting the prices could help us avoid all this pointless haggling. The queues in London move much quicker because we simply post the price."

"Did you hear that, Nick?" the girl said. "Our new best friend from London is going to buy our meal."

The wild-haired man grinned. "In that case, I want a hot pastrami sandwich, too. Why didn't you just put on a decent coat, London? It's December."

"Because it's not supposed to be so insanely cold here," he defended. "New York is ten latitude degrees south of England, so this freeze makes no sense."

"It's called the Gulf Stream," the girl replied. "Didn't they teach you about it in those fancy British schools?"

He suppressed a smile and tried to sound firm as he paid for their food. "The two of you are pure torture."

Of course he knew about the Gulf Stream, which carried warm air from the Caribbean all the way across the Atlantic and kept Britain warmer than other countries at the same latitude. But it was one thing to study it in a book, and quite another to freeze to death because he hadn't taken it seriously. Having spent the past two years in Africa, he had forgotten how miserable twenty degrees felt.

"Thanks, London," the wild-haired man replied. "We'll put up with your mangled pronunciation anytime if you keep treating us to free food."

"*I'm* mangling the language?" he asked.

"You said 'tow-cha' instead of torture," the girl observed as they moved farther down the path.

"Dearest, the British have been mangling our pronunciation since Shakespeare. Sadly for you, we get the final say. The proper pronunciation of the word is 'tow-cha.'"

She flashed a fantastic grin. "I think my brother and I need to give you a lesson on how to speak properly. Otherwise you're bound to make a fool of yourself over here."

"Go ahead." He heroically stopped the laughter from leaking into his voice. "I am dying to hear your insight into the mother tongue." He had gone to school with Queen Victoria's grandchildren. In England his lofty accent put people on notice of his class, and they tended to automatically defer to him. But he liked these two. They introduced themselves merely as Lucy and Nick, and when they learned he worked for Reuters, they thought it was hilarious.

"I don't believe you work for Reuters," Lucy said. "You can barely speak English. How can you possibly spell?"

They took a seat at a table near the bandstand and traded insults while they ate. It might have been the most fun Colin had ever had. His fingers and toes were so cold they could barely move, the hot chocolate was watery and the brass band badly out of tune, but it was a magical evening spent with two wonderfully irreverent people.

It came to an abrupt and mortifying end when Lucy made a play for him. When she found out he had never been to Steeplechase Park, nor had he ever ridden a Ferris wheel, she grabbed his arm.

"We must go!" she said, her eyes lively in the moonlight. "I could meet you there sometime. Couples pair up for the ride. Wouldn't that be fun?"

It would, but he was not a free man, and his attraction to her was growing by the minute. He couldn't afford this. He stared at the spot where her hand clutched his arm and wished every nerve ending in his body hadn't flared to life at her touch.

He hardened his face, and she withdrew her hand. "That is, if you like," she stammered.

"A fair like that really isn't my sort of thing," he said. "It sounds a bit riffraff, doesn't it?"

Lucy seemed to shrink within her heavy overcoat, but Nick's eyes narrowed. "Hey, Lucy," he said through clenched teeth, "are we riffraff and never noticed it before?"

An awkward silence descended. He hadn't meant to sound quite so arrogant, but he needed to put some distance between himself and this girl who disrupted his equilibrium.

"No offense, but I'm not exactly the type of man who can consort with any pretty girl he meets in a park."

Nick stood. "I don't know what 'consort' means over in London, but my sister didn't just ask to *consort* with you, mister."

True, the word had some unsavory connotations, but it was nothing worth coming to blows over, which was what it looked like Nick wanted.

Colin rose and excused himself just before the fireworks began, and hadn't spoken to Lucy since. In the intervening months, he'd seen her in the elevator and in the cafeteria on the first floor of their shared office building. He'd recognized her immediately, for her heart-shaped face and dark, flashing eyes were impossible to forget.

He only wished he could.

With a sigh, he turned his attention to the day's mail. A letter had arrived from the home office in London, and it deserved his full attention.

It wasn't good news. Reuters continued to lose subscribers to the AP, and it was beginning to affect morale. The previous director of the New York office had quit after hemorrhaging close to a hundred subscribers to the fledgling news agency, and it was Colin's job to stem the loss. Even worse than losing the subscriptions was that some of their correspondents were jumping ship and signing on with the AP. That had to stop.

He drummed his fingers on his desk. Until last year, Colin had been one of those correspondents in the field. He'd cut his teeth covering foreign wars for Reuters. This new management position was a challenge, but one he welcomed. Although he had no managerial experience, he had connections, charisma, and a desperate need to prove himself. He would do so.

A knock at the door broke his concentration. It was Albert Fergusson, one of their best telegraph operators, looking pale and nervous and clutching a slip of paper in his hands. "Are you ready for our appointment, sir?"

Colin had entirely forgotten their eleven o'clock meeting, but he stood and gestured to the chair across from his desk. "Of course. What can I do for you, Mr. Fergusson?"

"There's no easy way to say this, but I'm afraid I need to tender my resignation. I've accepted a position with the AP."

Colin wanted to mutter a curse, but he kept any trace of emotion from leaking onto his face as Mr. Fergusson set his resignation letter on the desk. Colin refused to touch it. He affected a pleasant smile. "May I ask why?"

"I got married to an American lady last month, so I'll be living in New York for good. I might as well throw my lot in with the local team, right?"

Quitting Reuters in favor of the AP was beyond appalling. It was opting for ground hamburger when prime steak was on the menu.

"And if I may be so bold," Mr. Fergusson continued, looking more uncomfortable than ever.

"Please."

"There's been a lot of grumbling out on the floor. People see more subscribers going over to the AP, and when the Pacific cable goes into service, everyone knows we will lose even more. Some are saying our best days are behind us."

That last line was a slap in the face. Colin had dedicated his life to this company. He'd fought and nearly died for it. Their best days would never be *over*. The sun would never set on the British Empire. The man standing before him was a lost cause, but Colin couldn't let this crumbling morale spread and infect the rest of the staff. He needed to handle the situation with dignity and aplomb. He rose and offered his hand.

"Congratulations, Mr. Fergusson. I wish you and Mrs. Fergusson the very best."

The moment the telegrapher left, Colin pressed the buzzer on his desk to summon his secretary.

"Tell the staff to close down their sounders at twelve o'clock. I have something to say."

His secretary looked surprised. Shutting down the telegraph machines was serious business, but it was Colin's duty to light a fire under his staff, and bringing the office to a standstill underscored the importance of his message. It was time to rally the troops. He wasn't going to let the AP best him in anything.

At twelve o'clock sharp, he stepped onto the main floor of Reuters, where five aisles contained sixty telegraphers, who received news wired in from all corners of the globe. Most of the telegraph operators had already stopped receiving messages and looked at him with curiosity and concern as he stood at the front of the office, waiting for the last of the operators to finish translating their stories, close their sounders, and prepare to listen. In addition to the operators, a dozen translators, ten secretaries, and a butler all awaited his announcement.

"Rumor has it that the AP is gaining on us in terms of newspaper subscribers," he began. "Although it is to be expected that newspapers here in the States might want to patronize our American competitor, it is our job to convince them otherwise. I've heard that some people fear the Pacific cable is going to be a problem for us. Please! It isn't a bunch of cable wires that makes us great—it is our writers, our telegraph operators, our willingness to venture into the wildest and most dangerous corners of the world and bring the stories back to the home front. Who cares if the Americans get a fancy new cable? It is decades of experience, centuries of empire, and a crusading spirit that make Reuters great, and no Pacific cable can ever undermine that."

He slowly scanned the room, making eye contact with his staff and injecting new energy into his voice. "Reuters is the greatest news agency in the world. Our territory spans the globe. Everywhere we go, we are examples of civilization and dignity. The Americans like to pretend they are the founders of democracy, but please—England is closing in on the 700th anniversary of the Magna Carta, the original breakthrough in democratic ideals. We have more creativity and imagination than the rest of the world combined. Shakespeare, Chaucer, Milton. King Arthur and Robin Hood. Cricket, the long bow, the steam engine. We discovered or invented them all."

His statement was greeted with a rumble of laughter and a little foot-stomping. One of the telegraph operators reached over a partition to shake Colin's hand, but he wasn't close to being finished yet.

"We can claim the sandwich and the world's best cup of tea. Proper queuing. Have you noticed how these Americans swarm like uncivilized beasts? Our dignified, single-file queue puts them to shame." His statement was met with huge grins and vigorous nods. A few in the back stood and clapped. His voice rose in volume to project all the way down the hall.

"We've faced down invasions from the Romans, the Huns, the Vikings, and the good Lord knows we have faced down the French." He stepped closer to the work floor, paused, and gave a slow smile of satisfaction. "My friends, we can handle the AP."

The room broke out in spontaneous applause.

*L*ucy snapped awake in the dead of night, uncertain what had roused her. She lay motionless in bed, holding her breath while listening for any disturbance in the apartment, but all was silent. Even so, her cloying sense of unease would make it impossible to sleep again. It felt as though someone was watching her, but that was foolish. Her bedroom door was closed, and since her window faced a brick wall across the narrow side alley, no one from the ground could possibly see into her fourth-story room. Rolling out of bed, she padded into the front room, where weak illumination from the gaslight outside was enough to read the clock. Four thirty in the morning.

She walked to the window and looked down into the street. During the last years of his life, her father often stood in this exact spot and stared into the street below. It was usually late at night or in the early predawn hours that she'd seen him here, always tense, always ill at ease. What had tormented him so?

She was certain it related to the lawsuit, for Uncle Thomas could be fiendishly clever in his attacks. The one time Lucy had a suitor brave enough to court her, a series of foul tricks brought the relationship to an abrupt end. Samuel had been her lawyer's legal assistant. He was smart and endlessly optimistic, the kind of man who walked between raindrops without getting wet. They courted for three months and were soon engaged to be married. How eager she'd been to begin sharing her life with someone! She might look prim on the outside, but inside she churned with a pent-up longing to take care of someone and *be* taken care of.

Samuel seemed perfect for her. He knew everything about the Saratoga Drakes and said he wasn't afraid of them. When a dead cat was placed in his mailbox, he shrugged it off. Then a dead cat arrived on his mother's doorstep, and he took it more seriously. A few days later, they attended a vaudeville show, and he'd been nervous and distracted, chewing his thumbnail the entire performance and never once cracking a smile.

The next day there had been broadsides with his photograph tacked on telephone poles up and down the street where he lived, accusing him of consorting with prostitutes and being a confidence man. Samuel was attending law school, and this sort of thing could make it impossible to be admitted to the bar in New York.

He severed ties with her the following day. She did her best to smile and say she understood, but she sobbed into her pillow for the next three nights.

That was the last time anyone had been brave enough to court her. Would she ever find a man who would stand alongside her and face down her uncle?

Lucy wrapped a blanket around her shoulders, chilled at the memory, as she stared into the street below. Early morning activity had already begun. A street sweeper guided a rotating brush pulled by a pair of horses, and a bread factory wagon lumbered toward the grocers on the neighboring block. These were normal sights, but the man who set her teeth on edge was leaning against a lamppost directly across the street from her apartment.

His features were entirely obscured by shadows, but she'd seen him before. He was tall and thin, dressed in a dark overcoat and a battered derby hat, the glow of a cigarette tip showing beneath the brim. It was hard to tell, since his coat was baggy, but it seemed one of his shoulders was a little higher than the other. Or maybe it was merely her imagination after hearing Mr. Garzelli's description of the man snooping around his tenement building.

It seemed like he was looking directly at her. She slid to the side of the window just to be safe. She was certain she'd seen him before, and there must be a reason he stood watch outside their apartment.

The temptation to wake Nick clawed at her, but he'd be annoyed if she did. She didn't want to admit it, but Nick was growing frustrated with her. The odds of the man leaning against the lamppost being affiliated with Uncle Thomas were minuscule, and what could he learn by staring at their darkened apartment, anyway?

She swallowed her sense of unease, and by the time she dressed and headed to work two hours later, the lamppost leaner was gone. She tried to banish him from her mind as she settled into her station and got to work.

Rattling clicks filled the air as information was piped in from all over the world. There had been a time when individual newspapers tried to send their own journalists to the major cities of the world, but it was an expensive endeavor few could afford. It soon became evident that the American newspapers ought to band together and follow the model created by Reuters, in which a single company sent journalists across the globe, and any newspaper willing to pay a subscription fee could have access to all the stories submitted by AP reporters.

Lucy opened a connection that carried all the way to San Francisco, beneath the sea to Hawaii, and then to the newest station added to the line on the tiny outpost island of Midway.

An uninhabited island between Hawaii and Japan, Midway was only two square miles in size and, until recently, a mere patch of sand without any trees or wildlife. But the government had selected it as the midway point for laying the undersea cable, so for the past year, the navy had helped settle the island by importing trees, farm animals, and plenty of supplies for building an outpost. An assignment on Midway was considered the least desirable post in the entire world. There was literally nothing to do other than drink or gamble with the other eleven men who'd been stationed there.

Lucy opened her sounder to summon the Midway operator. She clicked a four letter message. *"M B—P 4."* It was the code that identified the AP's Manhattan office, sending a message to the Pacific Four station on Midway.

Nine minutes later, her call was answered. *"P 4 Roland here. Who calls?"*

She smiled. Roland Montgomery was one of her favorite operators and always game for a little gossip. Chatter along the wires could be heard by any of the dozens of telegraph operators between here and Midway, and sometimes conversations got quite lively during slow news days. Should anyone need the wire for official business, they broke in and took over the wire, but as soon as the business was completed, the operators went back to gossiping.

"Lucy," she clicked back. *"Any news on completion of the cable to the Philippines?"* The moment the Pacific cable was completed, they would have no need to deal with Reuters or the insufferable Colin Beckwith ever again.

When Roland replied, it was not good news. *"Storms off the Mariana Islands slowing the ships. Two-month delay."*

She groaned. The mighty cable-laying ships were unwieldy, carrying tons of wire in enormous coils near the back of the ship, which made the vessels unsteady in rough water.

"*What news of TR?*" Roland asked, and Lucy rolled her eyes. While most of the operators on Midway wanted gossip from home, Roland followed politics with the zeal of a bloodhound and always wanted news of the president.

Another operator broke in on the conversation. "*TR is a wonderful, brave, and wise man. You have convinced me. He is the best president we have ever had.*"

"*That was not me!*" Lucy immediately keyed as fast as she could type.

One of the problems with chatting on the line was that unless operators identified themselves, it was impossible to know who sent the message or from where. She and Roland enjoyed a healthy debate about President Roosevelt, and most operators along the wire knew she could barely tolerate the president, while Roland idolized him as though he were King Arthur come to save the nation.

His response soon came from Midway. "*TR is the first real man to sit in the White House. News of Panama?*"

"*Hold,*" Lucy replied and closed the circuit while she ran to snatch a copy of today's *New York Times*. Of all the bold moves President Roosevelt had initiated, plans for a canal through the Isthmus of Panama was at the forefront. The narrow strip of land was part of Colombia, a nation reluctant to permit American engineers into their territory for the construction of the forty-eight-mile canal. Rumor had it that Roosevelt was encouraging rebels in the northern part of the nation to revolt and create their own independent country that would be called Panama. Lucy skimmed the paper, quickly landing on two stories about the topic, and summarized them as concisely as possible.

"*Plans for a canal moving forward. TR signed a treaty with Colombian diplomat to proceed, but Colombian Senate refuses to ratify. Standoff continues.*"

"*Bully!*" someone along the wire keyed.

A lively debate ensued among half a dozen operators sharing the line, with Roland on Midway being the most vocal. Lucy could only imagine the boredom of a man stuck on a desolate island, which might explain his eagerness to chat. He carried on a spirited discussion about presidential politics for a full ten minutes before another operator entered the line.

"*Breaking in with story from San Francisco.*"

Lucy immediately shifted her attention away from gossip and back to her job. She grabbed a notepad to write out the incoming bulletin about a shipwreck off the coast of California. The rest of the afternoon was busy as she transcribed a series of reports from Pittsburg about the ongoing strike of mineworkers, revolutionary sentiment in the Balkans, and the story of a man in Miami who crawled six miles in order to win a two-dollar bet.

The AP had over two hundred correspondents spread throughout the world, and they were encouraged to submit at least one story daily—more, if they were stationed in a major city. It didn't matter what Lucy thought of the stories as they came over the wire. She transcribed them into careful script, then sent them through the pneumatic tube to another floor, where each story would be made available to all of their subscribers.

She was transcribing an article about the arrival of a new diplomat from Mexico when a disturbance at the window caught her attention.

A bird seemed to be in distress. It flapped against the window glass and attempted to land, but the ledge was too narrow. It was strange for a bird to fly this high up, but she was too busy transcribing a message to spare a second glance at the bird.

Leonard, the operator at the booth next to hers, noticed and stood. "What's that bird doing?" he asked.

Another agent whose wire had gone silent stood and rapped on the glass to frighten the bird away.

"Something on the ledge is attracting it," Leonard said. "Dirty pigeons. They make a mess of the city." He joined the other agent at the window and rapped on the glass as well.

Pigeon? Lucy glanced at the window while trying to keep up with the incoming message from Mexico. The bird looked exactly like the homing pigeon she'd seen at Colin Beckwith's office, but her sounder continued to rattle out the message, and she had missed several words.

She opened her key to break the circuit. *"Please repeat last line."* Lucy almost never needed to ask an operator to repeat or slow down, but that pigeon was distracting her. The operator obliged and rekeyed the last sentence. When the transmission was complete, Lucy closed her circuit and hurried to the window. The bird still struggled to land on the narrow ledge, and sure enough, she spotted a tiny canister attached to its leg. There was a layer of suet and seed spread on the windowsill. Had this bird been trained to come here? She opened the window.

"Don't let it in," Leonard said, aghast. "Pigeons carry filth and disease."

"I think this one is trained." Lucy extended her hand the way she'd seen Colin Beckwith do last week.

Oh heavens. She was a city girl, and the leathery feet of the pigeon were unexpectedly cold and strong as it clasped her hand. The bird was heavy, too! She held her breath as she walked it back to her booth, the other operators watching in amazement.

"Yes, I have remarkable powers," she said in a nervous voice, feeling every eye in the office on her.

She had no perch, but the pigeon seemed game for being passed off onto the back of her chair. She carefully untied the tiny canister on its leg and wiggled the message out. It was in Morse code, but she read it quickly.

```
Greetings, Miss Drake. I send congratulations
on the triumph of the Reliance in the
America's Cup yachting race. The Shamrock
was clearly no match for the American yacht.
C.B.
```

Had the US won the America's Cup? Fancy yachting races weren't normally something she followed, but if America beat the British at something, she wanted to know. Reuters knew about the win, so someone in this room had probably gotten the story as well.

"Have we won the America's Cup?" she asked the room of telegraphers.

Ralph Boylston in the back of the room raised a slip of paper. "It came across the wire five minutes ago. The *Reliance* beat the UK yacht three to nothing."

A cheer went up from the room. Ever since Reuters moved in, there had been plenty of conflict between the rival agencies. Ralph proceeded to read the rest of the story aloud. The *Reliance* was built by Cornelius Vanderbilt with the sole intention of winning the America's Cup. It was a skeleton yacht, entirely unfinished below decks and had nothing aboard other than what it took to sail fast. It made the *Reliance* lighter and faster than any other ship on the water because it was nothing but a hollow shell.

"That doesn't seem too sporting," one of the older telegraphers said.

"All I care about is that we beat the British," Lucy replied. Colin Beckwith's smug attitude still stung, but at least he'd written a gracious note. She read the message to the assembled people in the office.

"Reuters is using homing pigeons?" Leonard asked in a voice as stunned as if they had gone back to using smoke signals. It did feel like stepping back in time, but in a fun way.

"I don't think it's a Reuters initiative, I think it's a Colin Beckwith quirk." She'd never used a homing pigeon before and wanted to try it. Flipping the strip of paper over, she wrote as small as possible in a series of dots and dashes.

```
Thank you. Strike a point for faster, better,
and cheaper.
```

After attaching the canister back onto the pigeon's leg, she carefully walked the bird to the open window and cautiously extended her arm. The bird needed no coaxing and lifted off to disappear from view somewhere above her window. Would it find its way home?

She shouldn't have worried, for less than five minutes later, the bird was flapping at the window again. She read the note for the office.

```
Vanderbilt cheated with the hollow yacht.
They are changing the rules next year so he
can't do it again.
```

A chorus of groans mixed with snickering filled the air. A few men suggested replies liberally laced with obscenities, but Lucy needed no help penning her one-word reply.

```
Bitter?
```

The bird returned two minutes after she sent it off.

```
Not bitter, just wish our civilized manners
had rubbed off on America. England's crew
drank from crystal and slept in beds with
```

`proper linen, while Vanderbilt's crew lived`
`like cattle in an empty hull.`

He'd gotten her with that one, for there was nothing she could say to defend Vanderbilt. She guided the pigeon back to the open window, leaned out, and looked up. Colin Beckwith was leaning out his window two floors up and grinning down at her.

"Hey, London!" she called out. "Here's your bird." She released the pigeon, and he lowered a hand to receive it.

Lucy was still smiling as she headed to the ladies' room to wash her hands. She'd never handled birds before, and it seemed a sensible thing to do.

Nellie Billingsford from the accounting department was straightening her hair before the mirror as Lucy walked in. "I just paid the bill for a copy of those photographs the *Harper's* reporter took of you," she said.

"Who?" Lucy turned on the tap and began lathering her hands with a bar of soap.

"Don't you remember?" Nellie asked. "That fellow from *Harper's Magazine* who did a profile about the AP. He took pictures all over the office."

Now Lucy remembered. Last month a photographer had set up his camera at several spots throughout the suite of AP offices and had asked to photograph her in particular because he wanted to show a woman operating a telegraph machine.

Nellie continued babbling as she adjusted the pins in her hair. "Mr. Tolland said he wanted copies of all the photographs for the company archives. We've been pestering the photographer incessantly because he never turned over copies, but I gather he's been sick. We finally got ahold of his assistant, who couldn't be nicer. He made copies of all the photographs and brought them right over."

Nellie turned to face Lucy and lowered her voice, even though they were the only people in the ladies' room. "Just between you and me, I think I know why the photographer was reluctant to turn them over. You appear in so many of the pictures that I think maybe he fancies you!"

Lucy remembered sitting for the *Harper's* photographer, but he'd only taken two pictures of her before moving on to take photographs elsewhere in the office. "Can I see?" she asked.

Two minutes later, she was in the accounting office, and everything Nellie said was correct. The pictures were almost all of her. Even when he was photographing from across the office, Lucy was in the center of the shot. Other photographs showed lunchtime at the cafeteria, employees waiting to board the elevator, and using the pneumatic tubes to send stories. She was in all of them.

She was ready to believe Nellie's assertion that the photographer might have a crush on her until she saw the pictures at the bottom of the stack, and her blood ran cold. One photograph showed her and Nick waiting at a streetcar stop. Another showed them at a German delicatessen a few blocks from their apartment.

An uncontrollable shiver raced down her arms. Someone was spying on her. He'd spent hours following her around, and she never even noticed.

A telephone call to *Harper's Magazine* confirmed her fears. The editor said there were no plans to feature the AP in any upcoming issue of the magazine, nor had they commissioned anyone to take photographs of the office. Someone had lied to gain access to her.

Lucy thanked the editor, hung up the telephone, and blew on her icy fingers to warm them. This had all the hallmarks of her Uncle Thomas, although his intention with these pictures was a mystery. It was frightening that but for the illness of the photographer, she never would have known anything about it.

❦❦❦

Lucy met Nick at their lawyer's office. They'd already had a meeting scheduled to go over their plans for the next day's court hearing, but now Lucy needed to know her rights about those disturbing photographs. She and Nick sat in flimsy wooden chairs before their lawyer's desk, noise from the fishmonger's stall on the street below floating through the open window.

"There's no law against someone taking photographs on a public street," Horace Pritchard said. He was not New York's finest attorney. He was overworked and understaffed, but he was the best they could afford. At least he was willing to meet with Lucy and Nick in the evenings, for neither of them could afford to take much time off work. "Unless he enters your home or other private property without permission, the photographer may take whatever pictures he likes."

Lucy folded her arms and scowled. She suspected the photographer might have violated the privacy of her apartment, but she had no proof other than the unnerving sense that someone was watching her. These photographs meant she couldn't even feel safe at work anymore.

Horace didn't seem worried about the photographs. All he wanted was to prepare for Uncle Thomas's latest motion. "So you know nothing about why your uncle filed a motion accusing you of bad faith?"

Lucy could not give him an honest answer, for if he had any idea of the "bad faith" she and Nick had been practicing, he would be duty-bound to report it to the judge. Besides, she couldn't imagine the Saratoga Drakes knew anything about her secret weapon. If they did, Uncle Thomas would have thrown her in jail long ago.

"I can't think of anything," she replied.

"Sometimes I wonder if we shouldn't just walk away," Nick said in a tired voice.

A stab of fear tugged at her. This wasn't the first time Nick seemed to be losing heart, but they couldn't give up. Theirs was a case of David versus Goliath, and in battles like that, the honorable people were supposed to persevere until they finally won.

She and Nick were part of a dispute that had begun decades before they were born, but some of her earliest memories were of watching her father wade through mounds of papers stacked on their apartment floor, the determination of a gladiator stamped on his grim face. So far they had lost every legal battle in the forty-year war, and with each appeal their prospects for winning grew dimmer, but Lucy could not stop. This lawsuit was in her blood and every breath she drew, because more than money was at stake. It was about decency and humanity and quality of life for millions of people packed into the burgeoning cities of the modern world.

It all began with two brothers who foolishly went into business together back in 1861. Jacob and Eustace Drake could not have been more different in character, ambition, or talent, but their unique skills combined to create what ought to have been a profitable business. Growing up in the shadow of Wall Street as the world's largest technological revolution was under way, Jacob wanted a piece of it. He had a natural aptitude for business and capitalizing on new technology. His brother Eustace was a plumber who had a knack for inventing things. Eustace designed a drain that was easier to clean and an enameled faucet that resisted rust. Jacob tried to market the inventions, but none produced more than a modest income. Eustace didn't care. He enjoyed tinkering, and Jacob gave him enough money to pay his rent and buy whatever technical equipment he needed to keep fiddling.

Jacob dreamed big and encouraged his brother to tackle a problem that bothered every single person in the overcrowded city of Manhattan. People in cramped urban environments needed water, requiring millions of gallons to be piped into the city. New York was already developing miles of underground tunnels to move water in and out, but the challenge was how to get water to move *up*.

As buildings got taller, it took a tremendous amount of pressure to send water to the upper stories, and most water systems usually failed. After the third or fourth floor, water barely dribbled from the tap. The challenge was in figuring out how to provide enough pressure to send water up ten, fifteen, or even twenty stories in a safe and reliable manner. Eustace Drake solved the problem by designing a pressure-regulating valve that was wildly successful.

Jacob provided the funding to mass produce the valve and sold it wherever he could. Eustace, meanwhile, turned his erratic attention to a new project, a hand-cranked auger that could be inserted down drainage pipes to unclog them.

Jacob became obsessed with selling the valve, the only one of Eustace's inventions likely to make a fortune. He needed Eustace to sign contracts to authorize the sale of the valves, but it was hard to get Eustace to pay attention to business matters.

Especially once the Civil War broke out. As the war dragged on, more and more men were called to serve, and Eustace's number came up in the autumn of 1863. Eustace wanted to complete his new auger before joining his regiment, but Jacob could not sell the valve without Eustace's approval. Eustace had no interest in reading exhaustive legal contracts as he raced to complete his newest invention.

"Tell you what," Eustace had said. "I have a hankering to buy my wife something nice before I head off to war. How about you give me enough money to buy a fancy pearl necklace, and in exchange you can do whatever you want with the valve while I'm at the front? We can straighten it all out when I get back."

That evening Jacob presented Eustace with enough money not only for a fine pearl necklace, but a pair of matching earrings as well. Eustace signed the half-page contract granting Jacob complete authority over the valve, and three days later Eustace joined his regiment.

He served until the war was over, enduring sweltering battlefields, deafening artillery charges, and crippling blisters from endless marches. He never once thought about the valve until he returned to Manhattan in the summer of 1865 and learned his brother had formed a separate corporation, Drake Industries, and its sole product was the pressure-regulating valve. Jacob split the proceeds of the valves sold in Manhattan on a fifty-fifty basis with his brother, which delighted Eustace, for the valves had been installed in hundreds of buildings in New York. As skyscrapers rose higher, they didn't merely require a single pressure-regulating valve—they needed six, eight, twelve, or more in each building, making them more profitable than Eustace could ever have imagined.

It took a while for Eustace to realize how badly he was being swindled, for while he earned a respectable profit from the Manhattan valves, Jacob claimed one hundred percent ownership of any valve sold outside of Manhattan. Jacob had begun selling the valves in every major city in the United States, as well as exporting them to Europe, Russia, and Latin America. While Eustace sweat and toiled on the battlefield, his brother had grown rich beyond all imagination. By the 1870s, Jacob had moved to an estate in the rolling countryside outside of Saratoga, where he built a mansion, raised quarter horses, and diversified his fortune into new industries.

Eustace hired a lawyer to sue, claiming he never intended to grant Jacob full ownership over the valve in perpetuity. He claimed he intended to deal with the legal aspects relating to the valve after the war, but the half-page contract technically granted Jacob the right to do whatever he wanted with the valve. The courts were generous with veterans and permitted the lawsuit to proceed, but it was hard to argue that Jacob had not fulfilled his part of the bargain. Eustace still possessed the pearl necklace, proof he had been compensated in precisely the manner he asked.

Eustace lost the lawsuit, but the appeals process dragged on until his dying day in 1893. Jacob Drake was still alive, but he was ninety-two and had long ago turned the business over to his son. Thomas Drake was even shrewder than his father. Uncle Thomas had been denying the Manhattan Drakes any part of their grandfather's legacy for decades. What was worse, Uncle Thomas jacked up the price of the Drake valve so high that it was out of reach for poor people.

The lawsuit was about more than money. Lucy still remembered the way her grandfather's face grew wistful when he spoke about why he worked so hard to create his devices. *"Talent is a gift from God,"* he would say. *"It's a sin to hoard our talent. There is nothing special about me except that I can build things to make life better for the people around me. And when I do that, I feel God smiling on me."*

Lucy felt the same way. When she and Nick installed homemade versions of the Drake valve in tenements, she felt like she had the blessing of her grandfather. Eustace had taught Nick how to build the valve, and to this day they sneaked them into the buildings of people who asked for it. It seemed like the right thing to do. Uncle Thomas might be earning a fortune from his mass-produced valves, but she and Nick helped people who could never afford the extravagant fees her uncle demanded.

Lucy and Nick rode the streetcar back home in silence. She was twenty-eight years old, and Nick was thirty-one. They both ought to be married and living a normal life, not working their fingers to the bone to pay a lawyer they couldn't afford.

"I'm sorry I can't be there tomorrow," Nick said as they sat side by side on the streetcar bench. "We're installing the new tidal doors in the tunnel, and I need to be there."

"I'll be okay," she said.

After all, she already knew how the Saratoga Drakes intended to proceed tomorrow. They were going to file a motion to get the suit dismissed, claiming that Lucy and Nick had no standing in the case. Since they had not been born when the original contract was signed in 1863, they had no vested interest in the valve. Their father had been alive and clearly had standing in the court's eyes, but with his death last year, the Saratoga Drakes wanted to call the lawsuit to an end.

The only thing that worried Lucy was Uncle Thomas's latest motion accusing them of bad faith. It had come out of the blue and hung over her head like a waiting vulture, frightening her with its vague sense of doom. Nevertheless, she had right on her side. She prayed each evening for wisdom in how to move forward with this ugly lawsuit. Almost four million people were crowded into New York City, and a third of them had no running water in their homes. If her uncle won, that was unlikely to change.

"I just feel like I'm letting you down," Nick said, his voice heavy with exhaustion. He leaned forward, bracing his forehead on his palms as he stared at the floor. "I really hate this," he whispered.

The fact that the Saratoga Drakes could make her brave, daring brother feel this low was discouraging, but she wouldn't let it stop them. This battle had begun before she was even born, but she would be leading the charge when it ended.

Colin smiled as he passed his coat and top hat to the butler at the Wooten family's Madison Avenue residence.

"The family is awaiting you in the drawing room, my lord," the butler murmured.

"Very good." He didn't correct the butler over the improper use of his title. He was technically a "sir," but servants in America weren't trained in the minutiae of hereditary titles. He rarely used his title in New York, but everyone in the Wooten household seemed to enjoy it.

Which was fine, especially if it impressed Miss Amelia Wooten, the quarry he was hunting this evening. Amelia was charming, nineteen years old, and her father was worth a cool sixty million dollars.

The scent of orange blossoms fragranced the air, and a violinist played music somewhere in the mansion glittering with hundreds of candles and cut-glass chandeliers.

"Welcome, Sir Beckwith!" Frank Wooten heartily greeted him as he entered the grand salon. Over a dozen people draped in the finest silks and broadcloth had already gathered, and he was introduced to the few people he did not already know.

He'd been paying steady court to Amelia ever since he met her last year in London, and he was eager to carry on here in the States. Mrs. Wooten was equally effusive in her greeting, as was the congressman from the 3rd District of New York.

These people could not have been more gracious, welcoming him as though he were actual royalty. If only they knew . . .

He pushed his misgivings aside and headed straight for Amelia, who looked lovely standing beside a towering vase of ivory camellias. Her flaxen blond hair had been coiled into an exquisite pattern that must have taken her maid hours to arrange. Tiny diamond pins nestled in her hair and shone like stars on a blanket of golden silk.

"You could not look lovelier if Leonardo had placed you there himself," he told her.

"What a silver-tongued flatterer," she said, beaming with delight. "I look no such thing."

He flashed her a devilish smile. "Oh, all right. You look a terrible hag, not even fit to be let out in public."

Amelia tapped his shoulder with her fan. "That makes two of us!"

Everyone laughed, even Amelia's mother. This was what he loved about Americans. They understood his reckless humor and kept pace without losing a beat.

"I think you look lovely, Miss Wooten," a thickly accented voice said. Colin stiffened at Count Demetri Ostrowski's voice. The Polish aristocrat wore round spectacles and an emerald green vest that made his skin look puffy and soft. There was plenty of competition for Amelia's hand, and Ostrowski had been pursuing Amelia with the zeal of a baby duckling waddling after its mother. A count outranked a baronet, which mattered to Amelia's mother, but her father clearly favored Colin. That meant Amelia's opinion would tip the balance.

Footmen in full livery circulated with trays of caviar and

imported cheese. Wine flowed freely, and soon the group drifted into the dining room, where the seating arrangements placed Colin beside Amelia. She delicately tugged at the tips of her long gloves, wiggling them off.

He leaned his head down to whisper in her ear. "Need any help?"

It was terribly forward to make such an offer, but Amelia blushed gorgeously as she finished the task on her own, laying the gloves in her lap.

"My maid still does not understand the language of gloves," she said. "She constantly confuses evening gloves with opera gloves."

He did not bother to inform her that they were one and the same. Amelia was a bit of a snob, but that trait would serve her well if they married. The British upper classes could be ferocious, and she would need plenty of armor were she to move to England as his wife.

The elderly matron across from him caught his attention. "I saw a photograph of Whitefriars in a guidebook of the English countryside," she said. "What a lovely home."

He gave a polite nod. "Indeed. It was a privilege to grow up in such a place." He could only pray the guidebook did not contain pictures of the inside of his house. Entire wings had been closed off due to plaster falling from the ceiling and floors sagging in the middle.

"Was it terribly lonely growing up in the countryside?" the matron asked.

He glanced at Amelia, who paid close attention. After all, if they married, she would be spending the better part of her life at the rambling, seventeenth-century estate in Yorkshire. They'd courted for two weeks in London, so she had never had a chance to see Whitefriars. From the outside it looked like a castle. Inside it was a wreck.

"It is six miles from the nearest village, and as a boy I remember feeling like I lived on the edge of the universe. We had a telegraph for communication, and I learned how to listen in so I could be connected to the rest of the world. Must keep up with the cricket scores, you know."

There wasn't much else to do for amusement in the middle of nowhere. He never cared for hunting, but cricket was his passion. It had been imperative to hear the scores the instant they were reported, prompting him to learn Morse code.

During the long hours while he awaited the incoming scores, he listened to the news of the world, and it changed his life. He heard about the discovery of gold and diamonds in Africa. He learned about Queen Liliuokalani and her tropical paradise in a place called Hawaii. The telegraph sounder became his portal into the wider world, opening his heart to adventure and possibility. When he was fourteen years old, a volcano on the island of Krakatoa exploded, and the eruptions lasted for days. It was spellbinding. He stayed plastered to the telegraph, listening by the hour as the extent of the devastation became clear. There were tidal waves, fires, and ash raining from the skies. A correspondent from Reuters risked death by going to the Indonesian island, sailing straight into the jaws of danger so he could gather information and send reports back to the world.

That reporter became Colin's hero, and from that moment, he vowed his life would amount to more than cricket games or living on a moldering estate. He wanted to see the world and experience its triumphs and catastrophes, reporting on everything he saw. He longed for the day he could join the army of Reuters correspondents, whose dauntless spirit helped illuminate the world with knowledge. During his years as a foreign correspondent, he asked Reuters to send him to the most exotic and dangerous postings. Nothing in his life had made him prouder.

"Did you really learn how to operate one of those rackety machines just to listen to cricket scores?" Mrs. Wooten asked from the far side of the table.

He pushed back the memories and flashed a wink at Amelia. "Yes. I learned Morse code for the sake of cricket."

After dinner they moved to the salon, where Amelia was going to entertain them all at the grand piano. He enjoyed music and vowed to wire his sister at Whitefriars to tell her to get their own piano tuned. No one had played it in decades, but it would be nice to have music at the estate again.

The ladies seated themselves along the rows of plush settees while he stood beside Amelia at the piano as she paged through a stack of sheet music.

"What would you like to hear?" she asked. "I can offer you Beethoven or Brahms, but please don't ask me to play Mozart. He adds too many—"

A gunshot rang out directly behind Colin, and he dove for cover. The goblet in his hand smashed to the floor, and wine splattered everywhere.

Before he could gather his wits, Amelia knelt beside him. "Colin? Good heavens . . ."

He covered his head, waiting for another explosion, but nothing happened. From his position on the floor, he saw feet gathering near but sensed no other signs of pandemonium.

False alarm. Again.

Silk rustled as people drew closer and murmured in concern, but his heart pumped too hard for him to stop quaking as he lay curled on the floor. He gathered his shattered nerves together and braced one hand on the piano bench. It was mortifying, but given the way his hand shook, he wasn't going to be able to stand up yet. He kept his eyes averted, counted his heartbeats to ten, then managed to get his feet beneath him and stand.

Directly behind him, a stunned footman held a freshly

uncorked bottle of champagne. Colin had mistaken it for a gunshot.

"Don't open champagne so close to me," he bit out on a low breath.

"Yes, sir. I'm sorry, sir."

He tried to stop the trembling of his hands, but it was going to be hopeless. He shoved them into his pockets. He forced a little levity into his tone, hoping it could mask his quaking breath. "Sorry. I slipped."

"Yes, of course," Amelia rushed to say. "Johnson, will you send Peter with a mop?"

How mortifying. Twenty people stood motionless in the salon, staring at him like he was a bomb about to detonate. Wine stained the floor and the skirt of Amelia's pale silk gown with splotches of red. Shards of crystal were everywhere. He and Amelia stepped away from the piano as a pair of servants mopped up the spilled wine and broken glass, but at least no one challenged his statement that he had slipped.

Not to his face, at least. A few gentlemen on the far side of the room spoke in low voices, but his hearing was excellent, and he heard them murmuring about the Boer War and rumors of him being shipped home early. He turned his attention to the ladies and did his best to ignore it, but sweat rolled down his face as though he'd just finished a mile-long race. Blotting his forehead with a handkerchief didn't help much. The sweating didn't stop, and he doubted anyone was fooled. Especially Count Ostrowski, who hid a smirk behind a raised champagne glass. So far the coddled Polish aristocrat hadn't been much competition for Amelia's hand, but tonight was a serious blow to Colin's prospects. If he was going to save Whitefriars and the ninety tenants living on his estate, he needed to win Amelia's hand and send the Polish count packing.

How long were these sudden fits going to plague him? Half

the reason he'd agreed to come to the United States was to be away from England until he could control these embarrassing episodes, for it didn't take much to spook him. A slammed door or the honking of an automobile horn could do it. Anything that sounded like a gun, an explosion, or the sound of men dying in agony beside him while he lay pinned and powerless in the dirt was enough to plunge his mind back into the stench of war.

Mrs. Wooten brought Amelia a long, floor-length wrap like the models in Pre-Raphaelite paintings wore, and it effectively covered the worst of the wine splotches on her skirt. Mrs. Wooten slanted a glower at him as she withdrew, but Frank Wooten wore a far different expression. It was a quizzical look, as though pondering the moves in a chess match.

Colin turned his attention to Amelia, who took her seat at the piano and played a few tunes, but the evening came to an early close. The laughing and easy conversation from earlier in the evening were gone, replaced by tentative smiles and forced jollity.

Amelia walked him to the front door. It was the first time they'd been alone since his embarrassing collapse.

"I don't 'slip' very often," he said.

She laid a hand on his arm. "My father told me a little about what happened when you were in the Boer War. It must have been terrible."

That was a surprise. He had no idea how Frank Wooten had come by the story, but he didn't want to talk about this. He hadn't even been a soldier, merely a reporter who got trapped behind the lines.

"Being here with you makes it all seem very far away," he said.

"You'll come again?" she asked, smiling up at him.

Thank heavens he had not frightened her off with his stunning display of cowardice. "Of course."

He would come again and again until he was confident Amelia was willing to become his bride and her father agreed to sign over an appalling amount of money to save Whitefriars. It was about more than just restoring a crumbling old pile of rocks. It was about the ninety people who lived on the estate and depended on him for their livelihood. If marrying an heiress would save the three-hundred-year heritage of Whitefriars, it was what he needed to do.

*L*ucy rose early on the morning of the court hearing in order to slip inside the chapel near her house and pray for wisdom. She never quite knew what to expect when confronting Uncle Thomas, and she needed the peace of prayer. As she knelt in the silent chapel, she could hear her grandfather's words in her mind. *"I can build things to make life better for the people around me. And when I do that, I feel God smiling on me."*

She had to believe she was doing God's will. She and Nick were making the world a better place, even if it meant she had to fight dragons like her uncle along the way. So far they had been keeping their head above water and were well-prepared for today's hearing. Only the vague threat of bad faith worried her. She hadn't seen that one coming, and it was troubling.

By nine o'clock she sat at the table before the judge's bench with only her lawyer, Horace Pritchard. The first time she'd ever been in this room, she was only nine years old. Her father wanted her and Nick to know exactly who they were up against, so he'd taken them to every legal briefing, hearing, and deposition. She'd been so amazed by the high-gloss shine on the mahogany table before her that she'd been tempted to stand up and look into it like a mirror.

Not today. Now she sat stiffly beside a single lawyer while Uncle Thomas sat on the opposite side of the room with three lawyers, two legal assistants, two secretaries, and a bodyguard. It was still five minutes before the judge would enter to hear Thomas's latest motion to get the case dismissed. Lucy had arrived as soon as the courtroom opened its doors this morning, for she would not put it past Thomas to reschedule the hearing and proceed in her absence. He had tried it once with their father.

Thomas's son, Tom Jr., was also there. She and Tom were the same age but as different as chalk from cheese. When they were younger, their parents went through a brief phase of trying to reach a truce. They all met in neutral territory at a fancy Manhattan hotel and went through the motions of friendly family gatherings. The youngsters were sent off to play while the grownups had dinner in the restaurant downstairs.

When Lucy was ten years old, Tom Jr. invited her and Nick upstairs to see his family's spacious hotel suite, so unlike their Greenwich Village apartment. They took off their shoes to slide across the marble floors and devoured the expensive chocolates the maid delivered to the room. They played with the dumbwaiter, raising and lowering the tiny platform built into the wall. Lucy remembered wondering what it must be like to have piping hot meals delivered from a fancy kitchen in the basement.

The moment Nick left the room to ride the elevator, Tom dared Lucy to get inside the dumbwaiter to see if she could fit. Never able to resist a challenge, Lucy clambered aboard, curling her knees up tightly and grinning in triumph. Tom slammed the door and locked her inside.

She couldn't get out. At first she thought it was a joke, but Tom taunted her from the other side of the door, and she knew there'd be no quick escape. It was pitch black and hot and stuffy. She started crying, mortified that Tom could reduce her to tears.

Then Nick came back. His roar of outrage was earsplitting the moment he realized what Tom had done. He flung the dumbwaiter door open and hauled her out, then lunged at Tom. A swift and brutal bludgeoning followed, and then it was Tom Jr. who was sniveling like a baby.

Tom looked very different today, sporting a three-piece suit identical to his father's, complete with a starched collar and gold watch chain. He even carried a walking stick with jewels set into the bronze handle, which seemed terribly pompous to Lucy, but the Saratoga Drakes were determined to use their money to buy all the trappings of class.

Aside from a few threads of silver in his black hair, her Uncle Thomas never seemed to age. At fifty-seven, Thomas Drake was tall, whiplash lean, and had piercing gray eyes. Most women found Thomas attractive, but Lucy knew him to be as oily as a snake, even though he consistently tried to make polite chitchat with her at every meeting.

"And how is your dear mother?" he inquired across the aisle as though this was a casual family get-together.

"My mother is fine." Her mother was a nervous wreck who had gone to live with her relatives in Boston to get as far away as possible from the Saratoga Drakes and this never-ending court case.

She stared straight ahead, reluctant to speak to Uncle Thomas without a court stenographer recording every word. Finally both the judge and the stenographer arrived, and Thomas began the hearing with his usual offer to settle the case for a flat fee of ten thousand dollars. Lucy politely declined. By her estimate, the Saratoga Drakes were now worth over thirty million dollars, so ten thousand wasn't tempting. Worse, it would do nothing to force Thomas to make the valve affordable to ordinary people.

Still, the offer made Thomas appear magnanimous before the judge, while she looked like a skinflint.

The judge's voice was as somber as his dark robes. "Mr. Drake? The court will now hear your motion to dismiss the lawsuit filed by Nicholas and Lucy Drake."

Lucy sat calmly while Felix Moreno, the Saratoga Drakes' lawyer, presented a motion to declare Lucy and Nick ineligible to proceed with this lawsuit due to their lack of standing in the eyes of the court. Mr. Moreno said that not only should the lawsuit be dismissed, but Lucy and Nick should reimburse Thomas Drake for the legal fees he'd paid defending against their illegal lawsuit.

Tom Jr. smirked at her from across the aisle. "I'll bet you didn't see that one coming, did you?"

Lucy stared straight ahead, refusing to let triumph show on her face. She knew all about their plans to declare her and Nick ineligible to proceed with the lawsuit, and already had a winning strategy mapped out with her lawyer. Uncle Thomas probably thought she would quake in fear at the threat to force her to pay his legal bills.

He was wrong. Mr. Pritchard approached the podium and smoothly cited three precedents from New York law that gave Lucy standing. One of the decisions was written by this very judge to support their position. The judge seemed impressed but still turned to her uncle's lawyer.

"Mr. Moreno? Have you an answer?"

Mr. Moreno asked for an extension to prepare an answer, but the judge was unsympathetic. "You brought this motion, and now you come into my courtroom unprepared?"

Her uncle's lawyer did his best to address the three cases but was unable to mount much of a counthercharge. After twenty minutes, the judge banged his gavel. "I am prepared to rule. The Drake cousins have standing to proceed with the lawsuit."

Triumph flared inside. The vague accusation of bad faith had not come up, so perhaps it had just been an empty threat. She began gathering the papers stacked before her, and the judge stood to leave.

"Not so fast," Uncle Thomas said. "We have another, more serious issue to raise, and I'd like to call Mr. Lorenzo Garzelli to join us."

Lucy could not stifle her gasp.

"We believe the plaintiffs are acting in bad faith and seeking to undermine Drake Industries," her uncle said. "We have proof."

Lucy swallowed hard and wished Nick were there. The way Tom Jr. snickered made her mouth go dry. Her palms began to sweat as Mr. Garzelli made his way into the chamber, nervously glancing about the room and rubbing his hands on his coveralls. He refused to meet her eyes as he took a seat at the witness stand.

"Please state your official residence for the benefit of the court reporter," Mr. Moreno instructed in a clipped voice. It should not surprise her that her uncle would hire a lawyer as nasty as Mr. Moreno. A small man who always dressed very dapper and had an oily politeness in front of distinguished people, he was the kind of person who hit his servants when no one was looking.

Mr. Garzelli swallowed twice and looked confused. "I don't understand," he said in his thick Italian accent.

"Where do you *live*?" the lawyer said, enunciating the words as though Mr. Garzelli was a simpleton. He wasn't. Mr. Garzelli was a proud man who had come to this country with nothing and worked hard enough to buy his own building just last year.

Mr. Garzelli stated his address, and then the attack began.

"How is water supplied to your building?" the lawyer demanded.

"Through the city water system."

"And did you do anything to your building to alter the manner in which your tenants receive their water?"

"Yes. A plumber friend of mine installed some fancy pumps so water flows to everyone in the building. Before that, they had to come down to the first floor and carry buckets up themselves."

"How many pumps?"

"Four."

"And the name of this plumber friend?"

Anxiety crossed Mr. Garzelli's face at the accusatory tone. "Nicholas Drake," he admitted.

"And what did you pay for the equipment?"

Mr. Garzelli began to perspire. "I paid for the materials and some extra copper tubes. I bought the Drakes lunch—"

"But you paid nothing for the actual valves?" the lawyer asked in an appalled voice. "Valves that cost thousands of dollars on the open market?"

Now Lucy saw where this was going. Uncle Thomas charged twelve times what it cost to produce the valve, but Nick knew how to make it, and he gave them to poor people for only the cost of the materials and equipment to fit them into the building. There was no law against what they were doing, but Uncle Thomas might be able to make them suffer for it anyway.

The lawyer changed tack with breathtaking speed. "Can you read English, Mr. Garzelli?"

"Yes, sir."

"Please read this document for the court stenographer." He slid a piece of paper onto the witness stand.

Mr. Garzelli's face went white. He knocked the page away, and it fluttered to the floor. "That was a long time ago," he stammered.

The lawyer picked up the paper and placed it back before Mr. Garzelli. "Please read it for the court."

Lucy started breathing fast and clenched her fists. One of the worst things about this lawsuit was what it did to innocent people she and Nick befriended. Uncle Thomas enjoyed his systematic campaign to bully, threaten, and frighten off their allies for no other reason than it made the Manhattan Drakes' lives uncomfortable.

Mr. Garzelli still refused to look at the paper. "That was a long time ago," he said. "I was desperate. I am not that boy anymore."

"Very well," the lawyer said smoothly. "Since Mr. Garzelli refuses to read the document, I shall summarize it for the court. It says that Mr. Garzelli was caught picking pockets on Mulberry Street. In other words, he was a common thief. Does your wife know about this?"

Mr. Garzelli folded his arms across his chest and glared at the lawyer.

"Fine," the lawyer continued. "As you say, it was a long time ago, and perhaps there is no need for your wife to know anything about it. Does she know you are a member of the Workingmen's Union? A group known to consort with socialists and other radicals dedicated to destroying the American way of life?"

"That's not true," Mr. Garzelli sputtered.

This hurt to watch. Lucy was accustomed to being on the receiving end of her uncle's vile tactics, but Mr. Garzelli had done nothing wrong other than supply his tenants with clean water and the chance to rise above the squalor of their neighborhood.

"This is irrelevant to the case," she protested. It wasn't Mr. Garzelli they wanted to destroy; it was her and Nick.

"We find it highly relevant," the lawyer said. "This man is accepting counterfeit goods, has a history of theft, and is consorting with known radical groups. We believe he is using his tenement to advertise the counterfeit Drake valves to his compatriots. Deportation from the country is a distinct possibility."

Mr. Pritchard stood. "Mr. Garzelli, I would advise you not to say anything else. You have the right to an attorney."

The hearing ended shortly after that. The judge ruled another delay for the Saratoga Drakes to gather evidence that she and Nick were selling counterfeit valves in an effort to undermine his business. Uncle Thomas had gotten exactly what he wanted.

She was still shaking in anger as she relayed the day's events to Nick in their apartment that evening. "Mr. Garzelli was waiting for me on the street as we left the courthouse. He wants us to take the pump and valves out of his building."

Nick let out a heavy sigh. He was already exhausted from a day of gritty labor, and learning that he'd be spending the entire weekend at the Garzelli tenement, uninstalling the valves, was demoralizing. "Doesn't he understand it's all just bluster?"

"He's terrified of being deported. I wouldn't put it past Thomas to press the case just to get beneath our skin."

For the hundredth time, she wondered if Horace Pritchard was the right lawyer. He was a kind and loyal man who worked doggedly on their behalf, but he'd never been able to mount much of a charge against the fleet of attorneys deployed by her uncle.

"Maybe we need a better attorney," she said, glancing pointedly at the kitchen floor.

Nick immediately understood the implication. "No," he said flatly.

The only thing of value they owned was carefully secreted beneath those floorboards. The triple-strand pearl necklace, bordered with hundreds of seed pearls woven together in a strand of unearthly beauty, had lain untouched for decades beneath that floor. It was an extravagant gift of love from a man to his wife just before leaving for war. Lucy had never worn it and wanted nothing to do with it, but Nick felt otherwise.

"If we sell the necklace, we can afford a better lawyer. One who won't let that man bully us or Mr. Garzelli."

"Someday I'm going to give that necklace to my wife," Nick said.

She sighed in exasperation. "We're not the sort of people who wear a fortune on our necks, and I doubt the woman you marry will be any different."

It was the wrong thing to say, stoking Nick's temper, which was never very far beneath the surface. "Do you think that because I'm a plumber I don't want to be able to give my wife something nice? If we sell the necklace, we get a couple days of a lawyer's time, but is that going to make any difference? That necklace is a symbol. It's proof that our family was once something great."

It was true, but she didn't need a necklace to prove it. All over the city, people enjoyed water pumped directly into their apartments because of Eustace Drake. That mattered to her more than a cluster of pearls.

But Nick felt otherwise. She could never have built or installed the valves throughout the city without Nick, and she needed to respect his decision.

"Okay, we keep the necklace, but we need to take the valves out of Mr. Garzelli's building."

It was a terrible compromise, one that made neither of them happy. Nick didn't say anything, but he slowly nodded. Two hundred people lived in Mr. Garzelli's building. Today those people had plenty of clean water to drink, cook, clean, and bathe. In a few days, it would be cut off, and they'd go back to lugging pails up the stairs each day.

Thomas Drake might have succeeded in intimidating Lorenzo Garzelli, but it only served to strengthen Lucy's resolve.

"I'm heading to the office," she said. "You know why."

Nick nodded and let her go. She was going to do the one

thing that had given them a fighting chance against the Drakes all these years. It was eight o'clock in the evening, but the AP office was still open. It operated around the clock seven days per week, and telegraphers were on duty at all hours.

Twenty minutes later, she had settled in to her station. Shoulder-high partitions enclosed each booth to help muffle sounds from other telegraph machines, but it also provided her with much-needed privacy. She opened the circuit on her telegraph sounder and directed the line to the secret wire Nick had helped her install two years ago. With literally thousands of telegraph and telephone wires bundled into thick coils coming in and out of the Western Union building, no one noticed that she and Nick had spliced a single wire in with the rest that led to Lucy's desk. That wire was bundled along with dozens of others that stretched across Broadway, down 6th Avenue, and directly into the law offices of Mr. Felix Moreno, her uncle's lawyer.

Every time the Moreno Law Office filed a motion, she knew about it. Every time Uncle Thomas wired a message or a planned strategy, she knew about it. For the past two years, Lucy had been able to eavesdrop on everything going in and out of that law office, and that wire was the lifeline that kept her one step ahead of her uncle all these years.

It was also entirely illegal. She wasn't proud of breaking the law, but all it took was the sort of dirty move Uncle Thomas had pulled in court this morning to strengthen her resolve.

This wire could land both her and Nick in jail, but it could also be the key to winning the lawsuit, and she was willing to run the risk.

I'm terribly sorry, sir. I take full responsibility and will
gladly tender my resignation if it will smooth matters."

The elderly butler stood in Colin's office, looking ready to
face a firing squad.

Colin waved his hand. "Don't be an idiot, Denby. This is an
easy enough matter to fix."

At least he hoped it would be. It appeared Lucy Drake's accusation about the sluggish delivery of Asian reports to the AP
was spot-on, and it was entirely his fault. Colin had appointed
the old butler to a position neither of them fully understood,
so he couldn't blame Denby for the mix-up.

Denby had been the butler at Whitefriars for thirty years, but
since Colin's sister no longer entertained, there wasn't enough
work for a butler at the estate. Denby had accompanied Colin
to New York, but there wasn't much to oversee at his Manhattan townhouse either. Sitting at home watching the plants grow
wasn't good for anyone's soul, and Denby gladly agreed to help
out at Reuters. Having a skilled butler in the office added a
touch of panache that secretly amused everyone working there.

Among the odd jobs Denby had taken over was handling

the mail. All of Reuters' outgoing mail was sent via pneumatic tube down to the sorting office in the basement. Denby failed to realize that anything addressed to the AP should have been sent by a different tube directly to the AP office two floors below. The unnecessary trip to the basement was causing a full day's delay in the delivery of the AP's stories received by Reuters.

Well, there was nothing for it but to go downstairs and tender a full apology. Besides, a strange compulsion urged him to see Lucy Drake again. The urge didn't warrant too much scrutiny, for there was nothing aboveboard about his interest in her. But then, it wasn't as if he had any sort of formal agreement with Amelia, who was still waffling between him and Count Ostrowski, so there was technically nothing stopping him from giving in to the impulse.

Knowing the staff at the AP were accustomed to little better than slop at the cafeteria, he had already asked Nanny Teresa to bake a batch of her incomparable lemon cream shortbread as a peace offering.

There weren't many female telegraphers in the office, making it easy to spot Lucy at a work station on the third row of operators in the cavernous AP office. He studied her from behind, noting her rigidly straight posture, her tailored jacket nipped in at the waist, and her dark hair coiled at the base of her neck. Her head tipped at a charming angle toward the sounding machine as she received a message and wrote out the translation.

What had driven a woman like her into this field? Did she work here from necessity or because she liked it? Given her intense expression as she transcribed, she seemed to be enjoying herself. There was something compelling about a woman so alive and engaged, as though she couldn't wait to interpret the next stream of dots and dashes coming off the wire.

He knew the feeling well.

At last she closed the circuit and finished transcribing the message on a tablet of paper. She stood to carry it to the end of the aisle for delivery via the pneumatic tube but froze when she spotted him.

When their gazes met, it was like a wallop to the chest. What kind of idiot was he to be affected by locking eyes with a woman across a crowded room of people? Nevertheless the mesmerizing charge did not fade as she made her way toward him.

"What brings you into enemy territory?" she asked as she opened the pneumatic tube, slipped her story inside the canister, then pulled the lever. A sucking sound shot through the air as her report was whisked to another floor.

"I've brought a peace offering," he said, extending the tin of lemon cream shortbread. "A new staff member has been inadvertently sending AP stories to the general sorting room in the basement rather than directly to the sixth floor, which caused the delay in delivery. My apologies."

The corners of her mouth turned down. "Does that usually work for you? A charming smile and something sweet to paste over an appalling lack of service?"

"I'd offer my firstborn child, but given the ferocity of your expression, I doubt even that shall suffice."

She still had a mutinous look as she eyed the tin skeptically. "What is it?"

"Lemon cream shortbread. Or 'cookies,' as Americans call them," he replied. "Nanny Teresa's recipe is world famous."

"You travel with your nanny's cookie recipe?"

It was worse than that, but he wasn't about to admit it. He lifted the cover from the tin, and the first hint of citrus aroma wafted into the office. "Try one. You'll understand."

Her fingers were hesitant as she reached inside, but her face lit with astonishment as she took her first bite. The movement of her jaw slowed, her eyes widened, and he knew exactly what she was experiencing—the buttery shortbread that practically melted in her mouth, mixed with the refreshing tang of lemon that captured a thousand days of Mediterranean sunshine. She actually moaned.

"Now do you understand why I travel with my nanny?" The confession slipped out before he could call it back.

She looked at him with curiosity. "Oh . . . you mean you have a nanny for your children, right? For a moment I thought *you* actually still had a nanny."

He smiled tightly. "I do, in fact, still have a nanny."

Keeping Nanny Teresa on the payroll probably looked odd to outsiders, but when he was a child, she had been the most important adult in his world. Like most children of aristocrats, he was brought downstairs to see his parents for no more than one hour per day. It was Nanny Teresa who taught him to tie his shoes and to read. She took him for walks in the countryside and encouraged him to look under rocks to study the strange and wonderful insects hiding beneath them. She was essentially both a mother and a father to him. Only a heartless man would turn out his aging nanny who had no family or any way of supporting herself.

He affected a lighthearted tone and tilted his nose up to precisely the right angle. "I adore Nanny Teresa. I simply refuse to give her up, or her lemon cream shortbread."

He needn't have worried about Lucy's reaction, for she had stopped paying attention to him as she stared at the shortbread in the tin, her lips moving silently as she scanned the contents. A guilty look came across her face.

"I hoped there would be enough for everyone in the office and still take some home to my brother," she whispered.

He replaced the lid and pressed the tin into her hands. "Let it be our secret. If you accept my apology for the delayed stories, I won't reveal your gluttony to your coworkers."

He followed her back to her work station, where it was a little quieter and he could ensure the air was clear between them. He held out her chair, and she sat.

"Truly," he said, "I apologize for the delayed stories traveling over Reuters' wires. We pride ourselves on being above reproach. We fully intend to trounce the AP in terms of newspaper subscribers, prestige, and quality—but we fight fair. I wouldn't work for Reuters if that weren't true."

Judging by the expression on her face, she accepted his apology. "Why did you go into this business?" she asked.

"The free newspapers."

Her eyes gleamed, but she shook her head. "Try again."

Normally he deflected personal questions with lighthearted quips. He wasn't exactly proud of the fact that he'd abandoned the management of his estate into the care of his sister. It was an arrangement few people understood, but he sensed a kindred spirit in Lucy Drake.

"I grew up on an isolated estate where the newspaper was my lifeline," he said simply. "Now I get to work in the business that opened up my world." The look of shared understanding on her face was captivating. He hunkered beside her chair so they could see eye to eye.

"Listen!" he said urgently as his eyes roamed the office, where dozens of operators were busily transcribing stories. "That cascade of dots and dashes pouring from the telegraph is the sound of history in the making. No symphony composed by human hands will ever sound more thrilling to me. Those rattling clicks are bringing accounts of political upheavals and financial intrigue. Of scientific discovery and athletic accomplishments. They tell of fortunes being made and dreams collapsing. Battles, disasters, triumph, scandal. Those clicks are the chronicle of human history being funneled into this room, where it can be written up and sent out to anyone curious enough to open a newspaper. And we're a part of that, Lucy."

He caught himself. Rhapsodizing like this was out of character, and he had no business growing closer to Lucy Drake. He stood and quickly erected a façade of breezy charm.

"And we shall ensure your future stories are submitted promptly with no more tedious detours to the basement, hmm?"

He left without looking back.

Clutching the tin of lemon cookies on her lap, Lucy stared sightlessly out the office window after Colin Beckwith left.

How long had it been since she'd been this drawn to a man? The enthusiasm in his voice as he spoke about working for Reuters was an echo of her own pride in working for the AP. It was a privilege to work in such an industry, and yet few of her coworkers seemed to share her fervor. Perhaps this surge of attraction was only because she was so pathetically lonely. She hadn't had a beau since Samuel broke their engagement, and the hollow feeling of being alone grew worse with each passing season. Inside she churned with energy, longing, and love that had no outlet. She was ready to share her life with someone, and how odd that Colin Beckwith managed to effortlessly tap into that well of emotion, drawing it out in a delightful flirtation and shared sense of curiosity.

At least Reuters was in good hands, for a man with that level of passion was an asset to any company. She hoped there was enough room in the newspaper industry for both Reuters and the AP. She worked for the upstart agency, and she knew that if only one of them could survive, it would be Reuters.

She shook herself and set the tin of cookies in her drawer, but her gaze couldn't help but follow Colin as he headed to Mr. Tolland's office, no doubt to deliver another apology.

The wires were lively, prompting her to open her sounder. She transcribed reports about a fire at the Philadelphia wharves and storms in Bermuda. Then came a story from a local reporter for the gossip pages. The gossip columnists identified their subjects by just their initials in order to avoid the potential for slander lawsuits, and the anonymity tended to make the stories even more salacious. As she transcribed the message onto her notepad, Lucy's eyes grew wide.

A splendid dinner was given by one of
Madison Avenue's finest residents in honor of
a British visitor, Sir C. B. To the assembled
guests' embarrassment, Sir B. was obviously
intoxicated, gulping wine and falling down
behind the piano. The gracious hostess
smoothed over the awkwardness, although her
dress, imported from Paris and designed by
Mr. Worth, was stained by the drunkard's
spilled drink. Rumor has it Sir B. is on the
hunt for a wealthy American wife, but the
verdict is still out on his character. Is he
England's finest? Or merely a boozy drunkard
come to steal another of our heiresses?

Lucy stared at the words she'd just transcribed. It was obvious who the story was about. Apprehension stiffened her spine. She'd seen worse gossip stories, but never about someone she knew. Someone who kept his nanny on the payroll and got a thrill from transcribing stories fresh off the wire.

A glance through the large windows of Mr. Tolland's office revealed that Colin was still there. The apology must have been accepted, for both men looked genial and relaxed as Mr. Tolland showed Colin a framed photograph of his two young children. Colin grinned and made a comment that caused Mr. Tolland to roar with laughter.

Colin wouldn't look so affable if he knew about the story she held clenched in her hands. A reputation for drunkenness could destroy a man's standing in the business community. A headache began pounding as she stared at the words she'd just written. There were enough identifying details in the story that Sir Beckwith could probably sue for slander if the story wasn't true.

But it wasn't her job to worry about being sued. Her job was to insert this piece of paper into a canister, slip it into the pneumatic tube, and send it to the fifth floor for distribution. Once this story was sent downstairs, it would be made available to over four hundred newspapers across the nation to print or ignore at their discretion.

It looked like Colin was preparing to leave as he loitered in the open doorway of Mr. Tolland's office, shaking hands and sharing a final clap on the shoulder. She instinctively turned the page over, as though he could see it across the crowded office space. Their gazes briefly met, and he sent her a friendly nod before heading out of the room.

She bit her lip and tapped her foot in a nervous rhythm. This story might not even be true. Should she follow him out into the hall and show it to him? It wasn't her responsibility to screen stories submitted to the AP, but wouldn't it be fair play to give him advance warning that this story was on the verge of being printed? Whoever submitted it worked for the AP, and it was impossible to know if a Reuters correspondent would submit a similar story, but it was unlikely. Reuters had a reputation for solid news over gossip, so if this story somehow disappeared, there was a chance it would never see the light of day.

She slid the story beneath a stack of telegraph manuals. It was almost the end of her shift, and she could delay submitting it until tomorrow morning. She might even warn Colin that it was in the wind. It seemed the decent thing to do, but she had the night to make her decision.

Chapter
SEVEN

Colin arrived at the office before dawn. It was only six in the morning in New York, but it was noon in London, and stories flooded the office early. His predecessor had rarely bothered keeping such a demanding schedule, but professional success was important to Colin. "Good enough" would never do. The respect he gleaned from his title was built on the efforts of a long-dead ancestor few people even remembered. Colin wanted to build his own name. He had sweat, bled, and nearly died in that effort. Reuters had taken pity on him when they appointed him to an office job after he returned home early from Africa. Maybe he was no longer fit to be a war correspondent, but he could ensure that Reuters' New York branch was as smoothly run as any in the world. Better, in fact.

He reviewed a list of newspapers in Brazil. If he played his cards right, he would win contracts with a handful of those newspapers. The AP had a lock on Mexico, but he intended to secure the South American market for Reuters. A smile tugged at his mouth as he started outlining a strategy, a surge of competitive instinct stirring to life. If he could make Reuters the dominant agency in South America, his standing with the company would soar. At the very least, it would help repair his reputation after what happened in Africa.

He had written a solid five pages of a proposal when the morning delivery of mail arrived. The interruption was frustrating, but a letter from his sister was at the top of the stack, and it was impossible to ignore.

Each line of Mary's letter caused his heart to sink further. He'd hoped the roof on the east wing of the house would last another year, but she reported that the ceiling in the music room had caved in from water damage. The worst of the disaster was confined to the music room, but blooms of mold were spreading throughout the entire wing.

Well. There was nothing to be done other than cancel the plans for draining the swamp on the Haddonfield grange. A shame, because as soon as it was drained, they might actually get the barley fields back into production and provide a few more jobs to the tenants. Maybe by this time next year, he'd be married and wouldn't have to choose if his sister was expected to live in a mold-infested slagheap or if his tenants would have work for the next year.

He rubbed the side of his rib cage, wishing the familiar tightness in his chest would ease. Deciding how to spend Whitefriars' dwindling resources usually awakened this crushing sense of dread. It was bad enough to have his sister and ninety tenants dependent on him for their livelihood, but always in the back of his mind were centuries of dead ancestors looking over his shoulder and second-guessing his every move. Time was running out to save the estate, and the fear of being the last Beckwith to live at Whitefriars haunted him. The prospect of marrying for money was revolting, but it wasn't as if marriage to Amelia Wooten would be a burden. She was an attractive woman with a sound head on her shoulders. Surely they could learn to rub along well enough together.

A knock sounded on his door, and his secretary entered. "A woman from the AP is here. She claims to have something you would be interested in."

His heart lifted at the sight of Lucy Drake. Wasn't that odd? She didn't even look happy to see him, but the sight of her was enough to lighten his mood.

"Looking for more lemon cream shortbread?"

"I'm afraid not," she said as she waited for the secretary to close the door behind her. Lucy's expression was pained as she handed him a single sheet of paper.

He read quickly, the damning words jumping out at him. *Boozy drunkard. Falling down behind the piano.* His mouth went dry, and his heart pounded so hard it could probably be heard across the room. He kept the muscles on his face frozen in a perfect mask of calm, but the corner of the page crumpled where he squeezed it.

"Is there any truth to it?" Lucy asked.

Anger made it difficult to speak, but he managed to block it from his voice as he handed the paper back to her. "Falling down behind the piano? Yes, that happened, but I wasn't drunk. I was . . . otherwise incapacitated."

He didn't even know the right word for what had happened to him. How could one describe the blinding panic, the inability to breathe, the sense of helplessness that came from nowhere and took hours to fully lift? All he knew was that it was shameful and embarrassing, and he had no intention of returning to England until he could control himself.

This story could destroy everything he'd worked for—not only his professional reputation but any hope for a decent marriage.

Lucy looked exquisitely uncomfortable, nibbling on her lower lip as she peered at him through worried eyes. Such a pretty girl, and how mortifying that she should learn this about him.

"Oh," she finally said. "I was hoping you would say it wasn't true."

"Why?"

"Because then I wouldn't feel so horrible if this message . . . I don't know . . . somehow got overlooked for a while."

He straightened, alert as a bloodhound on a scent. Would she really do that for him? It would be putting her job at risk for a virtual stranger, but his reputation was the only real thing of value he possessed, and that bulletin would take a wrecking ball to it. He didn't have a lot of money to throw around, but this would be an investment.

"How much?" he asked.

She looked confused. "What?"

"How much?" He enunciated slowly and precisely.

"I don't want your money," she said in an appalled voice. "I only wanted to warn you. And look, if you have a problem with drinking, no amount of money can protect you from that. There are things you can do—"

"I am not a drunk," he ground out.

"But you said you were incapacitated. . . ."

He turned away. Someone like Lucy Drake with her safe office job would have no experience with the kind of demons that haunted him. She had a healthy set of principles. He could tell that from her distaste when he'd tried to bribe her. But he wouldn't appeal to her sense of pity. A man had to have some pride. Sometimes it was the only thing left.

"If you expect me to bare my soul and expose all my vulner-abilities like your overwrought American poets, I'm afraid you shall be disappointed."

"Why do you have to be so frosty?" she demanded. "I came here to do you a favor by giving you a few hours' advance warn-ing. I'll hold the story until this evening, but then I'm sending it down to the fifth floor for distribution to anyone who wants to publish it. And don't ever try to bribe me again."

He glared at her. Goodness, she was impressive. He simultaneously wanted to strangle and applaud her. He wanted nothing so much as to rip that piece of paper from her hands and tear it to shreds, but she had done him a kindness in coming here, and he needed to acknowledge it.

"Thank you," he said stiffly, unable to soften the glacial anger in his face.

He sat frozen at his desk after she left. He had to stop that story. He didn't know how, but he had to think fast.

Lucy worked straight through the rest of the morning and afternoon without a break. In the days following a court battle with the Saratoga Drakes, activity was always lively on the wire from the law office of her uncle's attorney. Each time the telegraph line from the Moreno Law Office initiated a message, it caused a tiny electric bulb to light up on the corner of Lucy's desk. She kept the lightbulb concealed behind a potted geranium, and the instant it came to life, she leaned over to disconnect the bulb, then tapped into the law office wire to eavesdrop on the message.

Only a fraction of the messages related to the Drake case. Most were run-of-the-mill cases on inheritance law, real estate transactions, and other irrelevant chatter. Certain words and phrases immediately put her on alert that they were discussing the Drake lawsuit. *Appeal, adjusted value,* and most notably, *the mosquito.* It was the term always used to describe anything relating to the Manhattan Drakes' case.

Yesterday the law office wire had suggested the mosquitos were getting clever, but the Mr. G tactic had worked well to frustrate them. It had indeed. She and Nick were going to spend

the weekend disengaging those valves from Mr. Garzelli's building, depriving his tenants of the basic decency of running water.
Lucy remembered one tenant in particular, an elderly Italian
widow whose face was so wizened with age she looked like a
shriveled apple. The widow wore a rustic headscarf and looked
like she had stepped out of a different century, but she'd watched
with curiosity as Lucy helped Nick with the installation. That
old woman, whose hands were gnarled by arthritis, was going
to return to lugging buckets of water up the stairs thanks to
Lucy's uncle.

She tried not to let anger interfere with her concentration
as she transcribed a report coming from Minnesota about
a contested congressional race. Accusations of voter fraud
against a sitting congressman were proceeding to trial, and
Lucy wondered if anywhere was safe from corruption. Wasn't
Minnesota supposed to have only nice people? Wasn't there
anyplace where people could be counted on to be decent and
honorable?

The lightbulb turned on, indicating a message from the law
office. Lucy ached to switch wires immediately but finished
transcribing the Minnesota story before opening the sounder
to catch the law office message in the middle of a transmission.

```
—account overdrawn. Father furious and
threatening refusal to pay.
```

Lucy leaned in. Who wasn't paying their bills? It didn't sound
relevant to her case, but she couldn't be sure, so she scribbled
the message on a notepad in case it turned out to be important.

Whoever was on the other end of the conversation replied
with the amount of overdrawn funds and banking fees. It
sounded like a conversation between the law office and a banker.
Her hunch was confirmed when the law office replied.

```
Can we negotiate a lower fine structure? Our
client will pay.
```

The reply came quickly.

```
Bank will accept lower fines contingent on
immediacy of—
```

"What are you doing?"

The voice came directly above her shoulder, and she startled, dropping her notepad. Panic rushed through her at the sight of Colin Beckwith standing less than a yard away. The connection was still open, and his head tilted forward, listening to the rapid-fire dots and dashes coming over the wire that clearly weren't a news story.

She closed the connection to stop him from hearing more. It was a mistake. He looked stunned by her action, for disconnecting a message in transmission was a sure sign she was eavesdropping. Now she couldn't even claim to have been sending a personal message.

She hoped the guilt did not show on her face. "Just listening to operators chatter. Slow news day."

He remained motionless, staring at her with a keen look in his intelligent eyes. "Let's go for a walk," he said casually.

"I'm on the clock."

"Punch out."

He had no proof she was doing anything wrong, for there was no physical record of the message she was eavesdropping on, and it would take a skilled engineer to notice the stray wire nestled among the dozens of others attached to her sounding machine. Colin Beckwith might have translated enough of the conversation to learn something she wished he hadn't, but surely he wasn't an engineer. Was he? She swallowed hard, but the worst thing she could do right now was act guilty.

"Maybe aristocrats can afford to go off the clock at will, but I have bills to pay."

"Pay them later. Let's go for a walk." His voice was implacable, and worse, now he was scrutinizing her equipment. If she lost this connection to the Moreno Law Office, they would lose the only leverage they had in a forty-year war. She stood, blocking his view of her desk.

"Let me punch out, and I'll meet you at the front of the office."

She waited for him to step away before moving. She walked to the front of the office, her mind racing as she inserted her punch card into the brass slot, pulled the lever, and stamped her card.

"Let's go."

They were both silent as the elevator carried them to the first floor. It was a long ride, stopping at every floor as the uniformed attendant cranked open the doors to let additional workers crowd inside, for it was nearing the end of the work day.

Calm. She had to be calm. In all likelihood, Colin's sudden appearance at her office related to his drunken incident at the fancy dinner. It would be putting her job at risk to "lose" the story, but she'd been risking her job ever since she and Nick installed that wire two years ago.

Even after leaving the imposing Western Union building, they were silent as they walked along the crowded sidewalk. St. Paul's Chapel was only a block away and afforded a measure of privacy in the leafy cemetery plot surrounding the historic church. This was where George Washington prayed following his inauguration in 1789, and it seemed a timeless oasis of greenery amidst the bustle of Broadway.

Colin held the iron gateway open for her. The cemetery lawn was overgrown and lumpy as they wandered amidst the tombstones, seeking a little distance from the others strolling the grounds. The tombstones were smooth with age, the lettering worn away from centuries of weather. The people buried here had fought in the Revolution. They'd waged battles as fierce as her own. They knew heartache and deprivation and moral dilemmas.

Colin cleared his throat. "I believe I overheard enough of your conversation to know it could not be from an AP correspondent. It sounded like an entirely private conversation about some overdue bank accounts. Are you perhaps in some financial difficulty?"

"No!" The response was automatic, but after the word was out of her mouth, she realized she'd just closed off a possible explanation for being part of such a conversation. She shifted from the defense and moved to attack. "Were you drunk that night?"

He stopped beside a gnarled old sycamore tree and turned to face her. "I've told you that I was not."

"And I wasn't eavesdropping."

His smile was knowing. "The difference is that I'm not lying . . . and you are."

A little breeze ruffled his blond hair, and he looked flawless and intimidating in his elegant attire. He had the perfectly sculpted features that spoke of a long aristocratic heritage, but she sensed a hint of desperation in him. It was hard to imagine a man of his lofty status could ever want for anything, but did he have a medical condition that gave him fits? She knew a girl at school who had epilepsy, and disease did not respect rank.

"What happened that night?" she asked softly.

He turned and walked a few paces to brace his hands on the church fence, his knuckles clenched white as he glared into the distance. She followed, surprised by his troubled mood. When he finally spoke, his voice was low.

"I served in the Boer War as a foreign correspondent," he said. "I was under the mistaken impression that reporters attached to the army generally stayed behind the lines and wired their stories from a cozy inn after the fighting for the day had concluded. That was my experience during the Greek uprising. But this was no gentleman's war, and while traveling with a squad of soldiers, we found ourselves completely surrounded and trapped. The siege went on for weeks. I'd prefer not to go into details."

Lucy knew all about the Boer War, for the newspapers had been saturated with accounts of the conflict in the southern African colonies, which ended in a British victory over the Dutch only last year. The fighting had been brutal, made worse by the sweltering African climate.

"You were wounded?"

"No, but anyone who endures something like that does not care for the sound of gunshots. Or grenade detonations, cannon blasts, rocket flares, or artillery rounds." Maybe it was the chill in the air, but it seemed his face took on a pallor that hadn't been there moments ago. "When one is pinned down, unable to escape, and those noises are a constant companion for weeks, it can have a certain effect on a man. A bad one."

How interesting that he spoke in the third person, as if it had happened to someone else. She had no idea how this conversation had strayed from his drunken episode onto the dusty battlefields of the Boer War, but she'd rather discuss anything besides why she had an illegal wire monitoring her uncle's attorney.

"How does this relate to the dinner on Madison Avenue?"

He straightened and met her gaze. "A waiter uncorked a bottle of champagne a few feet behind me. It took me by surprise, and I responded badly."

"I see." She had no experience with war but didn't doubt

such things could leave a scar on a man's soul. "What about the other part of the story? About being on the hunt for an heiress?"

"Only a scoundrel would confess to such a thing." His expression was inscrutable, but he hadn't denied he was on the hunt for a rich wife.

"Why don't you simply tell people about it?"

He looked appalled, a series of emotions flashing across his face. "I am not the sort of person who lays my weaknesses out for all the world to see. Some things are better kept private."

Like why she needed to spy on her uncle and his legal maneuverings. "I agree."

She didn't know how to phrase her suggestion, so she turned to wander the cemetery grounds while trying to line up the right words. He followed. What she was about to propose was entirely illegal, but wasn't there a distinction between the letter of the law and what was morally right? Her family had been battling the law since before she was born; it came naturally to her, but she didn't trust outsiders. Especially not a rich, titled outsider who worked for Reuters. But sometimes necessity made unlikely allies.

"Perhaps we can help each other," she said as she wove between the gravestones.

"I'm listening."

"You need the world to believe that you do not quake in terror at the sound of loud noises, and I need access to a private wire that must remain secret. It seems we have each other over a barrel."

She risked a glance at him. He stared straight ahead as they walked, his face drawn and pensive. They reached the far side of the cemetery, and he braced his hands on the top of the iron fence, leaning on it as he stared at the towering office buildings across the street. What would she do if he refused to cooperate? The Saratoga Drakes would run roughshod over her and Nick if she could no longer anticipate Uncle Thomas's next move.

"Miss Drake, I may look superficial on the outside, but I try to maintain a modicum of honor beneath it all. I must understand why you have a private wire."

She told him everything. The Drake lawsuit had been covered in the press, and everything she told him of the forty-year battle could be easily verified. More difficult to prove was her uncle's sadistic delight in frightening off anyone who dared befriend them. She relayed Mr. Garzelli's story, how a decent man tried to provide something nice for his tenants and was being threatened with deportation as a result.

"It sounds appalling, but I need more information," he said. "For all I know, you could be involved in some kind of stock trading scheme."

She shot him a look. "If I were tapped into a stock trading scheme, I'd be a lot richer than I am."

"Nevertheless, I'll need to verify what you've told me about your uncle. You don't mind if I poke around a bit?"

"Poke away," she said. "Feel free to ask either me or Nick if anything isn't clear. We've got no secrets. Other than that wire, of course."

Colin folded his arms across his chest and looked at her down the length of his very aristocratic nose. "If I can confirm your assessment of your uncle's character, are you prepared to bury that story about me being a drunk?"

"What story?" she asked, and he smiled in return. They had an agreement.

Colin knew exactly where to find insight into Lucy's wild-eyed story about the long-running battle over a unique plumbing valve. Frank Wooten, the man he hoped would soon be his father-in-law, had made his fortune in the rough-and-tumble world of Manhattan industry, so he ought to know something about the case.

Even before Colin began courting Amelia, he went on regular fishing jaunts with Frank Wooten, first in England and now in New York. They both enjoyed the simple pleasure of a day in the country, fishing and catching their own dinner. Standing knee-deep in the cool water of a lake outside Mr. Wooten's summer retreat, surrounded by a thick pine forest, it was hard to believe they were only forty miles outside the city. These afternoons with Frank had been a godsend. Colin had no formal training in business, and the self-made millionaire was happy to share his thoughts on leading a corporation. He also knew plenty about the infamous Drake case.

"I met old Jacob Drake when I first came to New York," Frank said as he cast his line into the lake. "He was earning money hand-over-fist with that valve and started exporting them to Europe. He contracted with a stevedore who was new in the business to pack them up and get them loaded onto a ship. A storm delayed the packing, and the stevedore missed his deadline. Drake sued and won the cost of unfulfilled European contracts, which drove the stevedore into bankruptcy."

Colin had never had much interest in commerce or capitalism—a word with mildly revolutionary overtones he instinctively disliked—but he had always been fascinated by what drove men to strive, compete, fight, and die for a cause. He flicked his line to tug the bait along the surface of the water. "Is it true that a lawsuit has been waged by the inventor's heirs? That they were cut out of the profits?"

Mr. Wooten nodded. "It's a long shot, but any time there's that much money on the table, people will fight for it. It's ugly, and Thomas Drake has a reputation even more ruthless than his father's. I'm not exactly sure what happened there. The old man used to be the public face of the company, but no one has seen him for years. Everything gets negotiated through his son these days."

He went on to say that after Thomas Drake took over the company, the price of the valves had skyrocketed. Old Jacob had been difficult to do business with, but his son was impossible.

"Here's what I learned from the Drakes," Frank continued. "They're shrewd, tough, and know how to use the courts to their advantage. I don't think they've done anything illegal, but they aren't honorable people. The incident with the stevedore is proof of that. They were in the right, and the stevedore did miss his deadline, but an ounce of compassion would have brought far greater dividends in the long run. No one in Manhattan likes or trusts them. I think everyone is rooting for the poor relations to win that lawsuit."

As was Colin. Having learned a little about how the Saratoga Drakes did business, he would lose no sleep over Lucy's illegal wire. In return, she would bury the gossip about him.

Lucy squinted through the heavy rain trickling down her office window. The street below was already swamped, and Nick hated days like this. The sewers became overloaded, and men were taken off the fresh water pipe projects to manage outflow in the sewers, a wet and smelly job.

But she couldn't worry about Nick. All she could think about was Colin Beckwith and his pending decision about keeping her wire a secret. If he exposed her wire, Uncle Thomas would get away with all the devious things he'd done over the years. Her father had worried himself into an early grave over this lawsuit. For the hundredth time, she wondered about the location of that maroon satchel and its mysterious contents that had terrified her father. She was certain it related to the lawsuit, and if Colin decided to expose her . . .

As if her thoughts had conjured him, Colin entered the office. It was hard not to be impressed as he strode through the room, his lean form projecting a sense of confidence she wished wasn't so attractive. For pity's sake, she had no business being enthralled by the way a man *walked*.

His first words brought her wayward thoughts crashing back to earth.

"I hoped we could go for a stroll to discuss what I learned over the weekend, but the rain is going to make that a challenge."

Her heart seized. Whatever he had decided would have a drastic effect on her future, and she couldn't bear waiting another moment. "Let's head to the basement to talk," she said.

The basement housed the hub of the pneumatic tube operation, making it noisy and unpleasant. Aside from the people working in the sorting rooms, few people ventured down there. Since it was lunchtime, they would have plenty of privacy.

Colin followed her, riding the elevator all the way down

and stepping out into the dank air of the basement, which was brightly lit with bare electric bulbs hanging every few yards from the exposed ceiling. Down one hallway was the mail room and the hub of the tubes, so she headed in the other direction, toward the boiler room. Their footsteps echoed on the concrete floor as they rounded a corner and found an empty hallway. She turned her attention to Colin, who got straight to the point.

"Everything I've heard confirms what you said about the Drake valve," he said in a low voice, standing so close she could smell his pine-scented soap. "If your grandfather wasn't actually swindled, it certainly appears he was treated unfairly." The tension in her spine uncoiled a fraction, but he hadn't finished speaking. "Why do you suppose Jacob took such shameful advantage of his own brother? Especially while that brother was at war?"

"Easy," she replied. "Greed."

Colin shook his head. "I don't think so. From what I've been able to glean, old Jacob Drake charged a fair price for the valve. It wasn't until your uncle took over that the price skyrocketed, so I don't think it was greed."

"Are you sure about that?" Uncle Thomas had taken over when she was a baby, so she couldn't say how things changed under his administration. All she knew was that she distrusted every single member of the Saratoga branch of the family.

Colin's voice carried a combination of curiosity and frustration. "These kinds of questions drive me insane. I want to know what motivates people. How could your grandfather be so creative and brilliant, but careless at the same time?"

She tensed, sensing someone around the curve of the hallway behind her. The humming and hissing from the boiler made it hard to hear, but she gestured for Colin to be silent as she turned. Her back pressed flat against the cinderblock wall, she crept toward the bend in the hallway. Colin must have thought she was ridiculous, creeping like a bug along the wall, but he hadn't seen those photographs that proved someone had been spying on her here in the building.

Reaching the end of the short corridor, she peeked around the corner and gasped. A man stood not two feet away, his ear cocked toward her, but the distinctive twist of his shoulders sparked a memory.

"It's you!" she gasped. His tall, misshapen frame was unmistakable. It was the lamppost leaner who'd been spying on her apartment and lurking at Mr. Garzelli's tenement. Caught by surprise, he ran for the staircase at the far end of the basement.

She followed, hiking up her skirts and sprinting as fast as she could on the slick concrete floor. "Wait!" she hollered. "Why are you spying on me?"

Colin was just behind her, which was good, because the lamppost leaner was big, and she wouldn't be able to stop him without help. They were gaining on him. The corridor was a full city block long, snaking past the sorting room and heading toward the staircase.

Without warning, the lamppost leaner pivoted and charged her, his face fierce with determination. He slammed into her with enough force to knock the breath from her body, and then shoved her into a darkened room off the corridor. She stumbled and fell to the ground. A scuffle sounded behind her, but it was too dark to see. Colin tripped over her as he was shoved inside as well. The door slammed behind them. She still fought for air, but Colin got to his feet quickly and went to the door.

"What happened?" she gasped.

"It appears we've been locked in a closet." The jerky rattling of a door handle confirmed it. She rolled into a sitting position, struggling to draw a breath. A sliver of light came from the bottom of the door, but the closet was still oppressively dark.

"I think he's gone," Colin said, his ear pressed against the door.

"And we're locked in here." It suddenly felt like the walls were closing in.

"So we are." He sounded amused. He tugged on the door and wiggled the knob again. "And in rather over-the-top fashion, too. Americans never do anything halfway."

It wasn't funny. Ever since Tom Jr. locked her in the dumb-waiter when she was a child, Lucy had feared entrapment. Her breath came fast and ragged, sounding loud in the close confines of the room. How long were they going to be entombed here? The smell of tar paper was nauseating, and she couldn't get away.

"Are you all right?" Colin asked.

"Why should I be all right? That man has been spying on me, and I have no idea why. Now I'm trapped like a sardine in a tin, and I can barely breathe, and all my life I've been afraid of being trapped. So no. No, I'm *not* all right."

Her eyes were beginning to adjust to the dark, and she saw Colin cautiously step forward, hunkering down to sit beside her. "You realize that we are in no real danger, correct?"

"Other than being confined in a small space that smells like tar and stokes all my childhood fears simultaneously? Yes."

"This sounds like a good time to discuss the concept of a stiff upper lip," Colin said in a maddeningly calm voice as he twisted to sit beside her on the floor. "The British are famous for it. It doesn't matter what disaster befalls you, what sort of choking disappointments or tragedies knock you off balance. Those feelings must be repressed for the good of king and country. We're not like the French, who weep at the opera house, or heaven help us, the Italians, who sob over a spilled glass of port. Not the British! And with a name like Drake, you are descended straight from that glorious, sceptered isle. So chin up, Lucy. Make me proud."

His good humor was actually working. "Are you telling me the English aren't allowed to feel emotions?"

"Heavens, no. We feel as much as those wailing French and Italians. We just don't *show* it. Far more civilized, hmm?"

Since she was trembling on the floor and too queasy to stand up, yes, Colin seemed far more civilized. Then again, he probably hadn't been locked in a dumbwaiter by his cousin when he was ten years old. When she told Colin about the incident, he finally showed a bit of sympathy.

"He sounds like a snotty-nosed twit."

Lucy nodded. "While I was trapped, I hit the door and started crying. Tom taunted me the whole time from the other side, saying I sounded so crazy I ought to be locked up in Ridgemoor."

"What's Ridgemoor?"

"It's a lunatic asylum north of the city. When I was in school, grown-ups used Ridgemoor as a threat. Make good grades or you'll be shipped off to Ridgemoor. Finish your vegetables or you'll go to Ridgemoor." She hadn't needed to be threatened with Ridgemoor to behave. Any kind of entrapment terrified her. And now here she was, locked in a tiny room where no one could hear them call for help.

"You must think I'm an awful crybaby," she concluded.

He snorted. "Coming from a man who falls on the ground at the pop of a champagne cork?"

She scrambled for something to talk about besides their current entrapment. "Are you really going to marry for money?" It was a terribly personal question, but they had dropped all pretense, and she was curious.

"I really am." His voice was heavy with reluctant humor. "Here's the thing," he said slowly. "First, you've got to promise never to tell this to another living soul."

"I promise." It was easy, because she desperately wanted to hear what he had to say next.

He sighed and shifted position on the floor. "Sorry . . . let's just drop this."

"No! Go on! I promise never to tell."

She could hear his ironic laughter in the darkness. "All right. Since it's dark and you can't see my face flaming in embarrassment, here it comes. I inherited this glorious monstrosity of a house. Practically a palace. From a distance, it looks like someplace Henry VIII should live, with spires, mullioned windows, and miles of rolling hills. But my father was completely inept at turning its crumbling fortune around. He spent his life hunting grouse and perfecting his whist game."

There was a long silence, and Lucy wondered at the mild disapproval in his voice. She worshipped her father, but Colin obviously felt differently.

"Sometimes I fear I'm no better than my father. I dabble in Morse code and follow troops around the world. Watch revolutions, sit at grand dining tables and listen to the captains of industry plan the twentieth century . . . but I am only an observer."

In the darkness she reached for his hand, warm and solid in the chilly basement. "You're an observer who sends his eyewitness account out to the rest of the world," she said. "To the farmers in Nebraska or the power brokers in Washington. There is value in that. Without men like you, Reuters or the AP wouldn't exist."

He squeezed her hand. "I wish I didn't like you so much."

She pulled her hand away, for the feeling was mutual. "I wonder how much longer we'll be trapped in here."

Not long. Less than an hour later, employees returning from lunch walked past the closet, and Colin hollered loudly enough to get their attention. Lucy squinted against the flood of bright light as she stepped out of the closet. She'd overstayed her lunch break, but all she wanted to do was run to Nick and flaunt the fact that she now had *proof* the lamppost leaner was spying on them.

For once in her life, she didn't like being right.

❦

To her surprise, Colin offered to accompany her to see Nick, which was a relief. There was no way Nick could be dismissive of the lamppost leaner if Colin verified the frightening encounter.

It had stopped raining, and walking through the city alongside Colin was fascinating. She'd been born here, but watching his curiosity felt like being reintroduced to Manhattan, allowing her to see it anew through his eyes. He kept craning his neck to gape at the height of the buildings or gawk at the German vendor who heckled pedestrians to buy his bratwurst. He seemed riveted by the city, and it was unusually appealing. It was a delightful half hour until they arrived at the hog house where her brother worked.

Nick spent most of his day underground. Few people living on these crowded streets realized that each time they stepped outside, they walked above an underground city of tunnels where plumbers, electricians, gas line technicians, and engineers made their living. The men who dug and maintained the tunnels were known as *sandhogs*, and they took their breaks in buildings known as *hog houses*. Lucy put in a request at the front counter to summon Nick to the surface.

A few minutes later, Nick came above ground, wiping his hands on a grimy rag. He remembered Colin from their meeting on New Year's Eve.

"Hello, London," he said, looking skeptically between Lucy and Colin. When she told him about the alarming encounter with the lamppost leaner, instead of being sympathetic, Nick was incensed. He tugged her to the rear of the hog house, where the aboveground portion of the vertical turbine engine provided a loud and steady chugging noise to mask his voice. "What are you doing, bringing a stranger into our business?" he demanded.

Colin didn't feel like a stranger to her anymore, especially since the odd deal they'd struck about keeping each other's secrets.

"When a sinister prowler locked us in a basement closet, I thought I owed him an explanation," she said. "Quite frankly, I was terrified, and Colin kept me from losing my head. Unlike some people I know," she added in a pointed voice.

Nick's face twisted with regret. "I'm sorry, Luce." He gave a heavy sigh. "This whole thing makes me feel so helpless, and I hate it. Let's go talk to your fellow, and I'll hear the rest of it."

"Just be polite," she warned. She needed to hear Colin's observations about the lamppost leaner, for she hadn't gotten a good look at him, and Colin noticed far more than she did. He relayed that the lamppost leaner had a nose that had once been broken, wore a tweed jacket that had been patched on both elbows, and smelled of cigarette smoke. And he'd noticed one other crucial detail. The man had been afraid.

"All the color dropped from his face when he realized we'd spotted him," Colin said. "That was fear, not surprise."

"Why would anyone hired by the Saratoga Drakes fear *us*?" she asked.

"Maybe this doesn't have anything to do with the Saratoga Drakes," Nick said. "Maybe the guy is carrying a torch for you." She recoiled at the thought, but Nick kept speaking. "He followed you to the Western Union building. He loiters outside our apartment before dawn. Maybe it's all in hope of getting a glimpse of you."

"Then why was he sniffing around Mr. Garzelli's tenement?"

Nick didn't have an answer for that, and it was time for him to return to work. She and Colin had a long walk back to Broadway, during which Colin pressed her for more insight into the Saratoga Drakes.

"My uncle married a woman named Margaret," she said as they walked along a tree-shaded avenue. Margaret Drake seemed nice enough, but Lucy couldn't help but be suspicious of a woman who spoke with a trace of a British accent despite being born and raised in Yonkers. Sadly, Aunt Margaret seemed incapable of discussing anything other than her adored son. Tom Jr. suffered from the self-absorption of someone who grew up knowing he was the heir to a tremendous fortune and the apple of his parents' eyes. Tom had graduated from Princeton after only two years, so he was smart, but he still lived at the family estate, and she didn't think he'd ever held a job.

"If you and Nick win the lawsuit, what will happen?" Colin asked.

"It all depends on what the judge decides the damages are worth," she said. "Jacob was responsible for making the business flourish, and during the early years of their partnership, he and my grandfather split everything fifty-fifty. It's true my grandfather gave Jacob complete control until the end of the war, so if the judge decides Jacob's seizure of the valve was illegal, the court will have to determine how much my grandfather's valve has earned in the past forty years."

Colin drew her to a stop behind a boxwood hedge and turned her to face him. "And how much would that be?"

"About forty million dollars. My uncle is entitled to some, and my portion would be split with Nick, so I'd have to settle for a measly eight or ten million."

"Interesting." There was speculation in his eyes, as though she was suddenly a person of extraordinary fascination.

"Do *not* look at me like that," she said.

"Like what?"

"Like I might be a fallback candidate if your Madison Avenue heiress doesn't work out."

The roguish grin he beamed at her was wildly attractive. He didn't even pretend to deny her suggestion that he was on the hunt for a wealthy bride, and his good-natured banter made him even more appealing.

"Wouldn't you like living in a palace?" he asked. "If you bring over a few of those fancy valves, I can even rig up some running water. Nothing but the best for you, Lucy."

She couldn't suppress a grin as they resumed their walk to Broadway. "I'd be more tempted by the mouthwatering high tea you buy for the Reuters employees each afternoon. How much do you pay for those fancy watercress sandwiches?"

"Ah! A gentleman never worries over such tacky fiscal concerns."

"And an American never overlooks the ridiculous cost of a pound of watercress." It was fun being with someone so boundlessly cheerful.

"I bet your Saratoga cousins never worry about the cost of watercress. I'm still curious about the initial rift between the two brothers. Have you ever met Jacob Drake?"

"No. He turned control of the company over to Uncle Thomas ages ago. He used to live with them, but I don't know if he still does. He's ancient; at least ninety years old, I think."

"I want to meet him," Colin said.

She stifled a laugh. "I am not on cordial terms with the Saratoga branch of the family, so I can't get you an introduction."

Colin clucked his tongue. "One of the advantages of having a title is that I can get invited anywhere."

"So arrogant," she muttered.

"But also true," he countered. "You told me your Uncle Thomas lives in a grand country manor named Oakmonte. A man like that would be thrilled to host a visit from Sir Colin

Beckwith, 9th Baronet of Whitefriars. One of my responsibilities for Reuters is to visit our subscribing newspapers and make sure all is in good order. It's time for me to start making the rounds, and I suppose the newspaper in Saratoga might warrant a call. While I am there, I will finagle an invitation to Oakmonte."

She was flabbergasted. "You would do all this just to meet Jacob Drake?"

"Since it appears you are woefully under-informed about your own family history, it falls to me."

"But why?" she pressed.

"I'm curious. This is a fascinating story, and unless I learn what really happened, I'll keep obsessing over it. When investigating a story, nothing beats speaking to the parties themselves. You, my dear, are a highly partisan source. In the newspaper business, we would call you a 'biased witness.' Or perhaps an unreliable source. There's all kinds of terms I could think up for you."

"Clever and charming?"

"Clever, yes."

They walked several steps in silence. She could *hear* him grinning beside her, even as his mouth remained clamped shut.

"Charming?" she prodded.

He drew a deep breath mingled with laughter. "Why must you be so persistent? If I pay you a compliment, I'll be accused of chasing after your highly improbable fortune. Which is absurd. No self-respecting fortune hunter would gamble on a forty-year legal quagmire, no matter how *charming* the lady may be. And yet if I don't pay you a compliment, I'm arrogant and coldhearted. True?"

"The burdens of greatness."

They bickered all the way back to Broadway, and Lucy could not remember enjoying herself more.

It all came to an end the moment they stepped through the imposing doors of the Western Union building. Colin straightened his collar, assumed an aloof demeanor, and headed toward the Reuters office. The AP was located only two floors away, but she must never forget that an entire world separated them.

*W*hat Colin had told Lucy about the ease of wangling an invitation to her uncle's home was true. During his business meeting with the editor of a Saratoga newspaper, Colin mentioned the high praise he'd heard for the Drake mansion a few miles outside of town and that he would like a tour. An invitation to Oakmonte arrived from Thomas and Margaret Drake the next day.

Oakmonte. What kind of American gave their home a name? The Saratoga Drakes were new money and probably thought naming their estate would carry a whiff of old-world prestige. Colin didn't care what they did with their house; all he wanted was the chance to meet Jacob Drake. No one seemed to know where the old man lived, and there was no mention of him in the slim Saratoga telephone directory. Jacob Drake was now ninety-two years old, and in all likelihood, he lived with his son.

Colin was met at the Saratoga train station by Tom Jr., who was "taking a break" from employment in order to pursue his love of marksmanship. During the forty-minute carriage ride to Oakmonte, Tom Jr. did nothing but ramble on about shooting.

"There was no real competition at college," he said with

a knowing air. "Even the marksmanship instructors are little better than amateurs. Of course, I've been shooting since I was six years old, so perhaps I shouldn't expect real competition at Princeton. I intend to compete in the next Olympics. It will be a pleasure to vie against truly worthy competitors."

"Indeed." Colin was good at making small talk with strangers. Normally he loved asking endless questions to discover what motivated a man to study, conquer, and achieve. But there was no need to ask questions with Tom, who filled the air with a relentless monologue about himself. It was a relief when they passed through the gates of the Drake family home.

The splendor of Oakmonte had not been exaggerated. The red-brick Georgian mansion sat on a rolling green lawn as though it had been planted there a hundred years ago.

It hadn't. That much was apparent the moment Colin alighted from the carriage and approached the house, noting the fine condition of the mortar, which showed no sign of crumbling. Instead of wavering hand-blown glass, the windows looked smooth and sparkled in the sunlight.

The front door opened, and a tall man bounded down the short flight of stairs. "Welcome!" the elder Drake boomed in a confident voice. Thomas Drake's dark hair was threaded with a hint of silver, but he maintained the lean physique of an athlete. His wife was a predictably handsome woman with even features and a triple strand of pearls that hung to her waist.

"Thank you for hosting me," Colin said as he stepped inside. "Whenever I mention my desire to renovate my estate back home, people recommend a visit to Oakmonte as a chance to see the finest New York has to offer."

Margaret Drake beamed at the compliment, and Colin took the chance to admire the foyer, which was framed by a dramatic double staircase curving down from the second story, almost like a pair of welcoming arms. The foyer had elegant crown molding, gold-leaf wall sconces, and a series of arched windows stretching the length of the front hall. Mrs. Drake offered to take him on a tour as soon as he'd been settled into a room and had a chance to refresh himself.

A servant escorted him to a guest bedroom on the second floor. Colin had been invited to stay the night, since he didn't need to catch his train back to the city until the following afternoon. The guest room had a high ceiling and large windows framed with swaths of royal blue draperies held open by silken cords. It was a spacious and elegantly appointed room, but most impressive was the attached washroom with white tile, well-designed fixtures, and a narrow window of its own. Two ivory spigots on the pedestal sink brought a healthy stream of either cool or piping hot water pouring from the tap. Everything about this washroom was a miracle of modern plumbing.

Mr. and Mrs. Drake took him on a tour of the house. They were cordial and generous with information as they discussed building materials, how the house had been situated on the lawn to take advantage of the views, even the equipment in the kitchen. Mrs. Drake had plenty of questions about Whitefriars and what it was like to grow up in a house with so many centuries of history.

"I'd trade you a few of those generations of history for the engineering in one of your washrooms," he quipped.

Both Drakes laughed, but he was only partially jesting. Everything about this house was impressive. The mahogany floors were perfectly flush and gleamed with a high shine. The plaster moldings were carved by artisans and sported no cracks in the glossy paint. Not a hint of mustiness, sagging floorboards, or moldering tapestries anywhere in sight.

As they walked down the corridor to a conservatory, Mrs. Drake drew up alongside him and held his arm in genteel fashion. "I'd like to show you my animal tableau," she said. "I understand creative taxidermy is becoming quite popular in England."

It was true. Walter Potter had created a trend by stuffing small animals like rabbits and kittens, then dressing them in miniature costumes. The animals were posed in charming domestic settings such as a tea party, a classroom, or playing croquet. Colin found them mildly repugnant, but there was no accounting for taste, and he obligingly followed Mrs. Drake to the conservatory. The room was flooded with sunshine from banks of windows on three sides. Potted palms towered in the corners, and the green scents of moss and verbena filled the air.

The tableau was on display in the far corner of the room, with small animals gathered around a miniature tea table. The chintz-covered table sported tiny plates with remarkably life-like cakes and bowls of fruit. It was a charming display, if one could look past the bunnies and the kittens propped up in the chairs, teacups glued to their paws.

"Our taxidermist is a true artist," she murmured, gesturing to a kitten whose paws had been wired to hold a cracker to its mouth. A squirrel dressed as a butler stood to the side, a tray with creamer and sugar balanced between his outstretched limbs.

"Very impressive," Colin said. He'd seen a number of similar animal tableaux in England and never failed to marvel at their popularity. Over the centuries, Whitefriars had collected its share of mounted stag heads on its walls, so he was in no position to pass judgment on Mrs. Drake's taste.

"I understand there is a museum in Sussex featuring these animal displays," Thomas said. "One of them portrays a group of cats playing poker in a cardroom. Have you seen it?"

"I've never had the pleasure," Colin said. "But your taxidermist is to be commended. I've never seen dead creatures appear so delighted to be dead."

Both Drakes laughed, and they moved on to the next room. None of this was getting him any closer to meeting old Jacob Drake, but he decided to wait a little longer to see if his hosts brought up the topic on their own.

Besides, he had a genuine interest in the construction of the house. Its roof rivaled the size of Whitefriars', and he was brimming with curiosity to know how they prevented water damage on so huge a surface. Mr. and Mrs. Drake obligingly accompanied him to the attic, where the air was warm and dusty but without a hint of mold. The attics at Whitefriars were encrusted with centuries of mineral stains and corroded wood, and he had to admire this clean, well-ventilated space. After descending a flight of stairs from the attic, his hosts led him back toward the double staircase and its impressive foyer.

He paused at the top of the stairs. "What is down this hallway?" They'd gone into each of the bedrooms on the western side of the house, but the hallway on the other side of the staircase was closed off by a set of doors only a few yards away.

"We don't use the east wing much," Thomas said. "It's easier to simply keep it closed up."

Interesting. Among the numerous rooms on the two floors he'd been shown, none looked suitable for housing an elderly man, nor had any mention of Jacob been made all morning.

Colin would have enjoyed the chance to wander the grounds and learn how they managed their runoff drainage from the roof, but Mrs. Drake had planned a formal high tea, so it had to be delayed.

A neighboring couple, the McNallys, joined them for tea, along with their two daughters. Tom Jr. tried to flirt with the oldest and prettiest daughter, but Mrs. Drake engineered for the girl to have a seat immediately to Colin's left. Julia McNally carried on a lively conversation about life at Bryn Mawr College, where she'd been enrolled for the past two years. Despite attending university, her conversation seemed limited to the weather and horses. It made him long for Lucy's natural curiosity.

"Will your father be joining us for tea?" he asked Thomas. "I was looking forward to meeting Jacob Drake."

A hush settled over the gathering. Mrs. Drake coughed a little as she set her teacup down, but her husband recovered quickly.

"I was not aware you knew of my father," he said in a polite voice.

"I've heard of his invention. I understand the Drake valve has brought major improvements to the infrastructure of cities."

Thomas gave a small nod. "Indeed. We are all very proud of my father's work."

"Does he live here at the estate?"

"He is a private man and rarely has the energy for visits, but yes, my father does indeed live with us."

Julia set down her teacup. "I've never met him, but one of my college professors said the buildings of New York City would never have been built so high but for the inventions of reinforced steel and the Drake plumbing valve."

"It's just a piece of equipment," Tom Jr. mumbled. "And he didn't exactly invent it, now, did he? That was his brother, but Grandfather gets all the glory, doesn't he?"

Thomas sent a smoldering glare at his son. "That's enough," he said darkly. Tom Jr. looked as if he wanted to say more but managed to swallow it back, then put on a cheerful tone.

"Do you like shooting, Sir Beckwith?" he asked. "I'm training for next summer's Olympics and wouldn't mind a little sport tomorrow morning. How about it?"

Colin's mouth went dry. The prospect of gunfire prompted the beginning of a headache, but so long as he was prepared for the blasts, he ought to be able to handle the attack on his nerves. Both of the elder Drakes had immediately shut down the discussion of Jacob Drake, but perhaps the son would be more forthcoming.

"I'd like nothing better," he said with an artificially bright smile.

It was a cool morning, and the grounds were shrouded by a wispy layer of fog. Colin and Tom Jr. walked a fair distance from the house in deference to those who liked to sleep late in the mornings. A servant named Hastings accompanied them and would be responsible for launching clay discs into the air.

"Let's play doubles," Tom said as they chambered their shotguns, and Colin silently groaned. Even as a younger man, he had never enjoyed shooting, nor did he possess much skill. Trap shooting used an automated thrower to hurl a clay disc in a high arc over the field. It made for a challenging target. In doubles, the machine launched two discs simultaneously, requiring rapid-fire shooting to land both targets.

"You first," he said tensely. Shotgun blasts were deafening, and he braced himself for the assault. Perhaps this morning was a blessing in disguise, as it would help train him to maintain calm despite the explosive noise.

The machine hurled two discs into the air, and Tom fired off his shots, smashing one target, but the other fell to the ground intact.

"You spoiled my shot!" Tom accused.

It was true. After the first shotgun blast, Colin had flinched and reared back, startling Tom and making the second shot go wild.

"Sorry," Colin muttered as he clenched his shotgun. He had braced himself for the noise but forgot about the stench of gunpowder. It filled his nose and throat, gagging him. The reek of sulfur and saltpeter made him want to vomit. For the life of him, it felt like he smelled African dirt and sweaty bodies; heard the buzz of flies swarming above corpses.

He swallowed back his distaste, determined to get through this morning. Tom still muttered curses, swearing that Hastings had used a sloppy angle to eject the discs, but Colin ignored him as he stepped up to the line. The shotgun was heavy as he tucked it against his shoulder.

"Doubles it is," he said with a nod to Hastings. The machine let out a whoosh as the two discs hurled into the air. He squeezed off a shot, flinching at the blast, and tried to fire a second round but couldn't. His hand shook too badly. He missed both targets, and it delighted Tom.

"Better luck next time." Tom smirked as he gamely stepped back up for his round. He got both targets, and Colin hit only one on his next turn, but at least the match would not be a complete washout.

He hated every second of the morning punctuated with deafening shotgun blasts and the acrid stink of gunpowder. Tom fixated on shooting and had no interest in casual conversation, which was fine with Colin. He focused more on hanging on to his queasy stomach than trying to hit the target.

The match came to a merciful end after an hour, and Tom Jr. was delighted with the outcome, as he won 43 to 6. Frankly, Colin was lucky to have hit that many, given how badly his hand trembled most of the morning.

It was over, and they had a twenty-minute walk back to the house. Twenty minutes to learn as much as he could about Jacob Drake and the real story of what happened all those years ago.

"Your family must be very proud of your abilities," he said.

"Oh, they are," Tom agreed. "Everyone knows that I'm probably going to the Olympics next summer."

Wasn't it nice how Tom Jr. managed to squeeze that reference into almost every sentence? "It will be in St. Louis, correct?"

Tom's expression was sour as he kicked at a clump of overly long grass. "Yeah. It would have been better if it were in Paris like the last time, but what can a fellow do?"

"Will your family attend?"

"Of course. It's as close as they'll ever come to something like that."

"Your grandfather as well?"

Tom snorted. "He's too old. He's practically a hundred and completely out of his mind."

"Oh, really . . ." That would be a reasonable explanation for the family to keep him away from visitors.

"No, not really," Tom Jr. admitted. "He's just a royal pain in the neck and always has been. A complete zealot. He's impossible to be around, and frankly, I wouldn't want him to see me in the Olympics. Crazy old duffer; nobody can stand him. That's why my father keeps him tucked away behind closed doors in the east wing. Let the servants deal with him. Nobody else wants to."

Colin kept walking at a measured pace. "That seems a little cold, doesn't it?"

"Look, you don't know him like we do. I'm grateful that he made all that money and everything, but that doesn't give him the right to force his views down our throats."

They rounded a copse of willow trees, and the house came into view. Even the rear of the house was attractive, with a terraced patio overlooking a rose garden. Mrs. Drake was ensconced on a bench, wrapped in an angora throw and looking every inch the grand lady. Her husband sat a few feet away, smoking a morning cheroot.

She rose as they drew near and gestured to an impressive spread of breakfast pastries and pot of tea. "You must be hungry after a morning of shooting," she said with a welcoming smile.

"I won 43 to 6," Tom said as he scooped up a large wedge of blueberry bread.

Mrs. Drake winced and sent Colin a sympathetic smile. "Oh, dear. Then you must be even more eager for something to cleanse the palate."

"Actually, I'm eager to get the smell of gunpowder off me. Can I join you after a bath?" It was an unusual request, but people tended to grant ridiculous leeway to men with titles, and he was fully prepared to take advantage of it.

"Certainly." Mrs. Drake smiled, the teapot suspended over an empty cup she had been preparing to pour for him.

He wanted to dunk into a tub full of hot soapy water but was even more eager to take the opportunity to explore the east wing of the house while the family was outdoors on the patio.

He vaulted up the staircase two steps at a time. A quick glance down both sides of the hallway revealed he was alone, and he headed straight toward the closed double doors blocking the east wing of the second floor. The brass knob was cold in his palm as he gently twisted.

Locked.

He scanned the hallway and saw no obvious hiding places for a key, so he ran his fingers along the casement ledge above the door. It was coated with a fine layer of dust, and a key fell and clattered against the floor.

He held his breath, waiting for someone to investigate the noise. When no one appeared, he inserted the key, covering the mechanism with his hand to muffle the metallic clicks. The door twisted open easily, and he stepped through, closing it gently behind him.

The hallway mirrored the floorplan of the opposite wing. All the doors were open, and he'd be easily spotted if anyone was in those rooms. But nothing ventured, nothing gained. He strode forward with the entitlement he'd learned from decades of mingling with the British aristocracy. He strolled casually, looking from side to side as he passed each open door. There were six bedrooms, three on each side. All of them spacious, with neatly made beds and small sitting areas.

Only one looked different, for it had a wheelchair in the corner. Colin gently rapped on the open door. "Hello?"

There was no answer. He tipped his head inside, scanning the room quickly. It was the room of an older person, with extra coverlets mounded on the bed and a cane propped beside the wheelchair. In a house filled with well-appointed furniture and decorations, everything in this room seemed to come from another era. The furniture was old. A chipped mug advertising Brooklyn Tea rested on the bureau, filled with wrapped throat lozenges. Beside the bed was a bookshelf brimming with tattered novels. Colin pulled out a book by Victor Hugo and opened it. The nameplate on the inside cover said it came from the library of Jacob Drake.

A door led to a washroom identical to the one attached to Colin's own guest room. The washroom was spotless, the white tile gleaming in the sunlight from the narrow window. There was no sign of water droplets on the tub or basin. He ran a fingertip along the bottom of the sink and came away with a coating of dust.

There was only one possible conclusion. No one had used this room in months, and there was no sign of Jacob Drake.

After breakfast there were still a few hours before Colin needed to set off for the train station. Mrs. Drake had disappeared into the kitchen to scold the staff about something, leaving him alone with Thomas, who surprised him by suggesting a walk.

"I'd like to show you the fish pond," he said. "It's freshly stocked, and perhaps someday you can return for a morning of trout fishing."

"I'd like nothing better," Colin said, not only because he genuinely enjoyed fishing, but also because perhaps he'd find another opportunity to probe for information on the missing patriarch of the family.

To his surprise, Thomas was eager to initiate a business discussion the moment they set off on a gravel path toward the north end of the grounds.

"You are aware of the Drake valve," he said.

"I've heard something about it, yes."

"Do you have any connections with the Crown Building Agency in England?"

All it would take was a letter of interest, and Colin could establish whatever ties he wanted. Working for a newspaper opened doors like that, as did a title. "I do," he said.

"We've been running into a bit of a fuss lately," Thomas said. "At first our valves were selling quite well throughout the United Kingdom, but a British company has developed a competing product, and now the government is throwing obstacles in our way. If you have any influence, perhaps we can come to a mutually agreeable arrangement."

"I'm listening," Colin said. It was unusual for anyone to approach him with a business proposition. The aristocratic abhorrence of dabbling in trade was well known, but apparently Thomas Drake knew nothing of those unwritten rules, for which Colin was grateful. The entire roof at Whitefriars needed to be replaced, which would require a fortune and take years to accomplish, but in the short term, the roof over the music room needed immediate repair.

Thomas's offer was a generous four-percent commission on each Drake valve sold in the United Kingdom if Colin could lift the embargo. He smiled. He was close family friends with the current Chancellor of the Exchequer, and that friendship could help slice through red tape with ease. Colin might not even need to return to England to get the wheels moving.

But a four-percent commission wouldn't come fast enough for the immediate repair in the music room.

Thomas finished speaking and awaited his answer, but Colin allowed the silence to stretch for a full twenty paces. As they neared a wild mulberry hedge, Thomas held a branch aside and let Colin pass. The fishing pond was straight ahead, but neither commented on it as they came to a halt.

"If I get the embargo lifted, I'll need a five-thousand-dollar fee to be paid immediately," he stated. "Then the four-percent commission in perpetuity."

Thomas nearly choked. "That is a little richer than anticipated."

So was the cost of a new roof. "I remember my father telling me a story about the time the Crown cut a deal with a factory in Manchester to supply wool socks to soldiers fighting in the Napoleonic wars. The London manufacturer who'd been making army uniforms protested, claiming socks were part of the official uniform and the Crown had no right to buy the socks from an outside company. The Manchester factory put up a fuss and tried to enforce the contract. Quite a rumpus ensued. The Crown knows they were in the wrong but doesn't want to admit it. I believe that court case is still dragging on to this day."

Thomas was intelligent enough to understand exactly what Colin was saying. Each year, more and more tall buildings were being erected in cities throughout the United Kingdom. It could take decades to loosen the bureaucratic quagmire without the help of someone to grease the wheels. There was nothing illegal about it, and it would get Colin a new roof over the music room.

The pleasant façade Thomas Drake had been showing him for the past two days slipped, revealing the iron glint Lucy had warned him about. Thomas folded his arms and glared at the line of trees on the far side of the pond.

"I've always prided myself on being a shrewd man of business," Thomas said. "If I accept your terms, I'd want something more in exchange."

Colin raised a brow, and Thomas continued. "My wife does not feel our family has been warmly received by the local community. The prominent families in the vicinity have been here since before the American Revolution. Their roots are old and deep, as are their fortunes. Our money is new, and in their eyes, it carries a taint. That bothers my wife."

Given his terse tone, the chilly reception bothered Thomas as well.

"What are you suggesting?" Colin asked.

The frosty glare warmed, and the congenial host returned. "You have a name and a title that is bound to impress. If we form a business alliance, it would be natural for you to be an occasional visitor at Oakmonte. A few more visits such as this would be welcome. Margaret would enjoy having you as our guest of honor when we entertain the local community for a formal dinner or two. No more than that."

Colin smiled. Thomas Drake might be a viper, but he was a rich viper and willing to splash a little of his money around. Just because Lucy inherited an ax to grind didn't mean Colin couldn't establish a decent rapport with a man offering a tempting business alliance.

"We have a deal," he said.

Chapter
TEN

$\mathcal{L}$ucy sat on a hard wooden bench in Grand Central Station, watching thousands of people come and go. Colin would be arriving on the next train from Saratoga. He'd been gone on his business trip for a week, and during that time had visited Philadelphia, Boston, New Haven, and Saratoga. He'd seen more of the United States than she had, as she'd never even left the state.

What was it like in Saratoga? She'd heard about the rolling hills blanketed with verdant forests and sparkling lakes. Oakmonte sounded like such a grand place, and she was embarrassingly curious about what sort of life her Saratoga relatives lived when they weren't aiming darts at her from the other side of a courtroom. She doubted she would ever see it, though. Once, when her father was trying to find an amicable solution to the court case, he had visited Uncle Thomas at Oakmonte. The visit was supposed to last only two days, but her father was gone for a month and was a nervous wreck when he returned.

He'd had very little to say about what happened during his visit. "Oakmonte is a nice house," he'd said, but his hands trembled, and he didn't look anyone in the eyes. He seemed old and haggard. Even her mother noticed, but he brushed her concerns away. "I was ill and lost a little weight," her father said. "Nothing to worry about."

Lucy was only fourteen but could easily see that her father had lost more than a little weight. His trousers were so loose they looked ready to fall off, and his neck no longer filled his collar.

"Will you go back?" she had asked. "Can I come next time?"

Her father had shuddered, and the color drained from his face. "No. Oakmonte is a terrible place," he whispered on a shattered breath.

It had been confusing. Hadn't he just said it was nice? But he was adamant, and the conversation was never reopened.

That visit to Saratoga had been the last time her father tried to cooperate with Uncle Thomas. It seemed like everything got worse after that. They'd been bombarded with a hailstorm of new court motions as both sides hardened their positions.

The memory of her father's visit to Oakmonte caused a knot of tension to gather behind Lucy's forehead, made worse by the rumbling of trains in the terminal station. Surely Colin would have been well treated at Oakmonte, for Aunt Margaret craved social status like a hungry cat stalking prey.

"Looking for me?"

She whirled around. Colin stood directly behind her, grinning with reckless bravado. With his open collar and hair in disarray, he looked as dashing as Heathcliff coming in off the moors. But friendlier.

"How was your trip?" she asked, trying to ignore the zing of attraction that made her a little breathless.

"Profitable," he said. "You'll be glad to know that the American newspapers who have chosen to contract with Reuters instead of the AP are all first-class operations. They are not suffering from their lack of AP stories whatsoever."

"Probably because they don't know any better."

"No, no, they do," he rushed to say. "They're immensely grateful that the Crown allows them to partake of superior British reporting, for the AP journalists have little sense of style, nor can they spell. I was embarrassed for you."

A little girl nudged her way in between them, holding up a tray of cigarettes for sale. Colin declined the cigarettes but pushed a few coins into the girl's grubby palm.

A teenage boy pounced the moment the girl left. "Shoeshine, mister?"

"No, thank you," Colin said but still reached into his vest pocket, digging around but coming up empty.

Sensing a payoff, the boy moved closer. "Those shoes are a disgrace, mister. Think how disappointed your mother will be when she sees you looking so shabby. Sit down and let me shine 'em up for you."

"Lucy, have you got a few cents?" Colin asked. "It appears I'm flat broke until I can land that American heiress."

She shot the boy an annoyed glare and pushed a nickel into his hand. "Let's try to find somewhere private," she said. "There's a parcel room at the end of the lobby that shouldn't be crowded."

Rows of metal lockers provided a modicum of privacy in the cramped parcel room, and the few people inside were too busy storing their baggage to pay them any mind. Lucy strode to the end of the aisle, itching to learn what Colin had discovered about Jacob and Oakmonte. Colin wasted no time getting to the point.

"Jacob Drake was nowhere to be found," he said. "There is a locked wing where everyone claims he lives, but I got into it, and the rooms are empty. The only room that might belong to him was abandoned."

"Did he move out?"

"If he did, he left a wardrobe full of clothes behind." Colin went on to relay how Uncle Thomas claimed his father was too old to meet with visitors and Tom Jr.'s healthy dislike of his grandfather.

"I think Jacob may be dead," Colin said. "The family went out of their way to make me believe the old man had the run of the east wing. Can you think of any reason why your uncle would want to disguise his father's death? Are their implications for control of the company?"

"I have no idea." But this news was startling. She wouldn't put anything past Uncle Thomas, but Drake Industries was a privately run company and had no obligation to reveal their business dealings to anyone. Colin didn't have any insight into Jacob's mysterious disappearance, but he had plenty to say about the others.

"Your aunt is a marvel of nastiness. I overheard her scolding the cook over two spoiled oranges. The cook bought an entire crate of oranges but apparently failed to adequately inspect them, and those two oranges incensed Margaret to the point that she demanded the maid take them back to town for a refund. She wanted the maid to *walk* rather than tire the horses. I've heard of thrifty, I've heard of cheap, but this was just a mean spirit."

"Did she act that way to you?"

"Not at all. She couldn't have been nicer to my face, which makes me mistrust her even more. It wouldn't surprise me if she was goading your uncle into pursuing this lawsuit to absolute victory. Remember—the price of the valves did not get jacked up until after your uncle took control of the company. Is the greed driven by Thomas or Margaret?"

Lucy felt confidence gathering inside her. In the past five minutes, she had learned more about the Saratoga Drakes than she and Nick had gleaned in years.

"Tom Jr. has Olympic aspirations," Colin continued. "He felt compelled to take me on an early-morning shooting trip to demonstrate his prowess. I thought he might be an overconfident windbag, but he is in fact an exceptional marksman. He is also upholding the myth that his grandfather is living in the east wing of the house."

She'd been too distracted by the way the dim light played off the finely sculpted planes of his face to hear what he was saying, but his words eventually penetrated her haze of besotted musings.

"You went *shooting*?"

"Tom went shooting. I fumbled with a shotgun and tried not to embarrass myself by blowing off my own foot. Must uphold the reputation of king and country, and all that."

His tone was lighthearted, but tension lurked just beneath the cool tenor of his voice. Subjecting himself to a morning of shooting in order to investigate the Saratoga Drakes was genuinely admirable. She scrambled for the words to thank him, but it was hard to think when battling waves of attraction that suddenly threatened to overwhelm her.

"You're a very impressive man," she finally said.

"Really?" he asked. He wasn't being facetious; the flush of pleasure on his face was genuine, as though he was surprised at her compliment.

He shouldn't be. Colin was embarrassed by his fear of guns, but it was real, and he'd endured it for her. Nothing had ever been more flattering, and she beamed up at him in gratitude.

"You shouldn't look at me like that," he said on a shaking breath.

"Why not?"

"Because it makes me want to do this." He closed the space between them and kissed her.

This shouldn't be happening, but she mindlessly stood up on tiptoe to return the kiss. Oh, this was a bad idea. Terrible. She'd never be able to face him if she encountered him in the elevator at work. . . .

She tore herself away and tried to make light of what had just happened. "You know I'll have to split my vast inheritance with my brother. Right now I've only got about two hundred dollars to my name."

He regarded her with fondness and a hint of something else. Regret? Whatever it was, his voice was tender and funny as he replied. "That won't even buy the paint for a single room at Whitefriars. It looks as if we are doomed." He toyed with her fingers, triggering shivers through her arm. "I suppose I ought to apologize for the kiss," he continued. "I'm not free to pursue you and had no business behaving as if I were. If you would like to haul off for a good face-slapping, or if your brother would like to challenge me to a duel . . ."

She didn't regret it. No one had kissed her since Samuel broke their engagement more than a year earlier, and it felt good to believe, however briefly, that she was still desirable to a man.

"Maybe if we were different people, it would have been fun to see where this led," Lucy said. "As it is, it's time to go our separate ways. I need to thank you for going all the way to Oakmonte for me. Anyone facing down the Saratoga Drakes deserves a medal for heroism."

Colin shrugged. "It looks as if it will actually be a profitable trip. Your uncle had an interesting business proposition I could not resist."

At first she thought he was joking, but as he relayed the specifics of a deal in which he would regularly visit the Saratoga Drakes, a sense of betrayal warred with an urge to protect him. Didn't he realize how underhanded her uncle could be? It seemed so smarmy, showing up at Oakmonte for weekends in the sun in exchange for Colin's promise to smooth the way for the Drake valve in England. It was a stark reminder that Colin Beckwith was a man willing to barter his hand in marriage for a well-capitalized heiress.

"How much?" she asked tightly.

"How much . . . what?"

"How much is my uncle prepared to pay you in exchange for your sham friendship?"

He peered down at her with a raised brow. Centuries of breeding showed in that haughty look. "I'm not sure that's any of your concern."

This conversation was making her blood run cold. Uncle Thomas could be smooth and charming, but he was vile, and Colin seemed to be forgetting that.

"You don't know him like I do," she warned. "No amount of money is worth the price of your soul, and you're putting it in danger by getting into bed with that snake."

It was the wrong thing to say. The warmth in Colin's eyes evaporated, and his voice was coiled in ill-concealed anger.

"This is a business arrangement," he snapped. "It is perfectly legal and the sort of thing that happens all the time. I'm not getting into bed with anyone."

"Except possibly Amelia Wooten."

The accusation slipped out before Lucy considered how nasty it sounded.

Colin's eyes turned hard, and his mouth thinned. "I believe our business here is concluded."

He turned his back on her and headed toward the main terminal. She chased after him to apologize, but his long legs devoured distance while her narrow skirt forced her into mincing steps.

"Colin, wait! I'm sorry!"

He didn't turn around but raised an arm to acknowledge that he heard her. He disappeared into the thickening crowds, leaving her heartsick with guilt and unfulfilled dreams. It wasn't in her character to be so mean, but she simply *hurt*. Longing for Colin while he chased an heiress and a sketchy alliance with Thomas made her bitter; the kind of person who threw darts. It wasn't who she wanted to be.

She sagged against the lockers, the cold of the metal penetrating her blouse. How could she want a man who was selling his soul? The good Lord knew she wasn't perfect. Every day she eavesdropped on a wire that was entirely illegal, but she was fighting to carry out the wishes of her grandfather, a humble man who only wanted to bring the dignity of clean water to everyone, rich and poor. *I can build things to make life better for the people around me. And when I do that, I feel God smiling on me.*

She did, too. Each time she and Nick installed a Drake valve in a tenement, she felt God smiling on her. She didn't fight for personal gain, but Colin did, and he was willing to befriend the man who threatened Mr. Garzelli with deportation over a valve her grandfather would have given away for free.

It still didn't justify her nasty jab at Colin. She had been deliberately mean because she hankered after what could never be.

And for that there was no excuse.

Lucy sat at her booth, translating stories as they came over the wire from Europe. It was always busy at this time of day, which she liked, because it got her mind off Colin Beckwith. A flurry of dots and dashes came across the wire, reporting that the Queen of England paid nine cents for a cafeteria meal when she dined with a group of factory girls in London's East End. Two Italian revolutionaries had been arrested after trying to plant a bomb in an Austrian hotel, and there had been a riot at a bullfight in Madrid.

The rush of European news at the end of the day was always fascinating. Would she ever see Madrid? Or a bullfight? Sometimes the news made her feel a little low. She didn't have much of a life outside her job and the lawsuit. The closest she got was reading about other people.

And lately she was reading about Colin Beckwith escorting Amelia Wooten around town, so apparently his courtship was progressing at full steam. The story of his collapse at the Wooten dinner hadn't resurfaced, so whoever was responsible for it must have failed to notice it was never published.

After transcribing an epically long and dull story on German bankruptcy law, she was in need of a rest.

She bet Roland Montgomery would be at his post and happy for a little diversion on his remote Pacific island. She opened the connection.

"*M B—P 4*," she keyed. "*This is LD seeking bored Midway agent.*"

"*I'm here*" came Roland's reply a few minutes later. "*Losing my mind out here. Only excitement is watching the coconuts grow. Any good news from home?*"

She already knew what Roland would want to know. "*TR plowing ahead for the canal through Panama. Colombia resists. Standoff continues.*"

Before Roland's reply came, the tiny lightbulb nestled behind her potted geranium flashed to life. She immediately disconnected the bulb.

She sent a quick message to Roland. "*Stepping away. Incoming story.*" With a smooth flick of her wrist, she switched wires on her sounder to listen in on a message from the law office already in progress.

```
—hire droppers to bump him off. Best done
in Baltimore while he is traveling. TD will
arrange financing in August. Suggest using
foreign droppers to avoid detection. Over.
```

The line went dead, and Lucy furrowed her brow. What on earth did this message mean? She stared at the words she'd scribbled on the pad of paper, not certain this could possibly re-late to her case. It was normal for telegraphers to shorten words, use acronyms and slang, but she didn't know what to make of this snippet of text. It sounded . . . well, it sounded criminal.

She opened the connection to Midway. "*Roland, what is a dropper?*"

"*Eyedropper?*" he keyed back.

"*No. Is it a criminal term?*" Not that Roland was a criminal, but as a navy man, he would be familiar with blunt lingo.

"*Could mean a hired killer,*" Roland replied.

She swallowed hard. Looking at the message she'd jotted down, she swapped Roland's term into the first line. *Hire a killer to bump him off.*

Bump who off? Could she actually have just heard a plot to murder someone? She'd suspected her uncle of many things over the years, but even her rich imagination never suspected he could sink to murder. But the message clearly stated that TD wanted someone in Baltimore bumped off once financing could be arranged.

She clasped the seat of her chair and forced her breathing to slow down. It was far more likely she'd overheard meaningless talk about filing some legal briefs. Maybe lawyers had their own slang for legal terms.

Except she'd been eavesdropping on this law office for two years and never heard such strange language before.

Her palms began to tingle and itch, as they always did when she was flooded with uncertainty. If she told anyone about this, she'd have to explain the wire. She had no idea what she'd just heard, but it seemed ominous.

It was Wednesday, and she and Nick always met at the Western Union cafeteria for lunch on Wednesdays, as it was better than the mushy stew served at the hog house. She counted the minutes until noon when she could turn to him for help. She went down to the cafeteria a few minutes early to buy him a cheese sandwich, as they couldn't talk in the crowded lunchroom.

"What's going on?" Nick asked when he arrived, and she shoved the sandwich in his hands, then turned him toward the front door.

"I need your advice. We have to step outside for a walk."

His brows lowered in concern, but he didn't argue as she led him down the street until they found an unoccupied bench. Lucy passed Nick the message she'd recorded only an hour earlier. He read it three times, rubbing his jaw and shifting on the bench. After a few moments, he passed the note back.

"Well?" she whispered. "Do you agree it sounds like someone in Moreno's office might actually be planning a murder?"

"Maybe. I don't know." He unwrapped the sandwich and took a bite, staring gloomily ahead.

"What should we do about it?"

Nick looked taken aback. "What can we do? We don't know who, when, or where. All we know is that it might happen in Baltimore, so that leaves out you and me as the intended victims. It's not our problem."

Her jaw dropped open. "We're not talking about a *problem*, we're talking about *murder*."

A man strolling by slowed to stare at her, his brows rising so high they disappeared under his bowler hat. Lucy piped down, and the man continued past, but Nick's voice was low and annoyed.

"We *don't* know that it's murder. You heard a snippet of conversation, and everyone knows telegraphers are notorious for making up their own shorthand for common words. They could be talking about buying a racehorse for all you know."

Lucy stared at the note. It mentioned the initials TD, and she'd been eavesdropping long enough to know that her uncle was the only Moreno client with those initials.

"I don't think I could live with myself if someone gets killed and I didn't do anything to stop it."

Nick vaulted off the bench and started pacing on the sidewalk, his hands fisted. "What are we supposed to do? Go to the police? Confess that we've got an illegal wire? If anyone finds out about that wire, we're both headed for jail."

She wasn't used to hearing disdain in Nick's voice, and it hurt. "Nick . . . I've felt uneasy about that wire since the day we installed it. I told myself it was okay because Uncle Thomas is so awful and that if we win, a lot of people will have better lives. So I ignored my conscience, shut it down, and turned it off. Now I'm sitting here wondering if I can avert my eyes while someone gets killed."

"Stop saying that! You have no idea what that note means, and neither do I."

She flinched at the anger in his voice. He was right. What could the police possibly do with this incomplete bit of information? Revealing it could land them both in jail and everything they'd been fighting for in ashes.

Nick plopped down on the bench beside her, slumping forward and staring at the concrete beneath his feet. "I'm getting tired," he admitted. "I'm thirty-one years old and have nothing to show for it."

"Don't say that—"

"I used to have dreams, Lucy. I used to imagine that I would be remembered for doing something really great someday. I wanted to conquer mountains and invent things and settle down with a nice girl. Have some kids. Now I worry about how to keep my head above water until the next court date. I'm tired. I don't know how much longer I can keep going."

"Stop talking like that. We'll keep going as long as necessary because we are *right*."

He held out his hand. "Give me that piece of paper." It was an order, not a request.

"Why?"

"Because I'm going to destroy it and protect us both."

She bolted to her feet and took a step back. He followed. "What are you going to do, attack me for it?"

"Don't do it, Lucy. Don't tell anyone about that message." Nick's breath was ragged, his eyes desperate.

She swallowed hard. All her life, she and Nick had been a team. He taught her how to ride a bicycle and how to fix a leaky faucet. She leaned on him when her fiancé got spooked by Uncle Thomas and broke their engagement. When their father died and Nick had been inconsolable, she got him out of bed, put a wrench in his hand, and made sure he got to the hog house. Nick was the only person in the world she trusted to guard her back or come through for her in a storm.

But now that bond was fractured, all because of a note linked to Uncle Thomas. Her breathing came fast and hard. She didn't know what to do. Nick was probably right—the message she'd overheard probably meant nothing. All she knew for certain was that it was driving a wedge between her and Nick, and if she took the note to the police, they would learn about the wire. She couldn't ask Colin about it either, for the searing anger of their last meeting in the train station was a pretty good indication that she'd burned that bridge for good.

All that was left for her to do was return to work and see if she could catch another message from her uncle's law firm. If she could learn more, she'd know what to do.

She slipped the note into her skirt pocket, and Nick's shoulders sagged. He looked like he had aged ten years in the space of a few seconds. He picked up his uneaten sandwich and tossed it in the trash.

"You need to decide where your loyalties lie," he said in a

voice sapped of energy. "I'm not going to sacrifice the rest of my life to the valve or whatever is going on at that law firm. We can't save the world. I'm done, Luce. Don't ask me to keep wrestling with whirlwinds." He took a few steps toward the hog house before turning back to her. "And don't you dare reveal that note to anyone."

He left her standing in the middle of the sidewalk, alone and abandoned, still not knowing what to do.

As soon as she returned to her desk, she reconnected the tiny lightbulb to alert her when a message was sent on the illegal wire. Nick's coldness left her feeling hollow, but she couldn't shake the gnawing fear that something very bad was being plotted at the Moreno Law Office. If there were any follow-up messages to that cryptic note, she needed to hear them. In the meantime, she had to get ahold of herself, open her sounder, and do her job.

She translated a story about the declining cod liver oil harvest in Norway, and another about labor protests from Pittsburgh. It was a full hour before the tiny lightbulb flashed. She carefully wrote down every letter of the incoming message.

```
TD wants it to happen in August before
ICC meets. Cities are Baltimore Akron
Charlottesville Rochester Oyster Bay. TD
suggests dropping entire ICC. Only way to
save NCC. Bomb? Need funds. NCC dying.
```

Lucy stared at the message, her heart rate kicking up. It was too heavily laden with abbreviations to make sense, but was there any way to put a positive spin on a bomb?

She stood. The AP had a library on the floor below for precisely this sort of thing. Reporters in the field often lacked access to research materials and were prone to misspelling names or getting dates wrong, so the library was an invaluable tool for checking facts. She clocked out and made her way to the spacious library.

Where to begin? The reference shelves contained dictionaries for dozens of languages and directories for every major city in Europe and America. She checked the telephone directories from all the noted cities, looking for any man with the initials NCC, but found nothing. She grabbed the directory for Washington, DC, even though it was not on the list of cities mentioned and began searching. There were two men whose initials were NC, but what did that prove? She thumbed to the listing of government departments and agencies and turned to the N's.

Nicaragua Canal Commission.

Lucy sat back in her chair. She'd never heard of the Nicaragua Canal Commission, but it was the only thing so far whose initials perfectly matched. On a whim, she flipped back a few pages to see if there was anything that might correspond to the other set of initials, ICC. She quickly spotted one: the Isthmian Canal Commission.

Well, that was interesting. Lucy was well acquainted with the Isthmian Canal Commission, for it was the team of government experts the president had created to get the Panama Canal under way. The project had been stalled for decades, and Roosevelt had bluntly declared that he wanted a special commission of men to cut through the red tape and "make the dirt fly."

Could this telegram relate to the Panama Canal? It said "NCC dying." A little digging through the reference books confirmed the statement. In 1899, a group of investors proposed digging the canal through Nicaragua. The route would be longer than going through Panama, but the Nicaraguan option had flatter ground and would be an easier path to dig.

The message was making more sense. The NCC *was* dying, as Roosevelt pushed ever more aggressively for a canal through Panama instead of Nicaragua. She glanced back at the list of cities, and her heart froze. Oyster Bay was where the president lived when he wasn't in Washington. Just that morning she had translated a story about President Roosevelt's plan to deliver a speech at the University of Virginia in Charlottesville, and everyone knew he regularly visited Baltimore on business.

This message was tracking the movements of President Roosevelt and the ICC commission. It mentioned assassins and bombs.

Lucy didn't even bother returning to her desk but ran straight to the police department.

It took Lucy twenty minutes to get to the nearest police precinct. She tried to cut the line of people waiting to file reports by claiming her matter was urgent, but since she refused to explain to the harried clerk the nature of the problem, she was directed to wait her turn on a hard bench. Was she jumping to conclusions? She hoped so, as she took a seat between a dozing prostitute and a man wanting to file a reprimand against his landlord for serving cold porridge when he'd paid for hot.

What kind of porridge did they serve in prison? She might soon learn, for telling the police about this telegram could lead to the discovery of her illegal wire. Would President Roosevelt intervene if he learned she'd been sent to prison while trying to protect him? She wouldn't have voted for Roosevelt even if women had the privilege, but she wasn't going to stand aside and let someone plot against the President of the United States.

At last she was shown into an office, where a middle-aged sergeant listened to her outline the gist of the intercepted message. Sergeant Palmer studied her with a blank expression as he twirled the tip of his handlebar mustache.

"So you actually think someone is after President Roosevelt?"

he asked as she finished her statement. He spoke carefully, but it sounded as if he was trying not to laugh.

"Maybe. I couldn't live with myself if I didn't turn that note over."

The sergeant straightened. "And how is it you came by it? I'm still not quite clear on that."

This was it. If he probed, she would take sole responsibility for the wire. There was no need for Nick to be brought into this at all. She didn't want to go to jail. She *really* didn't want to go to jail, but she didn't want the president to get assassinated either. She cleared her throat and parsed her words carefully.

"It's not unusual for telegraph operators to listen in on other wires. I overheard a conversation sent from the Moreno Law Office that was directed to a village near Saratoga. They didn't know I could hear them."

The sergeant carefully noted her response on the bottom of the page before opening a file and slipping it inside. "All right, Miss Drake. The report will be handled in priority order, and you'll be notified of the outcome in due time."

That was it? This man's desk held a stack of files that looked like they'd been gathering dust since the turn of the century.

"You *will* turn it over to the proper authorities, right?"

"Yes, ma'am. Right alongside the other six threats on the president's life we received this month, the accusation that the Vanderbilts are plotting to conquer Canada, and a report that the man in the moon was spying on a widow in Columbus Park."

Only an idiot would miss the sarcasm in his voice, but she needed to underscore the urgency of the situation. "You did notice that the message referenced August, right? That means the issue must be addressed within the next two months."

The sergeant gave her a patient smile. "Thank you, Miss Drake. I was exposed to basic counting skills and the order of calendar months in grade school, so I am confident I can handle this."

She knew a dismissal when she heard one. She stood and spoke calmly.

"The next man waiting to see you is sadly disappointed with the quality of porridge served at his boardinghouse. It will be an easier task than defending the president, but I'm sure you know best how to prioritize your responsibilities."

She left before she lost her temper any further.

olin closed the file on the third performance review he'd written, a mind-numbing task he loathed, but a necessary one if he wanted to maintain his status within Reuters. He'd just reached for the next review on the stack when his butler knocked and entered.

"A woman from the AP, Miss Drake, is here to see you. Shall I send her in?"

Colin clenched his fists. He didn't want to see Lucy again. Her accusations in the train station had cut too close to home, and besides, there was no place in his future for a woman like her.

"Tell her our association is at an end," he said in an emotionless voice, but he couldn't help regretting it a little as Denby nodded and closed the door. Continuing any sort of relationship with Lucy would only be painful to them both. It had been fun while it lasted. A reluctant smile tugged at the corner of his mouth. He wished he didn't miss her so much.

A minute later Denby was back, followed by Lucy herself. She had a lot of gall, shoving her way into his office, and his nascent sentimental feelings instantly evaporated.

"I must see you!" she said as she nudged past Denby. "Please

. . . it will only take a few minutes of your time, and I desperately need your help."

He stood and tilted his chin to look down at her. "But your visit will interfere with my nonstop attempts to seduce American heiresses," he said in a frost-encrusted tone.

"Oh, please! I take it back."

"Sadly, that sort of remark isn't something that can be called back." The scar from her accusation still smarted and probably always would. Nothing hurt so much as the truth.

"Shall I escort the . . . lady out?" Denby asked, uncertainty heavy in his voice. Evicting unwelcome visitors was never something Denby had been called on to do at Whitefriars.

And Lucy looked ready to wage a battle. Her hands clenched a piece of paper, and Colin's natural curiosity got the better of him.

"That won't be necessary," he conceded, annoyed by the look of relief on his old butler's face. "Yes, Lucy, what is it?" he asked the moment Denby left. Courtesy dictated that he offer her a seat, and he gestured to a chair. She sat, but he remained standing. This meeting was not going to take long. He cast a pointed look at her and waited.

"Do you remember the wire I have installed at my desk?"

"Of course."

"I intercepted a couple of disturbing messages today, and the police aren't taking me seriously. I hope that I'm simply blowing this out of proportion. The messages contain codes I'm not sure of, but perhaps you're familiar with them." She handed him two slips of paper.

He studied both notes carefully, for the abbreviations made them a challenge to understand. He'd read enough detective novels to know that *dropper* was a slang term for an assassin. When Lucy told him that ICC and NCC were the two commissions investigating competing canals through Central America, his concern deepened.

"When did you receive this message?"

"This morning. The police sergeant I spoke with stuck my report in a file and dismissed me."

Colin sat down and rubbed his hands together, thinking how best to handle this. It would be disastrous for a Reuters executive to be illegally tapped into an American law firm's private wire, but Lucy was right to be concerned. What a frustrating, inconvenient, and fascinating mess. A spark of his old reporter's instincts flared to life, and he sat a little straighter. The note indicated that TD was funding this initiative, which certainly meant Thomas Drake.

"Did your uncle invest in NCC stock?" he asked.

"I have no idea."

He smiled grimly. Anytime a project of this magnitude was in the planning stages, investors gambled on the outcome. "Plenty of people invested in Nicaragua when it looked like that was where the canal would be built. Now that Roosevelt is backing a Panama route, those investors are liable to lose a fortune."

"That might explain why someone would want to eliminate all the members of the ICC," she said. The commission had just endorsed the president's recommendation for the Panama route.

"You told this to the police, and they didn't take you seriously?" he asked.

"Sergeant Palmer said he would look into it, but he didn't seem alarmed."

Perhaps there were ways Colin could gather information without police help. "What is the nearest telegraph station to your uncle's house in Saratoga?" he asked.

"There's a Western Union station at the Saratoga train depot and another at the local pharmacy. I think the messages are coming out of the pharmacy, because whoever is manning that station is an amateur. His transmissions are very slow. He often asks the telegrapher at the law office to repeat words. No one that slow would ever get hired by a train station."

Colin leaned forward, cracking his knuckles in frustration. He didn't have time for distractions like this. He had performance appraisals to write, but he desperately wanted to know more about that message. He *had* to know. Did Stanley delay his quest to find Dr. Livingston until he completed a stack of performance appraisals? Did the reporters who covered the explosion of the Krakatoa volcano wait until the dust had cleared? Or did they roll up their sleeves and pounce on the story, racing to the scene ahead of everyone else to provide Reuters with the scoop that made the agency world famous?

The annual performance appraisals could wait.

"I'm going back to Oakmonte," he said with resolve.

"You are?" Lucy asked in amazement.

His smile was tense. "As you recently noted, I have agreed to cozy up with a snake. I expect your uncle and his wife will be glad to host me."

Lucy looked suitably embarrassed, giving him a guilty rush of satisfaction. "Colin, I'm sorry——"

He cut her off. "If this message is what we suspect, I'm not going to let a personal tiff endanger the lives of the people serving on the ICC and perhaps the president himself. Of course I'm going to Oakmonte. Since the message indicates the event will happen in August, I've got plenty of time to see if I can uncover anything there that might spur the police into taking these notes seriously. Come to my office at seven o'clock this evening so we can start planning how this will work."

It was impossible to concentrate after Lucy left. Canceling his dinner plans, he impulsively paid a visit to Sergeant Palmer at the police department. He even used his title to cut straight to the sergeant's office and hopefully buy a little more credibility.

It was all for nothing. The sergeant's response was precisely as Lucy had reported.

"Sir Beckwith, it all sounds like idle gossip whipped up by a woman prone to over-emotionalism," the sergeant said. "You can't imagine the bizarre accusations I hear on a daily basis from people accusing the government of poisoning their water to suspecting—"

"But Miss Drake is a level-headed young lady," Colin interrupted. "She is not prone to exaggeration or emotionalism."

"And her complaint will be addressed in due course."

The encounter confirmed every one of Lucy's suspicions that the police were not taking her charge seriously. If a plot against the Panama Canal was brewing at Oakmonte, it was up to Colin and Lucy to smoke it out.

⇌❦⇋

Lucy was grateful to the marrow of her bones that Colin was willing to help her, even if every square inch of his starchy pride indicated he hadn't forgiven her for the insult at the train station. She stopped at the apothecary shop to buy a box of Hershey's chocolate as a peace offering before their meeting. No one could turn down chocolate, could they?

Colin could. When she arrived at his office at the appointed time, he peered at the box as though it pained him. "Hershey's?" he said skeptically. "You really haven't had chocolate until you've had Cadbury chocolate."

"If I ran out and bought a box of Cadbury, would you accept it?" she asked, even though it ran contrary to her thrifty spirit to spend twice as much on imported British chocolate.

"Probably not. I would urge you to share it with your colleagues downstairs so they could be introduced to quality chocolate. But come, I need to introduce you to my birds."

Two homing pigeons sat on the perch beside his desk. Colin

137

stood and coaxed one onto his finger. "This is Beatrice, and the other is Bianca. I've raised them since they were hatchlings, and they will allow us to communicate while I'm at Oakmonte. Every good spy needs a means of transmitting information, but we can't trust any telegraph operator near Oakmonte."

The chocolates were forgotten as Colin spent the next hour explaining how homing pigeons were trained to remember a route. He would have to ride to Saratoga on horseback in order to release Beatrice and Bianca to fly back home and imprint the landmarks in their memory. The birds would instinctively return to their loft in his Reuters office, where Mr. Denby would bring the messages to Lucy. She would then feed them, allow them a rest, and send them back to Colin. Once he arrived in Oakmonte, he would communicate with her solely through the pigeons.

He opened a jar of strange-smelling mash and showed it to her. "Beatrice and Bianca go absolutely mad for dried peas rolled in suet, so this is what I keep in my office. I'll bring a jar of it to Oakmonte as well."

"Couldn't you give it to me so they'll come straight to the AP office and save your butler the trouble of fetching me?"

A hint of amusement crinkled his eyes. "It doesn't quite work that way. And how can I be sure your ravenous coworkers won't devour the seed? They seem to have appallingly low standards when it comes to food."

She lifted a brow. "And you think a tin of congealed fat is going to tempt them?"

He wrinkled his nose and lowered his voice. "Well, Americans, you know."

"You're the one who seems to think it's a delicacy, London."

His laughter was reluctant, but warm and exhilarating to hear. She missed the camaraderie they once had.

"Colin . . . about what I said in the train station, I need to apologize."

As though an invisible wire had pulled every nerve ending in his body tight, he stiffened, and the temperature in the office dropped a few degrees. "What if I am not ready to accept an apology?"

"Then I would ask when you might be ready to do so." She twisted her hands in her lap. Who he married wasn't any of her business, but she deeply regretted the remark and had no right to pass judgment on him. "It was an ugly comment, and I wish I could take it back. Since I can't, only an apology will do."

A little of the frostiness melted, but his voice was sad. "Perhaps it would be best if we delayed it indefinitely. I find that I . . ." He swallowed hard. "I find it difficult to maintain proper decorum around you."

Her heart surged, but she tamped it back. "Then why are you helping me?"

He leaned forward to coax one of the pigeons onto his finger again and mindlessly stroked its back. His voice sounded as if it came from far away. "Sometime in the seventeenth century, one of my ancestors won a battle off the coast of Malta and was awarded a baronetcy by a grateful king. All my life I have been the beneficiary of that title, but I did nothing to deserve it. I'm no warrior, and neither was my father or grandfather. I can't even hear the sound of a gun without suffering a case of the vapors, and my only real friends in America are two overfed birds. So I need to prove myself. Sometimes I feel like my seventeenth-century forefather is looking over my shoulder, judging to see if I'm worthy of the title he earned. It's part of the reason I became a war reporter in the first place. Every instinct tells me that the messages you overheard are plotting something dangerous, and I can't stand down. I wouldn't be worthy of my heritage if I could overlook something like that."

The more time she spent with him, the more impressive Colin became. What an irony that she looked down on his pompous title from the moment he stepped into the building, and yet he had similar misgivings about it.

She met him at the public stables the next morning as he prepared to leave. The cage containing Beatrice and Bianca was secured to the back of his saddle. He would release them to fly back home every fifty miles. The time the birds needed to make the journey and the necessary rest afterward meant it would take Colin three days to reach Oakmonte, but he was doing so without complaint.

"I think your seventeenth-century forefather would approve," she said softly. "He fought with a broadsword, but you're fighting with your mind."

His expression gentled as he smiled down at her. "Thank you for that."

Why was she so apprehensive about this? It wasn't as if he were riding off into actual danger. No one at Oakmonte would suspect him of being a spy, but she still couldn't quell her sense of misgiving. As long as Uncle Thomas was in the picture, it was impossible to know what sort of quagmire Colin might be walking into.

"Will you please accept my apology before you leave?" she asked.

"Apology accepted, Yankee," he said without a hint of lingering bitterness. "You've helped awaken all my old reporter's instincts, and it will be good to get back out in the field again." He paused, as though struggling to find the right words. When he finally spoke, his tone was businesslike. "When I return, I'll report everything I've learned to Sergeant Palmer, and then you and I need to go our separate ways. I'm afraid I like you too much to keep playing with fire."

Her heart turned over, liking him even more for his honesty. "I understand," she said softly.

He didn't say anything, just scooped her into an embrace so tight it was hard to draw a breath. He released her, mounted the horse, and then he was gone.

Chapter
TWELVE

Colin arrived in Saratoga on the morning of his third day of travel. Before visiting Oakmonte, he had one very important stop to make.

Lucy suspected that the telegrams from the Saratoga Drakes were being sent from the Whittaker Pharmacy on the outskirts of town. Colin wanted to meet the telegraph operator to see if he might be part of the plot or an unwitting stooge. He would make an innocuous request to send a telegram to his secretary at Reuters to announce that he'd arrived. He dared not send a telegram to Lucy. Saratoga was a small town, and the last thing he wanted was for the Saratoga Drakes to learn of his friendship with Lucy. The doors at Oakmonte would slam shut the moment they suspected such an affiliation.

The bow window of the pharmacy was filled with soaps, glass jars of tea infusions, and colorful bottles of medicinal remedies. Most importantly, a small sign at the top advertised Western Union service. This was the place.

A bell jangled as Colin entered the shop, and he was engulfed in the scent of camphor and pipe tobacco. The store was empty except for a balding man behind the counter, reading a newspaper. He straightened and looked up. "Can I help you, sir?"

"Do you mind if I bring my birds inside?" Colin asked. "It's a hot day, and I don't like to leave them in the sun."

If the pharmacist was surprised, he masked it quickly. "It's not a problem if they stay in the cage," he said. "I'm Jack Whittaker. Can I help you?"

"I'd like to send a telegram, please."

The pharmacist frowned. "Floyd is the one who sends messages, and he's on a delivery right now. He should be back within a half hour. Can you wait?"

"Is he the only one who can send a message?"

"He's the only telegrapher on this end of town," Mr. Whittaker said. "There's another Western Union station at the train depot three miles from here, but I expect Floyd will be back before you could get there."

"I'll wait." Colin casually strolled to the counter. Colorful sticks of peppermints and licorice filled glass jars. To his delight, he saw a stack of Cadbury chocolates in their distinctive royal purple boxes. He impulsively bought a box for Lucy, since he doubted she had a proper understanding of how quality chocolate should taste.

"Have you lived in Saratoga long?" he asked Mr. Whittaker as he paid for the chocolate.

"Most of my life," the pharmacist said. "I lived in Albany for a few years, but when the owner of this pharmacy retired, I was eager to take it over. I've owned it for twenty-two years now."

Excellent. That meant the pharmacist would be a good source of information. Colin let his gaze wander out the front window. "It seems a charming town. I've come for a short visit to the Drakes up at Oakmonte. You know the family?"

There was a slight downturn of the pharmacist's mouth

before he forced a polite expression onto his face. "Goodness, yes. Everyone in town knows the Drakes. Fine people."

Sometimes words did not match tone, and Colin had just caught sight of it with the pharmacist. The flash of annoyance had been brief, but it was there. Pharmacists knew plenty about people, such as what ailments they suffered and who paid their bills promptly. If there was a man of Jacob Drake's age living at Oakmonte, Mr. Whittaker would know. As Colin tried to think of a delicate way of coaxing out the information, Mr. Whittaker picked up the conversation.

"You don't sound like you're from around here."

"My Brooklyn accent always gives me away," Colin joked, and the pharmacist laughed. Colin had spoken a little about growing up in the Yorkshire countryside and school in London when a bell dinged and a young boy came loping into the shop.

"Ah! Here's Floyd. He'll be happy to send your message for you."

This was Floyd? The boy looked no more than sixteen years old. He had a swath of sandy blond hair hanging over his eyes and a gap-toothed smile.

"You want to send a telegram, mister?" Floyd asked eagerly.

"Please." Colin handed Floyd a card with a brief message to his secretary. The boy vaulted around the counter and grabbed a station directory.

"Where to?" Floyd asked. The eagerness in his voice was endearing. Colin remembered what it was like to live in a rural village and crave a link to the wider world, even if only through a telegraph sounder.

"It's going to 195 Broadway." He resisted the impulse to tell the boy the official code, for he needed to hide his familiarity with telegraphing systems. Someone in this pharmacy might be part of the plot.

It took Floyd a while to locate the right code in the directory.

Colin affected a casual pose as he leaned against the counter and studied the modest telegraph station. The table had a small Morse sounder and a receiving wire. A training manual with practice exercises lay open beside the sounder, but Floyd closed it.

"I'm still learning," he said with a nervous smile. "I figure by this time next year, I'll be ready to apply for a railroad job."

Colin doubted it. It took years of practice before an operator could master the speed necessary for a railroad telegraph station. Floyd pecked out the code in painfully slow taps, but his eyes were fierce with concentration as he worked through Colin's message. After the message was sent and the connection closed, Floyd counted the words and calculated the cost, using a chart on the board above his desk.

"Twenty cents, please."

Colin slid the coins across the counter. "What are the other lists for?" he asked as he nodded to the pages tacked above the table.

"Oh, those are the codes for stations people in town use a lot. You'd be amazed how many thousands of telegraph stations there are in the country. It takes a while to look them up and figure out the right path to send the message, and some people can be so impatient, you know?"

Colin leaned over the counter as far as courtesy permitted, but he was too far away to decipher any of the frequent exchanges on Floyd's list. He pointed to the call box. "What's that metal disk?"

Floyd was eager to explain how the call box was connected to the local bank, and how it buzzed when bankers wanted him to come fetch a message to send.

"Can I come around and see?"

Floyd looked to Mr. Whittaker, who nodded permission. Colin moved behind the counter and let Floyd explain the system.

It gave him a close-up view of Floyd's list of frequently used exchanges.

The Moreno Law Office was at the top of the list. He was in the right place.

"So you are the only operator who mans this station?" Colin pressed. "What happens if a message comes in and you aren't here?"

"I live above the grocery right next door," Floyd said. "If I'm not here when the machine starts buzzing, Mr. Whittaker bangs on my door, and I come down and open the connection. The original operator is usually still on the line and will resend. I get to split the revenue with Mr. Whittaker, so I don't mind coming down anytime. I love sending messages. The more practice I get, the sooner I can move to Albany and get a real job with the railroad. And maybe someday even with one of the press associations. That would be my dream."

He was a good kid. It was impossible to imagine Floyd was anything more than an unwitting accomplice in the scheme.

"And after you receive a message, how does it get sent to the recipient?"

"I personally deliver. Most people give me a nice tip, especially if I have to go a distance or the weather is bad."

A perfect opening. "I'm heading out to Oakmonte this morning. Are there any deliveries I can take for you on my way out? Anything for old Mr. Drake?"

He addressed the question to the pharmacist. If Jacob Drake was still living at Oakmonte, the pharmacist would probably know.

"No, the Drakes rarely ask for delivery, for it involves a fee, and Mrs. Drake is very thrifty," the pharmacist said. "She always sends a serving girl when they have needs. It's best not to disrupt the system we have in place."

"Unless it's a telegram," Floyd interjected. "The Drakes own a fancy business and tip me extra to bring their telegrams right away. Nothing has come in for them today, though."

Colin nodded his thanks, picked up his birdcage and box of chocolate, and departed. He'd gleaned no insight into old Jacob Drake's whereabouts, but he'd confirmed other important details. Mrs. Drake was a skinflint, the family was disliked, and Floyd was an unwitting dupe in the scheme.

It had been a long three days getting to Oakmonte. Colin was tired, grubby, and looking forward to a long soak in one of Oakmonte's modern washrooms.

The greeting at the front door was a little awkward.

"You've brought your own meals?" Thomas said with a curious glance at the birdcage. It took Colin a moment to understand his meaning.

"Beatrice and Bianca are pets, not food," he said, trying not to shudder. He'd been raising pigeons since boyhood, and he would no more eat a pigeon than a pet dog. "I noticed the balcony outside the second story of the house on my last trip. Might I store my birds there whilst visiting?"

Thomas raised a quizzical brow. "I'll have to consult with my wife. I'm afraid Margaret can be particular about such things." Apparently Mrs. Drake had little tolerance for animals unless they were dead, stuffed, and dressed in outfits as part of a tableau.

A moment later, the lady of the house swept into the foyer in a rush of rustling Chantilly lace, chiffon, and lavender perfume. "Sir Beckwith, welcome!" She extended both hands toward him as though they were old friends and offered her cheek for a kiss. He obliged.

"You look like the first rose of spring," he said, and she beamed.

"Sir Beckwith has brought his pet birds along," Thomas said, and Mrs. Drake recoiled as she noticed the caged pigeons at his feet. It was only for a moment.

"How lovely," she said with an admirable recovery.

"They are homing pigeons," he said. "I'm old-fashioned and still like to practice the art. Might they stay on the balcony upstairs? They are clean birds, and I can assure you they will make no mess."

"Certainly! We'd be delighted to have them!" she said in a bright tone that didn't quite match her eyes.

They loitered in the foyer, making polite chitchat for a few moments, but all Colin really wanted was to take Beatrice and Bianca upstairs and release them back to Manhattan. They still needed to imprint the final twenty miles of the journey in their memory, and the longer he kept them in this enclosed foyer, the more likely they were to become disoriented.

"Can we offer you something to drink?" Thomas asked as he gestured to a formal tea service in the front parlor.

Margaret looked at a footman standing at the far end of the foyer. "Philip, please tell Cecelia to bring in the strawberry tarts and watercress sandwiches. And the tea."

"Actually, I was hoping for a chance to freshen up," Colin said. Anything to get the pigeons on their way back to Manhattan as soon as possible.

"But of course!" Margaret said in a rush. "Please! Take all the time you need."

It didn't take long at all. He was shown to the same bedroom he'd had on the previous visit, and he immediately stepped onto the balcony to set the cage on the railing. He opened the door and coaxed both pigeons out, giving them each a friendly rub and low murmurs of approval. They had a two-hundred-mile flight ahead of them but should be in Manhattan well before sundown. His message to Lucy was brief.

I have arrived at Oakmonte. Please water and feed the birds. Being female, they will also require a bit of praise and coddling.

He attached the canister to Bianca's leg, since Beatrice had carried the last message. Lucy had already been instructed to send only one bird back after he arrived in Oakmonte. Going forward, they would each keep a bird so they could initiate a message at will.

He released the birds and watched them fly confidently south. Soon they would reach the Hudson, and from there it was an easy journey to follow the river back to Manhattan.

Colin was about to walk back into the house when his gaze tracked down the balcony. It encompassed the length of the house, covering both the east and west wings. It would be an excellent way to get another glimpse inside those rooms in the closed-off wing.

That would have to be postponed until later. He did not want to keep his hosts waiting any longer.

It was during tea that Colin learned Mrs. Drake had planned a much more formal affair than he had been prepared for.

"A full Saturday to Monday, complete with formal dinners," Margaret said brightly.

He silently groaned. In England, a *Saturday to Monday* meant three days of cards, shooting, country walks, and fine dining in a house swarming with guests. All he wanted was a chance to poke around Oakmonte in hope of verifying his suspicions about the NCC and a possible assassination plot. That would be harder to do in a house full of people. He'd also like a shot at figuring out what had happened to the missing patriarch of the family, but he'd yet to learn anything more about Jacob Drake.

The Saturday to Monday looked like it was actually a Thursday to Monday, for within an hour, two house guests had joined them for tea. Dr. Friedrich Schroeder and his wife were visiting from Manhattan. They were an elderly couple, with the sort of gentle good cheer that made Colin immediately like them both. Two more places were set at the tea table, where Dr. Schroeder put a healthy dent in Mrs. Drake's supply of watercress sandwiches.

"Somehow everything always tastes better when it comes out of Oakmonte's kitchens," the doctor said as he reached for another sandwich.

Colin had to agree. The food here was excellent, but he believed there was something to be said for the power of association. He'd always thought food coming from the Whitefriars kitchen was ambrosia. He'd dined in the finest establishments in London, Berlin, and now New York, but anything served at Whitefriars simply tasted better to him. It was home, perhaps.

"Where is that handsome son of yours?" the doctor's wife asked Mrs. Drake.

There was a slight stiffening around Margaret's mouth, and Thomas scowled.

"Off to some political meeting," Thomas said. "Heaven only knows when he'll be back."

"That's all right, isn't it?" Dr. Schroeder asked. "I thought you wanted Tom to expand his horizons beyond shooting."

"I do, but it's rude to Sir Beckwith," Thomas said. "Colin has come all the way from the city for a visit. If Tom Jr. is serious about a political career, he needs to get accustomed to properly welcoming guests."

Margaret laid a soothing hand on her husband's fist. "I'm sure Tom will be here soon. Then we can all have a nice visit, hmm?"

Colin turned his attention to Dr. Schroeder, eager to smooth the ruffled feathers. "I imagine you have seen a world of change in the time you have been practicing medicine."

"Indeed," Dr. Schroeder agreed. "Of course, my specialty is psychology, the study of the human mind. Although science has made great strides in the treatment of the physical body, the human mind remains a mystery to us."

Colin leaned forward. "What do you mean?"

"The human mind is the most powerful organ in our body. It's what sets us apart from the animals. We can train it to learn languages, write a symphony, and build cathedrals. It can grasp theoretical concepts like justice, or algebra, or imagine the future. But for all its marvels, we have yet to understand how to control it. What makes us fall in love? Or *out* of love, for that matter? We don't know why some people are afraid of heights while others are exhilarated by them. When the mind overtakes our body, it can cause our heart rate to soar and the body to perspire. These are involuntary reactions triggered by nothing more than thoughts. We are getting better at figuring out how to manipulate the brain but still have plenty to learn."

Colin was entranced. None of his attempts to control his mortifying attacks of panic had worked, but he had no idea that doctors were beginning to specialize in this phenomenon.

"How does one do this?" he asked. "Train the mind? Tell me more."

Dr. Schroeder warmed to the topic, his eyes coming alive and his voice full of energy. "It can be done," he said. "I am convinced we have the power to control our emotions. All it takes is practice—"

A door slammed in the distance, cutting off Dr. Schroeder, and a moment later Tom Jr. swaggered into the room. Colin gritted his teeth in frustration. Everyone rose to greet Tom Jr. and another visitor, but all Colin wanted was to pull Dr. Schroeder away to continue the fascinating discussion on the science of controlling the brain.

"Nice of you to join us," the elder Drake said tersely, but Tom shrugged off his father's disapproval and reached across the tea table for a chocolate éclair.

"I had a meeting," he said casually. "Politics."

"You remember Sir Beckwith," Margaret said graciously. Colin had asked her repeatedly to call him by his given name, but apparently she enjoyed using the title.

Tom Jr. wiped his hand on a napkin and extended it gamely. "You bet. Want to go shooting tomorrow morning? We can talk then. Felix can join us."

Felix was the middle-aged man who had arrived with Tom. With a dusting of silver in his dark hair and a thick set of muttonchop whiskers, he seemed an old-fashioned companion for such a firebrand.

"Tom, please join us," Margaret said. "Felix as well. Sir Beckwith has been so gracious in coming all the way from New York to get to know us better."

The gentle rebuke was clear to everyone except Tom, who swallowed the last of the éclair and washed it down with a swig of milk. "Must be on our way," he said. "We just came to grab some papers and need to get back to town." He met Colin's eyes across the table. "Shooting? Tomorrow morning at eight?"

"I haven't made any plans yet," Colin hedged. "Let's speak again at dinner." While Tom Jr. could prove a treasure trove of information regarding who might have invested in the Nicaraguan canal, he'd rather learn more about Dr. Schroeder's insights into the human brain.

Thomas glared at his son's back as the young man dashed down the hall, his older companion in tow. Margaret seemed equally embarrassed by her son's behavior as she reached for the teapot and topped off everyone's cup.

"Forgive my son," Thomas said uneasily. "Like many young men, he is ambitious and has it in his head to run for Congress soon. His zeal for politics rivals his skill as a marksman."

"A political career is a natural extension of his interest in the Olympics," Dr. Schroeder said. "There is a glamour in the political world that appeals to young men. The desire to prove oneself in competition with other men can be an irresistible temptation for someone like Tom, be it in the Olympics or on the political stage."

"He'll have a far better shot at the Olympics than Congress," Thomas said, disapproval simmering in every word.

"We don't know that," Margaret said soothingly. "Tom's interest in politics is still so new, but I don't see any reason it can't develop into something lasting and meaningful. It's what we've always hoped for, right?"

Thomas seemed to take comfort in his wife's words, and the lines eased from his forehead. He turned his attention to Colin. "My son is competing in the Galliard shooting contest over the Fourth of July holiday. It's the most prestigious shooting match outside of the Olympics. The competition is supposedly the main thing, but most people attend for an excuse to enjoy three days of picnics, parties, and the chance to rub shoulders with the highest members of society. Perhaps you would like to attend as our guest?"

The question was tossed off casually, but Colin heard the command as though it came from the blast of a trumpet.

"I'd be delighted," he said with as much enthusiasm as he could muster. It was one thing to barter his hand in marriage, but now he was bartering his friendship as well.

Lucy's accusation at the train station stung worse than ever.

For Lucy, the days after Colin left for Oakmonte stretched out interminably. She feared he had stepped into a lion's den and there was nothing she could do to help. Still, her normal workaday chores had not evaporated. Her pantry at home was bare, and she had yet to settle up with her lawyer from last month's hearing. Shopping for groceries would have to wait, but on Thursday, she decided to use her lunch hour to walk the eight blocks to Mr. Pritchard's office and pay what she owed.

She entered the lawyer's tiny waiting area to the sound of laughter coming from behind his closed office door, which was odd. Horace Pritchard ran his business on a shoestring and had never hired another assistant after Samuel quit working for him. He must be meeting with a client, although legal meetings were rarely the subject of hilarity.

Lucy was about to slide the envelope containing her payment beneath the door when it suddenly opened. She almost collided with Samuel Ballard, her onetime fiancé, heading out the door.

"Lucy!" He looked stunned to see her, taking a step back and bumping into a tall lady standing directly behind him.

It had been a year since they'd seen each other. He looked

exactly the same, but seeing his quirky, funny face, with his too-big nose that didn't rob an ounce of his handsome appeal . . . She drew a heavy breath. She'd forgotten how dear his face was to her.

"How are you, Samuel?" she managed to ask.

"Fine. I'm fine." He turned and pulled the lady behind him forward. "I came to introduce Cecily to Mr. Pritchard. Cecily and I got married last week."

It was as though someone had kicked her in the chest. She couldn't draw a breath. They all stood in exquisite awkwardness, but for the life of her, she couldn't breathe.

"Are you all right, Lucy?" Mr. Pritchard asked, coming forward and putting an arm around her shoulders.

"Yes, of course," she stammered once she'd forced her lungs to function again.

But she wasn't. She was hot and sweaty and felt faint and like her heart had just been torn from her chest and stomped flat. She managed to send Samuel and the pretty lady beside him a wobbly smile.

"Congratulations," she said, wondering at the crushing sensation in her chest. It wasn't as if she still carried a torch for Samuel, but she'd once had such hopes. During those few months, she'd been so deliriously happy. Those dreams had come crashing down more than a year ago, but now the wound felt fresh all over again.

She shoved the envelope into Mr. Pritchard's hand. "This is what we owe you for the last court hearing. Good-bye!"

She couldn't get out of there fast enough. She'd hoped to discuss their next motion to clear away the bad faith issue. The Drake valves had been taken out of Mr. Garzelli's tenement, and she wanted the case to move forward as quickly as possible. It wouldn't happen today.

She scurried down the sidewalk, skirting pedestrians and

almost knocking over a newsboy she didn't spot until she bumped into him. She didn't even know where she was going or why she was so upset. She'd put Samuel behind her, hadn't she? Her ridiculous fascination with Colin Beckwith had pretty well dominated her every waking thought, so why did Samuel's marriage feel like a body blow?

Her life just felt so empty. So hopelessly, crushingly empty and hollow. She had so much love to give and nowhere to put it.

She headed for the hog house where Nick worked. It wouldn't do to let her nerves unravel here on the street. Mercifully, Jack Ellis was manning the clerk's desk at the hog house. Jack sometimes went to Brooklyn Dodgers games with her and Nick, and he was the attendant most likely to bend the rules for her.

She took three deep breaths before entering. If Jack sensed how rattled she was, he'd want to probe, and she didn't want to speak to anyone but Nick right now.

"Jack, I know it's after lunchtime, but could I ask Nick to come above ground? I need to speak with him."

Jack peered at her through concerned eyes. "You okay, Lucy? You don't sound good."

"I'm fine. I just want to talk to Nick. Please?"

"Wait here, kid." He went through the door, and she heard his footsteps echo on the metal bars as he descended a ladder to the tunnels below.

She paced the small open space before the lunch tables, wishing she had someone else in her life she could lean on aside from Nick. No man with a brain in his head would want to court her as long as Uncle Thomas was alive. Most women her age had a husband and children, while all she had was a lawsuit. She twisted her hands while she paced. What was taking so long? The pumping station where Nick worked was less than a block farther down from the hog house, so he should be here by now.

It took ten minutes for Jack to return. He sent her a regretful look and rubbed the back of his neck. "Sorry, Lucy, he's in a mood. Can't get him to come up."

She *knew* Nick was in a mood. He'd been freezing her out ever since they'd quarreled over the message she intercepted and took to the police. He'd been surly, rude, and even stopped cooking for her. Their recent squabbles aside, he was still her big brother, and if he knew how miserable she was, he'd want to help.

"Can I go down? I promise I won't be long."

Jack rubbed his jaw. Lucy was one of the few civilians who'd seen the waterworks beneath the streets, for Nick often took her below to show her the ongoing installations.

"Yeah, maybe you snuck down while I was stepping out for a smoke. I'm lookin' the other way for a minute."

"Thanks, Jack," she said, embarrassed by the wobble in her voice.

She hiked up her skirts to descend the ladder. Most people had no idea there was an entirely separate world beneath the streets of their city. Miles of tunnels, pump stations, and distribution pipes operated to move millions of gallons of water in and out of the city each day. Far from being the dank, cramped space most people assumed the underground world to be, there was a strange sort of beauty in the brick-lined tunnels that stood eleven feet tall and wide enough for five men to walk side by side. Gaslit lanterns along the walls gave it a gothic illumination.

It was easy to get lost down here. Signage was minimal, and most of the tunnels looked alike. Some led to freshwater supply pipes while others connected to the sewer system that carried wastewater to the filtering stations and then out to the river. Thousands of men earned a living in this underground world, and even vagrants managed to slip down via the manhole covers to seek shelter. It was hard to imagine that life could be so bad that people chose to make their home in this dank, gaslit world, but Nick swore that anytime he ventured too far away from a work site, he'd see tramps and vagabonds scavenging for coins or other treasures that rolled down into the sewers.

It was summer, but things always felt chilly in the clammy air down here. A little water pooled along the concrete floor of the tunnel as she followed it back to where Nick worked, installing a new water regulator. Sandhogs and plumbers sent her curious stares as she passed but made no effort to interfere as she headed to Nick's station.

Nick had his flashlight pointing at the valve he was adjusting. His back was to her as he squatted to work at the base of the regulator, but a plumber on the other side looked at her quizzically. Nick noticed and swiveled. Maybe it was only the dim gaslight that made the planes of his face look grim when he saw her.

"You look a little out of place down here, Luce." His voice was as stern as his expression.

It was too much. Against her will, the muscles of her face screwed up, and tears pooled, threatening to spill over.

Nick dropped his wrench and stood. "What's wrong?"

"Samuel Ballard got married."

"Aw, *Luce* . . ."

He tugged her into his arms, and she buried her face against his shoulder, but she held on and didn't cry. It wasn't that she loved Samuel anymore, but sometimes things just got so hard.

"I saw her," she mumbled against his shoulder. "The woman he married. She's got a big nose and a long face." Even so, Samuel's wife was pretty. She looked happy and healthy and like a good match for him.

"I pity their children," Nick said. "If she's got a snout as big as his, it's bound to get passed down. Poor kid won't even be able to lift his head."

158

A watery gulp of laughter escaped her. "Thanks, Nick," she managed to say. They shouldn't be teasing like this, but it helped put a little salve on her battered heart.

Nick extracted himself. "How did you find out?"

"I ran into them at the lawyer's office." An infinitesimal flash of tension crossed Nick's face, but she continued. "I went by to pay the bill and discuss what happens next. We can get the motion to delay on bad faith dismissed, I know—"

"I'm done, Luce."

"You can't be done. This is bigger than just us."

"I'm done. I don't care anymore." He glanced at the water regulator he'd been working on, a giant, complex piece of machinery only a skilled plumber could maintain. "I've got a good job, and I don't want to go through the rest of my life paying lawyers for the privilege of getting kicked in the face year after year."

"So you're going to let Uncle Thomas win?" Her voice echoed off the wet brick of the tunnel.

"I don't care what word you give it," Nick said, his voice tired but not angry. "I'm done. I want more from life than what we've had so far."

If it weren't for this lawsuit, Nick would have probably found some good woman and be settled by now. Certainly, she and Samuel would be married. A chill raced through her, and she tightened her arms around her middle. It was always so cold down here.

It was embarrassing to have collapsed like this, and it was time to pull herself back together. She was a Drake. A survivor. If she got knocked down ten times, she would stand up eleven. She needed Nick back in the fight, for the consequences were growing dangerous.

"I intercepted another message," she said in a low tone. "I've got more details about the plot, and it sounds like they are aiming at anyone involved with the Panama Canal. Maybe even the president."

Nick shook his head. "I think your imagination is out of control. I think you're so wrapped up in believing the worst of Uncle Thomas that you can't see straight anymore."

"I showed both notes to Colin Beckwith at Reuters, and he believes me."

Nick nearly exploded. "You told some limey we don't even know about that wire?" His voice echoed off the brick walls, and everyone in the tunnel turned to gape at them.

"Yes, Colin knows. He is an unbiased observer of everything that's been happening, and he thinks it warrants looking into. I'm not letting Uncle Thomas get away with *anything*. I'll keep fighting however long it takes, and I'll do it with or without you. I'm not a quitter."

Nick's glare was smoldering as she left him standing in the tunnel.

🙢❧🙠

Worries plagued her all day as she listened to the cascade of furious clicking coming across her sounder. She transcribed stories of a new steamship christened in the docks of Liverpool, of a royal wedding in Austria, and the discovery of oil in a Texas cow patch. There was a huge world of opportunity out there, but she wasn't part of it. She sat at a tiny workstation on the sixth floor of the Western Union building and listened to the rest of the world venturing into the future while she was mired in legal bills and a forty-year-old court case.

Maybe Nick was right.

To make it worse, as she walked into her apartment, she smelled cigarette smoke again. Nick was already home, his nose buried in the evening newspaper. The frostiness from their afternoon spat continued, for he didn't even bother to look up as she entered.

"Don't tell me you can't smell that," she said as she tossed her bag down.

"Smell what?"

"Cigarettes. Doesn't it bother you that this is the third time in a month our home has reeked of tobacco after no one was home all day?"

Nick jerked the newspaper shut and threw it on the table. He stalked to the hall closet and banged it open. "Come on. I'm blocking off the ceiling vent. It means we'll have stale air, but at least you can quit carping about the neighbor lady's cigarettes."

It was a good idea. At this time of year, they could leave the window open for fresh air. If they blocked the vent, she could learn for certain if someone was sneaking into their apartment or if Nick was right and the stink was all from the lady upstairs.

"I'll get the toolbox," she said. She also grabbed an old pillow small enough to fit into the vent.

She held the ladder while Nick unscrewed the plate on the ceiling. Clumps of dust fell as he pulled it away and handed it down to her. Her nose twitched, and she fought the impulse to sneeze. She was about to hand the pillow up to Nick when he stopped her.

"There's something up here," he said, twisting to reach inside. More clumps of dust fell as he dragged out a maroon canvas bag.

It was her father's missing satchel.

Her mouth went dry. How many times had they searched the apartment for that bag and come up empty? She met Nick's gaze, his somber face indicating he knew exactly what he held.

"Let's open it," he said grimly. They'd been looking for this satchel since the week her father died, but they both dreaded knowing its contents. The memory of her father's face, white with fear as he clutched the satchel, was still etched in her mind.

Nick lifted the flap and withdrew a photograph. It was a picture of her father, staring at the camera, all the sorrow in the world etched on his face. He was strapped into a chair and wearing a straitjacket.

Nick dropped the picture. "What is *that*?" he snarled.

Lucy didn't even want to touch it, but she needed to know. She picked up the photograph and drew it closer. Her father's eyes were frantic, pleading. She could make out nothing of the room, but lettering at the bottom of the photograph indicated where it was taken.

The Ridgemoor Insane Asylum.

Ridgemoor was north of the city, an ominous building surrounded by a wrought-iron fence and overgrown hedges to keep curious onlookers away. Schoolchildren were threatened with it if they did not behave. And her father had been in that horrible place? Her *father*?

An envelope peeked out from the satchel. She grabbed it and unfolded the letter inside. She read quickly:

Warren,

It pains me to learn you are suffering from the same insanity which affected your father, but I understand such conditions are often passed from one generation to the next. I hope your brief stay at Ridgemoor was of benefit to you. We can arrange additional visits if necessary. Furthermore, perhaps your children should be evaluated by a competent physician, for if either Nick or Lucy shows signs of mental volatility, it is best they receive treatment early, and the Ridgemoor Asylum is happy to accommodate children.

On another matter, I hope we can reach a speedy conclusion to the lawsuit over the valve. I fear the protracted lawsuit may have exacerbated your mental instability and

your intransigence is a sign of continuing mental illness.
Perhaps the judge would be interested in the attached
photograph. I have many copies.

Sincerely,

Thomas Drake

She tamped down a wave of nausea and glanced at the date on the letter. It was written in 1891, the same time her father had visited Oakmonte and did not return for a solid month. No wonder her father had been terrified of Uncle Thomas.

She passed the letter to Nick, too sickened to even speak. His face soured with revulsion as he read.

"How could Uncle Thomas have gotten away with this?" he demanded. "Dad suffered from moods, but he wasn't crazy."

"If you have enough money, you can buy anything," she said faintly. Including paying a physician to commit her father to an insane asylum. How could a man prove he was *not* insane? The frantic expression on her father's face certainly looked like a mentally unbalanced man. Anyone forced into a straitjacket and ripped away from his family would be frantic.

"I'm going to kill him," Nick said, his voice vibrating with anger. "Next time I see Thomas Drake, my hand to God, I'm going to kill him."

"Stop it," she said. "We have to be smart about this. Maybe there's some way we can use this letter. It's a clear case of blackmail." Not only did Uncle Thomas threaten to have her father committed if he failed to drop the lawsuit, he'd threatened to go after *children*.

Nick's hands curled into fists, and he took a series of long, slow breaths. "Uncle Thomas has no idea what kind of dragon he just awakened," he said, his voice vibrating with suppressed fury. "I'm back in the fight."

The first evening's dinner at Oakmonte was an informal affair, with only the Drakes, Dr. Schroeder and his wife, and Colin. Aperitifs were served on the outdoor terrace, where fresh flowers graced the table and a gentle breeze cooled the June evening. Although Colin had come in search of information on Lucy's ominous telegrams, his entire focus had shifted to the chance to delve into Dr. Schroeder's fascinating research about the human brain and what triggered its behavior.

The topic had to be handled gently, and he started with the wives, who were usually willing to follow his lead in answering meandering questions that ultimately led to his prime objective. Despite her age, Mrs. Schroeder had a willowy elegance that was probably the envy of women half her age.

He smiled as he approached her in the rose garden. "What is it like to be married to a doctor of psychology? Do you fear he is secretly scrutinizing your every move?"

"Fear it?" she asked with a smile. "After forty years of marriage, I am delighted that he still has the interest to be scrutinizing me at all."

Colin grinned, and Dr. Schroeder joined the conversation.

"Henrietta Schroeder, you shall have me spellbound until my dying breath," the old doctor said fondly. "An involuntary reaction, but I am helpless to resist."

Colin watched the pair interact. They were both vibrant and lively despite their age, but he wasn't here to enjoy the sight of a healthy marriage. He wanted access to Dr. Schroeder's knowledge.

"Tell me more about involuntary reactions," he said. "Do you truly believe there are parts of our brain we are powerless to control?"

"I don't believe so," the doctor quickly replied. "I think it is just a matter of willpower." He proceeded to outline the factors of self-discipline, a combination of suppressing instinctive urges, delayed gratification, and commitment to improving the mind through training. Colin hung on every word, wondering how he could put these principles into practice. He was about to ask when Tom Jr. and his companion arrived back home.

The entire dynamic of the conversation altered. Colin swallowed his frustration as Thomas stepped forward to offer formal introductions.

"Sir Beckwith, this is Felix Moreno, an attorney from Manhattan."

Centuries of inbred training helped Colin mask the shock from his face. This was the lawyer whose office was on the other end of Lucy's illegal wire.

"It's a pleasure to meet you," he said as he shook the lawyer's hand. This was excellent. Apparently Tom Jr. and Mr. Moreno were thick as thieves . . . perhaps literally. He'd assumed it was the elder Drake who was behind the messages Lucy intercepted, but perhaps it was Tom Jr.

The group went in to dinner, and Colin smoothly ignored Margaret's attempt to steer him into the chair beside her, heading toward Felix Moreno instead. It was time to start honing in on the enigmatic messages Lucy overheard.

"How's the law business in Manhattan these days?" he asked as soon as they were seated.

Felix sawed into his beef cutlet. "Aside from Mr. Drake, I've turned most of the firm's business over to junior members of the firm. I'm much more interested in politics these days."

Mrs. Schroeder joined the conversation. "Do you really think Tom has a chance at Congress?"

"I know it," Felix said. "Youth is no obstacle. What's needed is resolve, confidence, and vision. Tom has all three."

Colin turned to Tom. "And your vision is?"

Tom set down his fork, straightened, and recited an obviously prepared statement. "The president is overstepping, and we need strong men in Congress who can serve as the foundation of our government. Even after Roosevelt is defeated in the next election, we need to ensure this sort of roughshod treatment he is delivering can never happen again. Brave men in Congress are the first step."

"Well said," his mother murmured, approval glowing in her eyes. Even Tom's father had a proud smile as he listened to his son, but wasn't it natural for parents to dote on their children? Colin remembered his own father's pride when his newly born sister Mary was only a few hours old and she sneezed. Sneezed! And his father beamed like she had just discovered the secrets for harnessing electricity. Colin was four years old, and it was his first lesson in realizing that parents could be irrational about their children.

Less understandable was Mr. Moreno's overgenerous opinion of Tom Jr.'s natural brilliance for political office.

Although Colin thought he might have to finesse the discussion into something relating to the intercepted messages, the opportunity happened naturally the moment Felix learned Colin worked for Reuters.

166

"What do you think of all this Panama Canal hullabaloo?" Mr. Moreno asked. Before Colin could reply, Mr. Moreno answered his own question. "I think it's all nonsense. Everyone acts as if it's a done deal, when it is far from reality. There are other options for a canal rather than going through Panama. The Nicaraguan route makes more sense, but why do I rarely see it reported in the newspapers?"

Colin didn't even have time to open his mouth before Tom Jr. joined the fray. "Anytime that much money is wrapped up in a deal, someone is getting paid off. Half the congressmen in Washington couldn't even find Panama on a map, and they act as if it's the only route for a canal."

Colin parsed his words carefully. "Now that the president and the independent commission have both endorsed the Panama route, it seems to be the natural focus of scrutiny."

The statement caused Mr. Moreno to lower his chin and raise his voice. "That's because the press isn't doing its job. You are at the helm of Reuters. Why don't you *do* something about it?"

It seemed neither Tom nor his lawyer friend understood how a news agency worked. Reuters and the AP produced thousands of stories, but it was up to individual newspapers to select the handful they wanted to print.

"I merely manage a news agency," he said. "I'm paid to be politically neutral."

Tom Jr. smirked. "Neutral is just another word for 'neutered.' I'd rather die than suffer political castration. A real man must be permitted to make his mark on the world."

Both ladies at the table winced in embarrassment, but Colin had lived through far worse than potshots from a spoiled boy.

"Benjamin Franklin once said the pen is mightier than the sword, but he never met you, Tom. The world awaits your debut on the stage of history with breathless anticipation."

Margaret missed the irony in his voice. "Here, here," she said warmly.

Colin was coming to understand why Tom Jr. had such a high opinion of himself. As much as he longed to knock a bit of the smug off Tom, he needed to play this game carefully and wait.

❧

The sun had set by the time Colin returned to his room and stepped onto the balcony. To his delight, Beatrice had returned from the city. He found her beside the birdcage, happily gorging on suet and dried peas.

Lucy had attached a note to Beatrice's leg:

Your birds are valiant, tireless, and steadfast. They are female, so it comes with the territory.

He couldn't resist drafting a response.

My birds are indeed impressive. Please note: They were born and raised in England, so they are British. The American pigeons I see in Central Park have lost all drive. A tragedy, but not unforeseeable.

He would send the message as soon as he had something else noteworthy to report from Oakmonte. He coaxed Beatrice onto his finger.

"How are you this evening, love?" He stroked the downy feathers on the top of her head, listening to the warbling coo of her barely audible call. He loved that sound, which signaled perfect contentment. He continued stroking her head to coax it out again.

The door of the room next to his opened, and Dr. Schroeder

stepped outside to join him on the balcony. "It seems we are neighbors for the weekend," he said.

Colin put Beatrice inside her cage. "Indeed. You are a frequent visitor here?"

"Several times a year. My wife likes the countryside, so it's an enjoyable trip for her."

Colin braced a hand against the railing. Crickets chirped in the distance, and the soft rustle of leaves came from the nearby forest. This might be the best time to ask Dr. Schroeder's advice without others constantly underfoot to divert the conversation. He glanced both directions down the darkened balcony, as well as at the porch area beneath them. They were alone.

"I found your insight into involuntary responses of the brain very interesting," he began.

"You did?"

"Yes. I have a friend who served alongside me during the Boer War." He couldn't admit his own mortifying weaknesses, but by attributing the symptoms to an anonymous friend, perhaps he could learn what he needed to know. "My friend was trapped behind the lines while a battle raged. There was no escape, and the sound of gunfire and shelling went on for days. It was impossible to sleep or seek shelter from the barrage. The fear was the worst part, I gather. It went on for over a week with no let up."

Even discussing this made the night air stink like that hot, fetid battlefield. Overwhelming thirst descended upon him, and he wished he had something to drink, but this conversation was too important to walk away from. He forced his tone to remain casual.

"Everything turned out well in the end, but I continue to have—I mean, my friend continues to suffer." He glanced away, hoping Dr. Schroeder hadn't noticed his slip of the tongue. He swallowed hard and continued. "If something catches my friend by surprise, he panics and finds it difficult to breathe. A loud noise or even certain odors cause the anxiety to take over. He once vomited at the scent of gunpowder."

He clenched the balcony railing, unable to look at the doctor as he spoke, but to his relief, Dr. Schroeder's voice was calmly professional.

"We saw this following the Civil War," the old doctor said. "Sometimes soldiers suffered from acute mania for years following the war, even after the physical wounds were treated. Psychology was in its infancy then and very little could be done for such men, but I hope you assure your friend that his stress reaction is no reflection on his character. We have modern and effective treatments now."

Tension drained from Colin's neck and shoulders as hope took root. This visit to Oakmonte would prove to be a godsend if he could find a way to cure his mortifying weakness. "What sort of treatment?"

Dr. Schroeder had the kindly face of a grandfather as he gave a sad smile. "It all depends on how badly your friend wants to heal. A course of therapy in an institutionalized setting would be best, for the cure is not easy, and the patient may try to escape. Personally, I always secure them in a private cell to better monitor the situation. A straitjacket is standard in order to ensure the safety of the staff. Then a course of exposure therapy in which the patient is regularly subjected to the source of his fear. If his fear is gun blasts, that is easy enough to arrange. We'd secure the patient to a chair, then begin a series of gunshots to encourage gradual adjustment to the stimulus."

Colin's eyes widened at the barbaric images, but the doctor had not stopped speaking.

"Over time, we would expose the patient to traumatic situations when he least expects it. While sleeping or dining. These periodic exposures will gradually accustom the patient to the stimulus, at which point we would broaden his exposure to a variety of stressful situations that will train his brain to cope with trauma. I've had success with ice water baths and courses of electric shock. Now, now . . . no need to look at me like that. I would never subject the patient to this all at once. We are talking about a course of treatment over several weeks, during which he will be safely confined in Ridgemoor, where he would have the opportunity to strengthen his resolve and overcome his weakness."

Colin's face froze into a mask. At all costs, he would maintain his composure. What an irony that decades of good breeding prevented him from lashing out and telling Dr. Schroeder his true opinion of this sadistic cruelty.

Dr. Schroeder put a fatherly hand on his arm. "I hope you send your friend to me. With a few months of confinement at my facility, I am certain I can help him."

Colin withdrew to the door leading to his bedroom. He wouldn't send a dog to Dr. Schroeder, but he nodded politely. "Thank you for your insight. It was most enlightening."

ucy had never seen Nick descend into such grim resolve, but ever since discovering the satchel with the horrifying photograph of their father, he was like another person. A tougher, meaner person. They stayed up late that evening, strategizing.

"I'm going to hunt down every person who had anything to do with this photograph. Hunt down, incapacitate, and destroy them. The doctors, the photographer, even the nurses who tended him. There won't be enough to wipe off the floor for burial."

"Easy, Nick. We've got enough time to plan this carefully." They'd been patient all their lives in doggedly chipping away at this lawsuit. She wasn't going to let Nick lose his head now.

The first step was finding out who was breaking into their apartment and why. Lucy had a good hunch, which was why she and Nick now sat beside the window, the lights in the apartment darkened in the hour before dawn. The last time she saw him, the lamppost leaner had arrived in the early morning, the glow of his cigarette tip visible even from up here.

Sure enough, at five o'clock in the morning, he strolled along the empty, predawn street, a cigarette already dangling from his mouth. He glanced up at their apartment, and Lucy instinctively slid out of view, hugging the wall and holding her breath. Had he seen them?

Nick wasn't so timid. He stood behind the lacy drapes and squinted through the fabric. "He's making notes in a journal. Come on. I want to see what he's writing."

"Are you sure? He might be dangerous."

Nick opened the sideboard drawer and lifted out a revolver. "So am I." Popping open the cylinder, he checked to be sure it was loaded.

As soon as Nick stowed the gun in his coat pocket, he strode to the door. There was no stopping him, so Lucy followed, hurrying down the staircase after him. "Why don't you let me hold the gun? I'm less likely to lose my temper." After all, she'd suspected something shady about the lamppost leaner for months, but it was all new to Nick.

He paused at the second floor landing and gave her a quizzical look. "Do you think I'm stupid, Luce? I'll be calm and cold when necessary, but I'll scare the living daylights out of him if the time is right."

They left the building through the back door and headed down a block, then back up to the main street, and approached the lamppost leaner from behind. He was still making notes in a journal as they approached.

Nick grabbed him, hauling him up and two inches off the ground. The notebook splatted onto the pavement.

"Grab it, Luce," Nick growled. She prayed they weren't making a horrible mistake and attacking an innocent man. Nick whirled him by his shirt collar and slammed him against the lamppost.

She needn't have worried about the lamppost leaner's innocence. One glance at the notebook showed it to be full of references to the Manhattan Drakes' activities. Notes listed when they came and left the apartment and descriptions of their visitors. She read a few passages aloud to Nick, whose smile turned grim.

"Let's go behind the building and have a little chat," he growled.

"No need to be so hasty," the lamppost leaner stammered. Now that she could see him up close, he didn't look so threatening. Although he and Nick were the same height, Nick was all brawny muscle, and this man was skinny and soft. His bulging eyes had a spray of age lines in the corners.

Lucy casually stepped on the smoldering cigarette he'd dropped, extinguishing it before she followed Nick, who strong-armed the stammering man down the alley and behind the building. Once they were off the main street, Nick rifled the man's pockets while Lucy continued skimming the notebook, looking at page after page of their activities, almost all of them focusing on Nick. To her surprise, there was a list of each time Nick had gone absent from work. Some of them were for court dates or meetings with their lawyer, but twice it was because Nick was sick, and once because of their father's funeral. She turned the page, and her eyes widened as she read a list of books she'd checked out from the public library.

"What's this?" Nick snarled as he pulled something from the lamppost leaner's pocket.

"It's nothing," the terrified man stammered.

"Funny, it looks like a key to our apartment."

"I never took anything," the man said. "All I did was look around some. Honest."

"Why?" Nick demanded. When the man refused to answer, Nick gave him a mighty shake, pounding him against the brick wall. "*Why?*"

"I don't know why! I just do what I'm told."

"By who?"

"Some crazy guy up in Albany. I don't know his name. He wants to know everything about you, like where you eat and the names of the girls you squire around town. Look, this guy has the goods that could put my sister in prison for years. She's a good girl, she just got mixed up with the wrong people for a spell. He said I wouldn't have to do anything illegal, just watch the two of you and keep a record of things. That's all I've done."

"Why were you sniffing around Mr. Garzelli's tenement building?"

"The crazy guy wanted to know what you were up to in that basement. He wants reports on everything."

It had the whiff of Uncle Thomas. That didn't mean she trusted the lamppost leaner, but this was too good of an opportunity to miss. She stepped forward.

"Let's turn this to our advantage," she said quietly.

Nick's white-knuckled grasp on the man's collar eased. It was a tense few moments as he released the lamppost leaner and they both watched each other warily. They learned his name was Roscoe and his sister worked as a maid at a mental institution on the north end of the city.

"Ridgemoor?" Nick asked.

Roscoe nodded. "Yes. Ridgemoor."

Was someone trying to build a case for funneling Nick or herself into a straitjacket like their father? Her mouth went dry. Nick pressed, but Roscoe was reluctant to talk about the details of his association with "the crazy guy."

Nick wasn't shy about applying pressure. He nodded to the notebook. "You've been following me close enough to see the men I work with. They are big, smart, and tough. We risk our lives every day down in those tunnels, and we look out for each other. I trust them, and they'll back me up the instant I call. If

you double-cross me, there won't be a rock large enough for
you to hide beneath if we go in search of you."

Roscoe swallowed hard. "What do you want from me?"

Lucy answered. "We want to know how to get in contact
with the crazy guy up in Albany."

And then they could take action against the man who had
put their father in a mental institution.

Colin began his day by enjoying the copious hot water in the
spotless washroom attached to his bedroom. At Whitefriars,
a morning shave required lugging lukewarm water from the
kitchen hearth, then carrying it all back down once finished.

As he dragged the straight razor through the foam on his
face, he hummed a little and contemplated how to get Felix
Moreno alone for a few hours. He needed to separate Felix
from Tom, whose short attention span made it hard to focus
on the probing conversation Colin needed to identify an association between Oakmonte and the NCC. Manipulating the
conversation so that Felix would unwittingly reveal a motive for
scuttling the Panama Canal would be a challenge, but Colin was
good at asking questions. Most people loved the opportunity
to talk about themselves, and he was more than willing to let
them have the stage.

It was pure luck that he happened to glance out the narrow
washroom window and spot Tom Jr. heading off for a morning
of shooting, with Felix and Dr. Schroeder in tow. After wiping the shaving cream from his face, Colin threw on a pair of
trousers and made a mad dash downstairs and out the front
door, his bare feet sliding a little on the damp grass.

"Mr. Moreno!" he called as he loped across the lawn. All
three men turned toward him, rifles slung over their shoulders.
"I hear Mrs. Drake has a game of croquet planned this morn-

ing. Stick around and join us. I'm eager to hear more about practicing law in America."

Tom Jr.'s lip curled in barely concealed contempt. "Croquet is a girly game. Come on, Felix, let's go find something to shoot."

Felix flashed Tom a message Colin couldn't interpret, but whatever it was, Tom immediately backed down and wished them a good day, setting off toward the forest with Dr. Schroeder at his side. It was a relief to see the back of the doctor, for Colin suspected the man saw far too much.

An hour later, Colin was deep into a six-wicket croquet game. Margaret had to return to the house to handle a crisis in the kitchen, leaving only himself, Felix, and Mrs. Schroeder to enjoy the match. Mrs. Schroeder displayed a shocking amount of competitive spirit, and Colin had to admire her zeal as she lined up each ball before smacking it through the wickets.

He turned his attention to Felix. "How did you become acquainted with Tom Jr.?" he asked as he prepared for a shot.

"Tom and I go back years," Felix said. "Our firm has handled an ongoing lawsuit for the Drakes for decades, so when Tom Jr. ran into a bit of trouble at Princeton, I was called in to help. It was all hogwash and easily settled, but I've always been very impressed with the young man. He has a bright future in politics but needs guidance learning the political ropes. He's got everything—intelligence, drive, ambition. If he can medal at the Olympics, it will give him credibility on his own merits instead of simply inheriting a fortune."

Colin phrased his questions carefully as the morning unfolded. As suspected, Felix shared freely, supplying all the details of how he guided Tom in preparation for a congressional run, coaching him in debate, public speaking, and how to defuse the arguments of an opponent. He instructed Tom to read the *New York Times* daily in order to keep abreast of all current events.

"That explains your interest in the Panama Canal," Colin said.

Felix took the bait. "Absolutely! It is essential for Tom to have opinions on all contemporary events and be capable of defending his positions. We both agree that the Panamanian route is foolish and unlikely to succeed. The Nicaraguan route is longer but easier to dredge. Of course, that would rob our president of the chance to meddle in another nation's private business."

"Oh my, we've just veered into an awkward political discussion," Mrs. Schroeder said.

Felix gave a nod of appeasement. "My apologies, ma'am. I had forgotten you are an ardent supporter of our young president. Nevertheless, we must quell this reckless march through Panama."

They were getting to the heart of the matter, and Colin refused to let the topic be diverted. "How precisely can you quell the march?"

"In the long run? By getting men like Tom elected to Congress. But there are plenty of behind-the-scenes ways to convince current congressmen to see reason. It's why I've encouraged Tom to cultivate friendships among the political class."

Colin's insatiable curiosity got the better of him. "Why mentor another man for Congress? Have you never thought of running for office yourself?"

Felix snorted. "A man can become a millionaire through the practice of law. Not so by sitting in Congress. Having Tom win a seat would be the best of both worlds. I can still earn a lucrative living as a lawyer but guide Tom on how to cast his vote on important political decisions."

Mrs. Schroeder's smile was wistful. "Money can buy security and a few baubles, but it can't buy happiness. If your passion is in politics, you should run, not try to turn Tom into a puppet to do your bidding. Such a course will frustrate you both."

"So says a woman who has always had money," Felix said, not unkindly. "Money can disappear like that." He gave a brisk snap of his fingers. "I'm not so rich that I can afford to weather a financial tsunami just because we have a reckless young man sitting in the White House. It's only natural for a man to protect his investments, whether that is in a courtroom or by using influence in Congress."

Or by hiring a team of assassins to take out men on the verge of authorizing the Panama route. Colin blocked any hint of emotion from showing on his face, but inside a sense of triumph gathered momentum. It looked as if he'd just identified the person with a huge financial investment in making the Nicaraguan route succeed. Now all he had to do was find proof in order to convince Sergeant Palmer to take it seriously.

It was nearing lunchtime when the croquet game ended. Colin rested his mallet on his shoulder as he strode toward the back terrace where the family gathered in a tight cluster. Dr. Schroeder and Tom Jr. were there, as were both of Tom's parents. Whatever had them enthralled must be terribly interesting, for Tom was squatting on the slate tiles, and a good deal of laughter trickled up from the group. Colin's smile froze as he drew closer.

Bianca had returned, and they had removed the message tied to her leg. Tom had the strip of paper unfurled on his knee, reading aloud.

"Tom, you are a handsome and charming man. You deserve a bottle of French champagne served with your lunch."

Margaret's laughter rang out. "It says no such thing! Look, here is Sir Beckwith. Perhaps he can read it for us. We can't make sense out of all those dots and dashes."

His tension eased. He'd never expected a message to be

intercepted by the Drakes, but at least Lucy had the sense to write in Morse code. He held out his hand.

Good heavens, Lucy must have been in a chatty mood, for he rarely sent such lengthy messages via pigeon. His eyes traveled along the code, translating quickly.

He could actually feel the blood drain from his face. He felt light-headed and overheated at the same time. What Lucy had to say was a catastrophe.

I intercepted another message. Direct quote: In light of TR's progress with ICC, move up the date for action. Release additional funds to delay votes. Fire when ready.

"Well?" Margaret asked. "We have been dying of anticipation. What does it say?"

He felt the weight of six people staring at him while he scrambled for a suitable reply. He prayed no one here was disguising an ability to read Morse code, or this weekend party was about to become a dangerous operation.

"Just Reuters business," he said. "The quality of tea service often slips when I am not in the office, and my secretary thinks it warrants attention." He slid the note into his pocket. It appeared the team of conspirators was larger than just Tom and Mr. Moreno, because at least one other person in New York was involved in the plot and sending messages. "Forgive me, but Bianca has had a long flight, and I should ensure she has a proper meal."

"Oh, we've been feeding her bits of cookies with raspberry jam," Margaret said. "She seemed delighted."

His mouth turned down. That amount of sugar was the worst thing for a homing pigeon that had been flying for five solid hours. His bird needed plenty of water and nutrition-dense seed to restore her strength. He coaxed Bianca onto his finger.

"Nevertheless, she should be returned to her cage for some undisturbed rest. I will rejoin you all shortly."

He didn't care about his rude departure. He needed time to strategize, for the president's life might depend upon it.

Lucy had been working twelve-hour days ever since Colin left. She couldn't risk being away from her station if the tiny lightbulb tucked behind the geranium pot signaled a message from the Moreno Law Office. She also wanted to be here should a pigeon arrive from Colin.

Her thoughts were interrupted as a message came over the Moreno wire. She quickly opened the circuit and began translating. Within a few words, her heart was seized by plain, stark fear:

```
Urgent: NYC police here asking questions
about ICC. Denied all knowledge. Info came
from Colin Beckwith of Reuters. His secretary
says he is at Oakmonte. A spy? Stop him.
Shooting accident?
```

Good heavens. Oh, good heavens. So Sergeant Palmer had taken her seriously after all, apparently with Colin's help, but by beginning an investigation, he had inadvertently put Colin in terrible danger.

She had to warn Colin at once! Even now, he could be heading out for a shooting expedition with her loathsome cousin.

She left her lunch half-eaten at her station and dashed to Mr. Tolland's desk. "I need to leave for the day."

He glared over his glasses. "You're scheduled to work until seven o'clock this evening."

"I can't. Something came up."

She didn't even wait for a reply, but scurried to the far side of the room to punch her timecard. She might lose her job over this, but Colin might lose his *life* unless she warned him in time.

She had no bird with which to send an alert about the danger. Even if one arrived immediately, it would need to rest for several hours before heading back out. By then it would be nighttime, and homing pigeons couldn't navigate in the dark. Obviously telegrams were out, and there was no telephone at Oakmonte.

There was no help for it. The fastest way to get Colin out of danger was by boarding a train and telling him in person. She'd never been to Oakmonte, and the prospect of walking up to Uncle Thomas's front door and asking for admission was terrifying, but it had to be done.

It was time to head into the lion's den.

Chapter
SIXTEEN

olin was accustomed to weekend house parties, but hosting them was a new and terrifying affair for Mrs. Drake, and her anxiety was spilling over to infect the rest of the household. The harried servants were busy pressing linens, polishing silver, and carting in loads of fresh food. There was room for twelve people at Oakmonte's dining table, and the seats would be filled with guests coming from as far as Albany. It was Margaret's opportunity to shed the taint of new money by flaunting her titled old-world visitor before the people who had snubbed her. She desperately wanted to please, rolling out allegedly spontaneous entertainments with the rigidity of a general preparing for battle.

A special chef had arrived from Albany to handle the finer aspects of the Saturday evening feast, which would feature quail, a salmon soufflé, turtle bisque, steamed oysters, and two cuts of beef. Margaret's inexperience with gourmet preparations ratcheted her tension higher, leading her to hover over the kitchen staff.

Colin was tempted to suggest she try to relax and take pleasure in the weekend. How could guests enjoy themselves if the hostess was so tightly wound she might detonate on contact? The best hostesses displayed effortless charm and trusted their staff to keep the household running like well-oiled clockwork. Then again, those women had centuries of training behind them, whereas Margaret Drake was the daughter of a green-grocer and desperate to overcome it.

The mood darkened Saturday morning when Felix Moreno received a telegram, putting him into an unusually grim temper. Even Margaret noticed and asked if all was well, but Mr. Moreno simply gave a curt nod and glared out the window, his hands fisted in tension. It made the situation even more awkward. It did not ease until Mr. Moreno disappeared with Tom Jr. for a few hours to go skeet shooting. They didn't invite Colin, for which he was grateful.

Mr. Moreno's mood had not improved at lunch, and Tom's gauche behavior was even worse than usual. Colin tried to steer the conversation by asking seemingly innocent questions about their plans for the summer. Both men were curt and noncommittal, and Colin decided to escape the tension in the house by inviting Mrs. Schroeder to the grassy lawn behind Oakmonte before the local guests began arriving for that evening's grand dinner. There was nothing he could do to help, and his presence seemed to agitate Margaret even more, so a nice walk in the countryside with Mrs. Schroeder would be a welcome respite. As much as he despised her husband, he liked Henrietta and wondered if she had any idea what her husband did behind the walls of that sanitarium.

He used the pigeons as an excuse to coax Mrs. Schroeder outside. "We'll let them fly around a bit, and I'll show you how I call them back," he said. "It will be fun."

Mrs. Schroeder seemed relieved to join him. "Margaret is desperate to be accepted by the local community. Some of these families are very old indeed and quite proud of their heritage.

The Drakes' house is larger and grander than their colonial homesteads, and it's caused a bit of resentment."

A sundial on a granite pedestal rested at the far end of the formal lawn. It looked like it had been there since Adam and Eve left the garden, with its artificially aged copper face covered with a green patina and raised etchings. There was enough room to set the birdcage on the top of the pedestal. Colin opened the door, lifted Bianca out, and offered her to Mrs. Schroeder, who seemed delighted to accept the bird onto her outstretched hand.

"It's admirable how tenderly you care for these birds," she said.

"They work hard for me, and I am ridiculously fond of them," he said. "If taking them out for a bit of fresh air lets us escape the mayhem inside, I'm grateful for the excuse."

He showed Mrs. Schroeder how to raise her arm to summon the birds, and her laughter was as delighted as a young girl's as she practiced the movement. After a while, it was time to give the birds a rest, and he scattered a little seed on the face of the sundial. The pigeons lazily pecked away as he and Mrs. Schroeder reminisced about performances they had attended at Carnegie Hall.

Before long, he saw Tom Jr. striding across the lawn, a shotgun propped on his shoulder and a sour expression on his face.

"That's a six-hundred-dollar sundial your birds are pooping on." The rancor in his voice was excessive even for Tom.

Colin glanced at the sundial. Sure enough, one of the birds had made a mess. "My apologies. I'll rinse it off promptly."

Tom's lip curled. "As if some pampered aristocrat would ever lower himself to do real work like that. I'll bet you were planning on leaving it there, weren't you?"

He had been. It wasn't as if sundials didn't regularly get hit by wild birds all year long, but if the Drakes felt this piece was somehow special, of course he would rinse it off. The way Tom flexed and clenched the stock of the shotgun seemed odd.

"Take it easy, Tom. It's only a sundial."

"Which you don't mind defiling, just as you've come to our country to defile our women. Blue-blooded freeloader."

"Have you been drinking?" It could be the only explanation for such bizarre hostility. It seemed Tom was deliberately picking a fight, but Colin didn't pander to spoiled children.

"Why?" Tom demanded. "Is knocking back liquor what British aristocrats do in the middle of the day instead of rolling up their sleeves to make a mark in the world?"

Colin passed a tight smile to Mrs. Schroeder, who looked mortified at Tom's behavior. "Come along, ma'am. I think we'll find the air more pleasing back at the house."

"You do, do you?" Tom snarled.

He swung the shotgun like a bat at the sundial, startling Beatrice and Bianca into flight. Tom hoisted the gun and took aim.

"No!" Colin roared, but it was too late. Resounding blasts of the gun echoed over the clearing. Both birds fell from the sky, dead.

Without thinking, Colin hauled back to punch Tom, but the younger man sidestepped, the smirk on his face infuriating. The brat had come out here with the intention of shooting his birds. Tom pivoted to lope back to the house. Colin lunged forward, tackling him from behind, the shotgun flying off to the side. He delivered a series of swift punches to Tom's gut before rising and snatching the shotgun.

"Children shouldn't play with guns," he spat. "I'll return this to your father and let him decide if you're old enough to have it back."

Tom curled in the grass, gasping for breath, but Colin whirled away. If he lingered any longer, he'd do more than land a few punches. Blistering hot anger pulsed in his veins as he strode toward the first of his slain birds.

Beatrice lay on the grass, the pellet wound an ugly gash in the center of her soft feathers. The pain in his chest made it hard to breathe, but he couldn't simply leave her here. He rolled her onto her back and picked her up by the feet, then did the same for Bianca, carrying them both in one hand and the shotgun in the other. Mrs. Schroeder watched, dumbfounded, clasping a hand to her throat. He wished he hadn't lost his temper before her, but he loved these birds. He'd fed them through an eyedropper for weeks after they'd hatched.

Tom followed close on his heels all the way back to the house, where people had heard the gunshots and come running. Dr. Schroeder was on the patio, as were both elder Drakes.

"My heavens, what has happened?" Margaret asked, her voice appalled as she looked at Beatrice and Bianca dangling from his hand.

"Your son shot my birds," he said between clenched teeth.

"Oh dear," she gasped.

Thomas tried to smooth things over. "We'll gladly buy you a new pair."

"I don't want a new pair!" Colin roared. "These two birds had more valor, more endurance, and more sheer *heart* than your spoiled son has in his entire body." He turned to glare at Tom. "Good luck on your run for Congress. The rest of the world won't be so eager to kiss your rear end as your parents have been."

Thomas stepped forward to defend his son. "I beg your pardon! You are a guest in this home."

"This isn't a home, it's a trophy," Colin spat.

Margaret looked shocked, her jeweled hand flying to her throat. Her ring contained a diamond the size of an acorn. How many people paid exorbitant prices for the Drake valve so Margaret could enjoy that lump of rock on her finger?

Colin couldn't mask the acrimony from his voice. "Your money can buy diamonds and doctors and a fancy country estate." He swallowed hard. "I'm afraid it can even buy you friends, but it can never buy you decency or basic human compassion."

"Now then," Dr. Schroeder interrupted in a calming voice, "I have my medical bag and plenty of tonics for an overexcited temper."

"Keep away from me," Colin growled. "You're no better than the rest of them." By all that was holy, if that revolting psychiatrist took one step closer, Colin would flatten him.

"Calm down!" Mrs. Schroeder said, laying a gentle hand on his arm. "Do you hear me? Please! You must calm down."

Her face was white with alarm, and he understood. Henrietta Schroeder knew exactly what her husband did behind the walls of that sanitarium, and she was warning him.

He took a steadying breath. Time for a cool-blooded response and formal reserve. He'd been trained in it all his life. Anger pulsed, his heart raced, and he wanted to punch the lights out of Tom Jr., but he forced his tone to be calm as he looked at Margaret.

"Your son picked a fight and shot my birds for no reason," he said to both older Drakes. Even speaking the words brought a fresh surge of anger.

"I'm sure it was an accident," Mrs. Drake said.

Colin turned to Tom, whose face still smoldered. "Tom? Was it an accident?"

"I don't have accidents with guns."

"I didn't think so."

"Then you need to apologize, Tom," Margaret said, sounding as though she was reprimanding a six-year-old.

Tom didn't look like he was in the mood to apologize, and Colin didn't want to hear it.

"I'm afraid I am not yet ready to accept an apology from the future congressman. You must be so proud of your son."

An awkward silence descended on the group. The polite thing would be to smooth things over by following Margaret's lead and pretending it was a simple accident, but he wasn't feeling polite.

Margaret twisted a handkerchief between her clenched fingers. "I certainly hope this won't interfere with dinner tonight. You are the guest of honor."

Ah yes, the all-important dinner party to flaunt her titled friend before the local snobs. No wonder Margaret looked panicked. She sensed a storm cloud about to cast a pall over her glittering extravaganza all because of a silly argument with her son.

"I need to bury my birds."

"We can have a servant do that," she said quickly. "Don't worry about it at all."

"I'll do it myself. I wouldn't want to risk them ending up a featured attraction in your conservatory."

The insinuation that his birds might find their way to Margaret's taxidermist and her revolting animal tableau was clear to everyone. Margaret flushed in embarrassment, but he didn't care. She *should* be embarrassed.

"But then you'll come back and dress for dinner, won't you?"

"Of course he will," her husband said in a silky tone. "Sir Beckwith and I have an arrangement. Right?"

An agreement for five thousand dollars in exchange for being trotted out at just such a social event. Every instinct urged Colin to slam out of this house, but he couldn't afford to leave. Two birds in exchange for five thousand dollars. It would be enough to start the most urgent repairs at Whitefriars, even though it meant bartering his companionship in exchange for cold, hard cash.

"I will join you at six o'clock for dinner."

He swallowed back a wave of self-loathing and left to bury Beatrice and Bianca.

Colin carried the birds to a secluded copse of trees half a mile from the house for burial. A groundskeeper loaned him a shovel, and he selected a spot amidst a cluster of mulberry trees, for his pigeons had loved gorging on mulberries. Beatrice and Bianca weren't his first pair of birds. He'd had three sets of homing pigeons since training his first pair when he was fifteen years old, so he'd long known what it was to lose a pet. It was the way he'd lost them that was so infuriating.

After burying the birds, he walked for a solid hour to calm his nerves. The stench of gunpowder lingered in his nose, making him restless and on edge. He couldn't go back among the others until he felt more himself. Perhaps it had been irrational to make such a commotion over a pair of birds, but Tom's pointless act of brutality incensed him like nothing he'd ever experienced.

Tom was a gauche and conceited young man, but his hostility today was drastically out of step with his behavior earlier in the week. Something must have happened, and Colin suspected it related to the mysterious telegram Mr. Moreno received this morning. Maybe Tom had been passed over for the Olympics, spoiling his congressional aspirations.

Colin delayed joining the others for as long as possible by reading the local newspaper in the privacy of his bedroom. The sound of soft laughter and carriages rolling up the drive trickled up from below, but he ignored it. He'd be a lousy conversationalist with anger still roiling in his veins, and reading helped.

His eyes instinctively tracked to the bylines of the stories that had been reported by Reuters. He saw three—one about the untimely death of a thirty-five-year-old mayor, one on the failure of an Italian bank that lost the savings of its investors, and a third on the cholera outbreak in northern India.

His problems weren't so bad. He was giving himself an ulcer over a pair of birds while he sat in the lap of luxury and brooded like a sulky child. He snapped the newspaper closed and got dressed to perform as Margaret Drake's prized guest of honor.

The front hall was crowded with men in formal black suits, waistcoats, gloves, and white ties. The ladies wore fabulous confections of pastel-colored silks, satin, and lace. Perfume wafted through the air, and violin music came from somewhere deep in the house. Margaret spotted Colin the instant he started descending the staircase. The tension in her face eased and her expression was bathed in relief.

"Sir Beckwith," she purred, moving through the crowd with both hands outstretched like Cleopatra slicing through the peasants. After tilting her heavily powdered cheek for his kiss, she guided him straight toward a handsome middle-aged couple. She introduced them as Judge Mason and his wife, Caroline. Ah, descendants of a founding family of America and Mrs. Drake's bête noire.

Mrs. Mason was swathed in pearls while Mrs. Drake glittered in diamonds, but both of them had their knives carefully hidden behind polite smiles. Normally Colin would be fascinated by the sheer human spectacle of watching two privileged women battle for something as ridiculous as a little prestige, but a headache pounded in his skull. This was going to be a long evening. Other guests included the mayor of Saratoga and a bishop of the church. He cast his gaze about in search of Henrietta Schroeder and excused himself as soon as possible.

"There's a little too much drama in that corner," he whispered to Mrs. Schroeder, who smiled in silent understanding.

Mrs. Drake was to be commended. The candlelit rooms were exquisitely decorated with fresh flowers, the hors d'oeuvres were excellent, and despite the whiff of carefully veiled snobbery, everyone seemed to be enjoying themselves. Waiters circulated with trays of honeyed olives and pancetta with goat cheese. A string quartet played on the terrace, the music a perfect accompaniment on a summer's evening as it floated through the open doors.

Mrs. Schroeder sucked in a quick gasp beside Colin. "What is *that man* doing here?" she whispered fiercely.

He followed her gaze, surprised by the hostility in her voice. It was easy to spot the man to whom Henrietta referred. The bullnecked man wore a suit that was too small and a smile too wide. The last time Colin saw such odd stripes on a man's vest, it had been worn by a huckster selling peanuts at a carnival.

Margaret's smile looked frozen in place as she answered Henrietta's question. "I believe that's Mr. Sneed. He is someone Tom invited. I didn't expect him until later in the evening." She summoned a waiter and asked him to lay a thirteenth place setting at the table.

Henrietta's hand was unexpectedly strong as she reached for his. "Sir Beckwith, please . . . this man isn't someone I choose to dine with. If Mr. Drake cannot be persuaded to stand up to Tom Jr. and ask this man to leave, I believe you and I should be on our way. Immediately."

Colin looked down at her curiously. She obviously knew Mr. Sneed, and he suspected the man was here to somehow embarrass him, but Colin had grown up in elite British boarding schools. He knew a few things about how to stand up to a bully.

"Henrietta, you need not worry on my account."

To his surprise, Mr. Sneed inserted himself with no qualms into the glittering crowd, who pulled back at first, not sure what to make of the thickset man with the relentless grin. Tom proved his skill as a politician by smoothing over the situation, introducing Mr. Sneed as an old friend from college and recounting shooting matches he and Mr. Sneed had competed in. At one point, Tom even coaxed him into amusing the crowd by bending a fire iron with his bare hands. The crowd was suitably impressed, and a smattering of applause followed Mr. Sneed's efforts.

"What a . . . unique talent," the judge's wife said.

Mr. Sneed slapped his hands together and grinned directly at Colin. "I've been working real hard."

Henrietta slid closer to him. "Sir Beckwith, I really think it might be a good idea to summon a carriage."

A warning underlay her words. Perhaps Mr. Sneed was simply brought here by a spoiled boy bent on introducing mischief into his parents' assembly, but perhaps it was more sinister.

"Do you know why that man is here?"

She shook her head. "Mr. Sneed works for my husband and did not attend college with Tom Jr. I have no idea why he is here, but it isn't good, and I urge you to leave."

"Henrietta, you might be the kindest woman I've ever met."

"Don't say that." It looked as though her heart was about to break.

Colin would be a fool to ignore her warning, but he couldn't leave yet. Not before he learned enough to incriminate Felix or Tom in the NCC conspiracy. Other than his suspicions regarding an unwise investment in the Nicaraguan route, he had no concrete proof. He glanced around the room. It would be hard for Mr. Sneed to use brute force in front of a judge and the mayor of Saratoga, but Colin would still be on guard. He sent a reassuring smile down to Henrietta.

"No matter what happens, you are a kind woman who has offered me friendship, and it is deeply appreciated. Mr. Sneed is not a problem for me." No man who survived the Boer War could be intimidated by a bully like Mr. Sneed.

Couples proceeded into the dining room by order of rank, so naturally Margaret led him in first.

"Now, Sir Beckwith, let me show you to your seat," she murmured, reaching out to him with her icy hand. She'd been handling him as carefully as a grenade with the pin half-pulled ever since the incident with his pigeons.

The addition of a thirteenth place setting was barely noticeable, but the perfect alignment of the seats was now slightly off-kilter. At least Mr. Sneed was seated at the far end of the table, where Colin could keep an eye on him.

Colin was once again introduced to the guests sitting near him, including Judge Mason's wife and the wife of the mayor of Saratoga. He'd expected nothing less, as Margaret surely intended to milk every minute of the evening by flaunting his presence between the two highest-ranking ladies of the neighborhood.

But all he noticed was Henrietta Schroeder's anxious face opposite him, and he worried about the cause for her alarm.

*L*ucy stared out the carriage window as the sun slipped below the horizon and the countryside darkened. After arriving at the Saratoga train depot, she'd hired a carriage driver to take her to Oakmonte, and they would arrive within the next few minutes.

She already had a plan for talking her way into the mansion. All his life, the only thing Uncle Thomas wanted from her was an agreement to end the lawsuit. That would never happen, especially not after seeing the photograph of her father in a straitjacket, but Thomas didn't know that. She'd dangle the prospect of a settlement in front of him long enough to get inside and let Colin know he was in danger.

She gazed at the rolling green hills dotted with sheep and cattle. Even in the dimming twilight they looked so peaceful, slowly ambling behind their white picket fences, but they were only being fattened up for the slaughter. A part of her wanted to stop the carriage, open the gate, and tell them to run for their lives.

Well, she wasn't here to save cattle. She was here because it was the only way to get Colin out of the clutches of her uncle and his twisted network of associates.

The carriage slowed as it turned onto a narrow lane. The lawn before Oakmonte was brilliantly green, almost like a carpet of emerald velvet. Even in Central Park, the land was dotted with trees and shrubbery, but this lawn was abnormally perfect and unlike anything she'd ever seen. At the far end was a break in the tree line, displaying a wide brick mansion that looked like someplace a king would live.

Or her Uncle Thomas.

She raised her chin as the carriage pulled closer to the house, the clopping of the horse's hooves ratcheting her nerves higher. She could do this. She had no other choice.

The cabbie opened the slot behind the driver's bench and leaned down to speak. "Here or around back, ma'am?"

She pretended not to notice the way he glanced at her dress. It was a well-tailored gown of polished maroon cotton, the finest of all her work gowns, with a narrow band of lace at the collar. It still didn't seem like the sort of dress a lady visiting Oakmonte would wear, but timidity was not going to win her entrance into this house.

"I'll get off here," she said and allowed the cabbie to help her alight. "Please wait for me. It might be a few hours before I can return, but I promise you will be very well compensated." She handed him a few dollars to keep him interested.

She'd taken out the equivalent of a month's rent from her bank before leaving the city. She had no idea how long it would take her to break through to Colin, so she'd come well-supplied.

The cabbie seemed a little doubtful but nodded. "Of course, ma'am."

Her legs felt rubbery as she trudged up the half-flight of steps leading to the house, where a pair of torches illuminated each side of the grand front door. She lowered her head, trying to murmur a brief prayer for strength, but couldn't even find the words.

Please . . .

She raised her chin and pulled the chain of the doorbell. A servant who looked even scarier than Colin's butler opened the door.

"Ma'am?" he asked doubtfully.

Warm candlelight glowed in the foyer. The sounds of a string quartet mingled with laughter from deep in the house, and even from here, she could hear the clinking of silverware. She'd obviously interrupted a party in full swing. All the better.

"I apologize for being late," she said as she stepped into the foyer. "I hope my Uncle Thomas will forgive me."

"Are you an invited guest, ma'am?" the butler asked in an appalled tone.

"I'm Lucy Drake. My uncle has always said he would welcome my visit at any time. Will you let him know that I've arrived?"

There was no change in the butler's skeptical expression. "I will consult with Mr. Drake," he said. "Please wait here."

He turned and disappeared down the hallway, but she had no intention of waiting. She was here to see Colin Beckwith, and that was going to happen now.

She headed down the hall toward the music.

The center of the table was weighed down by an epergne, a massive silver sculpture sporting seven heavy arms laden with small dishes of pastries and fruit. Colin welcomed the ugly monstrosity, for it blocked his view of Tom Jr., who glowered at him from the far end of the table while a footman distributed bowls of turtle soup. It seemed the Drakes felt no need for a formal blessing, as everyone lifted their silverware and began dining immediately. He'd had no appetite all afternoon, but his first sip of delicately seasoned soup proved Margaret had made a good investment in her imported chef.

Mr. Sneed finished his soup in record time, then held the bowl up and asked for a refill. The judge near Colin rambled on about yachting, but Colin couldn't focus on the conversation. He was too busy paying attention to Mr. Sneed, for when the man raised his bowl, his jacket spread open to reveal a pair of handcuffs dangling from his belt.

Definitely not a typical accessory of formal attire.

A disturbance at the front of the room caught his attention. A late arrival? More henchmen from Dr. Schroeder's sanatorium? He turned to look at the woman in the maroon cotton dress and almost choked on his turtle soup. *Lucy?*

"I'm sorry I'm late," Lucy said as she pushed past a servant carrying another bowl of soup for Mr. Sneed. She took several steps into the dining room until she was only a few feet away, but she did not once look at him. "I would not dream of missing the celebration for Mr. Jacob's birthday. This *is* a birthday celebration, isn't it?"

"Get her out of here," Tom Jr. growled.

Colin was about to rise in Lucy's defense but paused just in time. Nobody at the table was aware he and Lucy knew each other, and it was probably important to maintain that impression, at least until he understood why she was here.

Thomas stood and cast a disapproving glance at Lucy. "This is neither the time nor the place, young lady."

"To celebrate your father's birthday?" She gazed at all the faces around the table, who stared at her in open-mouthed confusion. "Jacob Drake's birthday is at the end of June, so when I heard there was a grand celebration at Oakmonte, I simply assumed it was to honor your father. Where is he, if I might ask?"

"You may not—" Thomas began, but Lucy cut him off.

"Because I have a birthday present for him. My brother and I have come to a decision about the lawsuit and would like to talk about it. I think you and your father will be very pleased. May I invite myself to join you?"

"Of all the nerve," Margaret sputtered, but her husband cast her a warning glance.

He gestured to a servant. "Lay another plate," he said, scrutinizing Lucy with curiosity.

His wife was not so conciliatory. She came around the table to give Lucy a scorching glare that could have peeled paint. "Perhaps you would like to wait in the music room until my husband can join you."

"No, I'd actually like to have dinner. I'm so hungry I could eat a horse."

Colin hid a smile at her audacity, but Margaret was not finished. "Perhaps you would like to take a moment and change into something . . . more appropriate."

"Sorry, this is all I've got."

A servant squeezed in a place setting directly beside Uncle Thomas. Lucy was going to be revolted down to her knickers to sit next to a man who made her skin crawl, but she did it. She still wasn't looking at Colin. Why was she here?

Thomas made a grand gesture to the rest of the table. "Carry on, everyone," he said with forced congeniality. "Miss Drake is my niece, and I am looking forward to the chance to get caught up." He lowered his voice, but Colin could still hear him. "All is well in Manhattan, I take it?"

A waiter set a bowl of soup and a goblet of water before Lucy, but she remained tense as she made small talk with her uncle, hinting at a conclusion to the lawsuit. All the while, she fiddled with a spoon but made no attempt to eat.

"A poor relation, I take it?" the judge's wife whispered to

him, amusement dancing in her voice. "Perhaps she and Mr. Sneed can pair up after dinner for a tête-à-tête."

Colin made no response. This evening was turning into a triumph for the fine old families who despised the Drakes. He just wished their contempt didn't come at Lucy's expense. Whatever had driven her here was surely important, for she'd rather chitchat with Genghis Khan than her uncle.

Lucy's odd behavior wasn't doing her any favors. She nervously tapped her spoon against the tablecloth and only gave terse answers to her uncle. If only she would put down the spoon and quit that infernal tapping.

Colin froze, all senses on alert as he focused on Lucy's spoon. She was tapping out code! He turned his head to listen, but it was hard to focus on her taps amidst the clatter of people eating, talking, and laughing.

He closed his eyes and concentrated, finally able to screen out the background noise. She was repeating the same brief phrase over and over.

They know you are a spy.

He opened his eyes and met her gaze. He nodded, and she set the spoon down.

This explained Tom's behavior and why he'd shot the birds. Tom and Felix Moreno had started acting oddly after the delivery of that telegram this morning. Lucy must have intercepted the same telegram that warned them to be on the alert. The message was surely enough to get the police to open an investigation into Felix Moreno's investment in the Nicaraguan route, which meant Colin's responsibilities here were over. No more sick tableaux of stuffed kittens, petulant brats, or fiendish psychiatrists. He and Lucy could leave and take what they knew directly to the police.

He set down his napkin and stood. "Miss Drake, have you ever seen a stuffed-animal tableau?"

"No, I haven't," Lucy replied after only a moment's hesitation.

"Then allow me to show you. It is down the hall in the conservatory. I think you will find it fascinating."

It only took a few steps to reach Lucy's side, but Margaret intercepted them before they could get far from the table. "You're leaving?"

He gave her his most conciliatory smile. "I'm only showing Miss Drake your artistry, for it defies description. Carry on, everyone. We will return shortly."

Lucy needed no prodding to take his arm as he guided her down the hallway and toward the conservatory. He lengthened his stride, for he could hear someone following them. He reached the conservatory and stepped into the darkened interior. Torchlight from the terrace cast a weak illumination into the room. Once inside, he closed the French doors, but they were made entirely of glass panels, and Margaret was only a few steps behind and coming fast.

"What's going on?" he asked quickly.

"I've got a carriage outside," Lucy said. "We need to get away. Tom is planning a shooting accident—"

A rapping on the glass interrupted her. Margaret's face filled one of the small panels as she squinted to see inside, but at least she was alone.

He cracked the door. "I'd like a moment of privacy, please."

"But, Sir Beckwith! There will be plenty of time for this later."

He glanced over her shoulder to confirm no others were coming down the hallway. "I only need a few minutes."

"But the main course hasn't even been served. And we must have a formal toast to your health."

His fist tightened on the doorknob. "This," he said loudly as he pointed to the door, "is a closed door. It will remain closed until I have finished my discussion with Miss Drake. And I won't be returning to the dinner table until I do so."

Margaret's pleading expression soured and was replaced with cold venom. "You're going to regret this," she hissed. "Thomas and I will see to that!"

Colin yanked the door closed, the glass panes rattling in their frames. He didn't take his eyes from Margaret's retreating figure as she hurried back to the dining room, her spine rigid with purpose.

Lucy spoke in a low, hurried voice. "The police went to Mr. Moreno's law office to ask about a plot concerning the Panama Canal. They mentioned you called the matter to their attention. Someone at the law office sent a telegram to Oakmonte and suggested a shooting accident to silence you. The carriage is waiting for us; we should leave now."

He gestured to the door on the far end of the conservatory. "We can get out this way."

"What about Beatrice and Bianca? We need to fetch them."

He pulled her along. "They're dead. Don't ask why, just move."

But it was already too late. Through the glass doors, he spotted Tom Jr. and Mr. Sneed barreling down the hallway and toward the conservatory. Colin grabbed Lucy's hand and sprinted outside, their steps clattering on the flagstone patio. The waiting carriage was within sight, but the others were gaining on them.

"Going so soon?" Tom said.

Lucy's shriek pierced the night air. Tom had her by the elbow, dragging her back toward the conservatory. Colin tightened his grasp on her other arm, ignoring the panic on her face.

"Let her go," he ordered.

They were at a standstill, Lucy the anchor between them. Sneed had the handcuffs out, and Tom pulled back his jacket to reveal a pistol in his belt. It would be impossible to escape through force; Colin had to outsmart them.

"Make this easy on yourself," he began reasonably. "The last thing your mother wants this evening is an ugly scene."

Tom snorted, then let go of Lucy, who staggered a couple steps away. Tom stepped in so close to Colin that their chests almost bumped. His breath smelled of garlic and wine as he flung insults. "As if my mother's party matters when the fate of the nation hangs in the balance. Now I understand. The cops said you overheard messages coming out of the law firm, but it wasn't you who heard them, it was *Lucy*, wasn't it? The two of you have a very cozy arrangement, I see. Don't think you're getting out of this."

Tom backed up a step, pulled out the pistol, and pointed it directly at Colin's chest. Colin's mouth went dry, and he heard Lucy gasp. The barrel of the gun was less than a yard away. Tom was a hothead, but Colin hadn't expected this. Even Sneed looked surprised.

"Don't be a fool," Colin said, tamping down the rising panic. "Ten yards away are a judge, a mayor, and a bishop of the church. They are not your friends. Enough people know about those telegrams to put you in jail for decades. Or . . . you can look the other way while Lucy and I board that carriage. It will give you and Mr. Moreno plenty of time to fabricate an innocent explanation for those bizarre messages we've been hearing."

Tom's eyes sharpened, his face twisted in frustration. Lucy and Mr. Sneed stood motionless, and all Colin could do was wait. A bead of perspiration trickled down the side of his face, but he couldn't move lest he startle Tom into doing something stupid. Finally, Tom pivoted, cocked the pistol, and fired at a potted rosebush, the blast shattering the terra-cotta pot to pieces.

Colin ducked, the blast nearly deafening him. Four more systematic gunshots smashed into the other pots, one after the other. He curled over, muscles seizing so badly he fell to his knees. Panic froze his lungs. This couldn't happen. Not now, not when Lucy was in danger.

"I've still got one more shot," Tom said silkily.

Colin gagged, the stink of gunpowder clogging his throat, making it impossible to breathe. He still couldn't stand. Black spots speckled his vision.

Lucy sank to her knees beside him and put her hands on his shoulders. "Colin! Are you all right?" He wanted to reassure her, but he couldn't. Not yet. He couldn't breathe.

"What kind of *man* are you?" Tom sneered. "How does it feel to cower behind a woman's skirts?"

"Shut up, Tom," Lucy said.

Sweat stung Colin's eyes, but he ignored it, desperate to make his immobile lungs start working again. He finally managed to suck in a loud gulp of air. Then another, the rasping wheeze sounding horribly loud. He braced a hand on Lucy's shoulder, tried to stand, but couldn't quite manage it.

"This is absolutely fascinating," Tom murmured. "You're insane. A pathetic, shaking lunatic. And I've got a doctor here who can prove it."

Colin found his voice. "And you're a criminal. The judge inside will agree with me." He leaned on Lucy and managed to get back to his feet.

Footsteps came running. The door of the conservatory flew open with Thomas in the lead, followed closely by Judge Mason. "What's going on?" Thomas demanded.

Colin's heart still raced and sweat rolled down his face, but he narrowed his gaze and kept a calm tone. "Well, Tom? Shall I tell Judge Mason, or shall you?"

By now others had gathered, standing clustered near the doorway of the conservatory, looking at the decimated rose-bushes and the dirt and pottery shards sprayed across the patio.

Tom's face was twisted in fury as he opened and closed his mouth. Finally he spoke.

"Sir Beckwith didn't think I could hit all five rosebushes. I proved him wrong."

Colin waited to see if Tom would add anything more, but the younger man was already turning and heading back into the house. The assembled guests parted to let him through, their expressions a mix of bewilderment and disapproval. Colin didn't care. All he wanted was to get away. He grabbed his handkerchief to blot his face, making sure his voice was once again steady.

"I'm afraid Miss Drake and I have a pressing engagement back in the city, so we will make our farewells now."

Both Margaret and her husband looked dumbfounded, surely too horrified by Tom's behavior to challenge his departure. He grabbed Lucy's hand and trudged across the unlit grounds toward the carriage, feeling the gaze of a dozen people skewering him in the back, but they weren't going to stop him.

Mercifully, the carriage was already turned around and ready to leave. The cabbie saw them coming and opened the door of the carriage. One minute later, the wheels were rolling, and they were on their way. It was still hard to believe that only a few minutes earlier he'd been discussing yachts while eating turtle soup. Now he was in a race for his life.

"What next?" he asked.

Lucy's face was white in the dim carriage. "I have no idea."

"You don't have a plan?"

"Yes! My plan was to get us both out of Oakmonte alive, and I've done it. I don't know what comes next," she said in a voice bordering on hysteria. He knew the feeling well. The carriage jostled over the cobblestone path leading to the main road, and he craned his neck to peer through the back window, squinting in the darkness for any sign of pursuit. There was nothing.

He drew a steadying breath as the panic that had threatened to choke him only moments earlier began to ease. It wasn't until they passed the road leading toward Albany with no sign of pursuit that he breathed a sigh of relief and asked the cabbie to pull over. The trains had stopped running for the evening, so they offered the driver an obscene amount of money to drive them back to Manhattan.

Over the next hour, Colin listened in astonishment as Lucy told him about the horrifying photograph of her father shackled at Ridgemoor, which confirmed Colin's suspicions about the unholy alliance between the Drakes and Dr. Schroeder. She told him more about the telegram she intercepted and how Sergeant Palmer's investigation had inadvertently put him in danger at Oakmonte. He told her about Beatrice and Bianca.

"Tom was smart enough to figure out we were using the birds to pass information," he said. "It doesn't excuse what he did, but I won't underestimate him again. What really steams me is that I bought a very fine box of Cadbury chocolate for you, but I left it behind. Now your wretched family will feast on it, and you will *still* not appreciate the difference between British and American chocolate." He gave an ironic laugh. "This whole evening was like something out of *The Three Musketeers*. Fun to read about, but perfectly horrible to experience in reality."

"I never read it," Lucy confessed. "When I was a girl I was too engrossed in fairy tales about Prince Charming. Not very realistic, I suppose. I'm a plumber's daughter with calluses on my hands. I wouldn't know the first thing about how to act at a fancy ball or live in a castle."

He ached to think she was ashamed of those calluses. He knew how she'd earned them, and they made him respect her all the more. "The castle part is overrated. They're cold and drafty and cost a fortune in maintenance." Just like the boys' adventure tales, the reality did not live up to the dream.

"Maybe it's just as well, then," Lucy said quietly in the darkness. She didn't need to elaborate. They came from different worlds and could only briefly savor these fleeting, golden moments when their lives intersected. It was impossible to know what lay before them, but it was a certainty they would travel very different paths in life. To try for more would never work.

But it hurt. With everything he had, Colin longed for the freedom to carve out his own destiny rather than be responsible for the one he'd inherited.

"What happens to us once we get home?" she asked. The unquenchable yearning in her voice made it impossible to misinterpret what she was really asking.

"We go our separate ways. I marry some privileged heiress and wish you the very best."

Her chin dipped and she looked away, but in that fleeting moment, he'd seen the flash of disappointment in her eyes, and it hurt, knowing that he was the cause of it. How perfect they could have been together. He closed his eyes, already dreading his return to the real world.

"Lucy, I wish it could be you," he said in an aching voice.

"Me too." Her gaze was luminous as she looked at him in the darkness, a sad smile brimming with wistful longing on her face.

This was what he loved about her. They could be themselves without artifice or apology. The carriage bobbed and rocked over the jutted country roads, and they held hands in companionable silence as the moon rose high. Sometime in the early morning, Lucy slipped into a doze, her head resting on his shoulder and the weight of her body oddly soothing as she slept.

There wasn't another woman on this planet with whom he could simply be silent and not feel compelled to make clever conversation. Soon they would have to part ways, but the memory of his summer with her would never fade. She would forever be his greatest regret.

It was dawn when the cabbie let them off on the outskirts of the city, and they took a streetcar the rest of the way to Greenwich Village. After disembarking a few blocks from her home, he could not resist walking with her the rest of the way. He wanted to prolong this bittersweet interlude as long as possible. A gaggle of youngsters grew impatient with their slow, meandering walk and darted around them, their laughter echoing down the street.

His pace slowed even more as they reached the front steps of her brownstone. She turned to face him, and he smiled down into her face, wishing he were a poet so he could find the right words for what she meant to him.

A man wheeling a coffee pushcart struggled to angle around them, and Colin stepped back to make room on the sidewalk. His eyes followed the vendor as he trudged down the street, the scent of freshly ground coffee beans wafting in the air.

"Sometimes I wish I were a man with no more responsibilities than tending a coffee cart. I would have been free to follow wherever my heart or ambition led."

"You don't really understand," Lucy said as her gaze followed the coffee vendor down the street. "That man isn't free. He probably has a wife and children whose next meal depends on what he sells today. Bad weather or an overturned cart could land him in the poorhouse." Her smile was gentle as she touched his arm. "We're going to be okay, London. Sometimes it hurts to hanker after things that can never be, but I suppose that's the nature of dreamers. Thank you for going to Oakmonte for me. Twice! You were like a hero straight out of the storybooks. No one has ever gone out of their way for me like that, so thank you. A thousand times . . . thank you."

He touched the side of her face, loving her even more for the way she could smile as her heart was breaking. "Take care, Lucy," he said, then turned to walk away.

Lucy was dragging with exhaustion as she unlocked the door to her apartment. A bottle of milk had been delivered to their door, and every muscle ached as she leaned down to pick it up.

Nick must have been at Sunday services, for the apartment was empty when she let herself inside. It was a shame, because she was anxious to tell him everything she'd learned at Oakmonte and had been imagining his astonishment as she unloaded the wealth of information Colin had collected.

She carried the milk to the kitchen and unscrewed the lid. A rancid odor hit her, and she held the bottle at arm's length. It must have been sitting there more than a day for it to have gotten this bad. How could Nick let the milk spoil like this? She dumped it down the drain, running the faucet to rinse the stench away.

Despite her exhaustion, she needed to go to the police station to tell Sergeant Palmer what Colin had gleaned about Mr. Moreno's interest in the Nicaraguan canal. It didn't matter that her feet hurt from wearing these boots for the past twenty-four hours or that she was so tired she thought she could probably sleep straight through next week. If the president's life was in danger, she needed to do something about it. The irony was huge. Ever since he had taken office, Lucy had resented President Roosevelt and his high-handed tactics, but now she couldn't sleep for worrying about him. He was their country's leader, and she'd step in front of a bullet to protect him.

Sergeant Palmer was not in his office. The frazzled clerk at the front desk took her written report and promised to get it before the sergeant's attention "right away" on Monday morning. Given the way the clerk smirked when he said it, Lucy was not terribly optimistic.

Nick still wasn't home by the time she got back to her apartment, and it was after lunchtime. A niggling worry unfurled inside her. Maybe she was being paranoid, but what if Tom and Mr. Moreno had associates in Manhattan? And sent them after Nick? After all, the lamppost leaner had a key to her apartment until Nick pried it away. Maybe others had a key, too. It wasn't like Nick to let milk sit outside their door.

She locked the front door but still didn't feel safe. Blocking the door with the coffee table made her feel better. Though it wasn't heavy enough to stop a determined burglar, it would give her a little advance warning if someone tried to break in.

She plopped onto the sofa. She was exhausted, her heart ached, and her stomach felt full of acid as she worried over Nick. Her anxiety ratcheted higher as the sun set and the apartment darkened. Nick was never out this late on a Sunday evening. Something had happened to him, and she grew paralyzed with anxiety. Even the thought of going to bed was terrifying. How could she undress and sleep with the fear that some unknown force was out there?

It was cold and pitch-dark in the apartment when Lucy heard a scrape in the front door lock. She jerked into standing position. She'd fallen asleep on the sofa! The clock tower on the bank across the street said it was two o'clock in the morning, and someone was breaking in to the apartment. She darted to the kitchen, grabbed a knife, and squatted down behind the counter.

The doorknob twisted. A crack of light from the hallway slanted into the apartment as the door opened, silhouetting a man's shape in the darkness. He muttered a curse as he tripped over the coffee table. She recognized that voice.

"Nick?"

"What in all that is holy is this table doing here?" he groused, rubbing his shin.

"Where have you been?" she asked. "I've been worried sick."

Her worry got even worse when Nick turned on the lamp and she got a look at him. A huge bruise darkened one side of his face and a fresh cut split his lower lip.

It probably hurt when Nick grinned, but a gleam lit his face. "I've been following up on the address we pried out of the lamppost leaner. And surprise, surprise . . . it led me straight to old Jacob Drake."

Lucy listened with amazement as Nick relayed the story.

Far from the extravagant mansion he had expected, their great-uncle lived in a modest townhouse in a respectable neighborhood in Albany. Nick had thought it looked a lot like their own brownstone building here in Greenwich Village. That illusion came to an end when he knocked on the front door, and it was answered by a brick-shaped man wearing shirtsleeves and brass knuckles. He gruffly demanded Nick's name and business. Nick wasn't intimidated.

"Go tell your employer that Nicholas Drake is here, and I want to know why he's been spying on me."

A few minutes later, the old man himself had come into the foyer, propelling himself by pushing on the rims of his wheelchair. He displayed surprising vigor for a man of ninety-two. One might think that a rail-thin man confined to a wheelchair was no threat, but his iron-hard face and fierce eyes made it impossible to underestimate him.

"What do you want?" Jacob had barked.

Nick had glanced at the two henchmen standing on either side of the old man, plus the brass-knuckle-wearing butler who'd opened the door. He wasn't stupid enough to enter the lion's den on his own, and suggested a chat on the front stoop. There was plenty of room for the wheelchair, especially once Nick moved down a few steps toward the sidewalk. It let him be at eye-level with the old man, plus it would be easier to escape should the henchmen get any ideas. Nick wanted an audience, and there was enough foot traffic on the street to provide it.

He had waited until they were outside to tell Jacob that the lamppost leaner's cover had been blown, and demanded to know why Jacob had been spying on them.

Jacob's eyes had narrowed. "You've got a high opinion of yourself if you think I'm so fascinated by you that I'd pay good money to learn more."

"You have a copy of my work schedule, a list of the women I've courted, and the books my sister checked out from the library. You had some photographer follow Lucy around all day and take pictures of her. And that's only the things we know about."

Jacob had leaned forward in his chair, pointing a finger directly in Nick's face. "If I did those things, there's no law against it. Collecting publicly observable information is anyone's right."

"That man was *inside* our apartment!" Nick had fired back. "He stank the place up with cigarette smoke and rummaged through our belongings, and you don't think that's a crime?"

Jacob's sneer was contemptuous. "*If* I hired such a spy, and *if* I've been paying him for the past eighteen months to gather information, I am disappointed it took you so long to notice him. Sadly disappointed."

"You're disappointed in me, old man? I'm embarrassed that we even share the same blood. You stabbed your own brother in the back! No amount of money would ever tear Lucy and me apart like that. I'd live under a bridge before I'd be like you or the snakes living at Oakmonte."

Apparently, the conversation had deteriorated after that. Nick told Lucy how they'd slung insults at each other so vigorously that passersby on the street stopped to gawk.

Nick sat on the sofa, his forearms braced on his legs as he

stared at the carpet between his feet. "He didn't seem happy, Luce. All that money, and he lives in a house swarming with bodyguards but no family."

"So how did you get the black eye?"

Nick sighed. "I guess Jacob isn't used to dealing with anyone who's not interested in kissing his ring. He snapped his fingers, and the butler with the brass knuckles threw me out." At her sympathetic wince, he straightened. "Hey, it took two of them to wrestle me down the steps, and I planted a few bruises of my own."

"But why has Jacob been spying on us all this time?"

Nick glanced toward their dining table, where weak light from the street glinted off half-built plumbing valves. They were evidence that Nick was a worthy heir of their grandfather's talents. They had installed those valves in dozens of buildings, and since Jacob had been spying on them for a considerable amount of time, he knew about their activities and had done nothing to stop it. So what was his goal?

Nick shrugged. "Maybe as he gets closer to the end, he's worried about his legacy. I'd be more worried about the state of my soul, but frankly . . . I don't think he has one."

Colin sat at his desk, a contract for hiring a team of Portuguese translators untouched before him. His biggest professional coup since coming to America would be finalizing this deal to bring thirty Brazilian newspapers into the Reuters family, but his attention kept straying out the open window overlooking Broadway.

Strange—his homing pigeons were dead, but he still felt compelled to leave the window open for them, as though Beatrice and Bianca might fly in at any moment. It had been a week since his return from Oakmonte, but he couldn't bring himself to close that window.

He missed Lucy. He hadn't seen her since he walked her home, for which he was grateful. In a perfect world he would have the freedom to court whoever he pleased. He could find a wife whose curiosity and sense of humor matched his own. He wouldn't need to worry about what kind of dowry or continuing streams of revenue she'd bring to prop up a failing estate and keep ninety loyal tenants gainfully employed.

But it wasn't a perfect world, and he did have to worry about those things.

A knock sounded, and Denby entered. Colin was in no mood for tea, which was the only responsibility his butler was trusted with after the debacle with the AP wires, but the grim expression on Denby's face made it apparent that he wasn't here to deliver tea.

"The morning newspaper, sir." Denby extended the paper, folded open and doubled over to display the gossip column.

Colin's heart plummeted. The moment he'd been fearing had just arrived, and it was far worse than anticipated.

The erratic foibles of visiting British aristocrat Sir C. B. continue to perplex New Yorkers. Last month, in a drunken episode, he collapsed on the floor and sloshed wine on Miss A. W., a woman to whom he is rumored to be engaged. His inexplicable behavior continues to baffle at a fine estate in Saratoga County. This time, Sir C. B. hurled abuse at his hostess, threatened to murder her son, and needed to be placed into the care of a specialist in mental disorders. He stormed off in the middle of a dinner where he was the guest of honor, and some guests speculate incarceration in an asylum is warranted.

Heat gathered inside Colin, causing a sheen of perspiration to break out. This was bad. A glance at the byline showed that the story came through an AP wire, meaning it had already been distributed to over four hundred newspapers across America, and a few hundred in Europe as well. Lucy had saved him from the first story, but there was no way to stop this latest scandal from breaking across the world as fast as electrical currents could carry it.

"Is there anything I can do to assist?" Denby asked in his eternally professional voice. Smooth manners and a fancy title wouldn't be able to stem the tide of this one. He could only hope that Amelia would not believe this claptrap.

"Thank you, Denby. I'll handle this," Colin said in an offhand tone, but he left the office immediately and went straight to the Wooten mansion. There was a chance Amelia hadn't seen the story yet. It would be best if he could prepare her, although how did one put a positive spin on being a candidate for a mental institution?

"Miss Amelia is not at home," the butler said upon answering the door.

"Not at home, or not at home *to me*?" Colin pressed.

The butler was spared an answer when Frank Wooten came striding down the foyer, a grim expression on his face. Amelia's father was a tough man of business, but during their long hours fishing together, Colin liked to imagine they had become genuine friends. Frank's cordial demeanor was absent, a good sign that he'd already seen the gossip column.

"Sir Beckwith, if you would follow me to my office." It was a command, not a request.

Colin nodded and followed, hating the way he felt like a truant child beckoned to a scolding. Frank held open the office door, then tossed Colin the newspaper the instant the doors closed.

"Well?" Frank demanded.

Colin set the paper down on the desk and strolled to the far corner of the book-lined room. "You were there the night I had the accident. You know I wasn't drunk."

Frank gave a dismissive wave of his hand. "I know exactly what happened that night, which only confirmed the information I've gathered about your experience in the Boer War. Do you think I'd let any man get close to my daughter without an in-depth investigation on his character and his background? I don't look down upon a man who suffers aftershocks from having seen service. The world would be a better place if more of our leaders sweat it out on the same battlefields they send our young men to die upon. What I don't understand is the second half of the story. Is that an exaggeration as well?"

The tension in Colin's spine uncoiled a fraction as he strolled to the cold fireplace, braced his hand on the mantelpiece, and told his prospective father-in-law how Tom Jr. had shot his trained homing pigeons, sparing himself nothing in recounting his fury after the event.

"It was a senseless act by a spoiled brat, and I declined his mother's suggestion that I let it roll off my back."

There was a hint of understanding in Frank's expression. He demanded to know more, and Colin felt no embarrassment as he admitted to brooding in his room most of the afternoon. Although Dr. Schroeder had been in attendance, there had been no discussion of committing Colin to Ridgemoor or any other asylum. He knew his story had the ring of authenticity, and soon Frank was nodding in grudging acceptance.

"Here's the thing," the older man said as he twirled his cigar. "My wife wants Amelia to marry someone with a title, and Amelia does, too. I don't give a flying fig about a title. All I want for my daughter is a man who knows what an honest day of labor is like, and so far, you are the only man with a title who has demonstrated that quality. I also like a man who can stand up to bullies. But your title comes with 1.3 million dollars of debt and no viable prospect of bailing it out."

Colin's mouth went dry. He hadn't expected Frank to know quite so much about the situation at Whitefriars. As he scrambled for something to say, Frank continued to reveal an impressive knowledge of Whitefriars' history and condition.

"Two-thirds of the estate's four thousand acres are waterlogged and useless for crops or grazing. The roof is failing and will cost $200,000 to restore. You have ninety tenants, half of whom live in poverty because the land can no longer support crops, and what little comes in from sheep wool has plummeted in value in the face of competition from Australian ranching."

Colin squeezed the mantelpiece so hard his hand hurt. He

was done for. It was one thing for a man to be a bit strapped for cash, but quite another to be saddled with generations of crippling debt. For a man as hard-nosed as Frank Wooten, it was surely unforgiveable.

"Do you think I blame you for failing to work a miracle in the eight years since your father's death? I'm not worried about a few million to spiff up a moldering estate. I live in terror that my daughter will marry an effete aristocrat who will produce children in his image. I want my grandchildren to understand work. Accomplishment. I want them to know the satisfaction that comes from challenging giants and winning. I think you can be that man."

A day that had begun with such disaster was beginning to brighten. Colin needed to demonstrate that he had a plan for changing Whitefriars' fortunes. "There was a time when the back thousand acres supported barley. If I drain the land and plant—"

"Stop," Frank interrupted. "You're thinking like an aristocrat who only follows the model of the past. Think like an American."

Colin blinked. No one had ever asked that of him before. He reframed his plans with American attention to the bottom-line profit. "I could drain the land for cattle—"

An annoyed sigh from Frank cut him off. "Those sodden acres aren't what will make Whitefriars valuable in the coming century. You need to figure out how to capitalize on its real value."

Colin was baffled. If not cattle or crops . . . a horrible thought struck. The entail at Whitefriars could be broken, and it wouldn't be hard to start selling off pieces of the estate, but he cringed. The pittance to be had from selling plots of waterlogged land couldn't even pay to strip the roof, let alone purchase a new one. "If you're thinking of selling off parcels, I cannot approve of cannibalizing the estate."

"I agree. It would be a terrible decision and undermine the long-term stability of the property. I have better plans in mind. But first we have to talk my daughter around. She's in a fit over that newspaper article. Sit down, and let's start strategizing how we can make this work to our advantage."

The eagerness in Frank's eyes was reassuring, and Colin began to feel hope again. It was obvious Frank would be willing to provide the financial leverage to make Whitefriars sound again, but it would come at a cost. Colin had always known this and accepted it . . . so why did it suddenly seem so hard?

And after he listened to the older man outline his vision for Whitefriars, it got even harder. Frank was right—Colin wasn't thinking like an American, for never in a million years could he have envisioned such an audacious plan to rescue the estate and make it grander than it had been since its founding three centuries ago. Not only would Frank's plan restore the mansion, it would allow unheard-of opportunities for his sister and all the other tenants on the estate. The discussion lasted for hours and included everything from how to commence the renovations to starting production on an industry that would capitalize on the estate's strengths.

Men had been marrying for political and economic reasons for centuries, and this would be no different. It wasn't as if marriage to Amelia would be a burden. Whitefriars would become a thriving estate, and over time, Colin's feelings for Lucy would fade. Over time his tenants would have a way out of poverty.

Frank walked him to the door. "None of this will come to pass unless you can convince my daughter to overlook that newspaper article. She and my wife have gone for a ride in the park. Smooth over her ruffled feathers, then invite her to the piano recital at Carnegie Hall tonight. My wife and I will gladly host the two of you in our private box. There can be no better way to show we think the story is nonsense."

Frank's handshake was firm, lending Colin the confidence he needed to go out and start winning Amelia as the first step toward Whitefriars' future.

Amelia and her mother were still out for their ride when Colin arrived at the park's livery stable. Sweet-smelling hay filled the air as he paced, pausing only to stroke the mane of a quarter horse who poked his head outside his stall. Colin lacked the zealous love for riding shared by most of the British aristocracy, but the scent of the stable reminded him of Whitefriars and what he was fighting for.

Only about half the stalls were filled. Colin glanced at the young groom cleaning the hooves of a newly returned horse.

"Has it been a busy day?" he asked. Anything to get his mind off the exquisitely awkward conversation awaiting him the moment Amelia and her mother returned.

"Slow," the groom responded. "It was raining this morning, so I didn't get any tips at all. I'm hoping the afternoon stays clear."

Colin nodded. It seemed everyone had money worries, from those living in castles down to the groom in the stables.

Everyone except Frank Wooten. Colin idly stroked the quarter horse, wondering if the American millionaire's audacious plans for Whitefriars could ever come to pass. The prospect had been appalling at first, but the more Colin thought on it, the better it sounded.

A clatter of hooves heralded the arrival of riders. Amelia was in the forefront, perched in a sidesaddle and wearing a smartly tailored riding habit of cobalt blue. A transparent veil draped from her hat and protected her face from the elements. The vivacity in her flushed cheeks froze the moment she saw him.

Riding behind her came Mrs. Wooten, and disturbingly,

Count Ostrowski brought up the rear of the group. The count smirked when he saw Colin.

Colin raised a hand to assist Amelia from her mount, but she ignored it and dismounted on her own. "I'm surprised to see you here," she said coolly.

Two stable boys emerged to lead the horses back to the stalls. Colin would have preferred not to have an audience for this, but both Mrs. Wooten and the count showed no interest in granting them any privacy.

"Your father let me know you'd be here. Can I impose on you for a short walk?"

Amelia tossed a riding crop to one of the stable boys. "I don't think there'd be any point. I will be taking tea with Count Ostrowski as soon as I have the chance to freshen up."

Count Ostrowski was precisely the sort of effete aristocrat Frank Wooten loathed. The fine tailoring of his riding clothes gave him an impressive figure, but already signs of dissipation softened the lines of his jaw, testament to too much fine dining and endless rounds of weekend parties.

"Perhaps we can take a quick stroll down to the fountain and back," Colin pressed. "I need to speak to you in private."

"If it's about the story in the newspaper, there is no need."

He swallowed hard, sensing his worst fear was hurtling straight toward him.

Amelia still had not looked at him. She pinched the fingertips of her riding gloves to wiggle them off. "This morning was the first time I have ever seen myself alluded to in print, and it was associated with a man who appears to be a candidate for a lunatic asylum. I'm sure you can understand that I had hoped for more."

The count covered his laughter with a handkerchief in a poor attempt to pretend it was a cough. The stable boys listened with fascination, but at least they weren't laughing.

"You *know* I wasn't drunk that night," Colin whispered in an urgent tone.

"Does the rest of New York know that?" Amelia lifted her chin and met his gaze. She was furious.

"The rest of New York knows I have been holding down a demanding position at the most respected news agency in the world."

The count pressed his handkerchief closer to his nose. "Indeed. I thought I sensed the stink of newspaper ink spoiling the air."

To Colin's annoyance, Amelia flashed the count a quick smile. Apparently her father's work ethic had failed to make an impression on her.

"Yes, I carry the scent of newspaper ink," he said. "I love that smell. I love the smell of glue on a bookbinding and the sound it makes when I open a new book for the first time. I love walking into a library filled with a millennia of literature and inspiration and unanswered questions. And nothing makes me prouder than walking into the Reuters office where dozens of people work to spread insight about the world to anyone curious enough to open a newspaper."

The count rolled his eyes. "Buy him a bookstore and put the poor sot out of his misery."

Colin ignored him and glanced at Mrs. Wooten, who seemed to be in lockstep with her daughter. Amelia finally looked at him.

"Colin, I'm sure you can see that this situation has become untenable."

"Even though the insinuations in the articles aren't true?"

Her face softened, but her chin remained high. "Even so. I'm sure you understand that a woman's reputation hinges on her husband. This is the most important decision of my life, and I simply don't see a way forward for us."

He stood as still as if he'd been carved from stone as she passed her gloves to a groom and headed toward a carriage. Everything he'd hoped for was slipping away. Frank Wooten would not be interested in funding the grand renovation of Whitefriars if his daughter decided to be a Polish countess. Would Count Ostrowski make her happy? His title was older and grander than Colin's, but would he make her a good husband? Amelia had a spark of curiosity and intelligence that would wither if she had nothing to nourish it other than a title.

The trio left without leaving the stable boys a tip. Colin reached into his pocket and took care of it. This was probably the last time he would ever see Amelia, and she couldn't even spare him a parting word.

Chapter
NINETEEN

Colin headed straight to Lucy's office. It was quite possibly the last place he should be visiting, but she was the only real friend he had in New York, and he didn't want to be alone right now.

As usual, the AP's main office was alive with thousands of electronic clicks cascading through the air. Orderly rows of telegraph operators manned their stations like soldiers lined up for duty. None of them looked up as he wended his way toward Lucy's station. He stood directly behind her and admired her posture, so ramrod straight, as she transcribed the message on her wire. He waited until she closed the connection and wrote the final words on her pad of paper.

"Hello, Miss Drake."

She whirled around, and his heart tripped at the surprised delight in her eyes, but she regained her composure quickly.

"Hello, London," she said fondly. He had to stifle the impulse to haul her to her feet and sweep her into an embrace. The invisible thread that tied them together was electric and alive.

It was too crowded in here to talk, and he just wanted to be alone with her. "Can I buy you lunch? I'm dying to find out what's happening with your case."

Ten minutes later, they were downstairs in the building's cafeteria. He had to appreciate the gusto with which she attacked her plate of pork tenderloins with currant jelly. He'd been unimpressed when he sawed into the pork, and even less so after his first bite. He set down his fork, having no interest in finishing the meal, which she found amusing.

"You can be such a snob," she teased. "Everything served in the cafeteria is ambrosia compared to what Nick and I have for dinner, which usually comes out of a can."

"Well, finish quickly and give me an update on the case. If you hadn't noticed, I'm on tenterhooks over here."

She sighed. "I visited the police precinct on Monday, and the clerk told me Sergeant Palmer has turned the case over to the Secret Service. I haven't been able to see him again. I wanted to pass on that Tom knows I've overheard his messages and is probably fabricating some kind of story to explain his behavior, and not to fall for it. The clerk keeps saying the sergeant is very busy and I should wait for him to contact me. Maybe it would help if you came with me?"

Unlikely. His reputation had just taken quite a beating, and in the coming days it was going to get worse. Scandalous gossip tended to trigger plenty of speculation.

"Did you have a chance to peruse the newspapers this morning?" he asked. "The gossip column was lively. Plenty of salacious details about a visiting baronet misbehaving in public."

She dropped her fork with a clatter. "No!" The horror mingled with sympathy on her face made him feel even worse. He tried to affect a nonchalant tone.

"Miss Wooten was less than delighted with the story, as it alluded to her and hinted at a possible engagement. That's all in the past now."

Lucy pushed back her plate, as though she had lost her appetite. She looked truly sorry on his behalf, which was exceedingly generous of her. "What happens now?" she asked, and his wayward thoughts took flight.

You and I run off together. We head for the wilds of the Dakota territories and live like gypsies. We forget about responsibilities and live like we are the only two people in the world. Eat grapes straight off the vine; swim in the moonlight; dance until dawn.

He said none of it.

"I'll find somebody else," he finally replied. "New York is filled with young women who will bring a dowry along with them, and I'm afraid it is the primary criteria I need in a future wife." He'd have to lower his sights a notch, but even with a dinged-up reputation, he still had plenty of opportunity here.

It was hard to breathe with this crippling weight on his chest. He couldn't summon up a smile or a spark of energy, and Lucy seemed equally demoralized.

"And when shall the hunt for your next heiress begin?" she asked.

"Soon. This weekend I suppose I shall make the rounds on the social circuit."

"But not today . . ." The way her sentence dangled was a warning that she was up to something.

"Not today," he confirmed, and a hint of a smile lightened her features.

"Have you ever played hooky?" she asked.

"What's hooky?"

"Going absent without leave. Checking out from the office early. Escaping for the day."

Recognition dawned. "In England we call it French leave."

Lucy laughed. "Shall we play French leave? You look like you could use an escape from this place, and for once we can

226

have a few hours with a clean conscience. With no expectations of forever and no nagging guilt over heiresses or obligations to family responsibility. Just two people who want to steal some time together before the rest of the world takes us captive again."

He vaulted from the bench, abandoning their half-eaten lunches. She squealed in delight as he grabbed her arm and tugged her into a run toward the front door and out into a surprisingly cool June afternoon. They dashed to the nearest trolley stop.

"What shall we do?" he asked eagerly. This afternoon was going to be their one and only chance to be together, and he wanted it to be perfect for her. "Suggest your wildest daydreams, and I shall make it happen. Shopping on the Ladies' Mile? Fine dining at Delmonico's? Perhaps a private tour of the Brooklyn Museum? I know the director and can make it happen."

A light breeze tugged at the tendrils framing her face as she smiled up at him. Once again he was bowled over by her fresh-faced beauty. "I think I'd just like an ordinary day in the park. I don't want anything fancy. Just you."

Twenty minutes later, they wandered the trails of Central Park. They ate pretzels and fed the ducks on the pond. They tried to find the exact spot where they'd first met that snowy December night seven months earlier, when Colin stood half-frozen while she haggled over the price of chestnuts. Everything looked so different now, and after circling the pond twice, they couldn't be certain where they'd first met. Lucy put her foot down next to a blooming hydrangea bush and declared this was the spot, and he should kiss her immediately. He obliged, then found another spot a few acres later he thought might be the actual place, which required another round of kisses.

After a while they lay flat on their backs on Pilgrim Hill to stare at the cloud formations overhead.

"What did you dream of when you were a little girl?" he asked.

She laughed a little. "I wanted to grow up to be a great plumber." His eyes widened in surprise, and she rolled onto her side to grin at him. "Nick was training to be a plumber, my father was a plumber, and my grandfather was legendary in the field, so *of course* I wanted to be a plumber. But as much as I adore the men down at the hog house, I don't think they'd be ready to accept a woman working alongside them. I settled for telegraphy."

"Was it a better choice?" he asked.

"Absolutely! What other job lets me hear news from all over the world before it even hits the newspapers? I love it, actually."

He did, too. And he loved everything about this day. For a few hours there were no shackles or obligations, and no pretenses. He didn't have to disguise his emotions with Lucy or worry about revealing too much, for she already knew all his embarrassing secrets and didn't care. He didn't want this afternoon to end and kept careful watch on the shadows as they grew longer across the lawn. He traced patterns on the back of her hand.

"We'll need to head back soon," she finally said.

"Why?" he asked and managed to buy another lazy hour on the grass with her. As the sky darkened and it became impossible to linger any longer, they clasped hands and proceeded as slowly as possible toward Columbus Circle, where the park ended and the city began. There was no more avoiding it.

"This is it, then," Lucy said, trying to smile through the sadness in her voice.

"I suppose so." His mouth turned down, and for the life of him, he couldn't return her smile.

"Come on, London," she said with a nudge. "I need to see a little of that famous cool composure."

He shrugged helplessly. "I guess I've been in America too long."

They kissed like mad beneath the statue of Christopher Columbus. Pedestrians jostled them, and a couple of newsboys hooted, but they didn't care. For these last final seconds, the rest of the world simply didn't matter.

Colin pulled back and gazed down at her face. She smiled with humor and affection blazing in her incomparable flashing eyes. This was it. This was exactly how he wanted to remember her for all time.

"Good-bye, Lucy."

"Good-bye, Colin. Best of luck with everything."

Pulling away to walk toward his house was a physical ache he would never forget.

*N*ick plunked the dish of chipped beef on the table in front of Lucy, and she was grateful the bowl didn't shatter. He was still steaming mad at her for returning from the park so late, and he barely said a word to her as he slammed about the kitchen, opening the tin of meat and heating it for their dinner. Chipped beef in mushroom sauce was one of the better canned meals, but she didn't have much of an appetite. Parting from Colin for the final time was still too fresh. She poked at the chipped beef with the tines of her fork, wondering if she'd ever have an appetite again.

The knock at the door startled them both, especially when an authoritative voice called out, "New York City Police."

Nick opened the door to a uniformed officer.

"I'm looking for Lucy Drake," he said.

"That's me." She was disappointed it wasn't Sergeant Palmer, but her dismay vanished with his next words.

"Officer Garrett Wolfe," the heavy-set man introduced himself. "You are wanted down at the precinct. Sergeant Palmer is back and anxious to interview you. He's very interested in the report you made last week and needs to follow up."

Thank heavens! What a relief it would be to finally have the attention of someone who could get to the bottom of this. "He wants to meet with me now?"

"Now. We've got a carriage downstairs that will take you straight over."

"I'll go with you," Nick said, already reaching for his jacket. Lucy abandoned her uneaten chipped beef on the table and followed Nick and the officer downstairs.

An enclosed brougham carriage awaited them on the street. Another police officer was already on the driver's box, his horse whip propped at his side.

Officer Wolfe opened the door of the compact carriage, then turned to her. "We're taking this old gent to the station to file a report about a burglary. There won't be room for your brother."

A glance inside the carriage confirmed it. The dapper old gentleman was rail-thin and didn't take up much room, but another burly police officer took up the rest of the bench. Once she and Officer Wolfe were aboard, it would be impossible to fit a fifth person in the compact carriage. But she didn't want to leave without Nick.

He didn't want her to either. "I'll go hire a hack from the livery," Nick said. "It won't even take five minutes. Wait for me."

Lucy glanced at Officer Wolfe, who nodded in agreement. The livery always had cabbies lined up for hire, and it would only take a few moments for Nick to join them, but Officer Wolfe seemed impatient. He grumbled as Nick darted through the pedestrians on the street to get to the cabbies. When Nick was a few blocks down, the officer grasped her elbow.

"Let's get you onboard. We can leave as soon as your brother gets back."

She'd much rather wait on the street than inside a warm carriage. Lucy tried to tug her arm away, but instead of releasing her, Officer Wolfe squeezed tighter and propelled her toward the carriage.

"Let go of me," she sputtered, trying to pull away. The officer shoved harder, and panic set in. He was fighting her, using all of his weight to force her inside the cramped carriage.

"Nick!" she screamed. "Nick, help!"

But she was already inside the carriage, and it started moving even as Officer Wolfe hung out the open door. She kept screaming, banging on the side of the carriage, anything to get away. A couple people on the street turned to look with curiosity, but no one intervened.

The carriage door slammed shut, and Officer Wolfe's bulk pressed her against the side of the carriage, making it impossible to thrash her way toward the only exit on the other side of him.

"Just shut up, and you'll be okay," he growled.

She doubted it. The carriage sped through the streets as it weaved around lumbering wagons and slow-moving street trolleys. The elderly man across from her made no comment, nor did he seem particularly surprised by Officer Wolfe's aggressive actions. She scooted as far over on the bench as possible, glaring at the officer.

"Who are you?" she demanded. "Why are you doing this?" Although, heaven help her, she already knew. He'd probably been sent by the same people who'd suggested a "shooting accident" as a way to shut Colin up. Now they had her, and she had no prayer of overpowering these two brawny men.

"I told you to shut up," the man pretending to be a New York City police officer growled. Had Nick seen her being forced into the carriage? Or perhaps some of the bystanders would tell him what happened when he returned with a cab? It was her only hope.

She turned to the elderly man across from her, who watched her through pale gray eyes that seemed oddly kind. He was familiar to her, but she couldn't place him.

"It's going to be all right, my dear," he soothed.

"Have we met?"

"Not formally," he said in that cashmere voice. He gestured to the large man sitting next to him. "Officer Sneed and I are taking you someplace where you can be properly cared for. Where you can get the rest you've been needing."

Her heart nearly stopped, for she finally remembered him from that fancy dinner party at Oakmonte. He was the doctor in charge of the mental institution at Ridgemoor, and the hideous Mr. Sneed was his henchman.

Fear caused a tremble to begin deep inside. Her hands turned icy as they curled into fists, and every instinct urged her to run, but she was trapped in a space so confined she could barely draw a breath. The carriage continued to bump, jolt, and zigzag through the streets.

"You have no right to take me anywhere," she said.

A gentle spray of wrinkles fanned out from the old man's eyes as he smiled and took a sheaf of papers from his coat pocket. "These papers are signed by your uncle, who believes you are a danger both to yourself and others. As your legal guardian, Thomas Drake has the ability to authorize your incarceration. Therefore, under the state law of New York, I am obligated to take you to a secure facility immediately."

"Thomas Drake isn't my guardian," she sputtered. Fear caused her voice to quake. "I'm not his ward, I'm not a danger to anybody, and I am *not* going to Ridgemoor."

She lunged for the door handle, but both henchmen shoved her back onto the bench. Their combined bulk probably amounted to four times her weight, and she was no challenge for them. But she had to get out of this carriage before being delivered to Ridgemoor.

The carriage suddenly lurched sideways, dumping her against Officer Wolfe. Someone had jumped on the running board!

The carriage window shattered as a brick smashed through it, followed by a hand reaching for the door handle.

"Nick!" Lucy shouted.

"Back off," Wolfe yelled, pounding on Nick's hand as he tried to twist open the latch. The door swung open, and Nick dangled from it at a dangerous angle as the carriage careened down the street. Wolfe lunged at him, knocking them both out of the carriage and sending them rolling across the street.

"Jump, Lucy!"

She didn't hesitate. Her legs buckled at the impact, and she scraped her hands on the cobblestones, but she scrambled to her feet just in time to see Nick deliver a swift kick to Wolfe's groin and make a getaway.

"Run!" Nick yelled as he grabbed her hand and sprinted toward the sidewalk. They angled around two pushcarts and a vegetable stall. They had a head start, but Wolfe was gaining on them.

"Stop them!" Wolfe shouted. "Thieves!"

A fishmonger stepped away from his stall and moved into the center of the sidewalk, squatting low and stretching his arms wide to block them.

"Split apart," she told Nick.

He obeyed. The fishmonger lunged for Nick as they ran past, but Nick made a flying leap over a rack of newspapers and evaded him. Lucy crashed into an applecart as they rounded the corner. She hadn't meant to tip it over, but at least the apples scattered across the walkway would slow their pursuers.

"Thieves!" Sneed bellowed. "Stop them in the name of the law!"

A postman threw down his bag and made a grab for Nick, who barely escaped, but more onlookers had joined the chase.

"Down the alley," Nick panted. Everyone on the street was trying to stop them, but she and Nick had fear on their side as they dashed down the alley at a pace the bystanders couldn't match. The alley was almost deserted, and she hiked up her skirts and ran after Nick.

"They went that way," someone shouted behind her. Everyone was helping Sneed and Wolfe, while she and Nick couldn't look any guiltier as they fled like crooks. Nick cut across another alley and started tracking south again. Their pursuers were still a few blocks away, and Nick's haphazard flight through the back alleys bought them a little lead time, but bystanders continued pointing their pursuers in the right direction.

"Let's head back to the main street," Nick panted as he rounded a bend.

"Are you sure?" It didn't seem smart. There were so many more people there to intercept them.

"I know what I'm doing."

There was no choice but to trust him. She ran close behind him as they reached the main street again. Rather than stick to the sidewalk, Nick dashed straight into the middle of the street, veering around carriages and jumping over potholes. His long legs devoured the ground while she scrambled after him, hoisting her skirts high as she ran.

"Slow down!" she shouted, for getting separated terrified her. Nick was so far ahead he might not even know if Wolfe caught her.

"Can't!" Nick shouted without breaking his stride. They ran another five blocks before he squatted down in the middle of the street and she understood his plan. He worked his fingers beneath the grill of a manhole cover, tugging at it with all his might. By the time she reached him, he had it off and shoved aside.

"You first," Nick panted.

She stared down the hole. Beyond the first few feet, the sewer was completely black except for light glinting on some water far below.

"Go on," Nick urged. "It's only fifteen feet down, and it won't be too bad. We haven't got any choice, Luce."

He was right. From behind her she heard the shouting of the two henchmen. "Stop them!" Sneed shouted. "Thieves! Stop them!"

It was all she needed to hear. Draping her skirts over an arm, she turned and descended the ladder, sinking lower into the brick-lined tunnel. How much farther did this go down? Nick had said it was only fifteen feet, but it seemed forever. It got even darker when Nick's body blocked the opening as he followed her down.

She reached the bottom with a splash. It felt like only an inch or so, but she cringed at the thought of what she'd just stepped into. Within moments the damp seeped through the leather of her shoes, but there was nowhere else to stand.

Nick grunted as he dragged the manhole cover back into place, the clang echoing loudly in the tunnel. The metal rungs thrummed as Nick lowered himself, but she couldn't see a thing in the darkness. A splash sounded as he joined her at the bottom of the ladder.

"What now?" She was pressed against him shoulder to hip, squashed together in the small, damp chamber. He elbowed her in the ribs as he fumbled around, and a moment later a beam of light flared between them. Nick had his flashlight! He always took a dry-cell battery torch when working underground, and thank heavens he still had it from his work that day. They were in a brick-lined vertical shaft, a metal ladder anchored to the wall. Anyone looking through the grill of the manhole cover would see them trapped down here like sardines in a tin.

Nick leaned over to shine his flashlight down a horizontal tunnel leading both east and west. The arched opening wasn't even four feet high.

"This tunnel will join up with the main line within a few

blocks," he said. "If they follow us down, there's a fifty-percent chance they'll go down the wrong tunnel. Let's move. Fast."

"Are you serious?"

He grinned. "Look on the bright side . . . at least it rained this morning."

He was right. The stormy weather meant that fresh rainwater had flushed the sluggish waste that sometimes built up in the sewer system. The dank, musty air was bad but not unbearable.

Nick squatted onto his haunches, ducked his head, and disappeared into the tunnel, taking the light with him. She gathered her skirts up to her hips, for it was going to be a wet slog. She hunkered down and waded into the tunnel.

She braced one hand on a grainy brick wall for balance, while the other arm kept her skirts out of the way. It didn't take long for her legs to start trembling from the strain of their unnatural position as she waddled along the passageway.

"How far do we need to go?" she asked.

"Just keep moving. I doubt they'll follow us down, but if they do, I want us to escape into a sewer main."

Lucy wasn't exactly sure what that meant, but Nick knew his way around this underground city as well as anyone in the world. There were literally hundreds of miles of sewers, water tunnels, and work passageways snaking beneath the city, and it would be easy to get lost down here.

The tunnel sloped downward, and the water was getting deeper. The air carried a sulfuric scent, but it wasn't as awful as she feared it would be. More disconcerting was simply the knowledge that she was deep beneath the city street, with millions of pounds of earth, rock, and buildings above her head as she traveled through this underground labyrinth.

Every few yards an open pipe in the wall dribbled liquid into the sewer, leaving dark, algae-covered stains on the brick. The muscles in her neck and shoulders screamed, and she didn't know how much farther she could duck-walk through these cramped tunnels.

Nick slowed and turned to her, panting as he rested against the sewer wall. "Let's stop here," he said. "I'm guessing we're about halfway to the sewer main, but maybe they won't follow us."

She nodded, breathing too hard to respond. She pressed her back against the sewer wall, almost as if she were sitting in a chair, using the free moment to rub the abused muscles in her neck. The enclosed brick tunnel acted as an echo chamber, magnifying the sound of their ragged breaths. A few inches away, a pipe in the wall dribbled a steady rivulet of water. She wrinkled her nose and held her breath.

"Is that water coming from toilets?" she asked.

"Mostly not."

"Mostly?" She tried not to sound too appalled. "But some of it could be?"

"Just think of it as mostly rainwater, okay?" When she looked at him skeptically, he stifled a laugh. "Look, we're already up to our ankles in it, Luce. Might as well make the best of things. Just keep thinking of it as mostly rainwater."

He was right. She'd rather be in this underground maze than on her way to Ridgemoor.

The thin trickle of water at the bottom of the tunnel had grown to a more substantial stream. Each pipe fed more water into the system, and it would surely grow even deeper as they traveled down toward the sewer main.

A moment later, Lucy heard the heavy clang she'd feared coming from the far end of the tunnel. Wolfe and Sneed were still after them.

"Come on back, Miss Drake," one of them yelled, his voice echoing off the damp bricks. "If you make us go in after you, there's no telling what Dr. Schroeder will do once we catch you. Make it easy on yourself and come back."

She and Nick immediately set off farther down the tunnel, sloshing through the deepening water with renewed urgency. Every muscle in her body hurt, but at least they were both smaller and more nimble than the men following them.

A few minutes later, Nick said the words she'd been waiting for. "We're here."

They had arrived where the lateral tunnel opened into the sewer main. It actually hurt as she stood upright, her cramped neck muscles twinging in relief as she stepped inside. What a strange space they had just wandered into. It was at least ten feet tall and almost as wide, but it narrowed at both the top and the bottom, giving it an egg-shaped look. A few feet of water flowed in the bottom of the tunnel. Instead of brick, the walls were lined with concrete, and it wasn't pitch black in here. Yellow carbon arc lamps were attached to the walls, casting dim illumination down the cavernous space. Nick clicked off his flashlight.

"Who the heck are you?" a rough voice barked.

Lucy nearly jumped out of her skin, reaching for Nick in a panic. She followed the sound of the voice and saw two men slumped against the side of the wall. Vagabonds.

The two men lay sprawled atop some up-ended old crates nudged against the wall, but one rose to his feet, brandishing a knife. The other remained sprawled on his crate, peering at them through owlish eyes in his unshaven face.

"We're just passing through," Nick said. He surely had more experience with the desperate people who made their homes in this weird underworld.

"Then keep on passing," the vagabond with the knife growled. "This stretch is our territory, all the way up to the 59th Street sewer line."

Nick held up his hands in a placating gesture. "We don't mean to encroach. All I want to know is when the tidal gate was last opened."

"Why should I answer?"

Nick reached into his pocket and gave the man a dollar. That was all it took.

"Almost a day," the owlish man said.

"Then you and your friend might want to get moving," Nick said. "I have a feeling it's going to be opened in the very near future. It won't be pretty."

Lucy had a vague understanding of what they were talking about. The sewer system in New York depended on high tides from the rivers to wash the tunnels clean. Various screening chambers throughout the system filtered solid waste, where it was sent to pumping and lift stations for disposal. Then huge sluice gates opened, releasing the tidal water and flushing the system clean, carrying the water all the way out into the bay.

The vagabond put his knife away and scooped up his crate. The owlish one gathered a few bags of belongings, surely accustomed to avoiding the rush of discharge water. They headed for shelter in the side tunnel she and Nick had just traversed.

"There are some unsavory folks heading down that tunnel," Nick said, reaching into his pocket for a few more coins. "They're after us. I'd appreciate it if you sent them downstream instead of up."

The vagabond reached for the coins. "You got it. Just keep moving and don't come back. This is our territory." The pair disappeared into the intersecting tunnel.

"You're welcome to it," Nick muttered, already setting off upstream. "Let's hurry. It's not easy to open those tidal gates, and we need to put as much distance as possible between us and your friends."

There was no avoiding it. She hiked up her skirts and headed into the main sewer chamber, where the water reached above her knees, and began slogging forward. By heaven, it stank in there. The damp soaked into her clothes and her skin. This tunnel sloped uphill, and they were running against the stream, making the footing even more treacherous. Sounds of thrashing from the side tunnel behind them terrified her. Was it the two vagabonds or the henchmen from the insane asylum?

She couldn't worry about it, for it was hard enough maintaining her balance in the slick concrete tunnel as she waded forward. Flecks of water spattered onto her chest and face, but she couldn't slow down. Heaven only knew how long it would take Nick to figure out how to open the gate.

She was grateful for the light, but it made them painfully visible to their pursuers. She risked a quick backward glance. The henchmen hadn't reached the main tunnel yet, but she lost her balance and fell to her knees, spared from falling face first into the water only by dropping her skirts and bracing her hands on the slimy floor. It was so cold! Her teeth were chattering by the time she got upright and on her way again. Traveling was even harder with sodden skirts. Nick was quite a distance ahead of her, but at least she was in no danger of getting lost, for the sewer only went in one direction.

The water tapered off the higher they traveled. How far had they gone? A mile? Two? At least the water had become shallower, barely reaching her ankles.

She sighed in relief when she saw the mighty tidal gate ahead of her. Made of cast iron and timber beams, it blocked the entire sewer main. Nick scrambled up the concrete platform that framed either side of the gate and hunkered down to examine the hinges holding it closed. She staggered up the short flight of steps to stand beside him.

"Can I help?" she gasped with the last of her breath. Nick passed her the flashlight.

"Shine it on the hinges," he said in a low voice. His tone worried her. He didn't know what he was doing, and he didn't have any tools.

The gate looked like a portcullis that could be raised and lowered in place. The heavy metal door surely weighed hundreds of pounds, but coiled torsion springs would help lift it on the metal rails framing each side of the gate. If he could open it, they'd be protected here on the ledge as the flood released.

Nick unscrewed the caps protecting the levers from water, but tugged in vain on the iron lever. It wouldn't budge. This door held back thousands of pounds of water, and it was designed to withstand pressure.

Their pursuers came into view, slogging through the knee-deep water far down the tunnel, but they'd be here soon. Even now she could hear their grunts and splashing as they got closer. She bit back the temptation to urge Nick to hurry, for he was doing all he could, groaning with effort as he pulled on the lever. The cords in his neck bulged, and his face twisted into a grimace. This job usually required a crowbar to lift the lever, and Nick had only his bare hands.

Mr. Sneed was coming closer, his massive body lunging from side to side as he trudged up the tunnel. Wolfe was only a few yards behind.

"I need your skirt, Luce," Nick said. She squatted down, and he grabbed a hunk of wet fabric to wrap around the lever. *Please*, she prayed.

The men were less than fifty yards away, then forty. Nick bellowed, pulling on the lever with all his weight. The squeak from the lever was puny, but it sent her heart soaring. It must have renewed Nick's spirits too, for he roared louder as he tugged, the lever slowly moving forward. The torsion springs engaged, and the gate began lifting. Pressurized water spurted from the bottom few inches with a mighty hiss, foaming white in the dim chamber. As the springs fully engaged, the gate hauled upward to its fully open position.

A deafening wall of water thundered down the tunnel. She

caught a quick glimpse of the henchmen, their faces frozen in horror as the wall of water barreled toward them. She and Nick clung to each other on the raised platform, the spray of water soaking them as it gushed with the force of a waterfall. Through the mist, she spotted Sneed and Wolfe. They turned to flee but couldn't outrun the water that scooped them up, sending them bobbing down the tunnel like two corks in a whirlpool.

It took over a minute for the pressurized water to slow and finally ease to a trickle.

"What will happen to them?" she asked.

Nick snorted. "They've got a bumpy ride all the way to the river. If they manage to keep their head above water, that is."

She didn't pity them. They had been merciless in trying to slam her into an insane asylum, and only by Nick's efforts and the grace of God had she been spared. Exhaustion set in, and she sagged against the cold metal of the tidal gate frame, barely able to keep standing.

"What will happen to *us*?" she asked, for even though the immediate danger had passed, they were still deep underground in a maze of convoluted tunnels.

Nick's face was pensive as he scanned the dimly lit space. "We're near the East Side hog house, but the stairwell is locked until dawn. We'd better make ourselves comfortable until the morning crew gets here."

Her clothes were wet, cold, and filthy. She barely had the energy to lift her hand to wipe a drop of water from the end of her nose.

"Mostly rainwater, huh?"

Nick's teeth gleamed white in the dim light. "Mostly rainwater," he affirmed.

She nodded. It could be a lot worse.

olin tried to focus on a revised contract with a newspaper in Richmond, but his mind kept straying to Lucy Drake. Their stolen afternoon yesterday in Central Park had been the most magical and bittersweet few hours of his life. Had she felt the same? The way she clung to him on the edge of Columbus Circle seemed as if she was trying to memorize the perfection of the moment, just as he was.

Or perhaps he was reading too much into it. Perhaps she had gone to work this morning as usual and never thought twice about him.

The clang of the telephone interrupted his thoughts. It was a rude interruption, but just as well. He pressed the polished wood receiver to his ear. "Beckwith here."

An audible sigh of relief sounded through the telephone. "Thank heavens I've found you!"

"Who is this?"

"Henrietta Schroeder," the voice said. "You must hurry. Something very bad is in the works. Thomas Drake was over here last night, convincing my husband to do something terrible to that young lady who came to Oakmonte."

"Lucy?"

"Was that her name? Whoever she is, I'm afraid she is in danger. After speaking with Thomas, my husband summoned that awful Mr. Sneed, which only happens when a patient needs restraining at Ridgemoor."

She spoke so quickly it was hard to keep up with her, and the noise from his open window made it difficult to hear. He covered one ear and leaned in closer to the mouthpiece.

"Say it again and speak slowly," he ordered, panic beginning to set in.

"They are taking that young woman to Ridgemoor. I don't know why, but the Drakes intend to lock her away and ruin her reputation by having her declared insane. And I'm afraid my husband is quite capable of making that happen. You must hurry."

Fear gripped him as the plan became clear to him. The fastest way to discredit Lucy's allegations over the assassination plot would be to have her declared insane. After all, there was no proof other than the overheard messages she reported, and if the Saratoga Drakes could prove Lucy insane, it would be killing two birds with one stone. Suspicion of the assassination plot would vanish, and their lifelong enemy would be slammed into a lunatic asylum with little hope of escape.

Mrs. Schroeder's voice lost a bit of its panic as she relayed careful instructions. "The fastest way to Ridgemoor is to rent a hack at the Groverman Stables. Take it to the train station and ride the Ninth Avenue elevated train straight to Ridgemoor."

She seemed awfully eager to help . . . too eager. Was this all part of a plot to somehow entrap him into dashing off to Ridgemoor? With the most recent newspaper article casting aspersions on his own sanity, they'd have all the more reason to detain him. Was Lucy the prey, or was he?

It didn't matter. He couldn't go back to paperwork when

Lucy might be battling for her freedom. He vaulted from his seat and headed downstairs. For all he knew, Lucy might be happily ensconced at her station, dutifully translating messages like any other day.

He burst into the cavernous room where forty AP telegraphers swiveled to stare at the man who'd just come barreling into their office.

Lucy's station was empty. A cold fist squeezed Colin's heart, for the implications of that empty chair were chilling. He needed to move fast.

≈⟡≈

Colin was shown into the office of Sergeant Richard Palmer, the man who had been investigating the messages Lucy intercepted. Despite the wild-eyed nature of his fears, the overworked sergeant gave Colin his full attention, perking up at the mention of Ridgemoor.

"Thomas Drake is closely allied with the doctor in charge of Ridgemoor," Colin said. "I fear Dr. Schroeder won't hesitate to carry out Mr. Drake's wishes."

"Schroeder?" the sergeant asked. "The fellow in charge of the Ridgemoor Insane Asylum is named Dr. Schroeder?"

At Colin's nod, the sergeant grew grim. "The pieces are falling into place," he said, reaching for a file on the top of a cabinet and opening it for Colin.

Sergeant Palmer quickly brought him up to speed. Lucy's information had been turned over to the Secret Service in Washington, who had thrown substantial manpower at the case. A covert investigation into Tom Jr. had begun two months earlier when a congressman reported that Tom tried to bribe him regarding the Panama vote. It gave credibility to Lucy's report, especially since her information said Tom was tracking the president and members of the ICC. As part of the investigation, a Secret Service agent had interviewed Jacob Drake, who was on bad terms with his family and had been a wealth of information.

"Jacob Drake has been spying on both his son and grandson for years," Sergeant Palmer said. "The bad blood started when Thomas Drake tried to have his own father incarcerated in Ridgemoor over a business dispute. Jacob abruptly moved out, and the old man never travels without bodyguards so that his son doesn't try any of his old tricks. Oakmonte is swarming with Jacob's spies. He's also paid off employees at the local post office and telegraph station at a pharmacy in Saratoga."

Colin felt a pang for young Floyd, who was apparently not as innocent and idealistic as he seemed.

"For years he's been receiving a copy of all telegrams sent from or delivered to Oakmonte," Sergeant Palmer continued. "All he cared about was any efforts to have him declared mentally incompetent, but after Miss Drake reported the plot, those messages were able to confirm everything. A few days ago, the Secret Service intercepted a letter sent by Tom Jr. to Mr. Moreno. They steamed it open and read that Tom would make no more payments until 'the mosquito' was discredited. We gather he has been bribing congressmen to vote against the Panama route for the canal. He said that only after 'Schroeder swatted the mosquito' would they be safe enough to continue the plan. We had no idea who this Schroeder fellow was, but now it all makes sense."

Being certified a lunatic would do the trick. Colin leaned forward. "Then we need to get to Ridgemoor immediately."

Sergeant Palmer shook his head. "Not yet. We know there are at least three additional conspirators, but we don't know who they are. Tom's arrest may not foil the rest of the plot. If other men take over—"

A pounding on the door was quickly followed by a young officer. "Sir, you'll want to see this right away."

Before he could say anything more, the young officer was brushed aside, and Nick Drake shouldered into the room, followed closely by Lucy.

Colin shot to his feet. "Thank you, God!"

"Colin?" Lucy asked in a dazed voice. She looked filthy but alert and happy and *here*, not in a lunatic asylum. He leapt across the room and scooped her into a hug, lifting her from the floor and swinging her in a circle.

Then the stench hit him. Her clothes were damp, and she looked like she'd been sleeping under a bridge. Nick didn't look any better. Colin was delighted to see her, but honestly, that smell . . .

"Where have you been?" he managed to choke out.

She smiled weakly. "It's a long story, but to avoid a trip to Ridgemoor, Nick and I made our escape through the sewers. It was an adventure. Now that it's over, I'd like to file a police report and see if someone can be arrested for it."

He didn't want to help her file a police report. He wanted to hustle her into the nearest hotel with running water for a good hot scrub with soap. Nick, too.

"Not so fast," Sergeant Palmer said. "While I'm relieved you're no longer in danger, your escape has foiled some important plans. It would be best if you were actually admitted to Ridgemoor. Would you be willing?"

Lucy looked ready to explode. "Are you out of your mind?" she shrieked.

"Hear me out," the sergeant said, holding his hands up in self-defense. "Once Dr. Schroeder has you legally committed to the asylum, your cousin is going to initiate a series of events that will lead us to his fellow conspirators. We need to bait the trap for him, and you are the bait."

Sergeant Palmer continued to outline the plan, all of which required Tom Jr. to believe that Lucy had been incarcerated so he would once again contact his confederates to carry out the plan to stop the Panama vote. Until Lucy had been neutralized, Tom would remain on the sidelines. They needed Tom to believe he was entirely safe so they could catch everyone involved in the plot.

Lucy sagged as the implications sank in. Disbelief and exhaustion warred on her face, but she seemed resigned. Colin's heart turned over in pride as she gave her reluctant consent. "Tell me what I need to do," she said.

The plan came together quickly. The men who had kidnapped her, Sneed and Wolfe, were nowhere to be found and might not even be alive, but Dr. Schroeder had seen Lucy escape with the two henchmen hot on her trail. Sergeant Palmer concocted a story based mostly on the truth: that Sneed and Wolfe had followed Lucy down into the sewers, but in this version of events, they succeeded in capturing her and dragging her to the surface. Both men had been injured in the struggle and needed immediate medical treatment. They turned Lucy over to the local police, claiming she was an escaped inmate from Ridgemoor who needed to be returned. In order to make the story ring true, Lucy would need to be taken to Ridgemoor immediately.

"I can't even take a bath? Or change clothes?" Lucy asked.

The sergeant gave a reluctant shake of his head. "You are more convincing precisely as you are."

Colin grimaced in sympathy, wishing she had time for the world's longest, hottest bath. She deserved to be pampered like royalty for the ordeal she'd just endured. Instead, she would be carted off to yet another nightmarish trial, this time in an insane asylum.

It was a testament to Lucy's fortitude that she agreed without a fuss. She met Colin's gaze with sad resignation. "Sometimes challenges are sent to test us," she said.

Bedraggled, filthy, and smelling like the sewer she had just survived, Lucy was on her way to Ridgemoor.

❦

Lucy's initial reluctance to agree to Sergeant Palmer's plan was based on her screaming need to get out of this vile dress. Her skin was clammy, itched, and stank like a sewer. She'd give anything for a hot bath and a fresh set of clothing.

Instead, she agreed to board a carriage, drive to Ridgemoor, and turn herself over to Dr. Schroeder. The sense of camaraderie as she, Colin, Nick, and half a dozen police officers worked on the plan was exhilarating. A team of professionals were on her side. If all went well, not only would the ring of conspirators be arrested, but Uncle Thomas would suffer the consequences for forging a document claiming to be her guardian and forcing her into an insane asylum.

The plan was to station a police officer at the pharmacy across the street from Ridgemoor, where a telegraph message would be sent the moment Tom Jr. contacted his associates to authorize additional bribes. As soon as the telegram came through, the police would raid Ridgemoor and get her out.

The pharmacy closed each evening at eight o'clock, meaning there would be no telegraph operator to receive the message overnight. Colin wouldn't stand for it and insisted on being included in the operation.

"I will man the telegraph overnight," he said. "I don't want Lucy stuck in that asylum one minute longer than necessary."

Her heart turned over at his generosity. Just knowing Colin would be nearby made the ordeal seem not quite as horrific.

But her confidence began eroding as the officers peeled off to their respective tasks. Nick left to meet with the Secret Service and provide insight into the messages intercepted by Jacob Drake. Others prepared to monitor Tom Jr.'s activities in Albany. One by one they left, and the reality of what she was about to face was inescapable. She was going into Ridgemoor alone. There would be no way to communicate with the outside. She would be at the mercy of Dr. Schroeder and whatever sadistic treatments he used on the mentally disturbed.

She clenched Colin's hand on the walk outside to await the carriage. Everything seemed so normal on the sidewalk outside the police station, where the bustle of the city streets was achingly poignant. In a moment she would leave this comfortable world behind to venture into the complete unknown. It was a warm summer day, but a shiver of trepidation raced through her.

"It's not too late to back out," Colin said. "Just say the word, and I'll get Sergeant Palmer to come up with a different plan."

His face was gentle with concern, and she glanced away lest it sap her resolve. "I'll be all right," she said through chattering teeth, trying to make herself believe it.

Just before she boarded the carriage that would take her to the insane asylum, Sergeant Palmer approached her with regret in his eyes and a pair of handcuffs in his grip.

"It will be more convincing if you arrive wearing these," he said.

Colin looked appalled and ready to protest, but Sergeant Palmer was right. It was still alarming as the cold metal clamped around her wrists. Passersby on the street gawked at her, but she had other things to worry about.

"Next time we see each other, this will all be over," she said, meeting Colin's gaze and trying to smile.

His face was grim. "The next time we see each other, you'll be a hero."

The breath left her in a rush. She didn't feel like a hero. She felt small and weak and would give anything to run the other way. "All in a day's work, London."

He swept her into a hug. Despite how horrible she smelled, he squeezed her tightly, as if he never wanted to let her go.

A half hour later, she was approaching Ridgemoor, alone in the carriage except for a single policeman. Officer Jakes had drawn the short straw and had to share the interior of the carriage with her, while two others rode outside in the fresh air. He'd been a good sport about it, looking at her with a combination of sympathy and admiration. He tried not to recoil when he got a whiff of her, but she could hardly hold it against him. She'd shudder too.

"I've been told it's mostly rainwater," she said.

Officer Jakes looked dubious. "That so?"

The carriage slowed as it rolled through the gates of Ridgemoor. Fear caused an uncontrollable quaking deep inside Lucy, which might actually be a good thing, since it would help persuade Dr. Schroeder that she'd been dragged here against her will. The carriage bumped over the old, jutting cobblestones before finally coming to a stop before the front doors of the asylum.

Officer Jakes met her gaze from the opposite bench. "Ready?"

All she could do was nod.

Officer Jakes jerked open the door. "Out!"

She flinched at his tone. Even knowing it was an act, everything felt terrifyingly real as he dragged her from the carriage. The handcuffs robbed her of balance, and she stumbled onto the ground, banging a knee against a paving stone. With a firm grasp, Officer Jakes hauled her upright, and she got her first look at Ridgemoor.

The imposing fortress of granite block towered above her, iron bars over the windows. The sight froze the breath in her lungs. There could be no possible escape from this prison. A wrought-iron fence enclosed the property, with spiked finials at the top of each spoke. Even now, a pair of orderlies drew the gates at the front of the drive shut and secured them with a padlock, the clang hurting her ears.

Officer Jakes grabbed her elbow and propelled her forward, up the path and through the front doors into a lobby that smelled of camphor and mothballs. A uniformed orderly stood from behind the counter.

"We've got an escaped inmate," Officer Jakes growled.

The hospital orderly looked confused. "Are you sure she's one of ours? I've never seen her before."

"Then get Dr. Schroeder. He was bringing her in last night when she made a run for it."

Two minutes later, the doctor scurried into the lobby, his face a mix of astonishment and relief. Officer Jakes struck just the right tone, explaining the heroic efforts of Ridgemoor's orderlies in dragging the hysterical woman out of the sewers, where she'd fled like a lunatic. During the chase, Sneed broke his ankle and Wolfe got a nasty gash on his arm. Wolfe managed to drag the reluctant Miss Drake to the nearest police station before seeking hospital treatment. The police had reluctantly transported the escaped lunatic to the asylum.

"We're glad to get her off our hands," Officer Jakes said, nudging her deeper into the lobby.

"I don't belong here," she said in a shaking voice to the doctor.

"Your uncle's committal papers say otherwise," he said in that unnervingly calm voice before glancing at the orderly behind the counter. "Get two female attendants to strip her down for a scrubbing. Use plenty of lye, and don't let her out of the washroom until she's been scoured clean."

Her mouth went dry. She hadn't expected this. "I can wash myself," she said in a shaking voice, but the orderlies were already closing in, dragging her forward by both arms. A whimper escaped as her toes lifted from the ground. She was supposed to pretend fright, but this was the real thing.

She glanced at Officer Jakes. For a split second, she saw the sympathy in his eyes, then the orderly dragged her from the room. She was on her own.

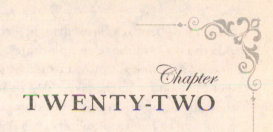

Colin glanced at his pocket watch. It had been ten hours since Lucy had walked into the Ridgemoor Insane Asylum. He'd spent that time loitering in the doorway of the pharmacy directly across the street from Ridgemoor. With its ominous granite blocks and bars over the windows, Ridgemoor looked like it belonged in a gothic horror story.

He'd never seen anything so courageous as when Lucy let herself be dragged through the heavy front doors that slammed behind her with such force that he heard them from across the street.

All afternoon he had stared at the windows, trying to get a glimpse of her. Every now and then, he'd see the pale face of an inmate gazing through the iron bars on the upper floors of the asylum. From this distance it was impossible to recognize if any of them were Lucy, but he wanted to remain here in the doorway where she could see him, just in case she was able to find her way to a window. Wearing his brown-tinted spectacles and a wool cap pulled low over his forehead, he was completely unrecognizable as the fashionable British aristocrat Dr. Schroeder had met at Oakmonte.

When the pharmacy closed at eight o'clock, Colin wandered inside to take over the telegraph duties. The instant Tom Jr. contacted his associates, word would be sent to the pharmacy to get Lucy out. It might take a day, or it might take a week. Either way, during the overnight hours, Colin would be here. He still had to report to Reuters each day, so he would try to steal a few snatches of sleep while he waited. The telegraph buzzer would rouse him the moment Lucy's ordeal was over.

Colin glared at the forbidding asylum across the street. He had borrowed Nick Drake's flashlight and fiddled with the switch on its side until he figured out how to work it properly. Angling the light in Ridgemoor's direction, he flicked it on and off, pressing out a simple message in Morse code.

```
Hang in there, Yankee.
```

He doubted she could see it, but merely sending the message made him feel better.

Lucy curled on a thin cot, shivering beneath a threadbare sheet. Every square inch of her skin hurt from the harsh scrubbing with lye soap, but at least it was over. She'd never been so humiliated in her life as when the orderlies dragged her into a tile lavatory, where a pair of female attendants stripped her naked and forced her to stand beneath an icy blast of water. After a thorough drenching, they brought out the lye soap and a long-handled boar bristle brush. They ignored her protests that she could wash herself and scrubbed until her skin was raw. It hurt even worse when they turned on the cold water to rinse the soap away. Then they washed her hair in the same rough manner.

She had no idea what they'd done with her clothing, but the

only thing she was given to wear was a loose cotton smock. It was identical to the shapeless smocks worn by the other three women sharing her cell. She'd been terrified when the matrons pushed her inside the room, which contained nothing but four iron bedsteads and three strange women. Each bed had a thin mattress, an oilcloth sheet, and a single pillow. The clang of the door as it locked behind her was chilling. The reality of her confinement made it hard to breathe.

It didn't take long to learn that two of the women sharing her cell were profoundly disturbed. One rocked incessantly on her cot as she gaped at Lucy through frightened eyes, while the other sang an endless lullaby into the palm of her hand.

"You don't have to talk to them if you don't want," the third woman said. She was a redheaded girl with a Brooklyn accent and hard eyes. Her name was Ruby. She was sixteen years old and had been sent here four months earlier after miscarrying a baby. It was the second time Ruby had miscarried, and her parents sent her to Ridgemoor for being incorrigible.

How many other men and women had been incarcerated here because they were inconvenient? It had happened to Lucy's father, and if it hadn't been for Nick's heroism, it would have happened to her as well. It sickened her, and for the hundredth time since stepping through Ridgemoor's doors, she wished Colin were here. It felt like she had entered another world, but she knew he was only a stone's throw away at the pharmacy across the street. When she got off her cot to look out the window for a glimpse of him, the girl singing into her palm went into hysterics, ordering Lucy back onto her cot with a firm shove and a smack across the face.

"No!" she snarled. "That's *my* window. Get away from it."

Lucy covered the side of her face, seeing stars. She'd never been hit like that before and hadn't realized how badly it hurt.

"Just do it," Ruby said with a resigned sigh. "We don't want the matrons in here, and Betty will change her mind eventually. She always does."

Lucy took Ruby's word for it, even though in the brief moment she'd stood before the window, she'd seen Colin leaning in the pharmacy doorway across the street. He was so close! Every cell in her body longed to lunge across the room and gaze out at him, desperate for the reminder that she wasn't really alone.

And she truly *wasn't* alone, she reminded herself. The Lord was with her, even at times like these when she felt isolated and abandoned. He'd even sent this hard-eyed adolescent girl to her, a small voice of sanity in this forsaken world.

The hours slipped past, and Lucy tensed each time footfalls sounded in the hallway outside their locked door. Would Dr. Schroeder come for her? Would she be forced into one of those hideous straitjackets like her father? Her mind rambled through the possibilities. Perhaps her uncle's plan was to lock her up indefinitely. It seemed impossible to believe, but Ruby's parents had done it.

An hour after sunset, Betty lay down and stopped singing. Lucy lay motionless, listening to the slowing of the madwoman's breathing. When she was sure Betty was asleep, she quietly lifted off her cot and tiptoed to the window across the icy tile floor. She almost wept when she saw Colin through the window of the pharmacy, reading a newspaper at a table in the waiting area at the front.

She slumped against the window frame as exhaustion pulled at every muscle, but seeing Colin gave her hope, especially since he repeatedly looked up from the newspaper to stare toward the asylum. She smiled. He hadn't forgotten about her.

She straightened as he set the folded paper down and reached inside his jacket for something. A moment later, a series of quick flashes came from the crook of his arm. He had Nick's flashlight!

It took a moment for her stunned mind to focus on decoding the message he sent her.

```
Oxford cricketers beat Cambridge by eight
wickets.
```

She covered her mouth lest her gasp of surprise wake crazy Betty. It seemed Colin was willing to share the evening newspaper with her. A moment later, he sent another message.

```
First woman went over Niagara Falls in a
barrel. I find you more admirable. You are
brave. She is merely stupid.
```

Even though the message was delivered in Morse code, she could hear Colin's charmingly smug British accent. She wilted a little when he returned the flashlight to his jacket and lifted the newspaper again. He went back to reading.

She couldn't blame him. She already verged on the edge of lunacy for want of anything to do other than half-hearted conversation with her one lucid cellmate. Nevertheless, it was comforting to watch him read, for she'd always admired his insatiable curiosity.

Less than twenty minutes later, he put the newspaper down and flashed her another message.

```
Last leg of transpacific cable successfully
laid. Inaugural message to be sent on the
Fourth of July.
```

A combination of joy and regret swirled through her. Once the cable running beneath the Pacific was working, the AP would no longer need Reuters for anything. How ironic that if Colin hadn't made that mistake in communicating the AP's Pacific messages, she never would have become friends with him.

She curled up on the windowsill, desperate not to lose a single message. He went back to reading his newspaper, but an hour later he picked up the flashlight again.

I love you.

"I love you, too," she whispered, her fingers touching the cold glass. Who could have guessed that the impossibly arrogant man who once chewed her out for taking too long to buy chestnuts would become so precious to her? No matter how long she lived, she would be forever grateful that during this most terrible of nights, Colin was with her throughout the ordeal.

At breakfast time a slot in the door opened, and four trays slid through the narrow opening. Ruby sprang off her cot to retrieve the trays and distribute them to the others. There were no words exchanged with the orderly on the other side of the door, only the squeaking of a metal cart as it wheeled down the hallway.

Lucy stared at her tray. Wherever Ridgemoor spent their money, it wasn't in the kitchen. A bowl of oatmeal, a cup of milk, and half an apple was what each woman received. Lucy had never cared for apples and offered hers to Ruby.

Which upset Betty. "Stop talking! No one is to talk while eating. It's forbidden."

It wasn't, but as Ruby explained after the trays were collected, Betty was liable to start throwing food if she got upset during meals. "And if that happens, we get nothing but bread and water until they're convinced we can all behave."

After breakfast, Betty went back to singing into the palm

of her hand, the other woman gazed vacantly into space, and Lucy turned to Ruby for a quiet word, speaking softly so as not to set off Betty.

"What are the days like here?"

The answer was depressing. It was three meals a day and a bath every fourth day. Dr. Schroeder was a big believer in the "rest cure," which meant complete physical and mental withdrawal from activity and stimulation. Patients were to lie on their cots in silence and concentrate on quelling unhealthy urges. External stimulation was limited, which was why interaction with the staff was prohibited and meals were bland. The same menu was served for seven days in a row. This week they would have oatmeal at breakfast, baked beans and stewed tomatoes at lunch, and broiled chicken with a wedge of bread for dinner.

Each patient met once per week with Dr. Schroeder for personalized treatment. Lucy's blood chilled as Ruby described the various treatments inflicted on the patients.

"He uses ice water baths that are supposed to slow circulation of blood to the brain and calm aggravated nerves. I've heard rumors he has a thing for electricity and sometimes uses it to shock patients who aren't doing what he wants. Then there is exposure therapy. That one's the worst. He tries to figure out what upsets you most in the world, and then he straps you down and makes you endure it. The lady who was here before you had an unholy fear of spiders. You could hear the screaming all the way up here on the third floor."

Lucy swallowed hard. She didn't expect to be locked up more than a few days, but if Sergeant Palmer didn't act quickly, she could find herself subjected to one of Dr. Schroeder's barbaric therapies.

It came sooner than expected. The door opened with a clang, and she whirled around, her mouth going dry at the sight of Dr. Schroeder and two male orderlies.

"You are to come with us, Miss Drake."

She backed away, clutching her gown. "Now?"

"Now." Dr. Schroeder's voice was implacable.

She would *not* scream or thrash like a madwoman. No matter what happened, she would endure it. This man couldn't break her spirit unless she gave him that power.

She felt naked walking through the wide hallways wearing nothing but a baggy cotton smock, but that was the least of her concerns as the orderlies guided her down the staircase, Dr. Schroeder close behind. She was shown into a comfortable office with plush oriental carpets and book-lined walls. No sign of a bathtub or electrical generator in sight.

Dr. Schroeder's face was welcoming as he gestured to a leather chair opposite his desk. "If you can comport yourself like a lady, I am willing to dismiss the orderlies, and we can have a pleasant conversation. It is entirely up to you."

"I can behave."

She stood stiffly by the chair as the two men left the room, the door clicking softly behind them. It was hard to believe Dr. Schroeder was actually willing to meet with her alone, and she glanced around the room, looking for additional guards lurking behind the potted palm or the velvet maroon panels framing the window.

"I assure you that we are alone, and the windows are secured from the outside, so there is no chance for escape. But come, let's have a chat and get better acquainted. All I want is to help you."

She lowered herself onto the chair, the cold of the leather quickly penetrating the thin fabric covering her legs. "The last time we met, you wanted to kidnap me."

His smile was pained. "People rarely choose to visit Ridgemoor on their own accord, which is a shame. We can help people become better adjusted to the world. While I understand you have achieved considerable success in your work as a telegrapher,

262

it does not exempt you from the normal psychological strains that often affect women who have no one to lean on. I can only imagine the stress you have been under, heading to the office each morning before the sun is even in the sky, then performing a man's work all day. I expect it is often dark by the time your workday is over. True?"

Of course it was true. Uncle Thomas managed to terrorize any man who dared court her, so of course she had to work to support herself. But she wasn't going to talk about her life with someone on Uncle Thomas's payroll. She opted to stare at the collection of miniature sculptures lined up on his desk. One was a hunting dog, another a child holding a shell to his ear, and another a woman cradled on a man's lap.

Dr. Schroeder noticed her gaze. "I see you are curious about the Rodin," he said as he rotated the figurine so she could see it from the front.

She caught her breath at the beauty of the sculpture. She'd seen it before, as Auguste Rodin's sculptures had been reproduced countless times in plaster, terra-cotta, and bronze. The plaster reproduction was wildly romantic, showing the hero's strong musculature as he sheltered the woman curled on his lap. He was leaning down and about to press a kiss to her face. It was possibly the most tender, romantic image she'd ever seen.

She looked away, and Dr. Schroeder rotated the sculpture back to face him. "Let's get to know one another a little better, hmm? Your uncle has serious concerns about your stability. He worries you have been working yourself to the bone, and who can blame him? A woman your age should have a man at her side, someone to lean on both for spiritual and material comfort. It must be exhausting to be on your own."

It was exhausting to be kidnapped and forced to run through a sewer system, but she kept her face carefully blank, refusing to engage with him.

"One of the things I do to get to know my new patients is to show them images and encourage them to tell me what they see. I find it so much easier than other examination techniques." Dr. Schroeder pushed the figurines on his desk to the side, then set a stack of full-color artistic prints on the desk before her.

She didn't want to look, but the first image was burned onto her mind before she could glance away. It showed a man at the head of a table, his head bowed in prayer, with his children gathered around him and his wife gazing at him through adoring eyes. It must have been a Thanksgiving meal, for the table was laden with a roasted turkey, freshly baked bread, and bowls of steaming vegetables.

"What sort of thoughts does this image evoke?" Dr. Schroeder asked.

She said nothing, just gazed at the elderberry leaves on the shrub outside the window. If she had to talk about the image in that picture, she might crack. The father looked healthy and strong but still humble as he bowed his head. The children were happy and secure, the wife content. She would give anything to be part of such a family.

"I hope you can cooperate with this examination," Dr. Schroeder said in a mournful voice. "The other examinations are so much less pleasant. Come. What is the first thought that comes to your mind when you see this picture?"

"It makes me wish your kitchen made meals that appetizing."

Dr. Schroeder threw back his head and laughed. "Excellent! I was hoping you had a sense of humor. Let's move on to the next image."

She glanced at it quickly. "Old people."

That was all she was going to say about the photograph of two people sitting on a bench in Central Park. She didn't want to comment on the quiet joy on the elderly woman's face or the laughter in the man's expression as he leaned forward to toss bread crumbs to the pigeons at his feet. The pigeons reminded her of Beatrice and Bianca. She'd had such fun with those birds during her fleeting time with Colin. Now the birds were dead, and Colin would marry someone else, and she would return to her desk at the AP, transcribing stories about other people living full and vibrant lives.

The rasp of paper cut through her thoughts as another image was set before her. "And this?" After she refused to look, he prodded softly. "Come, Miss Drake. I don't want to keep reminding you of what will happen if you don't cooperate."

This wouldn't be so painful if she wasn't so drained from the ordeal of the past few days. Why couldn't she look at some pretty pictures without the temptation to dissolve into tears? It was just that she was so tired. And alone. Even if she wasn't locked up in this horrible place, she was still mostly alone in this world. She didn't have a man in her life, and brothers didn't count. They didn't hold you protectively like in Rodin's sculpture.

The doctor slid the photograph to the bottom of the stack and nudged another image across the desk. She refused to look.

"Why does this experiment disturb you?" Dr. Schroeder asked. "There is no point denying it, for I can see the whites of your knuckles as you cling to the seat of the chair. Come. Have a look at this image and tell me what you feel."

As expected, it was another scene of domestic bliss, this time a mother nursing a baby as she laughed down at a little toddler at her feet. Lucy feared her own years for producing such a family were growing short, but she wouldn't give Dr. Schroeder the satisfaction of letting him know the image upset her. She looked him in the eye without flinching.

"The sight of that innocent boy looking up at his mother with such trust makes me wonder if he will grow up to be a man of honor, or if he will choose to become some rich man's lapdog."

The tightening of Dr. Schroeder's mouth was the only sign
that her arrow found its mark. He produced another picture.
"And this?"

It showed a gallant navy officer holding a woman in his arms
as they gazed at a warship on the horizon, an American flag
snapping in the breeze as clouds darkened the sky. Despite the
ominous tone, the image still radiated strength and the enduring power of love, dedication, and perseverance.

She straightened her spine to glare at Dr. Schroeder. "It makes
me proud to be an American. The people in that picture would
do whatever it takes, sacrifice anything, to protect the people
and the country they love. Too bad the artist doesn't show if
they are waging war against enemies abroad or the homegrown
sort. The kind who takes bribes, ignores common decency, and
debases himself to please his master. Next picture," she ordered.

He collected the pictures and slid them into a drawer. "That
will be all for this afternoon. I will have you escorted back to
your cell."

The hours blended into one another, the monotony of the
days broken only by the arrival of meals slid through the slot in
the door. Lucy soon realized Dr. Schroeder's test had been more
sadistic than she thought, for it revealed the huge, gaping hole
in her life. The full effect of the damage didn't hit her in the
book-lined office but in the endless hours after she was back in
her cell, with nothing to do but stare at the ceiling and remember
the burning sense of intimacy and love in those pictures. With
all her soul, she longed to trade places with the women in those
pictures. They lived in the shelter and protection of a loving
family. They probably didn't rise before dawn and make their
way across the city to work for countless hours transcribing the
stories of other people's newsworthy adventures.

If she and Ruby spent too much time in conversation, it was likely to send Betty into one of her rages, so Lucy did her best to sleep during the days. It would let her remain awake at night, when Colin arrived back at the pharmacy and sent her a few quick, covert messages by flashlight. They were always fleeting and usually pointless items from the evening's newspaper. A baseball score. Tomorrow's weather forecast. Once he told her that his nanny had made a batch of lemon cream shortbread for the team of police officers working with them.

The days were the worst. She tried to doze, but it was hard to sleep during the day, and she stared blankly up at a water stain on the plaster ceiling. The stain looked like a woman scrubbing the floor. Or was she crawling on her knees? Praying for mercy? If Lucy stared hard enough, her focus wavered, and it seemed the water stain moved a little, as though the woman crawled across the ceiling but never moved very far.

She had been here for three days. How much longer before the Secret Service located Tom's coconspirators? Fear crept around the edges of her vision, for she didn't know how much longer she could endure this.

Lucy was awakened before dawn for another session with Dr. Schroeder. The unusually early meeting time was worrisome as she followed an orderly to the doctor's office, still groggy and disoriented from a restless night.

Which seemed to be part of Dr. Schroeder's plan. He showed her more pictures of young lovers gazing wistfully into one another's eyes and happy families enjoying a picnic on a perfect spring day. Only this time he was shrewder.

Amidst the scenes of domestic bliss came the stark image of a single, sickly tree standing in a barren field. He asked Lucy how she felt seeing that isolated tree, twisted and battered by the wind and elements. All she could do was shrug before Dr. Schroeder moved on to a painting of a laughing couple on a sailboat. Picture after picture captured such loveliness that Lucy wanted to dissolve into them, and then came a photograph of a dozen women standing on a factory floor, their shoulders stooped in exhaustion and a blank look of resignation on their faces. Those women had no hope.

She looked away. She didn't need to stare at a picture to know that work was hard. For every carefree day in the sunshine she had spent with a man she loved, Lucy had spent a hundred days at a desk. A thousand days.

Ruby and the other women were awake by the time she was shown back to her cell. Lucy didn't even have the energy to smile as she crossed the room and sat on her thin mattress. Ruby sat down beside her, saying nothing but reaching out to hold Lucy's hand. Lucy felt almost guilty accepting comfort from her.

"I don't know how you can stand it here," Lucy whispered.

"What choice do I have?"

She sighed. No, Ruby hadn't had many choices in life. She had been taken out of school at the age of twelve to work in a shoelace factory, and the father of her baby had been the married, middle-aged manager of the factory. Ruby disliked him but did what she believed was necessary to keep her job.

It was a demoralizing thought. Lucy's life had been full of choices, but throughout it all, she'd marched in lockstep determination to bring Uncle Thomas down. She could have been like the women in Dr. Schroeder's photographs had she chosen love over retribution for a forty-year-old injustice. The resentment fueling her crusade against the Saratoga Drakes had never given her a sliver of the happiness she saw in those paintings.

She flopped back on her cot to stare at the water stain on the ceiling. Today it looked like the woman was weeping on her knees.

A noise at the slot signaled the arrival of breakfast, and Ruby crossed the room to retrieve it. Lucy dragged her attention from the water stain and rolled upright. She felt too demoralized to swallow the gloppy oatmeal.

Ruby stood holding the tray in confusion. "This is odd . . . lemon cookies for breakfast?"

She tilted the tray so Lucy could see. Instead of oatmeal, a dozen cookies were evenly spaced on a plate, their lemony yellow looking cheerful in the gloomy cell.

Lucy shot to her feet, too stunned to even move. Before she could speak, the slot opened again, and a narrow purple box filled the gap. She lunged across the room to grab the box with its familiar logo printed across the top. She held it out for Ruby to see.

"Cadbury chocolates?" Ruby gasped. "Now I think I really might be going crazy."

Lucy swallowed hard, her heart pounding but not daring to hope. She knelt on the floor to peer through the slot, but before she could get a good look, a bundle of green stems almost poked her in the eye. She reared back and pulled the stems through, the bouquet of daisies scattering petals on the floor and looking bedraggled but still delightfully cheerful.

She opened the slot again. "Colin? Are you out there?"

"I certainly hope you don't have other men courting you with flowers and chocolates in here." He tossed it off in his most charming voice. Which was a relief, because it meant he was in a good mood and this ordeal was about to come to an end.

She trembled so much she could barely get the words out. "Do you have a key? Am I getting out of here?"

Instead of answering, a click sounded in the lock, and the door pushed open. His smile was brighter than the sun, and he held a telegram aloft. "The Secret Service has everything they need. You are free."

She vaulted into his arms, and they clamped like steel bands around her back and lifted her from the ground. A sense of well-being flowed from Colin's warm strength and into her.

"You can't be in here!" Betty shrieked. "It's against the rules."

"Hush, Betty," Lucy murmured, not even lifting her head from Colin's shoulder. Amazingly, Betty retreated without complaint to sit on her cot and sing into her palm.

"Is it really over?" she asked, afraid to even hope.

"Sergeant Palmer is downstairs arresting Dr. Schroeder as we speak. He offered to let me witness the event, but I wanted to get you out of here as soon as possible. If there's anything you want to bring, collect it now. A carriage is waiting for us downstairs."

"There's nothing I want from here."

"What about me?" Ruby demanded, her voice hard.

Lucy caught her breath, momentarily speechless. Had she grown so callous in these few days that she could walk away and leave an obviously sane girl imprisoned in this madhouse? She looked at Colin. "Is there something we can do for her? She doesn't belong here."

Colin grew somber. "I have a feeling there are plenty of people who don't belong here. It's only a matter of time before a full investigation is done."

Ruby stepped forward, her chin thrust at a defiant angle. "I'm not waiting. I'm walking out of here with you, and if you want to see crazy, just try to stop me."

Colin's eyes widened a little, for Ruby appeared ready to ignite at the suggestion she would be forced to remain in this cell even another minute. "Let's go, then," he conceded.

They left the chocolates and flowers for Betty and the woman whose name Lucy had never learned.

As Ruby predicted, no one tried to stop her on their way out the door.

Colin couldn't understand Lucy's strange malaise. After the exhilaration of leaving Ridgemoor, her mood sobered quickly, and she became withdrawn and distant. Nick had provided him with clothes for her, and they went across the street to the pharmacy so she could change into something respectable as soon as possible.

The thin, tough-looking girl named Ruby looked painfully out of place in her shapeless smock as she fidgeted next to the display counter. The shop next door had a few ready-made dresses for women, and he took pity on her and bought her the smallest dress they had. It was so big it looked ready to slip off her bony shoulders, but the moment she was decently clothed, Ruby wanted to leave.

"Where will you go?" Lucy asked.

"Don't worry about me. I can look after myself. There's a church at the end of the street. I'll start there."

Before Ruby could make it to the door, Lucy stepped forward to hug the girl, who didn't seem to want the attention.

"I'll be on my way now." Ruby pushed out of Lucy's embrace.

She met his gaze with a brief nod. "Thanks for the dress," she said before heading out the door without looking back.

Lucy looked bereft after Ruby left, standing in the middle of the pharmacy. "What now?" she asked.

"Now we go to Albany so we can both witness Tom Jr.'s well-deserved takedown. The Secret Service are going to arrest him later today."

"Oh."

What was wrong with her? Shouldn't she be deliriously happy and running for the nearest train station to savor her cousin's downfall? Witnessing Tom's arrest was going to be more than a political necessity. It was going to be a pleasure, and Lucy deserved a front row seat.

"Are you hungry?" he asked. It looked like the waif who'd just left hadn't eaten in months, and perhaps Lucy's bewildering lack of energy was simple hunger.

"Yes . . . yes, I'd like something to eat."

"Excellent. We'll need to hurry in order to catch the twelve o'clock train. What are you in the mood for?"

For the first time since leaving the asylum, she laughed a little. "Anything besides a bowl of oatmeal or a plate of beans." It was a relief to see that the muscles in her face remembered how to smile. He'd been worried there for a moment.

Ten minutes later, they were seated at the back of a hotel restaurant. It was only ten o'clock, so the dining room was almost empty, and they had plenty of privacy to discuss the Secret Service's plan to arrest the remaining conspirators. Everything was going to happen quickly. News of Dr. Schroeder's arrest could only be suppressed for twenty-four hours, and the instant Tom Jr. got wind of it, he might go on the run and foil the carefully constructed plan to bring him down.

Lucy seemed strangely disinterested in hearing about the plan. Instead of pouncing on him for details the moment they were seated, she fingered the edge of the tablecloth, leaned forward to sniff the chrysanthemums in the table's centerpiece, and even peeked under the table to scrutinize the brass feet on the bottom of the table legs.

"I've never seen table legs with clawed feet," she said. When it appeared she was about to leave her seat for a better view, he grabbed her hand to stop her.

"Forgive me, but we have a great deal of business to discuss. We're taking the twelve o'clock train to Albany, and you need to know what's going on."

Did she just roll her eyes at him? He couldn't tell, because she quickly looked away to reach for a water glass, taking a deep drink while averting her gaze. He bit his tongue while waiting for her to set down the blasted glass. She still didn't look at him, just traced the patterns on the damask tablecloth.

"Agent Wilkes from the Secret Service took over the planning of the takedown operation," he began. "This afternoon, Tom is competing for the Galliard Cup, and his entire family will be on hand to watch."

The Galliard Cup was held each Fourth of July at the Albany Sporting Club. Drawing competitors from the entire East Coast, it was the most prestigious shooting event outside of the Olympics. It would draw lavish newspaper coverage, which was why the Secret Service decided to delay the arrest until the competition. They wanted plenty of publicity for foiling the plot. Best of all, Colin would be awarding the trophies and thus would play a prime role in bringing Tom down.

"I had to pull some strings. The Secret Service didn't want to risk Tom seeing you, since he assumes you are still locked up at Ridgemoor. It took some persuading, but I got them to agree that you of all people deserve to witness the event. They said you can watch everything from the private office near the stadium."

"Do I have to?"

He rocked back in his chair, stunned. "Of course you have to! You'll never forgive yourself if you aren't there to witness the final act." When she shifted uneasily and glanced at the exit of the restaurant, realization hit him, and he felt like an insensitive idiot. He reached out to cover her hand with his own. "There's no need to be afraid. We'll have eight Secret Service officers and a dozen policemen on hand. You'll be perfectly safe."

"I'm not afraid of Tom. I just don't want to be there. You can handle everything from here to the end, can't you?"

Before he could respond, a waiter arrived with two bowls of mushroom soup. Colin clamped his mouth shut, anxious for the waiter to finish grinding pepper over Lucy's bowl so that he could go back to shaking some sense into her.

When they were alone again, he leaned forward to speak in an urgent whisper. "Pull yourself together. All you have to do is finish your lunch, come with me to the train station, and then follow my lead. This is what you've been waiting for all your life."

"That's rather sad, isn't it?"

He didn't know how to respond. She couldn't have seemed more disinterested as she toyed with her spoon, dragging swirls in the pepper atop her soup.

This was unbelievable. Lucy had brought him into this scheme to take down the Saratoga branch of her family, and now she wanted no part of it? He'd had a sleepless three nights in order to man the pharmacy's telegraph station. He'd given himself an ulcer worrying about her and had a blister on the side of his thumb from sending her messages with Nick's flashlight. Which he *still* didn't know if Lucy had even seen, for she hadn't bothered to mention it. Which might be a good thing, since fear had driven him to confess that he loved her. Maybe that was best left unspoken, but he needed to know if she had seen that message.

"When you were in the asylum, by chance did you ever glance out the window and see the messages I sent using your brother's flashlight?"

"Yes."

He held his breath. She was the only woman he'd confessed love for, and this was exquisitely awful. "Were any of them particularly interesting to you?"

"I remember a lot of updates on cricket scores."

The silence stretched until it became obvious she did not intend to add anything else.

"That's all you remember?"

Her face crumpled a little, and she sent him a sad smile. "No . . . I saw them all. They were my lifeline. Every one of them is carved on my heart."

"Then why are you acting so cold?"

"I can say it in one word." He leaned forward, and she met his gaze directly. "Whitefriars."

His eyes narrowed. "What about Whitefriars?"

"You're going to sell your soul for that estate, and it breaks my heart to see it."

He threw down his spoon and dragged out his pocket watch. "Look, we don't have time for this. Are you hungry? You haven't touched your soup, so if you aren't hungry, we should be on our way. We might even be able to catch an earlier train." He stood, but she remained frozen in place. "Say something!" he finally burst out.

"Are you still seeing Amelia Wooten?"

The question took him aback. "You know I am not."

"Colin, please . . ." Her voice was so soft he could barely hear it. "Please don't sacrifice yourself for money. I lost the best years of my life to a ridiculous lawsuit, and I have nothing to show for it. You just said that I spent my whole life waiting to see the Saratoga Drakes brought low, *and you're right.* And I've suddenly realized how horrible that makes me. I lost my soul over it."

He had the strangest feeling that he wasn't looking at Lucy. This lost, broken woman was someone else. He sat back down and leaned forward, speaking in a low, bewildered tone.

"What did they do to you in there?" He dreaded the answer but needed to know.

Lucy had the oddest expression on her face, as though she couldn't decide if she was about to laugh or weep. "They showed me pretty pictures," she said. "Pictures of a man holding a woman, a mother nursing a child. The women in those pictures seemed so safe and content. Nurtured. It made me realize how barren my life has become. My world revolves around the next court date or attempts to evade my uncle's machinations. The women in those pictures had everything I've always longed for but never had. When Dr. Schroeder showed me those pictures, I wanted to step inside one of them and forget about the Saratoga Drakes. Those pictures made me realize that nothing I've done in my life amounts to very much."

Colin shook his head. "He showed you a fantasy, not the real world. Those pictures showed a single glimpse of intimacy and tenderness, but don't let that fool you. The real world is filled with challenges and obligations, and if you are very lucky, perhaps a little bit of joy to light your path. That's what you've been for me, Lucy. You've made every hour of each day a little more joyful. Just knowing you are out there gives a lift to my day . . . but make no mistake. People like you and me aren't free to step into a fantasy life or withdraw from the responsibilities of the world. We have obligations and heavy lifting, because there are Thomas Drakes in the world, and they will trample on helpless Italian widows or girls named Ruby if people like you aren't there to stop them."

She remained motionless, but a gleam lit in her eyes. He redoubled his effort, for this battle was too important to lose. She would regret it for the rest of her life if she didn't cross the finish line in this particular race.

"Three weeks ago, you noticed a message that might indicate someone's life was in danger. Every rational instinct in your body told you to ignore it, but you couldn't. You have a huge and generous heart that wouldn't let you look the other way, so you risked your job, you risked imprisonment and financial ruin to take action. Because of you, we've got a small army of policemen and Secret Service officers ready to dismantle a plot that threatened the president of the United States. By letting yourself be locked up, you allowed Tom to feel safe and lead the Secret Service to all four of his coconspirators. You've done what was necessary, and of course you don't have to go to Albany. You've paid a higher price than any of us and can return home to your safe world. But the final act of the play is about to take place, and I want you to be there."

The tension drained from Lucy's face, and she looked at him with new eyes. Happy eyes. It was as if a switch had been pulled and a surge of energy illuminated her. She looked so fresh and pretty that it was impossible to stop the smile from spreading across his face. Her next words brought it all crashing down.

"I'm not going," she said, confidence in her voice. "Don't you see, Colin? I don't *need this anymore*. I've wasted the best years of my life wallowing in resentment and anger. My only goal in life was to bring down the Saratoga Drakes, and it brought no happiness, only frustration and a life of loneliness. When I realized what Tom Jr.'s telegram messages meant, it became vital that I stop him, and thanks to you and the Secret Service, that's going to happen. But I'm done. I don't care anymore."

This would never do. He needed to shake Lucy out of this

strange mood and get her back in the game. He pushed the centerpiece of chrysanthemums aside to see her better. "You can't stop now. The Saratoga Drakes swindled your father and your grandfather. They've robbed poor people of the simple dignity of having hot water piped up to their apartments. They put your father in a lunatic asylum. They shot my birds!"

Lucy's tone was wistful. "And they cost me ten years and a thousand sleepless nights." She paused as emotion flickered across her face. "No, *they* didn't cost me those things; *I* did. I'm not going to let it cost me another day. Not another hour. My brother has wanted to abandon this case for a long time, but I couldn't let it go. Now I can, and it's like . . ." Her gaze trailed out the window, a look of unquenchable longing and hope lighting her from within.

"I feel like I'm about to take flight. The sun is breaking through the clouds, and I can't ever remember feeling this happy." Her voice bubbled with barely suppressed laughter and a hint of bewilderment, as though this moment was as much a surprise to her as to him. "It's like a mountain has been lifted from my shoulders, and for the first time in my life I can see the abundance God has given me. I can draw a breath of pure, clean air, and nothing has ever smelled sweeter. I've been admiring that etching of a pair of sparrows on the wall, and it occurs to me I've never enrolled in the bird-watching class in Central Park. I've wanted to go for years but never found the time. I want to start appreciating the simple blessings that are all around me. I want to find a husband and do things that normal women my age do. The Saratoga Drakes won't drag me down anymore, because I won't let them. So I can't go to Albany with you. There are too many other things I want to do with my life."

It was strange to see her looking so radiant while he was so furious. "I did all of this for *you*," he said, wadding up a napkin and throwing it on the table. "And now you tell me you don't want to be there? You *have* to go."

Her smile was serene as she stood. "No, I don't. And Colin . . . you don't have to marry for money. Don't let Whitefriars drag you down and turn your life into something you never wanted. You deserve better."

It was unbelievable, but she turned and walked out of the restaurant, leaving him standing like a poleaxed fool.

Colin fumed the entire train ride to Albany. Maybe it was the three days of sleep deprivation putting him in a surly mood, but it certainly seemed like Lucy had abandoned the war right before the final battle.

She had a lot of gall to suggest a parallel between Whitefriars and her revolting family drama. Caring for Whitefriars and the people who made a living on the estate was an honor, a privilege. Whitefriars came with responsibilities, and at least he understood that and wouldn't abandon them at a critical moment to go bird-watching or whatever else Lucy suddenly thought was so vital to her well-being.

It was a little after three o'clock by the time he arrived at the Albany Sporting Club. Set on the outskirts of town amidst miles of rolling countryside, the sprawling clubhouse looked like a hunting lodge from the Scottish Highlands. The periodic crack of a rifle blast indicated the trap contest was well under way. He clenched his teeth. Thanks to Lucy, he was going to have to endure an afternoon of shooting, his least favorite activity on earth.

The club was crowded with people celebrating the Fourth of July festivities. American flags snapped in the breeze, and a band played somewhere in the distance. Hundreds of spectators sat on the bleachers to watch the men on the shooting range. He scanned the audience until he spotted two Secret Service agents in the crowd. He blocked any hint of recognition or triumph from his face, but it looked as if everything was proceeding according to plan.

The back patio of the clubhouse was crowded with staff putting the finishing touches on a feast that would linger long into the evening. Bottles of sparkling wine cooled in tubs of ice, and tables were laden with platters of roast duckling, sirloin of beef, and baked haddock. A dessert table sported towering meringue cakes, chocolate tortes, and peaches drenched in raspberry wine.

He made his way to the spectator gallery, where people dressed in summer whites and wide-brimmed hats had gathered ostensibly to watch the shooting, but mostly to mingle with the elite of New York society. Clusters of people meandered along the lawn, drinking from flutes of champagne and socializing with abandon. The finest families of America were here, but beyond the carefully manicured grounds, others longed for a glimpse. Factory boys standing atop the nearby sugar mill cheered the shooters from afar. American society was not as stratified as England, but even here, there was an invisible line to keep the riffraff at bay.

Maybe someday that would change. After all, hadn't Frank Wooten and Jacob Drake climbed out of relative obscurity to amass a fortune?

Colin spotted Margaret and Thomas Drake crossing the lawn. Margaret's white straw hat was as wide as a wagon wheel and featured real orange blossoms encircling the crown. He wandered over, determined to present a charming façade and put them both at ease.

"Your hat is spectacular enough to call the angels down from the sky in admiration."

"Sir Beckwith," she murmured, caution rampant in her face

as she glanced around to see who might be witnessing the encounter. He couldn't blame her for being nervous. The last time they'd seen each other, he abandoned her dinner party during the first course, and shots had been fired.

He laid on the charm with a trowel. "I saw the feast being set out behind the clubhouse. Complete pig swill compared to the delicacies your cook serves at Oakmonte."

She smiled prettily. "We are indeed fortunate. Have you come alone today?"

He dialed his smile back to present the perfect degree of chagrin and self-deprecating wit. "I've been thrown over in rather dramatic fashion. And for a Polish count, no less."

Margaret set her hand on his arm. "Then Miss Wooten is a fool. Perhaps you should visit Oakmonte again and renew your acquaintance with the oldest McNally girl. What a lovely lady. And if you struck up a friendship, we would get to see more of you. Wouldn't that be splendid, Thomas?"

"Splendid," her husband agreed, although he seemed far more guarded than Margaret, who continued to prattle as though there'd been no hint of raised voices, murdered homing pigeons, or threats of incarceration during his last visit to Oakmonte. He suspected that Thomas and Margaret were completely unaware of their son's machinations regarding the Panama Canal and the assassination plot, but he couldn't be certain.

"Tom won the matched pairs this morning, did you hear?" she asked.

"You must be very proud."

"Oh, we are. Did you know he has Olympic ambitions?"

"I think he may have mentioned it during my last visit." He glanced over the crowd, spotting Sergeant Palmer sitting in the bleachers, pretending to watch the last of the trap shooters through a pair of field glasses. To the casual observer, this looked like any other elegant summer gathering, but scattered amidst the high society guests, the place crawled with law enforcement.

Margaret caught his arm again. "Why, here's Tom now," she said, gesturing madly to catch her son's attention. A sneer of contempt flashed across Tom's face, but he quickly masked it and strolled their way.

"Did you see the matched pair set?" he asked. "I won, but it was surprisingly close. Captain Bischoff from the army is a crack shot, but I'm younger, better, and faster. It all worked out in the end. I've got an hour before the pistol competition. Bischoff isn't competing, and I don't see any other worthy challengers today. That means I'll win the Galliard Cup. Again."

After four individual contests, the Galliard Cup went to the participant with the best overall score. It would be awarded just before the feasting. The Drakes didn't know it yet, but Colin had been tapped to present the award, and he dearly hoped Tom was right in his prediction. The Secret Service were ready to arrest him tonight no matter the outcome, but it would be so much sweeter if it happened on the award podium.

Lucy should be here to witness it.

He swallowed back his annoyance. He had his own scores to settle with Tom Jr. and wouldn't let Lucy's irrational mood interfere with that.

Margaret steered the conversation back to the best way to herd Colin back into the Oakmonte ring. "Colin has come on his own today," she said to Tom. "Perhaps you can show him around the club and introduce him to a few of your friends."

Colin would rather submit to dental surgery than spend the afternoon with this preening child, but it was important to set the Drakes at ease by making them assume all was forgiven. Tom gestured to the refreshment stand, and Colin obligingly followed. Tom had no compulsion to nurture the relationship but was smart enough to wait until he was out of his parents' hearing to begin slinging the insults.

"I'm surprised to see you here," Tom began. "Maybe I shouldn't be. I gather the only way a man like you can pay his bills is to cozy up to real men like my father."

Barbs that hit close to home were always the most hurtful, but Colin didn't let it show. "As ever, your discernment is the envy of all," he said. In a few hours, Tom would learn exactly the sort of man he was, and he was cool enough to be patient.

"Too bad about Amelia Wooten giving you the heave-ho," Tom continued. "Anyone can understand that losing a prize like Amelia would be a disappointment, but what germ of insanity convinced you to join forces with Lucy Drake?" He snorted. "I shouldn't say anything bad about my own cousin, but the girl is completely insane, and there are papers to prove it. But I suspect you've already heard about *that*." The smirk on his face was maddening.

"Insane? I'll own that she has made some pretty wild accusations, but I am not entirely convinced they are off base."

Tom reached the front of the line and scooped up two glasses of iced lemonade, a fiendish smile on his face as he passed one to Colin.

"The problem with telegraph messages is that they disappear into thin air so easily," he said in mock dismay. "They are no more than a series of electronic blips that spark across the wires, and then, poof! Lost to eternity for all time, with no documentation whatsoever. Tragic, really. Someday when the great events of history are written, those bits of electronic flashes could be worth something. As it is, there is no evidence they ever existed at all."

Tom's perception of his role in history continued to defy gravity. No matter how tempting, the real confrontation with Tom had to wait until this evening. Tom had never learned to rein in his impulses, whereas Colin had been doing it since infancy. He let the taunting words wash over him as though they were a cool summer breeze. Stiff upper lip and all that.

Tom knocked back his lemonade, passed the glass to a waiter, and straightened his lapels. "Time for me to go show the competition how to shoot."

Colin gave Tom his best smile. "Good luck," he said. "I expect it shall be fascinating."

As predicted, Tom Jr. won the pistol competition, which meant he had the best overall score of the day and had won the Galliard Cup. A hearty cheer went up from the crowd when it was announced that the awarding of the trophies would take place immediately. It was the final event before the lavish dinner would begin, which Colin suspected was the real cause for the enthusiastic applause.

Little did the crowd know that they were about to witness a most unusual award ceremony. Everything was in place. Colin stood next to the trophy table, but directly behind him were three Secret Service agents wearing sporting club jackets, and the front row of the audience was dominated by New York City police officers in street clothes. He suppressed a smile of satisfaction when he spotted a photographer and a pair of journalists from Reuters. He'd sent a tip to the local correspondents that this would be a newsworthy event, and he was pleased Reuters would get the scoop.

The president of the club awarded the second- and third-place trophies. Both men graciously accepted the small plaques, but the real prize was the Galliard Cup, a silver trophy with scrolled handles that gleamed on the table. At last it was time for Tom to receive his award, and it was going to be Colin's pleasure to present it to him. The president of the club introduced him.

"On this most patriotic of American holidays, the Albany Sporting Club has invited an aristocrat from the old country to present the honors. It is a mark of how far our countries have come that our one-time enemy is now our closest national ally and friend. We are honored to welcome Sir Colin Beckwith to award today's Galliard Cup."

He shook hands with the club's president before stepping up to the podium. The smattering of applause lasted long enough for him to scan the crowd, spotting Felix Moreno sitting unwittingly between the two undercover police officers who would be arresting him momentarily.

"Am I the only one who can smell the roasted duck and potatoes? I think I'd better get moving quickly before I lose my audience," Colin said to a little good-natured laughter. "I've had the unique experience of shooting alongside Tom Drake, and it is one I shall never forget. But before we officially hand over the Galliard Cup, a special visitor from Washington has requested the pleasure of Tom's company for a stint. Agent Wilkes?"

Tom looked at Colin quizzically, for events had just strayed from the script. Three men stood in tandem and began striding toward the podium, a pair of handcuffs dangling from Agent Wilkes' hand. Tom tried to step off the riser, but the agent blocked him, speaking loudly enough for everyone in the bleachers to hear.

"Thomas Andrew Drake, you are under arrest for conspiracy to bribe elected officials and for plotting the assassination of President Roosevelt."

"Are you mad?" Tom demanded. "You can't tell me you believe the ravings of that insane girl. She's been institutionalized."

Agent Wilkes had better things to do than get drawn into a verbal battle with a criminal. He grabbed Tom by both shoulders, spun him around, and forced him facedown on the podium. Another agent grabbed Tom's wrists and dragged them behind his back.

Colin took the handcuffs from Agent Wilkes. This was the only request he'd made in recognition of his service in exposing the conspiracy. He placed the first cuff around Tom's wrist, then leaned in close to speak softly into his ear.

"This is for Beatrice," he said as he heard the satisfying click of the cuff closing. "And this is for Bianca."

Click.

Tom was hauled away.

*I*t was early in the evening on the Fourth of July when Lucy set off to the Western Union building to witness the debut message sent across the transpacific cable. Traffic was heavy on the streetcars as revelers made their way to the city's parks for the celebration. After her third failed attempt to cram herself aboard an overflowing streetcar, she gave up and walked the final two miles to the office, where she would listen to President Roosevelt send the very first message across the new cable. If there was time afterward, she would go to Battery Park to watch the fireworks.

It was a new beginning. She was ready to enjoy the rest of her life.

She hadn't expected so many people to forgo the Fourth of July celebration to listen to a cable transmission, but thirty of her coworkers had gathered in the office, plus another dozen people from Reuters who invited themselves downstairs to witness the historic event. Bottles of champagne had been opened, and plenty of people were already toasting the event, even though President Roosevelt was not scheduled to send the initial message for another hour.

Anticipation hummed in the air, and she realized she was happy. This was what it felt like to break free of her inherited burdens and enjoy the present. She savored the sense of camaraderie as everyone in the room celebrated the culmination of the huge project.

She wandered to her desk, eyeing the secret wire tucked amidst the cluster of other cables. She had been a slave to that wire and never realized it before now. Leaning forward, she unscrewed the lightbulb, tugged at the illegal wire, and disconnected it from the switch. She was free.

Roy Collingsworth approached her, already flushed from the celebrations. "You look very pretty tonight," he said. She and Roy had been working ten feet from one another for six years, but he'd never hinted at such a thing in the past.

"I think that must be the champagne talking."

He grinned a little wider, but his eyes were speculative as he scrutinized her. "I'm nowhere close to being tipsy. You just look different tonight, and I can't put my finger on it. You look pretty."

"Careful, Roy," another man hollered from a few yards away. "You're liable to make her faint with all that sudden flattery."

Roy had the good grace to blush. "Heck, you've always been pretty, Lucy, you know that. You just look . . . different."

Probably because she was at peace. Forty years of bitterness had been lifted from her shoulders. She was never going to see a dime of the fortune her grandfather had been swindled out of, but she had her God-given talents and the ability to carve out a splendid life on her own.

Mr. Tolland, the office's longest-standing employee, had been selected for the honor of sitting at the telegrapher's station as the president's message was initiated at Oyster Bay. Ten minutes shy of the expected message, people began gathering in a large semicircle around Mr. Tolland's station. Someone tried to push a glass of champagne into his hand, but Mr. Tolland rose from his seat and carried it to the far side of the room.

"I am about to receive a message from the President of the United States," he said in a grave voice. "When it has been transmitted, I will raise a toast, but not a moment before."

Lucy smiled, knowing that at this exact moment, Roland Montgomery was eagerly awaiting the transmission of the same message at his post on barren Midway Island. The chance for this fleeting brush with his hero, albeit half a world away, would put wind in Roland's sails for years to come.

At 10:50 p.m., the telegraph machine came to life. Everyone in the office stilled as the rapid-fire stream of dots and dashes pierced the air. Mr. Tolland's face was fierce as he wrote down the words for publication in tomorrow's newspaper:

```
Oyster Bay, July 4. Governor Taft: I open the
American Pacific cable with greetings to you
and the people of the Philippines. Theodore
Roosevelt.
```

The wire fell silent, but nobody moved. Even now, the electronic pulses were speeding across the continent at thousands of miles per hour, and Lucy was certain hundreds of telegraphers along the line were listening in on this debut message. In her mind's eye, she could sense it flying across the wires through the American heartland until it finally reached San Francisco. Then it would be connected to the undersea Pacific cables to Honolulu and on to Midway, where Roland would receive the message from the president he idolized. Despite Roland's hero worship, she was confident he would maintain professional dignity as he switched the message onto the last leg of freshly laid cable, taking it to the American naval base in the Philippines.

Respectful silence reigned until Mr. Tolland finished writing out the president's words. Even after his fingers went still, the people assembled around him held their breath, amazed at the miracle of communication taking place. This moment would glimmer in Lucy's memory for as long as she lived.

"How long will it take for a reply to come back?" someone asked, and Mr. Tolland only shrugged. They weren't even one hundred percent certain the undersea cable would work, and how long it would take for a reply to cross the frigid, deep waters of the Pacific was anyone's guess.

They had their answer at 11:19 p.m., when a message from William Howard Taft, Governor of the Philippines, arrived over the wire.

```
The Filipino people and the American
residents in these islands are glad to
present their respectful greetings and
congratulations to the President of the
United States, conveyed over the cable with
which American enterprise has girded the
Pacific.
```

A cheer went up from the crowd. It had worked! In twenty-nine minutes, the president's message had been sent from a sleepy village in Long Island to the other side of the world and back again. Roy scooped Lucy up in a hug and whirled her around. The moment her toes touched the ground, stuffy Mr. Tolland reached out and did the same. Even the people from Reuters joined in the celebration, waving miniature American flags and toasting the accomplishment.

And amidst this temporary joyous moment of sleepy-eyed hysteria, she wondered where Colin was.

She forced herself to smile. It was going to take some time for Colin's memory and her ill-advised romance to fade, but it would happen. Life was too grand to waste it chasing after old grievances or impossible dreams.

It was after midnight as Lucy walked home. Even this late at night, the city was illuminated with the blaze of streetlamps and revelers carrying sparklers. She continued to relive the excitement of the first transpacific cable, playing it over in her mind so she could tell Nick about it. He'd probably be in bed by now, but she would report each moment of the historic event for him in the morning.

Her footsteps echoed in the stairwell as she climbed to the fourth floor of her building. A beam of light shone from beneath their door, so Nick must have left the front lamp on for her. She tried to be quiet as she turned her key in the lock and stepped inside.

"Where have you been?" Nick roared. "We've been worried sick."

She reeled back, stunned to see Nick and Colin Beckwith glowering at her from a few feet away.

"I've been at work," she stammered. "Tonight was the debut of the transpacific cable. I told you that."

"You told me you'd be back by ten o'clock!" Nick said. "We were just about to go on a search-and-rescue mission for you."

She cast a worried glance at Colin. "What's going on? Why are you here?" She didn't want to sound rude. Colin had been a hero over the past few weeks, but his presence here was worrisome. Before Colin could answer, Nick tore into her again.

"He spent the day in Albany, overseeing the arrest of our idiot cousin, since you couldn't be bothered to show up. Aunt Margaret pitched a fit when they led Tom Jr. away in handcuffs. She tried to bribe Agent Wilkes to let Tom go. When that didn't work, she slapped him in the face, then started kicking and screaming as another agent dragged her away."

Lucy was aghast, looking to Colin for confirmation. He nodded. "Your uncle seemed stunned, watching in horror as his world collapsed around him. He did nothing, letting your aunt lead the charge. I've always suspected your aunt was the more vicious of the pair. Sadly, we know of nothing illegal she can be charged with, but your uncle is another story."

Colin held aloft a piece of paper. "In questioning Dr. Schroeder, the police learned that the order to incarcerate you at Ridgemoor came from Thomas. Once Tom Jr. learned you had overheard the wire transmissions, he wanted you out of the picture and leaned on his father to make it happen. I've already filled out the paperwork. All you need to do is sign the complaint."

Merely looking at that form sapped the last of Lucy's energy. She'd just spent an exhilarating few hours alongside wonderful people while they got a tiny glimpse of the future. For those few hours, she hadn't worried about Uncle Thomas or the debilitating resentment that clouded so much of her life. Now Colin held a document that threatened to stoke the smoldering rancor back to life, making her feel old and tired.

She plopped onto the sofa, unable to meet the hopeful look in Colin's gaze. "I have no interest in pursuing that complaint," she said.

Colin's mouth compressed in annoyance. "You're the only one who can sign this document," he said. "The authorities could arrest Dr. Schroeder because he accepted a bribe to commit a sane woman and that's a violation of his professional ethics. With your uncle, it will require a complaining witness to bring charges against him. The police will ask nothing of you. After you sign this document, the case will be turned over to the district attorney for prosecution."

When she hesitated, Nick knelt on the floor beside her. "Don't you understand what that is?" His voice trembled with confused agitation. "That piece of paper is the key to bringing down Uncle Thomas. It's everything we've ever fought for."

This was awful. She hated disappointing Nick, but putting Uncle Thomas in prison wouldn't solve their problems.

"It's not everything we've wanted," she said softly. "All I really want is for the Italian widow at Mr. Garzelli's tenement to have running water in her apartment. I want the valve sold to the people who will never be able to afford it so long as Thomas Drake is determined to bleed every possible cent from our grandfather's invention. If we send Thomas to jail, he will still control the company through Aunt Margaret, and that woman will never lower the price." She paused as a new idea struck her. "I can negotiate with Thomas. We hold the linchpin, and he knows it. We can demand an affordable price for the valve as the condition for ignoring this document."

"And what about the fortune he and Jacob cheated us out of?" Nick pressed.

"We'll never see it. And I don't care. God gave me two hands and the ability to make my own way in this world. I don't think I ever appreciated that gift until this very day."

Nick's sigh was heavy, but that didn't stop a reluctant smile from gracing his face. "I still want to drive a stake through Uncle Thomas's heart, but you're a better man than I, Luce. And you're probably right. If we play our cards right, Thomas might cave about the price of the valve, but he'll fight hard to keep that pile of money he's been sitting on all these years."

Colin's anger had not faded. He stalked back and forth before the window, and his words were tight with aggravation. "You're quitting before the game is over," he snapped. "You've got the king in checkmate and won't finish the deed."

Except this wasn't a game to her. It had never been about

the money so much as fulfilling her grandfather's wild, generous dreams.

"I'd rather declare victory by lowering the price of the valve. If we try for a share of the money, it will drag things out for years. I want this to end now."

Colin looked flabbergasted. "Don't you understand what winning this lawsuit could mean for you? Mean for *us*?"

She flinched, for it was impossible to mistake his meaning. Even Nick looked appalled. Now that Amelia Wooten had thrown Colin over, it seemed he was already hankering over the Drake fortune to spend on Whitefriars.

Her mouth twisted in disappointment. "I'm not interested in being courted by fortune hunters. However charming or however fine his title might be."

Colin looked as if she'd struck him, and his voice lashed out like a whip. "I have been nothing but honest with you from the beginning. You know my every mortifying weakness and desperate need. I thought we trusted each other. I love you! And I thought maybe we could find a way forward—"

She cut him off. "If I roll the dice and go after the money too, how could I trust that it's really me you want, and not just saving Whitefriars?"

His shoulders sagged as the fire went out of his eyes. When he finally spoke, his voice sounded exhausted. "Strange. I would have trusted you with my life, and actually did so at Oakmonte. I'm sorry you don't feel the same."

He headed out the door without a backward glance. Every instinct urged her to rush after him, wipe the hurt from his face, and proclaim that she loved him too . . . but it was time to end this hopeless affair. The door shut behind Colin with a gentle click, but the sound still hurt.

Nick's face radiated with sympathy. "You'll feel better in the morning," he said gently.

She doubted it. Knowing that Colin might have married her if she'd managed to win the Drake money made her hurt even more. It was a scar she would carry until her dying day, but at least she had Nick's loyalty. He understood her bone-deep need to put this demoralizing lawsuit behind them forever, even if it meant walking away from a fortune.

There was only one more battle to fight. The police complaint Colin had left on the table was the weapon that could force Uncle Thomas to sell the valve at a decent price. The deck was stacked in their favor; she was ready to pull the trigger and make it happen.

At long last, her grandfather's dream was about to come true.

$\mathcal{L}$ucy's hope for a quick victory over Uncle Thomas came crashing down the next day when she and Nick met with their lawyer. The battle was going to be bigger and more dangerous than she'd realized.

"You can't threaten your uncle with imprisonment in exchange for lowering the price of the valve," Mr. Pritchard said. "That's called extortion. Your uncle is smart enough to know that. He'll send his team of attack-dog lawyers at us, and before the week is out, all three of us could end up in jail. I can't have anything to do with this."

"But we have honorable motives," Lucy pressed. She was prepared to walk away from vengeance and a fortune, all in exchange for requiring her uncle to do the decent thing. It didn't seem fair that the law could come down on *her* for such an action. Just speaking about the valve and contracts caused the weight to descend on her again. Already she could feel the tentacles of old nightmares snaking up to drag her back beneath the waves.

Frustration nearly suffocated her as she and Nick stepped

out onto the street. She wanted this over but couldn't abandon the fight until she'd won the battle for her grandfather.

"I'm not giving up," she vowed. "We'll get a better lawyer. One who understands criminal law and can help us navigate these waters without getting sunk."

"We don't have that kind of money, Luce."

"Yes, we do." In the form of a pearl necklace her grandfather had foolishly given his wife the night before leaving to fight in the Civil War. The only thing that necklace had ever brought their family was anguish, but Nick always resisted letting it go. "We need to sell the necklace," she said softly.

Nick said nothing as they walked along the sidewalk, but the way his shoulders slumped made it obvious he'd heard her.

"When I was a kid, I used to imagine how that necklace would look on my wife. I dreamed about squiring her around town, wearing that necklace and looking so fine." His voice was so low she could barely hear it. "Stupid. I know that, but still . . ."

It was the same rush of masculine pride that had prompted her grandfather to splurge on the necklace in the first place, and Nick seemed to realize that.

"I suppose I'll never have a wife and kids if I get sent to the slammer," he said. "Let's get rid of that necklace."

Twenty-four hours later, the deed was done. They sold the necklace and had enough money to hire one of New York's best attorneys. How ironic that the money they got from the necklace would ensure that the Drake valve would finally be sold for a reasonable price.

After paying the new lawyer's fees, they used the balance of the money to hire a private investigator to track the movements of Uncle Thomas. Ever since Tom Jr.'s arrest, their aunt and uncle had been spending their days meeting with attorneys and visiting Tom in jail here in Manhattan. They were both distracted and distraught. It was the perfect time to strike.

Attorney Vincent Ruskin was cagey, smart, and tough. He was also cunning enough to cover his own hide when preparing the contracts. Knowing full well he was helping Lucy carry out an extortion attempt, he drew up all the paperwork without once signing his name or listing the title of his firm anywhere in the documents. After their initial meeting, he even came to their apartment to finalize the plan, for he wanted to keep an arm's length away from the quasi-legal incident.

"The pair of you are smart enough to carry this out," he said as he handed them the two stacks of paperwork. "Just follow my instructions to the letter, and you'll have your uncle painted into a corner."

She swallowed hard. It was time to bring down the dragon who'd haunted her childhood. The stack of legal documents looked official and intimidating, and New York's finest attorney assured her the contracts were ironclad. It was time to slip a noose over the dragon's head.

It would take place at the Waldorf Astoria, the most elegant hotel in the city. It was where Uncle Thomas always stayed when he was in Manhattan, but it gave Lucy the chills. The last time she'd been here was when Tom Jr. locked her in the dumbwaiter.

Nick carried the paperwork as they crossed the lobby, drawing stares. They'd worn their best clothes, but Nick's too-long hair looked out of place, and Lucy's white lace gown couldn't compete with the satins and silks the other women wore. The check-in counter was a massive slab of curving marble jutting out into the stately lobby, its shape as impressive as the prow of a ship.

"We are here to meet with Thomas Drake," Nick told the clerk. "And I'd like to reserve a conference room for the meeting."

The clerk looked skeptical, but since their uncle was a regular guest and Nick was paying in cash, the clerk permitted them to reserve one of the meeting rooms. Their private investigator had said their aunt and uncle spent their days dealing with Tom Jr.'s legal quagmire and returned to the Waldorf Astoria sometime between five and seven o'clock each evening. Lucy picked a seat in the main foyer to keep an eye on the front door. Their lawyer had advised them to intercept Uncle Thomas immediately upon his return to the hotel. If he got to his room, he would have access to a telephone and might summon an attorney if he suspected what Lucy intended.

At least the seating was comfortable. The cushions on the baroque chairs were covered in velvet and felt like sitting on a cloud. Her gaze wandered over the marble columns that soared to the coffered ceiling. Everything in this foyer was gilded, lacquered, or draped in silk.

Nick leaned over to whisper in her ear. "Can you believe that an hour ago you were tending a telegraph machine and I was a hundred feet underground fitting sewer pipes?"

She stifled a snort of laughter. Neither one of them belonged here, and she'd much rather be opening a can of beef stew in the comfort of her own apartment, but she needed to get this agreement signed. Only then could she put the past behind her and venture into a new chapter of life.

As impressive as the surroundings were, the guests were even more so. The women were poured into custom-tailored gowns and wore broad-brimmed hats piled high with feathers and gemstones. They looked like exotic pieces of art. They didn't walk, they glided. They didn't work, they socialized. It was probably just as well Lucy wasn't going to marry Colin. She didn't feel comfortable in this lavish hotel and could never pretend to be a grand lady capable of presiding over Whitefriars.

She looked down at her hands clasped in her lap. Envy was such an ugly emotion. It wasn't that she envied these ladies.

She didn't covet their silks, their status, or their leisure . . . but she envied that they were the sort of women Colin would have courted for more than an afternoon flirtation in the park.

She couldn't wallow in regret about Colin, not when she had a dragon to confront. Her palms itched and her heart raced. She wished their lawyer was here. She wished the sight of her uncle didn't intimidate her so. She wished she was as smart as her grandfather or as brave as Nick, for the longer she sat in this opulent lobby, the harder it became to breathe. Everything depended on the next few minutes.

"Here they are," Nick whispered.

This was it. Lucy rose to her feet and spotted her aunt and uncle striding through the front doors. Margaret peeled off her gloves and hat, passing them to a bellhop without breaking stride or glancing at the young man. Lucy swallowed hard. The next few minutes would determine if poor people crowded into the towering buildings of Manhattan could enjoy fresh water the way rich people at this hotel took for granted.

Her boots clicked on the glossy tile as she and Nick scurried past the front counter to block Thomas and Margaret just before they got to the elevators.

"Uncle Thomas," Nick said in a loud voice that echoed across the marble lobby. "We have business to discuss."

Thomas looked surprised, but Margaret was incensed. Her eyes narrowed, and her voice was just as loud. "We have no business with you," she said. "We've just come from our son's side. He is prostrate with anxiety, unable to rise from his bed, unable to mount a defense against your despicable lies."

Heads swiveled, and the clerk at the front desk raised his hand, summoning a group of the hotel porters standing near the front door. Getting thrown out of the hotel would be a disaster, and they had to move quickly.

"If your husband doesn't cooperate with us, he will be equally prostrate with anxiety." Nick's voice was soft, making it even more threatening.

"Of all the loathsome things to say," Margaret spat. "I shouldn't expect better from a sewer rat, but I had hoped you would have the common decency—"

Thomas cut her off, raising his hand. "What are you suggesting?"

The cluster of intimidating hotel porters reached the front desk, and the clerk sent them over.

"I'm suggesting that you follow us into a meeting room so we can have some privacy," Lucy said with as much calmness as she could muster. Anything to escape the uniformed men heading their way.

"I wouldn't follow you into Buckingham Palace," Margaret said in a snarl that caused more heads to turn.

"Can I be of assistance?" A man in a formal suit backed by two hotel porters approached. His voice was polite, but his face was hard.

Thankfully, Uncle Thomas was more levelheaded than his wife. "Please forgive the disturbance. It has been a trying day. We'll repair to a meeting room to carry on this conversation in private."

Lucy breathed a sigh of relief. Nick led the way down the gilded hallway and toward the carved mahogany door of a meeting room. He waited until all four of them were inside before he closed the door with a gentle snick.

The room was dominated by a conference table surrounded by a dozen chairs, but everyone remained standing. Lucy had memorized the words the lawyer had instructed her to say, and spoke them verbatim.

"I have two sets of papers," she said calmly. "One is a contractual agreement to sell the Drake valve at no more than seventy-five percent markup from the cost of production. The other is a report I can sign and file with the police, complete with an account of my experience at Ridgemoor, an affidavit from Dr. Schroeder claiming he acted under your directive, and the letter you wrote to my father fourteen years ago, which proves your pattern of caging people in mental institutions. If I submit these documents to the police, you *will* be convicted of kidnapping. You might even be able to share a prison cell with Dr. Schroeder. On the other hand, you can sign the first set of papers to start selling the valves at a reasonable price. You can keep the money you've gouged out of people over the years; we don't want it. But make no mistake, one of these documents is going to be signed within the next ten minutes. You get to decide which one."

Uncle Thomas's face was chalk white, but his eyes were sharp. "I want a lawyer."

"Too bad," she replied. "You now have nine minutes to decide which of these papers gets signed. Otherwise I sign the complaint to the police." She set both stacks of paper on the table and pulled out a chair. "Please. Feel free to read them."

Uncle Thomas picked up the valve contract, his eyes moving over the pages of the ironclad agreement. Aunt Margaret seemed to realize the gravity of the situation and gaped in horror at her husband, her hand clutching the lace at her throat. That hand flashed a sapphire large enough to clog a sink drain. Lucy didn't feel sorry for her.

With two minutes left on the deadline, Uncle Thomas signed the contract lowering the price of the valve. The pen scratched in the silence of the room. He didn't speak a word and didn't look at them, but Margaret's glare was pure malice. After the papers were signed, Thomas rose and reached for her hand, but Margaret had a parting shot.

"Do you think you've won?" she spat. "Sometimes mosquitos can land a bite, but they always get slapped down in the end. I promise you, no matter how long it takes, I will see you and everyone you love swatted down like the nasty pests you are."

Lucy felt no need to reply, only an overwhelming sense of relief as the pair left the room without a backward glance.

It was over. The rest of her life could begin.

❧❧❧

She was wrong. A day after coercing Thomas into selling the valves at a decent price, a new and unexpected phase of the battle began. Like every Sunday, she and Nick rose early to attend services at the small church down the street. She bowed her head to give thanks and pray for wisdom as she ventured into the next chapter of her life.

Only ten minutes into the service, Nick stiffened beside her, triggering every nerve ending in her body. "What's wrong?" she whispered.

"Old Jacob Drake just walked in," he whispered back. "Don't turn around, but he's a few pews behind us. He's got a bunch of those henchmen with him. They're watching us."

Her mouth went dry, and her heart thumped with a force that made it hard to sit still. What did Jacob want with them? She sat pinned in the pew, helpless as poisonous old feelings came flooding back, urging her to fight, to flee, to strike out in vengeance. All she wanted was for this to be over. Jacob might be here to appeal for his son and grandson, or he might be jockeying to seize control of Drake Industries again. All she knew for sure was that if he meant them well, there would be no need for bodyguards. The nearest police station was six blocks away, and she doubted they could get there if Jacob's goons wanted to prevent it.

The service was interminable, and the words of the minister washed over her without penetrating the hard shell of her anxiety. At the end of the service, Nick's hand locked around her wrist to prevent her from rising.

"Let's see what they do," he said in a low voice.

The other parishioners filed out, but she and Nick remained motionless in their pew, her unease creeping higher with each passing minute. She tilted her head to peek behind her. Sure enough, the church was almost empty, but a flinty old man glared at her from four pews back. The entire row was filled by brawny men who made Sneed and Wolfe look like choirboys. After a few minutes, only the organist and an elderly man kneeling in prayer remained in the church. The voices of parishioners drifted in from the lobby, but soon they would disperse as well. Jacob and his henchmen showed no sign of moving.

"I don't want to be alone with them," she whispered to Nick, and he nodded.

"Let's meet them on the street," he said. "They wouldn't dare do anything in full view of the congregants."

They rose quickly and strode down the center aisle. As if on cue, the bodyguards all stood but made no effort to block her or Nick as they headed toward the front door. As soon as they passed Jacob's aisle, the men began shuffling out of the pew to follow them.

"Don't turn around, don't look at them," Nick urged.

She clasped his hand as they headed out the door and down the dozen steps leading to the street. Clusters of people mingled on the sidewalk. As soon as they reached the walkway, she and Nick joined the others and turned to face their great-uncle. A pair of his bodyguards lifted his wheelchair and began the treacherous journey down the steps. Despite herself, Lucy held her breath as Jacob swayed like the mast of a ship in a storm with each descending step. She breathed again when the wheels were safely back on solid ground. Jacob stared directly at Nick as one of his bodyguards wheeled him closer.

"Let's go somewhere private to talk," the old man said.

"Let's talk here," Nick replied.

Jacob shook his head. "Too many people, and we have business to discuss. Important business."

"I'm listening." Nick folded his arms across his chest but made no attempt to move.

Jacob's eyes narrowed. "In case you aren't aware, I despise young men who have no respect for their elders. It's a sign of stupidity and an inability to function in modern society." He reached into his coat pocket. Lucy and Nick instinctively took a step back, which seemed to amuse Jacob. "Oh, for pity's sake. If I wanted you dead, you'd both already be dead," he groused, then handed Nick an official-looking set of papers.

Nick unfolded it, his brow clouding in confusion. "What's this?"

"It's a report from my private investigator claiming you've been building reproductions of the Drake valve out of spare parts and installing them in tenement buildings."

"If you think I'm going to confess to anything illegal, you're both stupid and crazy."

Jacob raised a warning finger. "What did I just tell you about lack of respect?"

"You haven't exactly earned it, old man." Nick tossed the papers down on Jacob's lap. "Those papers prove I've got a functioning brain in my head, but I don't know the same about you, do I?"

"I built a forty-million-dollar fortune starting with nothing. You don't think I've got a functioning brain?"

Lucy couldn't remain silent. "But you didn't start with 'nothing,'" she snapped. "You started with my grandfather's valve."

Jacob didn't even turn to look at her, keeping his gaze locked on Nick. "We both know that without me, Eustace would have had a box full of half-completed inventions and nothing but two dimes to rub together."

"Fine, you're a smart man," Nick acknowledged. "That doesn't mean I have to like you."

Jacob braced his hands on the wheels of his chair and rolled it forward. Nick refused to step back, and their knees bumped before Jacob came to a stop.

"This is a copy of my last will and testament," Jacob said as he swatted another stack of papers against Nick's chest. "I am prepared to leave my entire fortune to you . . . provided you prove yourself worthy of it."

Lucy sucked in a quick breath, stunned at the magnitude of what she'd just heard. Given the way the bodyguards responded, this was news to them as well.

Even Nick looked surprised, but he masked it quickly and pointed to a vacant bench a block away. "Let's talk," he said grimly.

Two minutes later, Lucy and Nick were seated on the bench with Jacob in his wheelchair opposite them. Pedestrians had to navigate around him, but the old man didn't seem to care as he passed the copy of his will over. Sure enough, Nick's name was listed to inherit one hundred percent of Jacob's estate, and a paragraph specifically disinherited both Thomas Drake and Tom Jr.

"It's only fair that Lucy should get half," Nick said.

"No good," Jacob replied. "This fortune was built on the invention of a plumber, and it shall be inherited by a plumber. That's the way I want it, and how my brother would have wanted it. There is a poetic justice in it that appeals to me."

Nick locked gazes with Jacob. "If I inherit, I'm giving half to Lucy."

"Nick . . ." she tried to interrupt, but he silenced her with a raised hand. She didn't need half of Jacob's fortune, but she wouldn't mind seeing Nick get his hands on it. Jacob seemed like a volatile man, the sort who might change his mind if Nick proved difficult. And Nick could be very difficult.

For the first time, Jacob turned to look at her. His steel-gray gaze pierced her like a blade. "Show me your hands," he demanded.

She had nothing to be embarrassed about. She raised her hands, displaying her short nails, no jewelry, and a ridge of hard calluses on her thumb and forefinger. Jacob's eyes narrowed with satisfaction, but he turned back to Nick without saying another word to her.

"I won't have my money going to support a useless foreign aristocrat," he said to Nick. "Oh yes, I've heard about your sister gallivanting around town with a fortune hunter. I won't let a dime of my money support a freeloading aristocrat, so she's out of the will. She can't be trusted." He turned back to her. "Although I like the fact that you have those calluses," he added grudgingly, and Lucy had the strangest sensation that she'd just been paid a compliment.

"And how will you stop me from giving half to Lucy after you're dead?" Nick challenged, and it took an unusually long time for Jacob to respond.

"I'm afraid you will discover that ghosts have a way of haunting a man," he said.

A smile curved Nick's mouth, and it sounded like he was struggling to hold back laughter. "Are you telling me you have the power to haunt me from the grave? You're even more arrogant than I thought."

"You're a fast learner." Jacob looked up and down the street, then pointed to an Italian bakery on the corner. "Let's get something to eat. This sun is annoying."

He was already wheeling himself toward the bakery when Nick's voice stopped him.

"Are you going to treat my sister with respect?"

"Will you treat your elders with respect?" Jacob demanded.

"It depends on who's paying for breakfast."

Jacob's laugh was papery, as though it had been a long time since he'd found anything amusing.

The bakery was cramped, with small, round café tables packed so closely that diners were in constant danger of knocking elbows, but Jacob didn't seem to mind. He dismissed his bodyguards, keeping only the two men responsible for carrying his chair up and down stairs. It felt surreal as she, Nick, and Jacob squeezed around a tiny table with plates of Italian almond biscuits and strong black coffee. Jacob wasted time complaining about the biscotti before getting down to business, but when his offer finally came, it was stunning.

He wanted Nick to quit his job at the Water Authority, move to Albany, and learn the art of business. It was bound to be a deal-breaker. Not only did Nick love his job, but living under Jacob's roof would be like tossing a lit match into a powder keg. The two men were getting along at the moment, but they'd been in the bakery for less than ten minutes.

"Why can't Nick learn business here?" Lucy asked.

"Because I'm rich enough to demand what I want, and I want him in Albany," Jacob snapped.

This was going to be a disaster. Nick was a plumber, not a man of business or whatever Jacob wanted him to become.

"I want to go," Nick said.

Her jaw dropped. "But Nick! You love working for the Water Authority. What will you do if you can't build and fix things?"

"I don't know, Luce . . . but I want the freedom to find out."

And over the next hour, Lucy learned just how big that freedom would be. Although Jacob had been tricked out of sixty percent ownership of Drake Industries by his own son, it represented only a tiny fraction of his assets. Over the decades, Jacob had diversified into railroads, oil, and mining. The immensity of his holdings was why he insisted Nick come live in Albany to learn how to wield the reins.

Nick leaned forward to catch every syllable Jacob uttered. The spellbound concentration on his face was fascinating but worrisome. Even though Lucy and Nick sat as close together as sardines in a tin, a distance had taken root between them. Soon he would leave his workaday job and move upstate. Instead of fitting pipes, he would live in a fancy house and learn how to navigate in an entirely new world. Nothing would be the same after Nick left.

She toyed with her cold cup of coffee. Her world was changing quickly, and she didn't know if it would be for the better.

Chapter
TWENTY-SIX

*P*recisely one month after Colin's last break with Lucy, he forced himself back out into the social whirl by attending a gala celebration in the Egyptian wing of the Metropolitan Museum of Art.

Hundreds of the city's finest had flocked to the museum, where torches had been lit, musicians hired, and waiters carried silver platters of Middle Eastern delicacies as the crowd mingled among the sarcophagi, granite statues, and immense slabs of stone friezes taken from Egyptian temples. The dimmed lighting cast the monumental statues in flickering shadow, adding to the exotic appeal.

It made Colin feel stifled. He was determined to shake the gloomy mood that had haunted him ever since the night he'd quarreled with Lucy. In hindsight, he admired how she could walk away from the legacy of acrimony that haunted her life. A piece of him longed to do the same, but with ninety tenants depending on him, he couldn't blithely declare the game over the way she had. In his less proud moments, he admitted feeling jealousy. What must it be like to have the freedom she seized for herself?

She certainly looked happy. He'd seen her four times since that fateful night. Twice waiting for the elevator, once in the cafeteria, and once walking to the streetcar stop. Each time she sent him a tentative smile and a nod, which he managed to return without too much bitterness. What was there to be bitter about? They had made no promises to each other, and just because he desperately missed her was no cause to resent her newfound freedom.

A waiter approached with a tray of miniature teacups. "Sahlab, sir?"

Colin gathered that sahlab was an Arabic drink of hot milk with vanilla and rose water. Earlier in the evening, the waiters had been proffering seared monkfish filets and something made of sesame paste and pistachios. All of it tasted odd to him, but the guests had been scarfing down the delicacies faster than the waiters could supply them. Perhaps the association with the exotic made people excited, but he'd rather have some of Nanny Teresa's shortbread.

"No, thank you," he said to the waiter, then headed toward a cluster of people mingling by a re-creation of an Egyptian tomb. The Allentons were there, and Melanie Allenton was unattached, of sound mind and body, and most importantly, rich. There was nothing wrong with her, he just didn't feel an ounce of attraction.

It didn't matter. She was an eligible heiress, and Whitefriars needed a new roof. For the millionth time, he envied Lucy's freedom.

"There's the man of the hour!" the oldest Allenton brother boomed as Colin approached their group. Ever since Colin's name had been linked with the arrest of Tom Jr., he was the toast of New York. The combination of Tom's downfall, a foreign title, and a dash of derring-do was tailor-made for the gossip pages. Instead of having to seek out heiresses, women were now flocking to him.

"I hear the trial is scheduled for next month," George Allenton said. "The reporter covering the story for the *Times* expects Drake to plead guilty in hope of getting a shorter sentence. What do you think?"

"If Tom is smart, he'll take the deal," Colin replied. Felix Moreno had already pled guilty and confessed to his role in the scheme, so it was going to be hard for Tom to claim ignorance of the plot he'd been participating in.

Melanie Allenton's brown eyes warmed as she took a step closer to him. "What was it like to work with the Secret Service?" she asked in a breathless voice, gazing at him like he was actual royalty.

"It made me appreciate the joy of a boring office job."

The group pealed with laughter. They continued bombarding him with questions about the notorious assassination plot, but he didn't like claiming credit for bringing Tom down. He wasn't the hero, Lucy was. She was the one who first recognized the telegrams for what they were. She escaped through the sewers and voluntarily walked into Ridgemoor. She was the one brave enough to walk away from a lifelong obsession in order to do what was right.

Two weeks ago, he'd learned she had succeeded in lowering the price of the valve. There had been a series of newspaper stories about Thomas Drake's new pricing structure, in which he magnanimously announced his intention to improve the lives of the poor. Most people assumed it was a desperate attempt to buy public goodwill as his son's trial approached, but Colin knew otherwise.

A boom sounded outside, startling everyone in the gallery.

"Fireworks!" someone called, and most of the crowd rushed for the windows on the far side of the gallery. Colin remained motionless, a queasy feeling in his stomach roaring to life, a sheen of perspiration prickling across his skin. It was only fireworks. He'd known about the fireworks this evening, but still the racket took him by surprise. He concentrated on drawing in regular lungfuls of air and willing his heart to slow.

He grabbed a copy of the museum program, fanning himself. It was hot in here. Airless. At least he hadn't bolted for cover like he would have done a few months earlier. Maybe he would always be plagued by these awful, mortifying spells, but he was getting better.

He sensed someone staring at him. Across the gallery, beside a mammoth statue of an Egyptian pharaoh, Frank Wooten met his gaze. Colin shrugged a little helplessly, then went back to fanning himself. Frank gave a nod of understanding, then turned to watch the fireworks with the others.

How odd that Colin had always gotten along better with Frank Wooten than with his daughter. Amelia was here this evening, still hanging on the arm of Count Ostrowski and pretending that Colin didn't exist.

With most of the crowd clustered near the windows, a waiter bearing a tray of delicacies headed Colin's way. He eyed the blackened bits of meat with curiosity. "What are they?"

"Duck skewers with a date and tahini paste. The other is spiced cauliflower with lime yogurt sauce."

Colin politely declined and kept fanning himself. More than anything, he wished for a good cup of tea, the kind brewed in the Whitefriars kitchen. There was nothing quite like it available in America. Big, loosely chopped tea leaves infused with oil from bergamot oranges. It tasted like home and comfort, and he'd trade every Middle Eastern delicacy served here for a cup of that tea right now.

Ten minutes later, the fireworks were over, and the crowd moved back to mingle throughout the gallery. Colin gathered his wits, ready to try a flirtation with Melanie Allenton in hope of finding a bit of common ground or hint of attraction. Even though it would never be like when he met Lucy. Magnetism had flared within five seconds and only burned brighter the longer he knew her.

But Lucy had moved on. He was still mired in the same spot he'd been a year ago, searching for an heiress and wondering how to save Whitefriars.

Think like an American.

It was what Frank had urged him to do when he was still courting Amelia. The idea Frank had outlined was daring . . . and just because the potential marriage had collapsed, did that mean the business plan needed to as well?

Another waiter approached, this time presenting a tray of miniature cakes. "Lemon basbousa cake," the waiter said. "A favorite in Egypt."

"How exotic," Melanie purred as she helped herself to one.

Colin did as well. Now *this* was more to his liking. Sweet, its lemony flavor mixed with a hint of coconut and almonds. It paled in comparison with Nanny Teresa's lemon cream short-bread, but it was still good. Serving it amidst the Egyptian exhibit made it taste even better. Frank would probably say it was all in the packaging and presentation. That was what Frank had been obsessing over back when they were contemplating a business alliance.

Except Frank was thinking about how to upgrade his canned fruit business. What if . . .

The idea hit Colin like a bolt of lightning. It was an audacious idea, but maybe he was finally learning to think like an American.

"The music will be starting in the first-floor gallery," Melanie said, her sentence dangling, clearly waiting for him to offer to escort her downstairs.

"Excellent," he said. "But I'm afraid I must get home immediately."

It wasn't the most delicate way to excuse himself, but he needed to wake up Nanny Teresa and get her to make as much lemon cream shortbread as their tiny kitchen could produce.

He'd just had an idea for how to save Whitefriars, and it would begin tonight.

After a telephone call to Frank Wooten's secretary, Colin had an appointment with the man he once hoped would become his father-in-law. Now he wanted Frank as a business partner. The proposal he was about to make was a gamble, but the only thing he risked losing was a pan of lemon cream shortbread, and with luck he could be saving both his dignity and Whitefriars.

At four o'clock, he was shown into Mr. Wooten's office with its view of the Manhattan skyline. The self-made millionaire sat at a desk weighed down with neatly organized stacks of files and financial statements. Colin came armed with a basket of lemon cream shortbread and a tin of tea he'd brought from Whitefriars. Frank's welcoming smile turned confused, then appalled as Colin began outlining his proposal. Mr. Wooten's famously impatient demeanor got the better of him, and he cut Colin off before he could finish explaining his plan.

"You want me to drop everything, sail across the ocean, and invest a fortune in a floundering estate? The crumbling fortunes of European aristocrats are everywhere. Why should I invest in Whitefriars?"

"Because it is a once-in-a-lifetime investment you won't find anywhere else," Colin said, determined to start thinking and sounding like an American. "You need the prestige of the White-friars name, and we need your experience. You and I think alike. We don't need to resort to the antiquated custom of a marriage alliance to solidify the deal. I have a property, a name, and an estate that can add instant prestige to your company. And I'm not talking only about jars of fancy fruit or jam. I'm proposing an entire line of delicacies inspired by the English countryside. You know how to can and bottle fruit, but you're competing with dozens of other companies who want to do everything faster and cheaper. Go high-end. I'll sell you the rights to use the Whitefriars name and image, but it will have to happen quickly." The repairs to the music room could not wait.

Nor could Lucy. If this deal worked, he would be free to pursue her, to cut free of his past just as she had done and embark on a new life of his own choosing.

"How quickly?" Frank demanded.

"I want it done before the end of September. By Christmastime, your company can reinvent itself with an aristocratic lineage behind it."

Frank leaned back in his chair, the friendliness gone. "I'm not interested in licensing the Whitefriars name. I want the house. The land. Everything."

Colin blanched. That hadn't been part of the deal they were negotiating earlier this summer, but when he said as much, Frank's reply was brusque.

"Back then I was considering you as a potential son-in-law. That's off the table now, so we're discussing a straightforward business deal. I have no interest in paying a fortune for nothing more than a name and an image. I want the house. I want this deal locked down so it's watertight, and that means I have to be in complete control. This is an all-or-nothing deal, Sir Beckwith."

This would never work. It would mean he had to walk away from his heritage, his sister's sense of security. His home. Whitefriars was an albatross around his neck, but he still loved every stone, every squeaky floorboard, the view from every window. If he signed a deal with Frank, it would all be gone. He could already hear his ancestors howling in dismay as he proposed linking their name to an American fruit canning company, but pride wasn't going to pay for a new roof on his house. The fortunes of his family had been sinking for generations. He wasn't so arrogant as to think that only someone with a Beckwith lineage could do right by Whitefriars, but he didn't want to sell it out of the family.

He affected an indifferent tone. "Why would you want a drafty old house? It's in the middle of nowhere. It doesn't even have running water or telephone lines. Someone like you could never live there."

"I won't invest a fortune in a line of products based on something I don't own." Frank opened a leather-bound calendar and began flipping through the pages. "I need to see the property again. We can sail at the end of the week. I'll have an agent assess the estate's value and set a fair price. Those are my terms. Do we have a deal or not?"

Colin clenched his fists. This was going to hurt. It was going to break his sister's heart and cut the foundation of his world out from beneath him. But it was also going to save ninety tenants. It would restore Whitefriars to the magnificent home it once had been. It would secure his future without having to sell his soul or hand in marriage. It would set him free.

"When do we sail?" he said.

There were still dozens of hurdles to clear and his sister to persuade, but with luck and hard work, he could save Whitefriars.

Chapter
TWENTY-SEVEN

To her profound embarrassment, Lucy found herself irresistibly drawn to tracking the movements of Colin Beckwith as his star rose in Manhattan. He was the city's newest luminary. His role in bringing Tom Jr. down had completely overshadowed earlier rumors about his erratic behavior. Each day she turned straight to the society pages, which often featured Colin's attendance at various high-society gatherings, probably on the hunt for another heiress. This daily ritual of stalking his activities was a unique form of torture she was helpless to resist. Her better half wished him well and hoped he found happiness; the other half was tempted to mound these newspapers into a dramatic pyre and set them aflame whenever she read about him in the company of another lady.

Then, in early September, as if someone had turned off the spigot, the stories about Colin evaporated. At first she was grateful not to be subjected to the mental images of him flirting in perfume-scented ballrooms, but that was soon replaced by concern. He wasn't coming to the office anymore, either. Twice she had gone up to Reuters to do repairs on the pneumatic tubes, and she'd risked a peek through the window in his office door.

The room had been empty, and the stack of mail on his desk had grown alarmingly high.

Her curiosity regarding his whereabouts tormented her like an itch she couldn't scratch. Three weeks after he disappeared, she couldn't take it any longer. As she entered the elevator at the end of a long day, she spotted one of the few female telegraph operators who worked at Reuters. Lucy nudged through the others in the elevator until she was alongside the operator.

"Was Sir Beckwith in today?" she asked.

"Heavens, no. He's gone back to England."

She sucked in a little breath. "He did? Why?"

The operator shrugged. "It's all been very hush-hush. He said it was 'family business' before he left, but most people think it's because he's getting married to some fine lady back home."

A physical weight landed on Lucy's chest, making it hard to breathe in the tight, confined elevator. When the doors opened, she strode as fast as her legs could carry her until she reached the blissfully cool air outside the building.

Her brief but exhilarating fling with Colin would probably hurt until her dying day, but she wasn't going to wallow in it. No more! Now that her life had been liberated from the court case, she had the time to turn herself into a better, more interesting person. She had already begun broadening her horizons by signing up for a class on how to operate a radio. She wasn't even sure what a radio was, but the AP was about to get one for sending wireless telegraph messages, and she wanted to learn about it.

Just as she'd already started learning how to cook. Ever since Nick moved to Albany, it seemed pointless to cook for only one person, but life was too precious to waste doing nothing. Each day for the rest of her life, she was going to learn something new, do something charitable, or simply try something different. Even if all she wanted to do on this awful evening was curl up in the safety of her apartment and weep over the fact that Colin might be getting married. But moping would never do. Stagnating was forbidden. If she wasn't moving forward, she was slipping into the bad habits of her past.

She bought some vegetables and a pound of potatoes on the way home from work. She would drag out a recipe book and make a pot of homemade soup instead of opening a can for dinner. After cutting up the vegetables and putting them on the stove to simmer, she grabbed the book about bird-watching she'd checked out from the public library. She had already begun attending weekly bird-watching talks given by an ornithologist in Central Park each Saturday morning. Anything to get her out of her lonely apartment and meeting new people.

So hard was she concentrating on trying to master the migration patterns of northern birds that she completely forgot about the soup until the scent of burning potatoes demanded her attention. She leapt off the sofa and ran to the kitchen, scorching her hand as she lifted the lid from the pot. Who knew it was possible to burn soup? The pot was heavy as she lifted it off the flame, then began scraping it with a wooden spoon to dislodge the layer of potatoes and onions that had fused to the bottom.

The reek of burnt vegetables stank up the apartment, and she was waving a towel to diffuse the stench when a loud knock sounded on the door. She startled but relaxed at the sound of Nick's familiar voice.

"It's just me, Luce."

She opened the door and gasped. "You cut your hair!"

"I figured it was time." He nudged his way inside their apartment, lugging a valise and an oversized box under one arm. Nick's hair wasn't the only thing that was different. She was used to seeing him in a plain white shirt and suspenders, but today he wore a tailored wool coat and a shirt collar that looked uncomfortable.

"I brought you a telephone," he said as he set the box on their kitchen table with a thud. "I'm afraid that one of these days I'll be tempted to strangle Jacob Drake. I'll need you to talk me down, so I want a telephone in this apartment. I'll pay the monthly bill."

"Are you *that* miserable in Albany?" she asked.

It was worrisome that Nick didn't answer right away. He just hauled his valise back to his old room and hefted it onto the bed, the mattress springs squeaking as the bag bounced. He came back and plopped down at the kitchen table.

"It's pretty bad," he said. "Jacob may be a brilliant business-man, but he's a mean piece of work. I needed to get away for a week or two. And we need to talk about the money. Jacob says he's ready to start transferring lump sums to me, and I want to split it with you. Have you got a bank account set up for it?"

She tried to reiterate that she didn't need any of Jacob's money, especially if sharing it with her was going to further antagonize their great-uncle, but Nick cut her off.

"Shut up, Luce," he said in a worn-out voice. "Money has caused a rift in our family for generations, and I want that to end now. Everything I get is going to be shared fifty-fifty with you. I won't let money drive a wedge between us, too."

Like it had driven a wedge between her and Colin. What would he do if he learned that the Drake fortune was finally starting to find its way to her? Would it have made a difference? It was too late to worry about it, for he could be standing at the altar in England at this very moment.

She turned away so Nick wouldn't notice the despair on her face. "Did Jacob make you cut your hair?"

"Jacob can't *make* me do anything I don't want to do. I'm just trying to learn how to operate in this new line of work and . . ." He glanced out the window, his face a mask of exhaustion. "And

I've got enough real battles ahead without asking for more with a stupid thing like hair that's too long."

The frustration in Nick's voice was another blow. He was supposed to be the strong one, the one who was never afraid of anything and could power through whatever obstacle stood in his way. The gloom in his voice got to her.

"Oh, Nick," she sighed. "We're both a mess."

His laugh came from deep in his chest. "Why do you think I bought us a telephone?"

She couldn't help but laugh in return, even if it was mixed with a few sniffles. Nothing had been the same since Nick had left. Now that they had no money worries, they were supposed to be deliriously happy, right? It looked like they would just have to keep reminding themselves of that.

A week later, Lucy accompanied Nick to the train station for his return trip to Albany, then headed off to Central Park for her bird-watching class. An ornithologist from Cornell led the group of bird watchers on a tromp through the park each Saturday morning, and they always met here at the Ladies' Pavilion. Lucy had attended for the past four weeks and liked to arrive early to enjoy the fresh air and some time to sink into the pages of a novel.

After settling into a spot in the corner of the Ladies' Pavilion, she opened her novel and braced herself for the best of times and the worst of times in *A Tale of Two Cities*. Would she ever see London or Paris? Maybe not, but at least the pages of a book could transport her there for a few hours. The nattering of the women on the other side of the pavilion faded away, as did the brisk autumn breeze that tugged a strand of hair free. All of it vanished as she sank into the drama of Paris gripped in the throes of revolution.

Only the pigeon bothered her. It was too close, pecking away at the pavilion railing a few feet away. Without looking up from her book, she slid farther down the bench, but the pigeon kept scattering seed and distracting her. Before she'd met Colin, she'd thought pigeons were dirty, lazy creatures. Now she knew differently. Casting a wistful smile at the pigeon, she wondered—

It had a canister on its leg!

What on earth was a carrier pigeon doing in Central Park? But the bird seemed to have reached its final destination and was happily gorging on the seed spread along the railing. Someone must have sent that pigeon here. Could it be part of today's bird-watching class? That was surely it, but her heart still beat a little faster as she extended a hand and the pigeon climbed aboard. Holding her breath, she unlatched the canister, scolding herself for getting her hopes up. She probably shouldn't even be reading this message.

She wiggled the slip of paper free and nearly froze when she saw the note was written in Morse code. She skimmed the series of dots and dashes.

Miss Drake, would you join me for tea?

Her heart raced so hard she felt dizzy. Well! It seemed Colin was back from England, but where was he? She glanced around the park, scanning the open spaces and the pedestrians on the footpaths, but he was nowhere to be seen. Maybe he'd launched the bird from his office or even from his townhouse. He obviously had a good memory, for he recalled her vow in the hotel restaurant to start attending these bird-watching classes in Central Park. He had enclosed a blank strip of paper for her reply, and she drew a few calming breaths before she wrote her answer.

```
Sorry. I no longer have tea with men
courting heiresses.
```

She inserted the reply in the tube, lifted the pigeon, and watched as it took flight and careened behind a stand of fir trees on the other side of the grassy lawn. She loved Colin but could no longer play second fiddle while he searched for a rich wife. She deserved more than that.

The pigeon returned from the same location less than five minutes later. The message this time was masterfully short and dramatic.

```
No more heiresses. Sold Whitefriars.
```

Oh good heavens. Now her heart pounded so fast she had to sit down. He'd sold Whitefriars? And still came back to New York? If he'd sold Whitefriars, it meant he had no need for a rich wife.

She mustn't read too much into this. He'd probably returned to wrap up business at Reuters before heading back to England for good. It was foolish to imagine he'd come back for any other reason. She read the note three times. There was no mistake. He had sold Whitefriars.

There was no slip of paper for her to send a reply. She watched the pigeon happily peck at the seed on the railing, wishing her heart could stop racing.

As if her yearning had conjured him, Colin emerged from behind the stand of trees, striding toward her with confidence and purpose. Another pigeon rode on his shoulder. He looked happy, not like a man getting ready to tell her good-bye for a final time before sailing back to England forever. He locked gazes with her for his entire walk across the lawn, his eyes ablaze. Finally, he stood before her, fresh, windblown, and vibrantly alive. She rose to meet him.

"Hello, Lucy."

Even the sound of his voice made her heart squeeze. "I'm sorry you had to sell Whitefriars."

"I'm not," he said without losing a beat. "If I wanted it desperately enough, I could have married Amelia, for she's lost interest in her Polish count. She sent me a very conciliatory note, suggesting a renewal of our friendship, but that is the past. I sold Whitefriars and have no need of a wealthy heiress. I intend to stay in the United States permanently. I find that I am homeless in England, and the girl I love lives in New York."

She went so light-headed it was hard to see straight, and she had to sit down. She didn't even want to speak, for fear this moment would pop and vanish like a soap bubble.

Colin smiled widely as he braced his forearms on the railing so they could be eye-level with one another. "I figured I would find you here," he continued. "The first thing I wanted to do now that I'm back was seek you out and tell you I love you. Only you, not your highly unlikely Drake fortune."

That was good, since it was anyone's guess if Jacob Drake would actually deliver on his decision to leave his fortune to Nick.

This moment was so overwhelming that she couldn't think of what to say. She took the coward's way out by nodding toward the pigeon on his shoulder. "And you have a new pair of birds."

He grinned. "Yes! They are a delight. Lucy, meet George and Martha."

She blanched, not quite sure that even Colin would have the gall. "As in George and Martha Washington?"

"Well, they *are* American birds."

"I'm not certain if that's an insult or a compliment."

His eyes warmed with reluctant admiration. "George and Martha are valiant, tireless, and clever. Of course it is a compliment."

The wind blew again, and she used it as an excuse to swipe at a wayward tendril of hair. She didn't know what to say. How odd, since they'd been refreshingly forthright from the instant they first met on that snowy New Year's Eve.

As the silence lengthened, he seemed equally awkward. "I'm sorry I lost my temper on that last night in your apartment. When you refused to come watch Tom Jr. get his comeuppance, I was furious. But I was also amazed and humbled. With everything I have, I admire how you broke free and started anew. I wanted to find a way to walk away, too. Selling Whitefriars wasn't my first choice, but it was the right thing to do. We live in the twentieth century, and I've been trying to live in my seventeenth-century ancestor's world. It won't work."

He pushed away from the pavilion to stand upright. "So, Miss Drake . . . I repeat my original invitation. Will you join me for tea? I've brought something interesting to show you."

For the first time, she noticed a canvas sack slung over his shoulder. He held out his hand, palm up, and treated her like a great lady as he helped her rise and walked her out of the pavilion. From the sack he removed a blanket and tossed it on the ground. He placed an assortment of boxes, tins, and jars on the blanket. Heavens, it looked like a delightful spread.

A gust of wind knocked over one of the boxes, sending it tumbling across the lawn. Colin lunged after it, but it traveled several yards before he was able to scoop it up and carry it back to her.

"I'm afraid it's empty," he said, wiggling the box in the air. "But someday soon people all over America will be able to buy Nanny Teresa's lemon cream shortbread."

He handed her the box. It featured a vibrant watercolor of a platter of the familiar cookies on a lace doily. At the top of the box was an oval etching of a stately castle.

"Whitefriars?" she asked.

"Whitefriars," he confirmed. "There will be an entire line. Fancy tea, jam sold in hand-blown jars, shortbread. Maybe some candies, since Frank says the profit margin for candy is hard to beat. All of it manufactured by Frank's facility, but using the Whitefriars name and traditional English recipes."

She picked up a tin promising fine tea. It was empty too, but the tin featured a profusion of brilliantly colored orange blossoms, tea leaves, and trailing vines that made her want to buy it for the charming package alone. The jars were clear glass, but heavy and cut in the shape of an octagon. The label contained the same oval etching of Whitefriars.

"The label on the jam is smaller so the color of the fruit will be the backdrop," Colin said.

She set the jar back on the blanket. "I am in awe. Never in a million years would I have imagined you could be so business-like. Weren't you the one who suggested the word *capitalism* sounded like *dangerous and revolutionary* to your ears?"

"Now it sounds like *survival*," he said with a grin. "I'll be making a one-percent commission on every product we sell." He flicked the empty box of shortbread. "Of course, I invited you to a fancy English tea and don't have a morsel of food to offer. But I do have a hand to offer. And a heart, although that's already yours. I love you and would be honored if you would consent to be my wife."

The breath left her in a rush. She had no money of her own and nothing to offer him, but he was willing to marry her anyway. "Oh, Colin . . ." she said in a voice so shaky it sounded like a butterfly caught in a gale-force wind. "I love you, too. And I think I might be able to make a go of being your wife if I don't have to preside over some fancy castle."

He grinned but held up a hand to stop her. "Before you say anything else, you should probably get a look at the ring that comes with the job." He dug into his vest pocket and retrieved a plain, dark metal band.

"The first baron of Whitefriars was up to his eyeballs in debt when he won that battle off the coast of Malta. This was the ring he had given his wife years earlier. A plain band forged of iron. Even after he struck it rich, I guess she never wanted to trade it in for something else. All the subsequent wives went in for something flashier, but I am turning over a new leaf and am of a mind not to buy things until I've earned the money to pay for it. So for the moment, this is what I have to offer."

He dropped the ring into her palm. The metal was humble, but the blacksmith must have been a master, for the filigree ring had swirls forged into it, and a tiny, simple cross in the center of the design. She could understand why the first lady of Whitefriars wanted to keep it. This ring spoke not of glamour or status, but of enduring strength and beauty. It was the ring of a strong woman.

"I wouldn't want any other ring," she stammered. It suited her. Forged in fire. Resilient. It was bound to fit her to perfection. Her hand trembled as she held it out and Colin slipped the ring on her finger.

It was way too big and slipped off to bounce in the grass.

"We'll get it fitted!" they both said simultaneously, then burst out in laughter.

Colin leaned forward and caught her up in a kiss, and Lucy wrapped her arms around his neck and pulled him closer.

They would make this ring work, for there was nothing they couldn't do. They had crossed oceans, foiled an assassination, and overcome class differences. They had both broken free of a dangerous legacy, and together they would embark on a new life they would forge for themselves.

EPILOGUE

One Year Later

*L*ucy eyed the platter laden with German sausages and fermented cabbage as it was passed down the length of the table. Nick had rented the entire outdoor biergarten for his birthday celebration. With lights strung through the trees and platters of hearty German food circulating the shared tables, the mood was boisterous and loud.

Which was a problem, since Lucy had come here with the goal of getting to know Bridget O'Malley better. It looked as though Nick had serious intentions toward the pretty seamstress he had been courting for the past three months.

Bridget reared back, her eyes widening at the platter of pale meat passed beneath her nose.

"Have you tried the braunschweiger?" Lucy asked. "Colin isn't brave enough, but I'm game if you are."

Bridget flinched as she looked at the array of sausages on the plate. Bregenwurst, knackwurst, bratwurst, and liverwurst. The restaurant's host had tried to explain them earlier to Lucy, but they all seemed to have the same pale beige coloring and smell.

Colin raised his chin a notch. "I'm not trying any sausage soft enough to be spread with a knife."

Lucy grinned. Colin was always such a snob about food, especially since the extravagantly priced Whitefriars brand of shortbread, teas, and candies had debuted on the market. The public had eagerly embraced the gourmet delicacies, but Nick didn't want anything elegant at his party. Most of the guests here were the men Nick once worked with in the tunnels beneath Manhattan, along with their wives and children. Over two hundred people crammed the biergarten, for Nick was picking up the bill for everyone. When Jacob Drake died earlier in the year, he'd left his entire fortune to Nick. Although Nick tried to split it with Lucy, Colin was adamant that he intended to live off the money he earned through his own work with Reuters and the products sold under the Whitefriars brand.

Each morning, Lucy and Colin still walked hand in hand into the Western Union building, where they rode the elevator to the sixth floor. He escorted her to the AP telegraph office, kissed her hand, and bid her farewell.

"Have a good day, Lady Beckwith. I shall return at five o'clock to escort you home," he would say, then they parted ways and went to work at their rival news agencies. Until they had children, she intended to keep working at the AP. She had a fulfilling career, a man who loved her, and the knowledge that she was making the most of her God-given talents.

At the end of the table, Nick sat amidst a crowd of his old plumber friends. One would never know from his plain clothes and suspenders that he was one of the wealthiest men in Manhattan, for he never flaunted his money and still seemed most comfortable in his old stomping grounds. Lucy worried about him. His face was flushed in laughter as he watched a fellow plumber balance a mug of ale on his nose, and Lucy realized this was the first time she'd seen Nick looking genuinely happy in months.

"Come, let's be brave," she whispered conspiratorially to Bridget. "I'm trying the bratwurst. If we slather it with enough mustard, surely we'll be able to get it down."

Bridget smiled shyly back. "Okay," she said a little breathlessly. She certainly seemed a sweet young lady, but Lucy wished they had a quieter venue for getting to know each other.

A man in a herringbone vest not far from Nick snagged her attention. In an evening of rollicking good cheer, loud voices, and plentiful food, he looked out of place.

She elbowed Colin and spoke in a low voice. "Do you know that man over beneath the tent pole? The one scribbling in a notebook?"

Colin's eyes narrowed as he leaned forward to scrutinize the man in question. "I can't be sure, but it looks like Count Demetri Ostrowski. He was once my rival in courting Amelia Wooten."

The heiress's name caused an involuntary stab of jealousy in Lucy, and Colin noticed.

"Sheathe your claws, Yankee," he said with a wink. "The battle is over. You won."

She had indeed, but she didn't like the way the count was eyeing Nick with a mild sneer on his face. She rose and grabbed Colin's hand. "Come on," she said. "Introduce me."

Colin obliged, weaving among the long tables and around waitresses balancing trays filled with platters of meat and bowls of sauerkraut. When they reached the count, he tucked his notepad into his jacket and stood.

"It's been a while," Colin said with a casual smile. "Allow me to introduce my wife, Lady—"

"Mrs. Beckwith," she interrupted. She would probably never wear Colin's title with ease, and since they lived in America, she preferred the simple joy of being Mrs. Beckwith.

The count gave a slight bow. "Ma'am," he murmured politely.

"I'm glad you could join us," she said. "Nick rented out the entire restaurant, but I don't believe we've ever met. How do you know my brother?"

The count shifted his weight. "Your brother is a popular man. He has many acquaintances."

All true, but Count Ostrowski definitely wasn't the type of man Nick normally associated with.

"It was you, wasn't it?" Colin's voice was coiled with tension, and it cut through the celebratory air of the party. She looked at him curiously, surprised by the hint of anger on his face.

"I beg your pardon?" the count asked.

"It was you who wrote those gossip stories about me. You were at the Wooten residence that night, and somehow you must have had a spy planted at Oakmonte, didn't you?"

Lucy gasped. They had never discovered the source of those vicious rumors, but she'd always wondered. As if sensing the sudden tension, Nick showed up beside them. He extended a hand to the count.

"Hello, Demetri. I see you've met my sister." Nick turned to her. "Demetri was loitering outside when Bridget and I got here. He looked hungry, so we invited him inside."

"He's only hungry for gossip," Colin said. "You'll want to watch out for men like this. I suppose we are going to enjoy an account of this party in tomorrow's newspapers?"

Count Ostrowski smirked as he scanned the hundreds of people in the outdoor biergarten. "I'm not sure anything here would make the cut," he said dismissively. "Money can't buy class, now can it?"

Nick's friendly attitude vanished. "I've never tried to buy class, and I don't care what people say about me in the papers. If you've got a problem with me, throw a punch. Write your dirt. Take a stab at me. But if you print one bad word about my family, I'm coming after you."

"Is this fellow giving you trouble?" Ruby Malone inserted

herself into the group, her hands fisted, ready for battle. The hard-eyed girl Lucy had met at Ridgemoor now did office work for the Whitefriars brand of delicacies. Despite the genteel image of the product line, their chief clerk was a tough girl from Brooklyn who would fight to the death to make it succeed.

Count Ostrowski was about to respond, but Lucy held up a hand. She sensed he was doing his best to goad Nick into losing his temper, and that would be a disaster. "I don't care what people *say* about us," she told the count. "I care about who we *are*. My brother offered a stranger hospitality, and you are repaying it by digging up dirt about him."

"One doesn't have to dig very deep to find it," the count said as his gaze tracked to Bridget, sitting alone at the end of the table and opening her mouth wide in an attempt to take a bite of an oversized sandwich.

Nick grabbed the count by his lapels and shoved him against the side of the restaurant. "You write one bad thing about Bridget, and I'll stuff that notepad down your throat."

Colin grabbed Nick around the waist and hauled him back. "He's not worth it, my friend. There are things you can control in the world, and things you can't."

Nick's breathing was ragged, but Colin's words must have penetrated, for he straightened his collar and gave a nod of understanding. When he spoke to the count, his words were calm.

"You can say whatever you want about me, but leave Bridget out of it. She's a nice girl who isn't cut out for the spotlight. Leave her alone."

Count Ostrowski affected a pleasant smile. "I imagine a man of your wealth will kindly remember a hardworking journalist who overlooks the shortcomings of a woman who is . . . not cut out for the spotlight."

"You suppose correctly," Nick said tightly.

In all honesty, Lucy worried Nick wasn't cut out for the spotlight, either. The reading of Jacob Drake's will had caused a sensation when a vast fortune was inherited by a plumber. Americans loved to see an underdog rise to power, but they were just as eager to watch him stumble. Nick no longer worked in the tunnels beneath Manhattan. Instead he had taken a government position that planned the construction of new aqueducts to bring water into the city. Instead of plumbers, now Nick worked alongside politicians, engineers, lawyers, and yes, if he was going to make it in this new world, he was going to have to learn how to deal with journalists. Colin had done his best to guide Nick in this new and rarefied world, but her brother was a force of nature who was difficult to tame.

After the count turned to leave the biergarten, Colin put his arm around Nick's shoulders.

"Come on. Let's have one of those revolting blood sausages, and you can tell me about the new apartment you're about to buy."

Nick's face was flushed as he glared at the departing count's back. He swallowed hard. "Give me a second to cool down."

It didn't take long. Nick was naturally buoyant and soon swallowed back his annoyance, took a bracing breath of air, then flashed the reckless smile Lucy knew so well.

"Okay, I'm good!" he said, clapping Colin on the back. "Let's go set the night on fire."

They rejoined Bridget at the table. She had given up on the bratwurst but managed to flag down a serving girl and finagled an apple pie for the four of them to share. Their laughter lingered long into the night.

Over the past year, Lucy had known fear, hope, joy, and despair, but tonight was perfect. Would tomorrow be? Probably not, but she would seize this beautiful, star-speckled night while it lasted, for these fleeting moments of fellowship gave her the fortitude to venture toward whatever new challenges lay ahead.

HISTORICAL NOTE

Reuters and the Associated Press occupied different floors of the Western Union Telegraph Building until it was demolished in 1914. Although they were competing news agencies, they had a remarkable level of professional respect and cooperation as they sent their reporters into dangerous postings all over the world. The best example of their collaboration was the AP's leasing of Reuters' telegraph wires through the British colonies in Asia, an agreement that was in effect until the Pacific cable was completed in 1903.

The route for a canal through Central America was controversial for decades. Although the shortest path was through the Isthmus of Panama, the rugged terrain required numerous expensive locks. French engineers broke ground in 1879, but tropical diseases, an earthquake, and a financial scandal brought construction of the French canal to a halt in 1889. Negotiations with the Colombian government for the United States to resume the abandoned French canal proved difficult, causing a Nicaraguan route to become a tempting alternative. Numerous investors lost a fortune in Nicaragua when Roosevelt backed the Panamanian route through Colombia instead. The

United States quietly aided a Panamanian revolution against Colombia, resulting in Panama's independence in late 1903. Construction on the canal began in 1904, and the Panama Canal opened in 1914.

Over time, the new generation of ships became too large to use the canal, and a second, larger canal was built alongside the original Panama Canal and opened in 2016. Ironically, the Nicaraguan canal route is once again under consideration after a Chinese billionaire won approval for the project in 2013. Ecological concerns and mounting expenses have put the project on hold, but the path through Nicaragua continues to be a powerful lure.

DISCUSSION QUESTIONS

1. Lucy's wiretap into the lawyer's office is illegal, but she justifies her actions by claiming a distinction between the letter of the law and what was morally right. Was her choice truly honorable? Since she clearly stood to benefit by winning the lawsuit, can she genuinely claim to be acting in a selfless manner?

2. The friendships formed among telegraph operators as they chatted with one another during slow times is similar to online friendships over the internet. Have you ever formed an online friendship with someone you've never met?

3. Mrs. Schroeder knows that her husband is engaged in illegal activities at Ridgemoor. What is the moral obligation of a good woman married to a corrupt man?

4. When Lucy believes Colin has left to get married, she redoubles her efforts to broaden her horizons. Has heartbreak or other disappointment ever inspired you to become a better person?

5. Eustace Drake believed that his inventions were his contribution to making the world a better place. He said, "When I do this, I feel God smiling on me." Are there any special gifts or tasks you perform that make it feel like God is smiling on you?

6. Tom Jr. is intelligent and a talented marksman but suffers from an inflated view of himself fueled by his parents' gushing praise. Do you know any well-intentioned parents who have inadvertently puffed up their children? Tom's lack of moral compass aside, what other consequences can excessive parental praise have on a child?

7. The deal Jacob and Eustace struck was loosely modeled on Jacob and Esau (Genesis 25:29–34). In both cases, the deal was binding, albeit foolishly entered into. Was either Jacob morally justified in asserting the deal?

8. Lucy dislikes President Roosevelt but is incensed when she learns of the plot against him and is willing to risk everything on his behalf. In our own era when distrust of political figures runs high, how do you feel about her lockstep loyalty to the office rather than the man?

9. Even though Colin and Lucy eagerly embrace technological advances, they both find charm and value in the lost art of homing pigeons. We live in a similar age of technology-driven change. Are there any obsolete traditions or technologies for which you feel a genuine sense of loss?

10. Frank Wooten favors Colin over the Polish count as a husband for his daughter because Colin has a solid history of

accomplishment. When a parent has qualms about their child's pick of a spouse, what is the appropriate level of intervention, if any?

In 2018,
Look for Nicholas Drake's Story
in *A Daring Venture*

Amidst the glamour of turn-of-the century New York, Dr. Rosalind Werner is at the forefront of an innovative but risky experiment to eliminate waterborne disease from the nation's water supply. This brings her into direct confrontation with Nicholas Drake, the newly appointed Commissioner of Water for the state of New York. As scientists and engineers line up to take sides in a battle that will be fought in the courts, the streets, and in college laboratories across the nation, Rosalind and Nick wage their own personal war as their reluctant attraction becomes impossible to ignore. When the conflict grows into an inflammatory public controversy, can these two rivals overcome their differences to prevail against the opposition coming at them from all sides?

Elizabeth Camden is the author of ten historical novels and two historical novellas and has been honored with both the RITA Award and the Christy Award. With a master's in history and a master's in library science, she is a research librarian by day and scribbles away on her next novel by night. She lives with her husband in Florida. Learn more at www.elizabethcamden.com.

Sign Up for Elizabeth's Newsletter!

Keep up to date with Elizabeth's news on book releases and events by signing up for her email list at elizabethcamden.com.

More from Elizabeth Camden

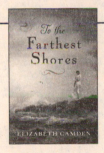

Naval officer Ryan Gallagher broke nurse Jenny Bennett's heart six years ago when he abruptly disappeared. Now he's returned. However, with lives still at risk, he can't tell Jenny the truth about his overseas mission—but he can't bear to lose her again either.

To the Farthest Shores

More from Elizabeth Camden

Visit elizabethcamden.com for a full list of her books.

Artist Stella West has moved to Boston to solve the mysterious death of her sister, but she is in need of a well-connected ally. Fortunately, magazine owner Romulus White has been trying to hire her for years. Sparks fly when they join forces, but will her questions cost him everything?

From This Moment

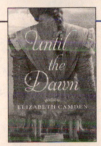

National Weather Bureau volunteer Sophie van Riijn has used the abandoned mansion Dierenpark as a resource and a refuge for years, but now the Vandermark heir has returned. When old secrets come to light, will tragedy triumph or can hope and love prevail?

Until the Dawn

When a map librarian and a young congressman join forces to solve a mystery, they become entangled in secrets more perilous than they could have imagined.

Beyond All Dreams

United in a quest to cure tuberculosis, physician Trevor McDonough and statistician Kate Livingston must overcome past secrets and current threats to find hope for their cause—and their futures.

With Every Breath

⬧ BETHANYHOUSE

You May Also Like . . .

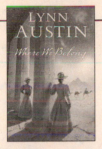

Accompanied by their young butler and their maid, two sisters defy society's expectations as they search for a biblical manuscript. On their exotic journey to the Sinai Desert, they experience challenges and wonders, and recall the events that brought them to this time and place.

Where We Belong by Lynn Austin
lynnaustin.org

After a terrible mine accident in 1954, Judd Markley abandons his Appalachian town for Myrtle Beach. There he meets the privileged Larkin Heyward. Drawn together amid a hurricane, they wonder what tomorrow will bring—and realize that it may take a miracle for them to be together.

The Sound of Rain by Sarah Loudin Thomas
sarahloudinthomas.com

After being unjustly imprisoned, Julianne Chevalier trades her life sentence for marriage and exile to the French colony of Louisiana in 1720. But soon she must find her own way in this dangerous new land while bearing the brand of a criminal.

The Mark of the King by Jocelyn Green
jocelyngreen.com

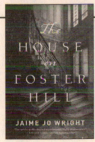

Fleeing a stalker, Kaine Prescott purchases an old house with a dark history: a century earlier, an unidentified woman was found dead on the grounds. As Kaine tries to settle in, she learns the story of her ancestor Ivy Thorpe, who, with the help of a man from her past, tried to uncover the truth about the death.

The House on Foster Hill by Jaime Jo Wright
jaimewrightbooks.com

◈ BETHANYHOUSE